SHIFTER WARS

SUPERNATURAL BATTLE: WEREWOLF DENS

KELLY ST. CLARE

Shifter Wars
by Kelly St. Clare
Copyright © October, 2020
All rights reserved
This is a work of fiction. Names, characters, organizations, places, events, media, and incidents are either products of the authors' imagination, or are used fictitiously. No part of this book may be reproduced, or stored in a retrieval system, or transmitted in any form or by any means, electronic, mechanical, photocopying, recording, or otherwise, without express written permission of the author.

Edited by Hot Tree Editing
Cover design by Covers by Christian

The unauthorized reproduction or distribution of a copyrighted work is illegal. Criminal copyright infringement, including infringement without monetary gain, is investigated by the FBI and is punishable by fines and federal imprisonment

ABOUT THE AUTHOR

When Kelly is not reading or writing, she is lost in her latest reverie. Books have always been magical and mysterious to her. One day she decided to unravel this mystery and began writing.

Her works include *The Tainted Accords, Last Battle for Earth, Pirates of Felicity, Supernatural Battle,* and *The Darkest Drae.*

Kelly resides in New Zealand with her ginger-haired husband, a great group of friends, and whatever animals she can add to her horde.

Join her newsletter tribe for sneak peeks, release news, and disjointed musings at kellystclare.com/free-gifts/

SHIFTER WARS

1

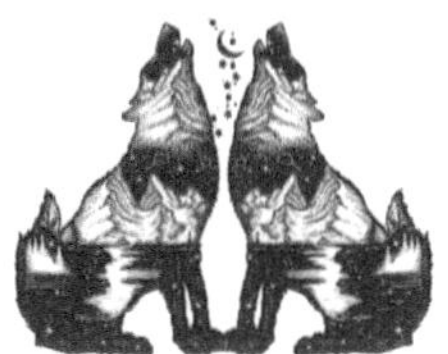

Dressed in black, I watched the phone ring.

It was the first sound in days—now my mother's laboured breaths had stopped. Somehow, after returning from collecting her ashes, the silence was heavier.

I leaned forward on the kitchen stool and answered.

"Hello?" My whisper echoed in the empty house.

A woman chirped, "Good morning, I'm calling from Eastway Bank. My name is Sarah. Miss Booker, I presume?"

"Yes."

She sighed in response. The kind of salesperson sigh people did when empathy was required but, really, the person was wondering about what to feed their kids for dinner.

"My condolences on the recent passing of your mother."

I rubbed my forehead. "Where did you say you're from?"

A pause. "Eastway Bank. There's never a good time for these calls, so I won't keep you long. It has to do with the debt your mother held with us."

That pierced the numbness. "My mother doesn't have any debt. Her treatments were covered by insurance." I'd know, seeing as I'd paid the outrageous bills since seventeen.

The woman's voice firmed. "This isn't in regard to her treatments, Miss Booker."

"Well, we don't have any credit cards." I paid and closed them off long ago.

"Your mother reopened a mortgage against her property. However, she stopped paying monthly payments on this some time ago. It appears the loaned funds went to a gambling app called WinEasy."

I stared at the half-filled cardboard boxes littering the benchtops.

"*Miss Booker?*"

"There must be some mistake. My mother hasn't gambled in years."

"The transactions date back eighteen months. The last deduction was two weeks ago, the 7th of May at 2:00 p.m."

The 7th of May. I worked an afternoon shift that day. She opened the app as soon as I walked out the door. My chest tightened to painful levels. Closing my eyes, I listened to the silence on the other end. "How much?"

The woman's tone was genuinely empathetic this time. "Four hundred and ten thousand dollars."

My mouth dried. "That can't be right. That's—"

That's a fortune.

"We'll need to discuss repayment options with you at your earliest convenience, Miss Booker."

Eighteen months. She'd gambled for eighteen *months* as I broke my back caring for her around my full-time job and study.

"I can't pay," Panic closed my throat.

My savings were a speck on that. Saving just two thousand dollars took me four years. I already had three years' worth of student loans from my business and communications degree to worry about.

The bank woman typed in the background. "The property 373A Belgrave Close is listed against the mortgage of course. I understand you're now the owner of that property?"

The floor fell out from beneath me. "Y-Yes."

"If that property was sold at rateable value, it would cover the repayment," she said brightly.

Sell the house.

I'd intended to anyway. So I could downsize and—for the first time in my life—not worry about an emergency pushing me to the brim of homelessness.

Fresh tears stung my scratchy eyes. How could Mum keep this from me?

Eighteen fucking months.

My breath struggled past the lump in my throat. "I can't talk about this right now."

"I understand you're in mourning. How about we schedule a time for you to come into the branch next week and—"

I hung up, feeling the phone tumble from my cold grip to the tiled floor.

One dead mother.

No family to invite to the funeral.

And a four-hundred-and-ten-thousand-dollar debt.

Dragging another box of chipped picture frames closer, I sneezed through the dust in the attic for the umpteenth time. I rubbed my dripping nose on my sleeve. *Gross*, but the outfit was ruined by now and manners could get fucked today.

Two years had passed since I had time to get up here to clean. Mum wasn't so sick back then, and I'd even gone out with friends and acted like a nineteen-year-old sometimes.

Those were the days.

I worked the age-faded pictures free, placing them on one pile and the wooden frames in another. People paid good coin for those.

Picking up the last frame, I studied the picture of my mother. She stood next to a man I didn't recognise—he wasn't the asshole who abandoned us when I was three. This man had dark auburn hair like my mother and me. A cousin of hers, perhaps? She didn't have any siblings.

In my life, I'd seen three pictures of my mother before my birth. Three, *including* this one.

I traced my finger over the man. "Who are you?"

Working the photo free, I placed it on the picture pile, then rolled my neck and shoulders to relieve the ache from days of packing and cleaning.

This was the last room to clear.

Ugh, I really didn't want to contemplate returning to my reception job at the accountancy firm next Tuesday.

As I walked to the far end, my shin connected with a container. "Mother*shitter.*"

I kicked the offending black piece of furniture and rubbed my leg. Crouching, I worked off the lid and rifled through the contents.

Sales and Purchase Agreement.

Loan Approval.

Tax Return.

I pulled out a crumbled document from the very bottom, working it flat.

Mum's birth certificate.

Snorting, I shook my head. I'd spent *days* looking for this last year. So like Mum.

I sat back on my heels, sighing.

Death confused things. I should be pissed about the gambling debt. Except my mother was dead and gone, and sadness overwhelmed any anger I might have felt. Addiction didn't discriminate, and terminal illness was a lot to handle without relapsing.

I just wish she hadn't lied to me.

A heaviness settled on my heart as I read her name on the birth certificate. "Ragna Eloise Booker," I read aloud.

In other words, the only person to stay with me. Now she was gone, but at least that wasn't by choice.

I studied the box directly beneath her name.

Previous name(s): Thana

"Her maiden name was Booker though," I murmured. My mother and Dropkick didn't marry.

Thana.

The surname was printed as plain as day.

She lied to you for eighteen months about gambling.

Brushing back my long hair, I set the certificate aside, then riffled through the other envelopes and papers in the container, seemingly a collection of a decade's worth of bills.

Last Will & Testament
Of
Ragna Eloise Booker

Age had faded the words.

"Another will?" But she made such a fuss about having her *first* will drawn up when doctors gave her the cancer diagnosis. Even for my scatterbrained mother, this level of forgetfulness was extreme.

The legal document was dated twenty-two years ago—before my birth.

Skimming through the jargon on the first page, I wrinkled my nose at the paragraph naming Dropkick as the sole beneficiary.

No wonder she'd changed it.

I paused on the "last wish" section. Mum requested cremation in her recent will. I received her ashes two days ago. *This* will stated Mum wanted her ashes spread at Deception Valley.

"Where's that?" I asked the attic.

It didn't answer.

My phone blared and I dropped the paper.

Fumbling to answer, I sneezed my greeting.

"Andie? That you? Roy here."

I wiped my nose on my sleeve again. *So sexy.* "Roy. Hey. What's the verdict?"

"Pretty good overall. The bank was right. If we hit rateable value with the sale, it will cover the amount owed."

I blew out a quiet breath. "That's definitely good news. Interest is sky high, so I'll need you to move on the sale ASAP."

"Can do. Where are you at with moving?"

"I hired a truck for tomorrow to put everything in storage. The cleaner is in the day after."

I'd have to dip into my savings to pay those bills, but if I could focus my attention on the sorry-looking garden while others worked inside, I'd lose two or three days *less* money from the ridiculous interest.

"I'll schedule photos for Friday," he said. "Then we'll need three days to get it online. I'll put out feelers now to see if we can get an early sale."

So much change. And so fast. My life hadn't altered in the last three years.

I peered around the dirty attic and steeled myself for how much things were about to overturn. "Perfect. Thanks for that, Roy."

"No problem. I'm just sorry this fell on you."

"What do you mean?" As far as he *should* know, we'd used our mortgage and a personal loan on cancer treatments.

He answered in the same sombre tone. "I'm sorry Ragna's addiction has impacted your life so much."

A telling heat crept up my neck. Mum always said I had the temper to match my dark auburn hair. "I'm not sure what you've heard, Roy. You've been misinformed."

Over my dead body would people gossip about my mother.

"Oh... the person must have their wires crossed."

"Must have," I said coolly.

He rushed to say, "I'll make sure to set the matter straight."

Sure he would. Still, I needed him. "I'd appreciate that, Roy. See you on Friday for photos."

Disconnecting, I strangled my phone in place of Roy's neck.

Gossiping bastards. They had no idea. My mother was a lot more than her disease, *either* disease.

I crouched over her old will, studying her last wish again. *Deception Valley.* If this place was once so important, how come she never mentioned it? Rummaging for her certificate, I squinted at the almost faded *Place of Birth*. I could make out *cep* in the first word.

The second word was definitely *Valley*.

She was born in this place, too, *not* in Queen's Way Public Hospital as she'd always maintained.

Opening Maps, I typed in Deception Valley.

Jesus. "Nine hours away."

Zooming in, I squinted at the route, tracing it to the destination. The town was in the middle of nowhere, past Frankton Gorge.

No wonder I'd never heard of it.

Tapping on the bus, train, and flight icons yielded the same message.

No options found.

"What the hell, Mum?" I stared at the screen as if it could solve the mystery for me.

Carefully folding the two documents, I hesitated and grabbed the photo of her with auburn cousin guy too.

I slid all three into my back pocket.

2

I wiped sweat from my brow, probably smearing more dirt across my face.

"Thanks for your help, Marie," I said, ready for a shower and bed. The last ten days officially caught up this morning.

At least the seasoned cleaner had put in a day as big as mine. The house was sparkling. Except *now* I regretted not doing the cleaning because aside from dropping a last load at the storage container, there was nothing more to do.

That left me contemplating my future with mounting dread.

Ten days ago, I didn't mind my life.

But ten days ago, my mother was here.

"You're welcome, dear. I enjoy cleaning when the house is empty."

I grabbed her vacuum. "Let me help you."

She took her mop and a toolbox filled with cleaning equipment, falling in beside me.

"I've heard the house market is slow," she said. "I hope you get the place sold quickly. Took my niece four months to sell hers. People just don't move to Queen's Way as much with that new bypass in."

I really hoped the house didn't take four months to sell. Thinking of the interest I'd accrue made me feel sick. Mum grabbed at a personal loan with sky-high rates—with a bank, at least, and not a loan shark as she'd done in the past.

Should I be thankful for that? Well, I was.

Loan sharks were more likely to be the *kicking in doors* type.

"Fingers crossed it's quick," I replied as she opened the boot of her small car.

Handing over the vacuum, I stood back. A piece of paper with the words FOR SALE was plastered in the back window.

"Selling your car?" I crossed my arms.

She closed the boot. "Too small to fit my grandbabies in now. I need something bigger. A shame, because this one's as economical as they come. I considered keeping it just for work, but I can't justify paying two registrations."

"Understandable."

I'd always relied on my legs or trusty bike to get me around. A car was always out of the question, though Logan let me drive his sometimes and a neighbour let me borrow their car to practice for my license.

"Why? You looking for something?"

No. Buying a car wasn't practical. It would be an additional cost. I didn't need a car to get to work or to study. To see Logan. Or anything, really.

Nothing at all...

...except Deception Valley.

Public transportation didn't run anywhere near the tiny town. I could only get there by driving nine hours. Logan needed his car for work, so I couldn't borrow that. And he'd want to come along.

More than anything, I wanted to be alone to understand why Mum's death had only uncovered a series of lies so far.

"Maybe." The word slid from my lips.

Oh my god. I just said maybe.

My heart raced.

She joined me on the pavement. "The annual safety check and

registration were just done. I've priced it at $1600, but there's wiggle room if you can take it off my hands quick. You have my number if you're interested."

My heart beat faster still.

This was crazy. I'd lined up two viewings for rental properties tomorrow. To rent a place, I'd need a bond and a month's rent upfront, around $1500. If I bought this car, I'd have $500 left in savings.

I couldn't afford a car.

Entertaining this was... insane—a totally, *totally* rash thing to do. As the adult in our household since eleven, I understood rash decisions led to angry knocks on the front door.

And yet.

And yet.

I could slide into this car and drive away. I could escape. The lure of that enticed me.

That future wasn't bleak. It didn't fill me with dread. What if I left for a few days? What if I had a destination to drive to instead of aimlessly wandering around Queen's Way?

For the first time in ten days, I felt something else.

"I'll take it off your hands for $1500?" I tried to swallow the words.

Shit.

The cleaner peered at me and laughed. "Don't you want to give it a whirl around the block?"

What the fuck did I know about cars? "Is it automatic?"

"Yep, and eight years old. Never had a problem with it—I can show you the annual check reports."

People made impulse decisions all the time, right? Habit was such a bitch.

I tried to embrace the feeling of newness, which was about as natural as hugging a mall Santa at Christmas time.

"If you say it works—" I took a deep breath. "I'll take it."

She shook her head, smiling. "You young folk are so spontaneous. If you're sure, I can sell for $1500."

Spontaneous?

I almost laughed despite my slight queasiness. "That's me. Spontaneous Andie. Is it okay to pay in cash?" With the bank breathing down my neck, I hadn't trusted them not to freeze my accounts. After their call, I withdrew every cent to my name.

The woman extended her hand. "You've got yourself a deal."

No wonder public transport didn't come out here. I eyed the sheer cliffs rising on one side of the narrow, winding road, more worried about the steep drop on the *other* side. At least the powder-blue Corolla I'd dubbed *Ella Fitzgerald* hadn't conked out.

Cleaners were trustworthy mofos.

The raw beauty of the area couldn't be denied as I worked deeper into the valley. Over the steep drop, enormous lush trees were visible as far as the eye could see. I caught occasional glimpses of a wide river.

I consulted Maps again.

Another five minutes. Supposedly. I hadn't seen a house or car since Frankton Gorge, and if this town didn't have a petrol station, I was screwed.

"Nearly there, Mum," I told the bright purple urn strapped to the passenger seat.

The set-up was borderline creepy, but the thought of the urn smashing and sending her body ashes spilling everywhere was worse.

My alto saxophone occupied the passenger seat foot space. Two suitcases, my bedding, and photo frames filled every inch of the Corolla's back seat. By the time I got a spare key to Realtor Roy for the upcoming house photos, I was eager to leave and couldn't be bothered with a final run to the storage place.

I eased Ella F around a tight curve, and the road slopped down. We started descending into a huge gully.

House lights were visible at the bottom.

"Thank fuck." I did not want to find myself in a *Without a Paddle* situation tonight. Or probably ever.

I slowed to read a sign around the bend.

Deception Valley
EST. 1870
POPULATION: 11,400

Huh. Bigger than I thought.

A few more bends, and the massive trees receded to better outline the valley below.

Wow.

Just wow.

On my left and right, two towering mountain ranges extended into the distance, creating the border of the gully. While the space between them was narrow here, the valley floor steadily widened in a V to become an enormous basin. A river stretched through the middle as far as my eyes could see, cutting the valley neatly in two.

In the dying light, I glimpsed what looked like a huge lake.

I once watched a documentary on Denali Park, and this had that same untouched appearance. I couldn't even tell if the gully eventually ended or if it kept going forever and ever.

"*Beautiful*," I murmured, oddly emotional at the sight.

My holidays away from Queen's Way numbered nil. I'd never seen anything like this off the television. The thick forest and the houses dotting the river were pretty beyond words.

I glanced at Mum's urn. "Why did you leave this place? Seriously."

She'd concealed so much. The gambling, I could process, as messed up as it was. But this?

Why did Mum bury her past, even from *me*?

She felt like a stranger in death, which made mourning her properly impossible. Because how could someone who loved me also lie to me for twenty-one years?

I had to reconcile Mum's past with the mum I'd known.

Closure. That's what I needed.

My phone complained in a series of chimes and beeps as I reached the bottom of the winding descent.

Back in reception, obviously.

Ignoring the noise, I took in the surrounding scene. On one side of what I assumed was the main road, old stone buildings stood proud, shoulder to shoulder with their neighbours as they looked across the road to the river.

This place was straight out of a children's movie. Peering back, I could see that the river ran down from the gorge in three large steps like something from *El Dorado*. The streetlamps reminded me of *Lady and the Tramp*.

Cobbled roads.

Slots in the doors for mail.

No rubbish in sight.

This town cast the graffiti-spattered walls and chewing gum-covered pavements in Queen's Way to shame.

"Still not understanding, Mum."

A couple of cars were parked farther up the street, and it was just after 7:00 p.m., but maybe this was normal for a Wednesday night.

Pulling over, I blew out a breath.

Focused on getting here, I hadn't put thought into my next step.

I scrolled through my messages and missed calls. *Eek.* Logan wasn't overjoyed with the hasty message informing him I was boosting for a long weekend.

Dialling his number, I put the phone on speaker.

"Andie."

I relaxed at his familiar voice amidst the crazy new I'd launched myself into.

"Logan. Reception was out for most of the drive. I'm here now."

The silence was leaden. "And where is here exactly?"

"I texted it to you. Deception Valley. That's where Mum was from."

"You decided to buy a car and drive all the way there? By yourself."

"My name is Spontaneous Andie now. I had to get away from everything for a few days."

He sighed. "Understandable, babe. I just wish you took me with you."

I studied the jam-packed car. "Would you have fit between two suitcases?"

My boyfriend of the last year wasn't exactly fun-sized. I had a penchant for tall, loud, and confident men. Of course, going for the alpha type hadn't *ever* worked for me in the past, but Logan was steadily changing my mind. And attraction was attraction.

His deep chuckle made me regret leaving.

"When will you be in my bed again?" he asked.

"I have work on Tuesday, so I'll be back for that. It could be sooner. I just want to find out as much about Mum as possible."

"Call me each night to let me know you're alright."

I rose a brow. "I'll think about it if you say please."

"Night, babe."

So stubborn. "Night, Lo."

After locking the car, I snapped a few photos of the river and street. The full moon painted the calm parts of the water silver. I sent a quick selfie to Logan because, honestly, I had no friends. School buddies hung around at first, but when I couldn't find time for them, ever, they disappeared in a steady trickle.

Whatever. People weren't reliable. I stopped crying myself to sleep over that a long time ago.

A man hobbled down the road, walking his Dachshund.

"Evening," I said, leaning against the iron fence with the river at my back.

He displayed his teeth in a smile that had to be dentures. "And to you, miss. Can I help you find somewhere in town? I'm afraid if you're here for The Dens, they're closed on a Wednesday. I hope you didn't make a special trip over."

"Uh, no. Not here for that." This guy was a quarter of the way to dust and seemed like a local. If anyone remembered my mother, it'd be someone like him. I wet my lips. "I'm actually visiting because my mother was from here. I'm hoping to find out more about her during my stay."

I leaned down to pet the wiggling Dachshund.

"What was your mother's name?" the man asked, excitement painting his features. Couldn't blame him. How many visitors could they really get here?

The name *Booker* hovered on my lips.

"Thana," I said instead.

His eyes widened. "*Thana?* Sure. The Thanas own this valley. You don't know them?" Before I could answer, he leaned in, scrutinising me. "Oh, a Thana for sure. Spitting image of Rhona. How bizarre."

There were Thanas living here? For some reason, I didn't expect that.

"What was your mother's first name?" he asked.

I blinked. "Uh. Ragna, sir."

His eyes nearly disappeared in his wrinkles as he squinted to ponder that. "Ragna. *Ragna.* Rings a bell. When about did she leave the valley for the big wide?"

No idea. "At least twenty-one years ago."

He hummed. "My memory ain't the greatest, I'm afraid. It's why I started scrapbooking paper clippings. I'd be happy to dig through my records for you, but in all truth, the Thanas are the people to ask."

The Thanas. Did he say it that way on purpose?

I rubbed my arm. "I don't know. They might not know anything about me. I'd hate to just show up at this hour. I'd rather call—"

"We don't stand on ceremony here, miss! You'll see. Plus, on a Wednesday, the Thanas play laser tag."

Uh... what now?

"Really?" That was... pretty random.

"8:00 p.m. Every Wednesday. There's time to track down Hercules Thana before they start though."

Hercules. Serious name o'clock.

Though, in saying that, Mum's name was Ragna.

"Could you hold on a second, please?" I said quickly.

At his stupefied nod, I jogged to Ella F and reached into the glovebox. Returning to the old man, I unfolded the picture of Mum and cousin guy.

"Is that Hercules Thana?" I asked, slightly out of breath.

Angling the photo to catch the light of the moon, the old man pressed his large nose to the age-crinkled paper. "Sure is. Red hair. Blue eyes. About your height, maybe a little less."

This Hercules guy knew my mother. With the resemblance, they *had* to be related.

Shit.

I brushed my hair behind my ear. "They really wouldn't mind me showing up?"

The alternative was to sit in a car until morning. Might as well kill some time.

The man crossed his heart. "Really. Or my name isn't Walter Nash."

Was it though?

He recited the address, and I plugged the street into my phone. Another fifteen-minute drive. I'd get there twenty minutes before laser tag began.

Thanking the man, I slid into Ella F, biting back a grin.

Opening my messages, I typed to Logan:

Wth. The town plays laser tag on Wednesdays. LOL.

I checked the direction, pulling away from the curb. Their address was registered in Maps as *The Manor, Deception Valley*.

So that wasn't intimidating at all.

Shoot, what was I wearing? Dark jeans and a black long sleeve. Gold necklace.

Could be worse.

Fussing with my hair as I left the stone building, I nearly missed the turn-off.

Gnarled trees lined the wide road. Beyond, the forest rose in a wall of impenetrable black. Huge gates rose up in the distance.

Oh my god. This wasn't a road.

"*No one* needs a driveway this big," I muttered.

The ominous gates blocked the way in a pretty clear witch coven statement of *Unsolicited Visitors Will Be Cursed and Eaten.* Except Walter Nash crossed his heart and assured me the Thanas would be welcoming.

Plus, these people played a game every Wednesday. This was probably a religious camp or something.

I slowed in front of the iron gates, noting the ornate crests on the stone columns. One of them could reimburse me the cost of this car.

I jerked at a tap on the window.

A torch shone on my eyes, and eyes watering, I made out a hulking man in uniform.

I cracked the window. "Hey."

"Rhona? What's with the car?"

He stepped into a hut covered by ivy, slapping his hand on a button. The gates opened as the man threw his hulking body into a cushioned seat and consulted his flashing tablet.

Okay.

Apparently, I had a twin called Rhona.

Shrugging, I wound up the window and drove on.

Wiping my clammy hands, I guided Ella F down the driveway, mouth bobbing when the *house* came into view.

House, my butthole!

I was in the wrong place.

These people would take one look at the Corolla and suitcases and think I'd come to swindle a chunk of their wealth. Of course, now the driveway was, indeed, of actual driveway proportions, turning around was impossible.

I idled outside the mansion. Should I write a letter to Hogwarts and tell them I'd found the building's long-lost sister?

Stone and iron like the gate, soft lights illuminated the sheer size of the one, two, three... *five*-story building. A wide stone staircase lead to the front doors. One door wasn't enough, clearly.

"What the hell, Mum?" I said, glaring at her urn.

I thumped my head back.

Fuck it. I'd come to get answers.

I locked the car—which was laughable considering the surrounding opulence—and marched toward the stairs. Jogging up, I tensed as the doors flew open and a crowd of people poured out.

Oh my god.

They had guns.

A scream hovered on my lips before I recalled laser tag Wednesdays. I swallowed hard as people of all ages streamed past, not pausing at my wide-eyed presence.

Catching a teen's gaze, I fell into step beside him. "I don't suppose you could tell me where to find Hercules—?"

"Herc? He'll just be in the normal place."

"And that is?" I asked.

He looked at me closely. "Who did you say you are?"

"Uhm, Andie... Thana."

The guy stopped short. "No shit? For real? Are you playing tonight?"

Nope.

"I just need to talk with Hercules."

"Always happy to help a Thana. Follow me. He's probably there already."

Walking beside him, I surreptitiously studied his gun. How *real* did laser tag guns look? I'd never played, but this one was *hella* lifelike. Each person had a flat backpack and torch too. I spotted coiled ropes, nets, and some shovels.

Whoa. Intense was an understatement.

They were dressed in black cargos and black tanks. Some wore leather jackets, but their happy chatter put me at ease that I wouldn't be tied up and killed.

Sliding my phone free, I turned on the torch to navigate the huge tree roots in the thickening forest. Soon after, we entered a cleared area filled with more black-clad players.

I had to admit, no matter how diehard these people were, the setting for their laser tag was *badass*.

Towering trees provided a lush canopy. Dried pine needles covered the ground like a blanket only interrupted by enormous roots.

The smell was incredible.

"Hmm," the teen said. "I can't see him."

"I don't want to hold you up. Just let me know where to search." Their game started in ten minutes.

Shooting me a relieved smile, he pointed to the far back. "Thanks. I'll get in trouble if I'm late. Herc stands there with the marshal when we're in Timber."

I let his weird game lingo wash over me. "Thanks for your help."

Pine needles crackled underfoot as I wound through the swelling crowd. How many people played this damn thing? There had to be *hundreds* gathered.

A walkie-talkie crackled from the vest of a willowy brunette. "*Little Red. West team in position. Over.*"

She replied coolly, "Roger that. This is Snow. South team in position. Over."

This was just *one* of the teams? *Shit balls.* In the alternative universe where I was a badass bitch, I might want to get in on this.

"Where's your mask?" asked a woman who appeared a few years younger than me.

A quick check told me the entire crowd were donning black masks. I stared at the black number she shoved into my hands. It had hard clear shells over the eyes that gave it a bug-like appearance, but otherwise mimicked Batman's mask.

"Oh, I'm not—" The words died in my throat as she left.

I surveyed the masses.

The mood had changed. The chatter was gone. The sea of black masks was borderline freaky. Returning to the car was the safest option. I'd come out again tomorrow. Or preferably, call first—no matter that Walter Nash crossed his heart and swore his name on the matter.

On the other hand, if I spoke to this guy now, it could save me petrol money.

One more try.

"Excuse me, do you know where Hercules is?" I hushed to a short male in the eerie tension.

"Rhona?" the man replied. "Why are you being so nice?"

Okay, he was the third one to say it. Was it the emerald eyes or the red hair?

"He's running maintenance on ground traps tonight," he continued. "He was over there a few minutes ago."

Mumbling my thanks, I followed the direction of his arm.

"Mask on," someone hissed.

Jesus. Would it stop everyone staring?

I held the mask between my teeth, pulling my hair into a messy bun before slipping the stupid thing overhead and tightening the strap. To my surprise, my vision wasn't impeded whatsoever by the bug lenses. If anything, the lenses countered the darkness.

Fancy...

Judging eyes returned their attention to the front, and I released a breath.

Approaching the forest line, I whispered. "Does anyone know where, uh, *Herc* is?"

An older woman cast me a curious look. "Over there."

The best and worst thing about being a redhead? Spotting us was easy. The only red head in the crowd stood straight-backed beside a massive pine.

I took a step in his direction. *Shoot*, what would I say to the guy?

Hey, I pretended to be a Thana to crash your laser tag game.

Herc? I'm Andie. No, not Rhona. Yes, I look like her. Also, are we related in any way?

A thunderous *boom* shook the ground, and I jumped as the mob of people surged forward.

"Watch out."

Someone jostled me, and I sidestepped another, frantically trying to find Hercules again. Shoving my way forward, I spotted him dodging deeper into the trees as the younger part of the horde overtook him.

Shit.

"Hey," I called, giving chase. Stampeding feet and the grunted breaths of hundreds buried the sound of my shout.

Crap, the guy was fast.

Wait.

Wait.

I was chasing a grown man through the damn forest. What was I going to do? Spear-tackle him to the ground and kindly ask that he return to the manor for a lengthy conversation?

I slapped the closest tree—redhead temper—halting in my tracks. The laser tag goers passed me, and I watched their disappearing backs, listening to the rumbling thunder of their feet.

This had officially become the strangest night of my life.

Choking on a laugh, I patted the tree I'd just slapped. Sue me, I felt bad for hitting the thing. Mum always had a deep respect for nature and instilled it in me well and truly.

Ugh, back to Ella F it was. I'd find a quiet street to park and sleep for the night, then return tomorrow.

I turned in a slow circle.

These trees were really thick. I couldn't see the manor or clearing from here. I set off the way I came, snorting again at the turn of events. Sliding my phone out, I snapped another picture to send to Logan.

Tried to.

"No reception," I grumbled. Maybe that's why Mum left the valley. Wouldn't blame her if so.

I didn't run that far. Where was the clearing?

Getting lost was *not* on my list of fun things to do tonight.

I retreated to the slapped tree—or one pretty close—and tried a slightly different direction.

The sounds of the laser tag mob were gone. The odd shout

echoed through the trees as I walked, but otherwise, a heavy quiet had descended. The stridulating chirp of crickets soon after was almost a relief.

After walking for several minutes without success, I threaded my fingers into my hair. "Okay, Andie. Where are you?"

I consulted my phone again. *No reception.*

Tracking back a second time, I stared at the slapped tree. Was this actually it?

Maybe I should just sit here and wait.

Oh! My phone had a compass app. At least I could be methodical about my search.

The woman had called this side the south team. Assuming that meant we'd entered from the south, I had to walk north to find the clearing.

Theoretically.

Selecting a dead branch, I leaned it against my starting tree. Not to brag, but my old Girl Guide sash was covered with badges. If a person wanted a knot tied, I was their girl.

"Be prepared," I told the trees, holding up my hand in the Girl Guide salute.

The problem had to be that I wasn't walking far enough before turning back. If the moon wasn't full tonight and I didn't have these bug lens things, I'd be too scared to move.

"From the top," I said, teeth gritted as I set off north *again.*

I was never telling anyone about this.

The crickets cut off and I froze.

Hundreds of people ran into this forest an hour ago, but it was night, and—*yep*—my imagination was in the driver's seat. The crowd probably scared off the wild animals with their passing, but I shouldn't take any chances.

Sinking into a crouch, I placed my back to the nearest tree.

Crack.

My heart thumped. Something was fucking out there.

I pressed a palm against my mouth, trying not to scrape against the tree as I leaned forward to look.

The moonlight beamed down on the man. Clad in dark jeans and a flannel shirt, he wore hiking boots but barely made a sound on the pine needles.

He wasn't trying to hide. That much was obvious.

I sagged in relief, standing. But I paused, one foot raised to step out from cover, as the massive man tensed, sniffing the air.

Uh... what?

He was muscular and in shape. Being five ten, I didn't always notice a person's height, but he was other-level big. The guy continued sniffing, only the tip of his nose visible through the shadows shrouding his face. Hay fever aside, he would take me in a fight no problem—there wasn't a Girl Guide badge for kicking ass when I attended.

Maybe I should wait until a larger group arrived.

Flannel Man stepped forward, and I jerked behind the tree, covering my mouth again. Or was hiding weird?

I should just say something. It was *laser tag* for fuck's sake.

Where was he now?

I eased forward again to steal another peek. I squinted. He'd moved. *Jesus,* the bastard was crazy quiet.

The hairs on the back of my neck rose.

Whirling, I screamed as a huge hand encircled my throat.

"I'm—" My words cut off in a pathetic wheeze at the painful grip.

"Too easy, little bird," he growled in my ear.

He yanked on a vine near my head. The ground underfoot gave way, and I clawed for a hold on him, screaming as I fell.

The bottom arrived rudely, and my knees bounced up to clip my chin. The shock of landing reverberated through my feet, and crying out, I sprawled against the dirt wall of the... of the *pit.*

Fuck. *Fuck.*

My hands shook.

He'd put me in a hole. It was a trap.

"What are you doing?" I gasped through the pain in my legs.

Moonlight gleamed off his jaw, but the rest of his face was cast in shadow. I rubbed dirt from my mask, squinting up through the dirt-streaked lenses.

He inhaled, sniffing again before freezing. A high-pitched whine left him.

I pressed myself against the wall of the pit. There was something wrong with this guy.

Seriously wrong.

He sniffed again, and a lengthy curse slipped from between his gleaming teeth.

Nuh-uh, he didn't get to sound confused, shocked, and psychotic. That was my role.

Cheeks flushing, I opened my mouth.

"Reach for my hand," he ordered, the tone harsh and clipped.

My mouth bobbed.

Was he fucking serious?

"No way, you're insane!" I snapped. "My family knows where I am, by the way. You better hope you're gone by the time they find me. They'll bury you."

Another whine slipping from him. He was *actually* whining—like a dog.

"Please, I'm not going to hurt you. I'd *never* hurt you," he rasped.

My hands shook. Okay, I was beyond freaked out. Violent to pleading to fervent in the space of a minute.

This guy was unsafe.

He'd put me in a *hole*. In the *ground*. My chest tightened, and I splayed my hands against the dirt wall. "What are you going to do to me?"

He boomed in a gravelled voice. "Take my hand."

Maybe I should take him up on that. My chances of escape were better out of the pit.

I stepped into the middle, glaring upward. Not that he'd be able to see it through my bug mask.

His breath hitched.

I wanted to see his face. I wanted to know what the bastard looked like before he got on with whatever he planned for me. The moonlight had disappeared behind a cloud—or maybe the oversized imbecile was blocking it himself. I reached to remove my mask.

Shouts echoed from close by.

"Help," I screamed. "Help me!"

"Fuck." The man kicked something over the top of the hole and pitched me in complete and utter darkness.

3

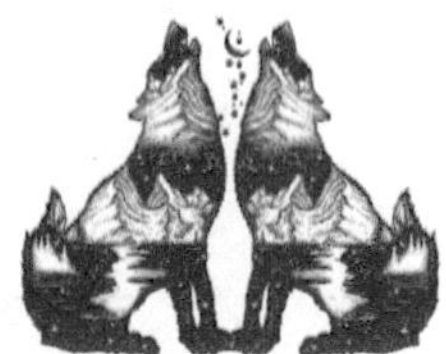

"Please help me," I shrieked.

My phone. *My phone.*

I turned the torch on, spinning in the tight confines. My breath rattled with my desperate inhales.

I screamed again. *Surely*, the group could hear my screams. "I need help! I'm trapped down here!"

Maybe I could carve some foothold in the dirt to climb out. I scoured the ground for a stone. That failing, I gouged at the wall with my fingers, digging out an indent.

One.

I yelled for help again, gasping pants echoing in the small space. I clawed out another hold. And a third.

Taking my fake Converse off, followed by my socks, I shoved my foot into the first hold, reaching for the highest indent. I placed my phone between my teeth and pressed myself flat against the side. Grunting, I probed with my toes for the second foothold.

Got it.

The pit wasn't that deep.

Two more holds should do it. I stretched up to carve another foothold, face down to avoid the falling dirt, then moved higher. Gripping tight, I pulled myself up.

"You aren't taking me down, you fucker," I puffed.

Clinging to the wall, I dug out the last hold and then used one hand to push against the lid.

It didn't budge.

Not even a whisper.

But he kicked it in place like the top weighed *nothing*. Did he put a rock on top?

I shoved with all my strength.

This wasn't happening.

"Help me! Please," I spluttered as dirt and leaves showered me.

My grip on the wall disappeared. I squealed, falling to sprawl on the bottom of the pit again.

A fresh shower of dirt and pine needles rained down on me as the lid was lifted.

Coughing, I squinted through the glaring moonlight.

"Steward?"

This voice was different. I sat, voice shaking. "Please get me out of here."

"Why was the lid on?" someone asked.

I shrieked. "Get me the fuck out of here!"

"Oh, it's Rhona."

There were sniggers. Multiple people were here. And they knew Rhona.

I sagged.

A rope ladder thudded against the wall. I snatched for it, taking a rung in an iron grip. Heaving myself up, I nearly burst into tears after crawling onto the forest floor.

I stared at the small group. "My name isn't Rhona. It's Andie. A man trapped me in that hole. He kicked the lid over the top. I couldn't get out. I didn't think anyone would find me." The pitch of my voice catapulted into hysterical territory, and finally, the group seemed to take me seriously.

A man boomed, "You're *not* a steward?"

"No," I snapped, struggling to confine my temper.

"*How did she get in?*"

The group exchanged a long glance, and a woman approached.

"You're not from Deception Valley?" she asked.

I held up both hands. "If someone can please show me the way back to the manor, I'll leave straightaway."

And never come back. This whole thing had turned into a nightmare.

I sat in a chair, filthy and seething. A steaming mug of tea sat before me that I hadn't touched out of sheer stubbornness.

"Do you want a blanket?"

Jerking, I glanced up at Eleanor, the woman who'd brought me here. She walked way too quietly. She shrugged at my glare and retreated with the blanket as silently as she'd arrived.

I crossed my arms, scanning my surroundings. The manor was all polished wood and studded, leather furniture. In another situation, the stateliness might have intimidated. This office room was all *Beauty and the Beast* with floor-to-ceiling bookshelves—and a ladder I'd love to perch on while singing Disney songs.

As it was, they had about five minutes before I stormed out and called the police or lit a fire. I only agreed to come inside because they'd mentioned talking to Herc and it felt like a failure to leave Deception Valley without meeting him once.

"Andie, is it?"

The temptation to reply with *No, I'm Rhona*, was real.

The red-haired man I knew to be Hercules Thana moved past my chair to the heavyset desk that occupied most of the huge study.

He faced me, and I clutched the armrests.

Oh. My. God.

His expression mirrored my shock.

My fingers itched toward the picture in my pocket. The similarities between Hercules and my mother—his hair, for starters, and the sloped shape of his face—were more obvious in person. She'd had emerald irises like mine, and his were a clear blue, but the shape was the same.

This guy was just shorter than me, the same height as Mum.

"Yes, I'm Andie. I came to see you. I—" Quickly reaching into my back pocket, I drew out the picture, laying it flat. "You're in this picture with my mother. Did you know her? Her name was Ragna Booker?"

I held my breath.

The man seemed stuck in a trance.

Did he not remember her?

"I'm—" He broke off, shaking his head. "—so sorry. This is a shock. Ragna, your mother is my sister."

Shoot. I really hadn't considered this next part. "I'm sorry to be the bearer of bad news. She passed around ten days ago. Mum battled bone cancer for five years."

The man squeezed his blue eyes shut, turning to the large windows that looked out over expansive and manicured lawn.

I studied his back.

Such an emotional response. Yet Mum didn't keep in touch with him. Judging by his surprise, Hercules never knew I existed until this moment.

"Was she in pain at the end?" he asked.

Did he want the honest answer?

Hercules cut me a flat look over his shoulder. "The truth, please."

In my experience, people mostly wanted the nice, tidy answer. "It takes a lot of morphine to lessen pain that deep. She wasn't always lucid in the last few weeks because of the medication. She's out of pain now."

The matter-of-fact words rolled off my tongue—the only way I could deliver them. Cancer was a bitch like that. I'd lost my mother and she'd left a gaping hole in my heart. But my grief encompassed the five years I'd cared for her, the times I thought I couldn't make it through the day, and the constant nagging guilt that I could have eased her pain by trying harder.

Her cancer killed her in five years. The sickness would go on in my heart.

I watched his shoulders shake and had to dig my nails into my thigh to avoid joining him. After the terrifying ordeal and a long day driving, bawling seemed like a fucking great idea.

Hercules drew a hand over his face. Grabbing a tissue from the desk, he blew his nose.

"I didn't expect that," the early-fifties man croaked. "Andie, I'm so very sorry for your loss."

His reaction wasn't faked. He was distraught. It just didn't jive given the situation.

What happened here, Mum?

Standing, I extended a hand. "I'm Andie Charise Booker."

That floored the poor guy all over again, and sympathy panged deep for him. At least I'd had a few days to process that my mother had a life I knew nothing about.

"Hercules Thana," he murmured. "Charise was our mother's name."

Oddly, I did know that. Mum always told stories about her.

He rubbed his forehead. "Sorry, your last name's Booker. Did Ragna marry?"

"No. My father left us when I was three. I guess she just changed it."

People didn't just *change* their damn name. And Mum purposely hid the truth, lying to me about her birth certificate all those years ago. Then there was the first will too.

Mum didn't *want* me to find Deception Valley.

I could only fathom the reason was to do with Dropkick. But I shouldn't discount that it was to do with Hercules.

"I see. It sounds like your life hasn't been easy," he said slowly.

I couldn't recall anyone speaking those words to me. The comment was something a responsible adult said to a child. If not an abandoned one, then one whose mother had a rampant gambling addiction, or one caring single-handedly for her ill mother.

Shifting my attention to the shelves, I put more space between us.

"I came because of the picture," I replied, ignoring his comment. "Her birth certificate mentioned Deception Valley and the name Thana too." I'd keep the discovery of the old will to myself for now. My mother's last wish seemed too personal to share with her estranged brother. "I'd like to find out more about the place my mother's from while I'm here."

"I'm happy to tell you everything I know." He perched on the desk. "You may also be interested to learn why she left and why I didn't know you existed?"

Okay, I liked his straight-forward manner. "Yes. I would. As far as I was aware, Mum had no family."

A shadow crossed his gaze. "I'd be curious about it too. However, it's late, and I want to make sure our conversation isn't rushed. Could you meet here tomorrow at, say, ten?"

Hmm, could I fit that into my crazy schedule? "Not a problem."

His faced turned grim. "Now, Eleanor told me you were attacked in the forest. Could you tell me what happened?"

Shit, I'd genuinely forgotten that dirt covered me from head to toe and I spent most of my evening lost and trapped. I exhaled. "Right, yeah. I came here to talk to you, and someone offered to help, but laser tag started before I found you. I ended up lost in the forest, then some huge guy attacked me and shoved me in a hole."

"Was he wearing black?" he asked.

I frowned. "Dark jeans and a dark-green flannel shirt. Why?"

"He wasn't from our side."

"I mean, I'm more concerned with what he did, actually. Not what side he was from."

Hercules leaned back in the leather chair. "You know that we play laser tag every Wednesday?"

I cocked a brow. "Yes."

"It's an old tradition here due to a long-held grudge between the two families in this town. A hundred years back, the feud was tearing Deception Valley in half. They decided to focus the anger into something that wouldn't affect other families in the area."

"Laser tag," I said doubtfully.

A shadow of a smile graced his face. "It used to be a far more violent version of the game. Even now, our version of laser tag is far more complex than the one you may know."

Me? *Know* laser tag? Laser tag cost money, so that was a big, fat no.

His blue gaze bore into mine. "In our game, teams win points for hitting the other side with their laser fire. They also win points for trapping members of the opposing team. Most often, the traps involve nets or rope, but some traps have been built into the playing field over the years. We're usually very careful about ensuring other members of town aren't caught in the crossfire. I imagine you were granted access to the grounds because you look a lot like one of our players, Rhona."

Tell me about it. "Yeah, I possibly didn't correct anyone on that front."

Turned out the terror and fury I'd felt in the last hour had a simple explanation. *Awkward.* I must have looked like a freakin' idiot.

Laughter trembled on my lips.

"The gate guard will be spoken with, I assure you. This can't be allowed to happen. Those in town know well enough to stay away on a Wednesday night, but your ordeal must have been terrifying. I apologise sincerely on behalf of both sides for what you went through."

Most of me was glad Flannel Guy wasn't a raging serial killer who trapped young women in holes and then begged to free them for twisted reasons. But seriously, he whispered creepy words in my ear. What was I meant to think?

"That kind of thing *only* happens on a Wednesday night?" I asked.

He spread his hands wide. "Deception Valley is the safest town this side of Bluff City."

It certainly felt that way when I drove into town.

I studied Hercules, heart squeezing at his resemblance to my mother. "Why do you keep playing the game? Are the two families still fighting? Don't people get hurt?"

I was lucky not to have a sprained ankle or worse after dropping into that pit.

Smiling slightly, he lifted a shoulder. "It's a lot different when you know what's going on. There's nothing more exhilarating. Perhaps we don't need the game now, but it's part of our culture at this point. Deception Valley thrives because of the game. I'd even go as far as to say that the area depends on it."

Strange answer, but I wasn't from a small community. Queen's Way didn't have any traditions—aside from an annual craft market that no one under fifty-five attended.

"If you like," he said, "I'm happy to find out the name of the man who trapped you."

The memory of the huge Flannel Man sent a shiver down my spine.

Too easy, little bird.

Actually though, such a serial killer thing to say.

"No need," I rushed to say. "Tonight was a series of extremely unlucky events. In a different context, I can see how it would all be normal-ish."

Oops, didn't mean to add the *ish*.

Hercules scanned my face. "If you change your mind, please let me know. We'd hate for the valley to get a bad reputation in neighbouring areas."

I checked my watch, nodding. *10:30 p.m.*

"I'll say goodnight," I said. "It's been a long day."

Hercules straightened. "Can I offer you a place to stay while you're in town?"

I longed to sleep in a real bed, and the thought of sleeping while this dirty was kind of horrible. I only got good vibes from this guy, but until I knew why Mum left, I'd keep my distance. "Thanks. I've got a place to stay."

"Oh?"

"Yep, in town," I lied, "Thanks for the offer though, Hercules."

"Just Herc, please," he answered. "I try to forget my real name as much as I can."

He extended a hand, and I shook it, grinning.

"It's out there, but Mum's was too. What does your name mean?" I asked as we walked to the manor entrance. Mum's name meant goddess or warrior—something like that. I'd heard of the hero, Hercules, but that was about it.

Mum's brother pulled a face, shoving open a heavy wooden door. "It means *Glory of Hera*, but I was given the name because Hercules captured Cerberus."

Specific.

The pine scent from the forest flooded my senses as I stepped outside. I took in the full orb in the sky, grateful again for the extra comfort after the night I'd had.

"Who was Cerberus again?" I really wasn't down with mythology.

The moonlight brightened Herc's face, lending his red hair a fiery glow. "Cerberus was the three-headed dog."

4

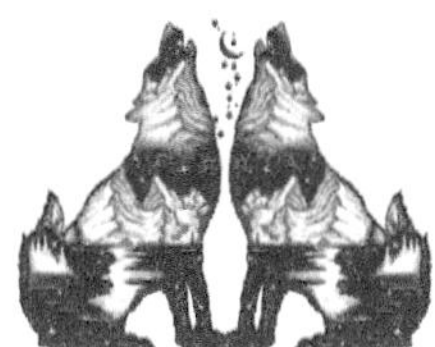

Sleeping in cars was so much fun.

Really.

Not really.

I wrung my hair, shivering against the early morning chill. Dawn awoke me an hour ago, and I'd hurried to find a private spot on the riverside to wash so the locals didn't get a wildlife sighting they never bargained for.

I picked my way over the pebbled shore to where my towel and clean clothes waited. Wrapping my hair, I donned fresh underwear, moaning as I slid into jeans and a jumper. Being clean was everything.

"Hygiene is sexy," I told the trees. They didn't seem convinced.

This place, the whole area, was seriously, *seriously* awe-inspiring. The forest was wild in a way I'd never seen. I could appreciate why Mum always respected nature so much. People dressed up like Elizabeth Bennet and Mr Darcy could have stood here having a damn picnic, trappers could have washed off the grime of a day's work, and this forest had seen it all—silent observers.

These trees would witness my life and be here long after.

That boggled my mind.

The air was crisp and unpolluted. The water, clear and cool. Last night's incident aside, I felt... in sync with this place. I'd never felt that with Queen's.

Or ever.

Bagging my dirty clothes, I checked the time—just after *7:00 a.m.* I had a few hours to kill.

Trekking back up the hill to Ella F, I dusted her driver's seat off, apologising under my breath.

Back in town, I stopped at the petrol station, wincing at the cost of filling the Corolla. *Crap.* Unless I really wanted to screw myself back in Queen's Way, I'd have to keep an eye on that.

It would take one-and-a-bit tanks to get back, and I couldn't eat into much more of my savings.

Maybe I'd walk into town from here.

Just a block down, the shoulder-to-shoulder stone buildings rose in a steady row facing the river. Small iron signs swung above the doorways, and most here appeared to be family names—*Wright, Rousseau, Paton, Irvin, Kay.*

At the end of the block, a road branched up the incline and stone buildings lined either side of that street, too, until the gradient became too sheer for construction.

I set off up the street, soon puffing.

Yeah, Queen's Way was flat.

Jesus. I gasped for air.

The signs here were for shops—*Grey Beaver, Growling Bear Brewery, Valley Designs.*

I forced myself to keep climbing, shoving my hands in my jacket pockets. On the next block, the business signs stopped entirely.

Was this one big building?

I reached the middle where a gigantic sign read *The Dens*. The massive lettering made the small door seem all the smaller.

How come these guys got such a huge sign?

The Dens.

Hmm, Walter Nash mentioned this place last night.

From a branding perspective, the name didn't give much away—

which my studies told me wasn't always a bad thing. An air of mystery shrouded the name, like a person would enter an underground club and see impossible things they could never speak about. Clearly the branding worked if Walter Nash said people made special trips up to visit *The Dens* all the time.

No one was out and about yet.

I strode to the nearest window, cupping my hands around my eyes to peek in. A bar. Stools. Pendant lights. Dark décor. I pursed my lips. Pretty cool layout.

I moved to the next window, but a notice in the window obstructed my peeking.

Now HIRING!
Please enquire inside during work hours.
Or contact Hairy.

Below his name was a number. Maybe I shouldn't assume Hairy was a male though...

I continued on, walking to the very last shop.

An older woman with curled white hair gasped at the sight of me.

"Sorry," I grimaced, "Didn't mean to frighten you."

She blew out a breath. "You just caught me off guard. We don't often see people outside this early."

"It's pretty chilly," I replied. Hard to remember summer was nearly here. Winter must be freezing.

"Always is in the valley until the sun rises over the east ranges. Then we have sun all day long."

The woman started setting out chairs and tables. "What brings you to the valley?"

Not an easy question to answer. "My mother was from here. I'm meeting with Hercules Thana to learn more about her. She was his sister."

She paused, expression sobering at the clear past tense I used in reference to my mother. "If you want answers, Herc is the man to give them to you. Your mother was a Thana?" She squinted at me. "Oh, yes. Definitely. A hearty welcome to you!"

"Oh, uh, thanks. This is a lovely place. Everyone seems to know Mum's family."

Her voice muffled as she returned inside to bring out more chairs. "Everyone knows everyone here, as I'm sure you can imagine. The Thanas run the town though. The town is built on their tribal lands, and they maintain everything here with our council fees and do a beautiful job of it. My husband and I have lived here over twenty years now."

Her response helped to relieve the last of the niggling uncertainty about last night. She was the second person who'd only had great things to say about the Thanas.

"Is this a café?" I asked. Food was the next item on my agenda.

"Sure is." She gestured at the uniform stone building—which confirmed nothing.

My stomach rumbled. "How much is it for breakfast?"

A supermarket would be more cost effective on my budget, but I could swing five bucks.

The older woman winked. "You're a Thana. First meal is on me."

"Wow, Ella F," I muttered. Driving to the manor during the day was so much less *witch coven*.

In the soft morning light, the gnarled trees had morphed to mature maples that glimmered deep purple. A low stone wall bordered the road, containing the lush and wild forest beyond.

A different guard was on duty today.

I wound down the window as she strode over.

"Andie is it?" the beanpole woman enquired. "Shoot, you do look like Herc's daughter."

"Rhona is his daughter?" I replied. Did he mention that?

The woman nodded. "She just got back from a course in Bluff City, which is why people were so confused last night. Sorry about that, by the way. We heard what happened and feel really bad you got caught up in things."

That was nice. "Thanks, it was freaky, but I just feel embarrassed now."

"Don't be. It would be terrifying to stumble into that without knowing a damn thing."

I smiled at the woman, and she winked, slapping the red button to open the gates.

"Might see you around," she called.

"Might do," I said quietly, driving on.

Damn, talking to someone my own age was really nice. Maybe the loss of my friends in Queen's Way affected me more than I thought. Though, really, did I want friends who left as I struggled to care for my mother? Her cancer wasn't their burden, but some support would have been everything.

I pulled into the same spot as yesterday, noting a few people working in the gardens. The Thanas were rich as shit.

Hopefully they didn't think I was here for a chunk of gold.

The doors were open at the top of the wide stone stairs, and light streamed into the manor.

I stared down at a rug that could probably pay my rent for a year.

"Andie."

I jerked. "Christ, Eleanor. Make a noise or something."

She pursed her lips against a smile, shrugging a shoulder. "Toe walker. Can't help it. Don't want to help it."

Fair enough. I'd focus my efforts to not having a heart attack then. "Listen. Thanks for taking me to Herc last night. I was pretty pissed off, and I shouldn't have taken it out on you."

"Don't apologise. You took the whole thing well, considering. Between you and me, the guy from the other team got in shit for kicking the lid over the pit. That's against the rules."

Ice coated my insides. "It is?"

"He should have secured a net and put up a flag, so we knew you were in there."

Frowning, I recalled the way he'd cursed and shut the top of the trap. "He did it when he heard you guys coming."

Eleanor cut me a look. "I'm guessing he realised you weren't part of the game and freaked out."

That theory didn't jive with Flannel Man's behaviour. I recalled his hot breath in my ear, and the firmness of his body pressed against my back. His voice was entirely calm—aside from the moment he'd apparently changed his mind about shoving me in the pit. But the arrival of the group didn't freak him out. Annoyance was a better word.

"Maybe," I hedged. "Is Herc around?"

"In his office," she answered. "Nice to see you, Andie."

I knocked on the office door a moment later. "Morning."

Herc looked up, and my heart panged for my mother all over again.

A warm smile spread across his face. "Andie. I thought we'd talk in the gardens, unless it's too cold for you. I'm cooped up in this office too much and take any excuse to get outside."

"Mum was the same." Her daily request when she could no longer walk was to be wheeled into the gardens. She'd always refused to prune the plants and trees, and now I could see why. Allowing something to grow naturally was beautiful.

I walked beside him through the manor, trying to sneak covert glances at the grandeur when he wasn't looking.

"My immediate family lives here," he said, casting me an amused glance. "We also rent out the other rooms. Living in a mostly empty manor never appealed to me. I like the sound of people around the place."

"It must help with running costs too."

Or maybe this place came with an inheritance.

"It does. I also work from home. So it's more the company that drives me to open my home to others."

He gestured out a glass door that led to a conservatory. We continued through the other side into a wildflower garden I'd associate with a forest cottage. I trailed my fingers through the fireweed and purple harebells.

"Breathtaking," I said before recalling I wasn't alone.

"I see you feel the call of nature. That's common in our family."

I tilted my head. "What do you mean?"

He met my gaze. "This manor—actually, this entire valley and the land surrounding it are our family's tribal lands. We have acted as guardians over them for centuries. And that's just what we've found written proof of."

Was that why I felt so in tune with Deception Valley?

A small table sat in the middle of an herb garden. I breathed in the basil and mint, listening to the pleasant chitter of birds.

"I admit," Herc said, pulling out my seat, "I was nervous you wouldn't return after your ordeal last night."

No kidding. "It occurred to me. But only embarrassment would have kept me away. The Thanas are quite the celebrities in town. I got glowing reports of you from the only two people I met."

He cleared his throat, rubbing an invisible spot on his cheek. "They can come on a bit strong."

I grinned at the thought of Walter Nash's gleaming excitement. "Perhaps. They clearly feel valued."

My mother's brother smiled again, the curve fading as he sat and contemplated me. "I spent most of the night thinking of where to start. There's so much to tell you."

Reaching into his jacket, he extracted a wad of photographs. Some of the edges were rolled and torn.

He set the stack in front of me, and I eagerly reached for them as he dragged his chair closer.

"I'm four years older than Ragna," he murmured as I brushed my thumb over a picture of a young boy next to a chubby baby.

My mother.

I had no pictures of Mum as a baby.

I set it aside with care, glancing at the next photo. Mum was older in this one and standing on a platform, hand in hand with a woman I knew to be my grandmother, Charise.

He murmured, "It's fair to say our childhood wasn't normal. Being

Thanas, certain behaviours and duties were expected of us from a young age. Yet, I like to think Ragna and I were happy in our early years. The manor provided a playground most children can only dream of—'

The next photo was of Herc and Mum at a lake surrounded by other young teens. I smiled at their vintage swimsuits.

"—we had the lake and the rivers, hunting and fishing, and nature. The community we grew up in was tightknit because of the town's isolation."

What would it be like to grow up like that? I couldn't even imagine it. Nothing could be further from my lonesome upbringing.

I traced the picture of my mother dressed for a dance. A giant corsage adorned her wrist. My slight smile disappeared at the sight of the man standing next to her.

"Dropkick," I muttered.

"You know him?" Herc said.

I'd only seen one photo of him in my life. A few years back, I found one in Mum's bedside table along with the photo of Grandmother that I'd seen many times prior.

"He's my father. I think. I don't have any memories of him."

Except for one.

I still remembered him looking at me before walking out. I'd never told anyone for fear they'd tell me recalling anything from three years old was impossible. But I swear the memory wasn't invented. We'd regarded each other so seriously.

I'd known something wasn't right. Enough to forget about the toy truck gripped in my hand.

The thing that tortured me for so long was his expression in that memory. For a while, I interpreted the shine in his eyes and the flat line of his mouth to mean he hadn't wanted to leave and would return. Then I realised that's what guilt looked like. Dropkick knew that was the last time he'd see me.

"Murphy," Herc said, watching me intently.

Oh, I knew his name. "To me, he's just Dropkick."

"I couldn't agree with you more, especially for learning he's your father. It might interest you to know he's dead."

My brows rose. "He is? When? How?"

Perhaps that information should trigger some emotion in me. But honestly? How could I mourn a stranger who'd only hurt me and Mum?

"A rock-climbing accident. Years ago."

Murphy returned here after leaving us. "So he left with Mum, then came back here?"

A wrinkle appeared between Herc's brows. "Murphy worked transporting goods from Frankton Gorge to the valley. Ragna left after one of his runs. None of us ever thought the two were connected."

"You never knew she was pregnant with me?" I asked, studying the photo of my mother and the grandmother I'd never known.

"Never," he said vehemently. "She had to have been pregnant with you before leaving, given your age, but she wasn't showing." He broke off, looking past the gardens to the forest. "I could never make sense of her leaving except for our mother's death shortly before. Ragna loved her dearly."

I nodded. "She always spoke about Charise. And sometimes your father. She never mentioned you though. She hid the pregnancy from you too." Glancing up, I met his gaze. "Why is that?"

He closed his blue eyes briefly. "Ragna often felt trapped by the weight of being a Thana. As you've already found, the community places us on somewhat of a pedestal. That's not always easy to bear. When our father passed several years before our mother's death, responsibility for the valley fell on my shoulders. I'm afraid that, being rather young and inexperienced myself, I wasn't as adept as my father at helping my sister to manage her feelings. She rebelled more and more, spurning family responsibilities to engage in activities that I saw as selfish—or at the very least, detrimental to our family's standing in the community." He sighed and leaned back. "That's perhaps too honest. I loved my sister, but... she had her faults just the same as anyone else."

I was well aware of my mother's faults. Not that I liked her being shot down, but I'd rather all the facts than the edited version. "Don't filter anything, please."

"We said things to each other during those years that I'm not proud of. I can only use the stress of sudden leadership as an excuse. Looking back, I see my sister was floundering. Being more sensitive than me, she was hit hard by Father's death. When our *mother* died, I was afraid of what grief might do to Ragna. She handled it... surprisingly well. She began to pull her weight again. I thought, foolishly, she'd found her way again."

He paused, hands tight on his knees.

This had to be opening old scars for him, but I sat still, afraid he'd stop. I wanted to know *everything*. My mother's past couldn't die a secret. It had to be passed on through me or she'd be forgotten forever.

Herc's voice was hoarse. "I guess that was her preparing to leave. Meanwhile, like an idiot, I was over the moon because I had my sister back and we weren't fighting. Then I woke to find her gone. She'd posted a letter to say she wouldn't be back. I had no way to find her. Worst of all, no explanation for her decision. Days turned to weeks and months to years, and it was obvious she wouldn't return. If not for the note, I would have scoured the valley to find her, assuming someone had harmed her. *That's* how shocked we were. None of us saw the signs. Even now, I can remember how hurt and abandoned I felt."

Welcome to the club.

I tapped a finger on the glass table. The explanation gave me a lot to go on, but the conclusion was that Herc didn't know why Mum left. For whatever reason, they'd drifted apart when he became the head of the Thana family. I didn't see anything nefarious in that. I knew my mother and her faults, and his words rang of truth. Herc could only have been a few years older than me when he inherited responsibility of this valley. With both parents dead, and so much responsibility, both my mother and Herc could be forgiven a lot.

People fucked up.

"Thank you," I told him. "I appreciate your honesty. I don't suppose any of my mother's old friends are still around to talk to? I'd love to meet with them before I leave."

His blue eyes flickered. "Some were as hurt as I was by Ragna's decision to leave, but I can see if they're willing to speak with you."

"I'd appreciate that."

He searched my face. "How have you been since your mother's death? You look tired."

I clamped down on the urge to fidget. He was doing the responsible adult thing again. "I didn't sleep well last night."

Herc's steady gaze didn't leave my face. "Probably because you slept in your car."

"You *followed* me?"

He grinned. "You mentioned staying somewhere in the valley, but we own all the accommodation in town. Everything was empty last night."

Oh...

"Sorry for my assumption. Yes, I slept in my car. I don't know you, and I didn't feel comfortable staying here."

"Fair enough. A smart choice. You seem like a very focused young woman. I'd like to know more about you, if that's okay?"

I liked his mild manner and patience. Responsible adult questions aside, I did want to know my... well, I guess he was my *uncle*.

Gross.

That concept felt like trying on pants three sizes too small.

Taking a breath, I said, "I'm about to start my final year of a business and communications degree. I took the course online so I could care for Mum. That's pretty much it."

"I'm certain there's much more to you," he said, turning away to pull the heads off a rampantly growing chive. "How are you doing in your degree?"

Heat crept into my cheeks. *Straight As.* Only due to my sad social life and Logan's long hours. "Pretty well."

"Is there a special someone at home?"

I shrugged. "I have a boyfriend. And a reception job at an accounting firm."

Herc called over his shoulder as he worked a few weeds free. "How long do you plan to stay in the valley for?"

"I'll need to return Monday at the latest." I stared at my hands.

He sat again, hands full of weeds. "So soon? I'm sorry to hear that. Let me know if there's any way I can convince you to extend your stay."

Sell off a chunk of land to pay Mum's gambling debts? "Gotta pay the bills and get back to Logan."

"Of course. Please, let me at least put you up in one of our town accommodations while you're here."

I hesitated. I couldn't recall being offered something like this ever.

Jesus, I must look poor and desperate. The discomfort was real.

"Free of charge, of course," he rushed to add. "There's a place right in town. You'd be within walking distance of everything. The concept of being an uncle is a new one for me, but I believe this is the kind of things uncles do for their nieces?"

I laughed despite the *niece* curveball. "Are you asking me?"

He snorted. "Well, yes. Between us, I'm sure we'll figure out how this works in time."

The word *no* lurked on my lips as I prepared to slam the door closed. Though he'd offered me a place in town, so I wouldn't be living in the manor.

Discomfort aside, why would I say no when the alternative was sleeping in Ella F?

I managed to swallow the word back, pointy corners and all. "Okay, thanks. That'd be great."

5

I dusted off my hands and scanned the apartment.

This was officially the nicest place I'd ever been in. Patio doors opened to reveal river views. Even the sound of pouring water just outside was like a meditation tape. En suite, lounge, and kitchen, this place wasn't accommodation—it was a gorgeous apartment.

Beaming, I watched people milling along the road below. Thursday nights were a stark contrast to Wednesdays. Where did all these fancy people come from? Decked with jewels, they promenaded up and down the riverside, laughing with their friends.

They looked ready to spend money.

Oh, to be a waitress tonight.

Straightening, I glanced at my saxophone case.

Actually…

I hadn't busked in a long time, but I could make a killing off the crowd tonight. Of course, the town might have rules regulating buskers, but I could sneak in thirty minutes before someone stopped me, surely.

Kicking off my jeans and discarding my thick, cable sweater, I yanked on my only black dress—a first date number—and shrugged into a jean jacket, slipping into white strappy block heels I'd scored at a secondhand store last year. Tearing the tie from my hair, I ran the plastic glitter brush I'd had since age twelve through the long strands and tied the top half in a bun.

I tightened the neck strap of my sax, shoving a 3.0 reed in my mouth as I assembled my beloved instrument. The sax wasn't cheap —Mum saw me looking at it in a shop window and could only afford it because of a win on the slot machines. Later, when we'd desperately needed the thousands she'd spent, I'd offered to sell the thing, but she wouldn't hear of it.

Maybe I only started playing at thirteen to justify her spending that money, but playing had morphed into so much more.

Fixing the reed in place, I tucked my chin, drawing my lips in tight and launched into a D scale.

Ahh.

The soulful sound touched something in me no one else ever had. Tears squeezed at the corners of my eyes, and I embraced the ache.

I limbered my fingers and embouchure with scales and exercises learned off YouTube.

Dropping my phone, keys, and card sleeve into my purse, I slung the bag over my head, snatched up an old cap, and pulled the apartment door closed after me. A communal stairway led down to street level, and I shut the front entrance, crossing the cobbled street to the river side.

Crap. Finding a free spot on the pavement would be difficult. Deception Valley was pumping tonight. I spotted an empty bench seat, and beelined for it, clambering atop.

Better.

A few people in the crowd stopped in anticipation, and I didn't waste a beat. I wanted eggs on toast from the café for breakfast again. If I could make enough for a tank of petrol, that would be awesome.

Tossing my old cap on the bench next to me, I closed my eyes, setting my top teeth on the mouthpiece and drawing my lips tight.

"Perfect" by Ed Sheeran suited the vibe.

I began, letting my exhale flow into the brass instrument. I loved this song because it was so simple. Adding my own spin to the ballad was easy.

Trying to ignore the sudden silence, I continued through the verse to the pre-chorus, keeping my eyes closed as I did my best to imagine I was alone.

Not that I didn't like playing for people, but they were a distraction. To feel the music, *really* feel it, I had to pretend no one was around.

With the river at my back, and the fresh air, envisioning my empty forest wasn't hard.

I held the last note, moving my jaw to add vibrato. Closing the song, I opened my eyes.

I had a crowd. *Good.*

Smiling and thanking those who dropped in coins and notes, I settled into the next song, "The Edge of Glory" by Lady Gaga.

The money came in a steady trickle, and my stomach rumbled at the thought of tomorrow's meal. *Hell yeah!* If I got enough for petrol, maybe I could explore the area a little tomorrow.

Blasting the final note, I lowered my sax.

"You can't play that here."

Standing on the bench brought me to the guy's chin. *Whoa.* Handsome. Twin dimples. *Yum.* I'd have to scope out his body if he didn't annoy me too much with his next words.

"Oh, really?" I said. "Not even for half an hour?"

His face firmed. "The council restricts busking after 5:00 p.m. As you know."

I nearly groaned. "You must know Rhona. My name is Andie. I'm visiting Deception Valley for a long weekend. So no, I wasn't aware."

The blond giant jerked as though I'd physically struck him. "You're *not* Rhona? Wait, don't answer that. You have manners. But you must be a Thana."

He was the first person to not sound overjoyed about Mum's family. *Interesting.* "I'm a Booker. And I've never met Rhona, but I can assure you, I'm not her."

Seriously though. I wanted to meet this chick.

The guy studied me as though wondering which box to place me in. Giving into temptation, I let my eyes wander. *Yep*, firm body. Bit of an attitude. Tall. *Mmm-mmm*. I might be a taken woman but looking was free.

He folded his arms, biceps popping. “Same answer for you, miss. It’s past five. As nice as your music sounds, you’ll need to stop.”

“But why?” I pressed. “People are enjoying it.”

“Because they’re staying on the street instead of entering our establishment,” he answered.

I cocked a hip, resting my sax on top. “The only reason I have to stop is because your business isn’t entertaining enough? No deal.”

In line with that sentiment, I launched into “Fuck You” by Ceelo Green.

Some of the eavesdropping members in the crowd recognized the song and sang along. I held tight to the mouthpiece with my lips against the urge to grin. Smiling and playing sax wasn’t a great combination.

The man bristled, and I averted my gaze at the sudden brightness there. More coins and notes flowed into my cap.

Just a little more. Then I’d listen to Dimples.

Turning my back on him, I played to a young couple, then winked at a small group of middle-aged women. One of them gasped, pointing.

I spun. The music cut off as my jaw dropped as I took in the empty bench. The fucker had swiped up my hat!

“That’s my money, asshole,” I shouted after him.

The crowd reared back as I launched off the bench seat, booking after the huge guy. I squeezed between the hordes. “Come back! That’s mine.”

That mother*shitter*.

That was my breakfast money.

I puffed, protecting my sax as I chased him down the main road and up a damn hill. Why didn’t people separate for me like that?

Oh, fuck. I was not made for inclines. Sweating, I placed my hands on my knees, panting as I glared up at the huge sign.

The Dens.

I sucked in breath after breath, clutching my side.

He'd gone inside.

I was going to kick his ass.

Linguistically.

An arm barred the way. "ID."

"A guy went in here. He stole my money," I panted at the bouncer. My mouth bobbed as I took him in. What the hell? *Another* hot guy? Did this valley have a magic spring they bathed male babies in?

Dark hair flopped over his eyes, and he brushed it back. "ID. And the cover charge is ten bucks."

Was it now? I narrowed my gaze. "Do you have card? I don't have any cash."

"Sure." He turned to grab the machine.

Ha!

Gripping my saxophone, I leaped the cordon and dodged into the stone building. The bouncer shouted after me.

I spotted Dimples immediately. Though, on second thought, he could be downgraded to Asshole.

The thief leaned against the bar without a care in the world.

He'd rue the day he angered a redhead.

Storming up to the bar, I snatched at the open hat on the bar top. "What the fuck is your problem?"

The female bartender sneered. "You're not welcome here, Rhona."

"Not her," Asshole grunted. "Some lookalike. Not even a Thana."

Well... perhaps he'd overinterpreted *that* part, but they clearly weren't keen on Rhona *or* the Thanas, so I wouldn't correct them.

The woman's expression wiped clean. "Huh. You're shitting me? Uncanny. And I'm glad. She's a mega bitch."

A hand gripped my upper arm.

I scowled over my shoulder at the bouncer. "Yeah, yeah. Keep your pants on. I've got what I came for."

"You need to pay the cover charge," he seethed.

I jerked a thumb at Asshole. "He offered to pay." Pursing my lips, I pointed at the patrons streaming in the unmanned front door. "I don't think they got the cover charge memo."

Cursing, the bouncer let me go, racing back to the door.

The bartender snickered.

"Where the fuck is Hairy?" a quiet voice asked.

I stilled. I just stopped.

After a beat, my chest loosened, and I sucked in a ragged breath.

Whoa.

Asshole answered, "Sorry, boss. We've had some trouble with this one."

"Pretty sure you know my name," I retorted. "But you can forget it. *This one* is leaving."

I whirled and smacked into a wall of man. Rubbing my nose, I stepped back.

The wall spoke. "This is?"

I froze again. *Completely.* Like a car stalling.

Restarting, I shivered. How on earth could I hear such a quiet voice over the music anyway? I'd never heard anything like his smooth tones—maybe my saxophone, but that didn't really compare.

Craning my neck, I studied the man's face. He had to be the tallest man I'd ever seen. Dressed in a black shirt and black pants that marked him as a businessman, his dark brown hair extended to just above his shoulders. The stubble lining his sharp jaw was a day past groomed.

Totally, *totally* pulling off the look.

I swallowed hard at the sight of his uncompromising mouth, trailing my gaze up the full plains of his face.

Our eyes met, and something slammed into my chest. He grunted, doubling slightly as I gasped, falling back against the bar. Arms whipped out to catch me, and I sagged against Asshole, sucking in gulps of air.

"Ah... what's going on?" The bartender's voice cut through my buzzing senses.

I seconded that.

What the *hell*?

Holding a hand to my head, I struggled to stand. "I—"

"Are you alright?" The quiet voice filled my ears again.

No!

Heat flooded me, and I shifted on the spot, wishing I could put my sax down and remove my jean jacket.

"What just happened?" I asked.

I almost didn't want to meet his eyes again. But that was *ridiculous*. His *eyes* didn't make my legs give way. Squaring my shoulders, I looked into his direct, brown gaze.

Not brown.

I'd never seen his colour iris before, but the word honey came to mind.

More importantly, I didn't feel like a horse had kicked me in the chest again when our gazes met. My shoulders eased.

The trio watched me in silence.

"I haven't eaten much today," I hedged. That didn't explain what just happened. My legs had never given out from hunger. Or at all.

"Please, have a meal at the bar on me," he answered, never breaking in scanning my face. His eyes dipped down lower, and where usually I'd take the chance to return the perving favour, his face was too fascinating for me to shift my attention just yet.

And that was... crazy.

The silence in our neck of the bar grew heavy.

"Andie was the saxophone culprit, boss," Asshole murmured. He caught me when my legs gave way, so maybe I'd suspend his Asshole status.

I crossed my arms. "Seriously. I was only going to play for thirty minutes. It's not my problem the music in here sucks."

"Finding entertainers to come to the valley is difficult," *he* answered.

His voice. Why did it affect me so much? Maybe it was the tone, honey like his gaze, and as smooth as Sam Smith's songs.

I lifted my hair off my neck. Didn't this place have any damn windows?

Air.

I needed air.

Breaking eye contact made me realise we'd been locked in a staring contest. Shaking my head, I dragged my purse around and poured the contents of my old cap inside. I jammed the nautical hat over my wavy curls, all the better to block the sight of honey eyes with.

"Would you be interested in playing here Thursdays through Sundays?" he asked, stepping forward.

Every inch of me was aware of the smaller space between us. I eyed the exit around the giant. "I'm leaving on Monday. Thanks for the offer."

Unable to resist, I peeked up and glimpsed the struggle on his face.

"If you change your mind, you know where we are," he said eventually, jaw clenched.

If I had to pick an emotion, I'd say he was horrified.

This just catapulted into *nope* territory.

A quick peek told me Dimples's mouth was ajar and the bartender had forgotten about pouring a beer.

Yeah, something was up. And I wasn't sticking around to figure out what.

Spinning on my heel, I hurried for the door, ignoring the bouncer's glower as I burst from *The Dens.*

6

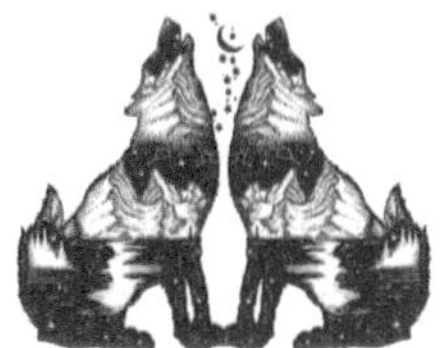

I answered my phone.

"Andie? Hey, it's Herc here. How are you finding the apartment?"

The apartment was freakin' amazing. "It's great. Are you sure I don't need to pay you anything for staying here?"

Because I have two dollars to spare.

"No, really. I won't hear of it. So I spoke with two of your mother's old friends. One returns to the valley on Tuesday, and the other is sick, but she'd love to chat once she's better. When did you say that you needed to return home?"

My heart sank. "Monday at the latest. It takes nine hours to drive there."

The word *home* felt strange in relation to Queen's Way. I'd lived there my entire life yet didn't feel one scrap of the belonging I felt here. There had to be something wrong with that.

The line went quiet. "I suppose they could always call you, but reception isn't great out where they are. There's no way you could extend your visit?"

I was out of grievance, holiday, *and* sick leave. My workplace had been more than understanding of my situation. More understanding than any other job I'd worked. But their understanding was growing thin.

With Mum's ginormous debt to pay, I really, *really* needed that job. "I wish staying longer was possible, but I can't swing it."

A booming knock at the front door made me jump.

"Shit," I blurted.

"What's that?" Herc asked.

Crap. "Sorry, someone's knocking."

Herc sighed. "Loudly bordering on obnoxiously?"

"That about sums it up."

"I expect my daughter is on the other side. I told her to give you space—"

I arched a brow. "Not a problem, but I'll hang up before she succeeds in teaching the door a lesson."

Tossing the phone on the bed, I straightened and marched to the entrance, swinging it wide.

"Whoa," we chorused.

Mirrors aside, who was used to seeing themselves?

"Freaky," I whispered.

The young woman added, "Very. You're my cousin, Andie."

Her emerald green eyes didn't move from mine as she invaded my personal space. *Yeah*, I could see how some people could take her manner the wrong way.

"I am," I quipped. "You're my cousin, Rhona."

She sent me a dry look. "I squeezed the details of you from Father last night. I had to see my lookalike with my own eyes." She circled me. "Shoot. We *really* look similar. Creepy."

"I think so. Should I circle you after?"

She blinked before laughing. "I'm glad you're not a weakling. I'm not sure how that would have worked."

The woman couldn't be more different from her mild-mannered father. "How old are you?" I asked.

"Twenty."

Only a year apart. *Cool.* And weird. Extra strange because Rhona was an *overstepper of boundaries*. I struggled to deal with those people for long being the exact opposite in personality.

She glanced around the apartment, facing me after. "I've just returned from a course in Bluff City, and I'm catching up with my friends at the lake today. Wanna come?"

My plans for the day included finding the elusive supermarket, calling Logan, and exploring the town. That plan was comfortable, but I had a number of days to know Rhona better.

Maybe the time had come to actually act twenty-one.

"Thanks for the invite," I said. "Sure."

She kicked back the top of one suitcase. "Got a swimsuit?"

"I do. But don't go through my stuff," I said calmly.

Rhona peered back at me. "Sorry."

"Not a problem. I'm just used to my own space." I opened the other suitcase and rummaged for my black bikini, dragging out a jean skirt and flip-flops.

"That'd be nice," she replied, shooting a look at my sax. "Can't say I've ever had much of that."

"I guess the manor gets pretty busy."

"*That's one word for it.*"

I partially closed the bathroom door, ripping off my tank and shorts. Slipping into the bikini, I tied the strings, adjusting my boobs in the mirror. I had awesome cleavage according to a survey carried out on three past boyfriends. I stepped into the jean skirt and flip-flops, mussing my hair.

"Hey, I only brought my bike, but Dad said you have a car. Is it alright if we take that to the lake? I can buddy ride you, but it's a decent bike out there."

I lowered my hands. *Dang.* "How far away is the lake?"

"Forty-five minutes by bike," she called.

Double dang. Ella F was on petrol rations. But with the small amount of money from busking, I could make it work without breaking into my savings more. "That's fine."

She arched a brow. "Are you sure? Because we can bike. I'm used to it—we bike whenever we can."

Yikes, I was the poor cousin. "I just need to keep an eye on how much petrol I use. I usually walk, so I'm not sure how much my car drinks. Driving to the lake should be fine."

The drive was, thankfully, only twenty minutes, including a bumpy five minutes down a dirt road.

I followed Rhona through the trees to the lake, listening to the shouts and laughter ahead.

Thick trees opened into a sandy beach, and I gasped at the glistening water.

The mountain ranges bordering the valley were reflected on the calm surface. All manner of trees bordered the lake. Some had toppled into the lake recently and the logs bobbed in clusters on the opposite side.

"Beautiful, huh?" Rhona said. After her big show entering the apartment, she didn't speak much on the drive here.

"That's one word for it," I replied.

Rhona was quickly surrounded when we reached the water.

For everyone being a little scared of her, she had more friends than I'd had in my *life*. I murmured hellos to the sea of strangers. This lake gathering was exactly like the one in the photo of Herc and Mum. Every single person here knew everyone else. They'd grown up together. For them, a lake day like this was a regular occurrence.

The entire situation blew my mind.

Boggled my mind. And not in a good way.

I untangled myself from the hoard and found a spot to sit apart from the—what had to be—thirty young people.

The amount of change was the problem. Mum died two weeks ago. Then the debt. Vacating the house. The car. The road trip. Forest attack craziness. The talk with Hercules, and meeting Rhona today.

More change within *days* than my entire life put together.

I was literally quaking inside, but when I was back in Queen's, I'd kick myself for not making the most of this.

"Hey, Andie."

Glancing up, I recognised the female guard from the manor gates. "Hey..."

Shit. What was her name?

She grinned. "Don't worry. I don't think I told you my name. I'm Cameron."

"You're part of the boy's name for girls' club too." I raised my clenched hand for a fist bump, which she didn't hesitate to deliver.

She sat. "We've got to stick together."

I eyed the gorgeous male beside her. He wasn't as tall as *The Dens* men—or, perhaps, as old—but he'd definitely bathed in the magic man spring.

"This is Wade," Cameron said. "He wanted to talk to you but was too scared to come without me."

The curly blond shot her a glare and she smirked.

What was the dynamic there? "You guys are together?"

They both shook with laughter.

Cameron raised a hand. "Women for me. Don't suppose you're interested? The lesbian population in Deception Valley is almost non-existent."

"Not on the market," I replied, smiling. "I'm straight anyway."

She sighed dramatically.

"Nice to meet you," Wade said, outstretching his hand.

I took it, liking his open expression and grey eyes. "So how long have you guys known Rhona?"

Their expressions smoothed. Wade sat on my other side.

"Our entire lives," Cameron said, clearing her throat.

My lips twitched. "You don't like her."

"*Like*," Wade repeated as though tasting the word. "I'm not sure I like or dislike Rhona. She's like pepper. Pepper is a necessary seasoning. You couldn't do without it, but get some up your nose and you'll choke. That's how I feel."

Laughter burst from my lips as I checked Rhona wasn't nearby. "That kind of sounds like dislike."

"She's fine," Cameron said, tipping her face to the sky, eyes closed.

Wade leaned back on his hands. "We heard your mother recently passed away. I'm really sorry for your pain."

People here had a way of letting me know they cared. It was so *new*.

"I appreciate that. She suffered for a long time, and I'm glad she's free now." A lump rose in my throat.

Cameron lay flat, flicking her sunnies into place. "How long have we got you for?"

"Until Monday. I'm staying as long as possible, but I have a job to get back to." I added, "Oh, and a boyfriend."

Both grinned.

"Sounds like he's super important to you." Wade cast me a look.

"There's just a lot going on. We've been together a year."

Wade leaned in, taking my hands as he stared into my eyes. "The sex is great, but your heart is untouched."

My jaw dropped as he resumed his reclined position.

"Magic, right?" Cameron murmured.

"Some of us are born with ability," Wade replied.

That wasn't how I felt about Logan at all.

Cameron peered at me over her sunnies. "Do you think you'll be back?"

The thought of never returning here made me feel ill. I'd caught myself daydreaming about living in the valley this morning. Maybe one day that could become a reality. "If I didn't have to leave, I wouldn't."

"That's nice to hear," she said, smiling. "We love this place."

I love it too. "I can see why."

"Let us know if we can convince you to stay." Wade nudged me.

My phone blared.

"It's Logan," I said.

"We'll see you later," Cameron hollered after me.

Walking toward the tree line, I answered, "Hey, Lo."

"Hey, babe. Where's the phone love been? You were meant to call last night."

"I didn't realise these things only worked one way," I teased.

He exhaled. "Please tell me you're halfway back."

"I'm halfway back."

"Thank—" He cut off. "You're joking."

I bit back a smirk. "Sorry, couldn't resist it. But no, I'm here until Monday."

"Found some stuff about Ragna?"

"Yep. And an uncle and cousin."

"Whoa. Heavy stuff."

I toed the sand. "Tell me about it, but it's probably nice. Or will be when I wrap my head around them. This valley is so beautiful, Lo. Seriously. I wish I didn't have to leave."

"... Okay, but you *are* coming back."

His question sounded more like a demand, something I'd always found sexy and irritating at the same time. Alas, bossiness was the downside to my *type*.

I watched the joking group splashing in the lake. Most were swimming. A few paddled kayaks. They felt like an alien species.

One million responsibilities lay between me and them. "I'm coming back."

"Fuck. I thought you were about to break up with me."

"The sex is too good."

His voice lowered. "Just good?"

"Hmm, what?" I hung up, laughing at his incoming text.

**Great ;)*

My skin flushed as my thoughts turned directly to the bedroom. There was a definite itch to scratch at this point. We usually saw each other every couple of days.

"Andie," Rhona said breathlessly. A guy with curly white-blond hair had his arm draped over her shoulders. "Could we give Foley a lift back into town?"

"As long as he's not far off the main road, sure."

Rhona mouthed, "Thank you," dragging the guy away as he stammered a hello.

My phone pinged again, and I bit my lip in readiness of another text from Logan.

Hi, Andie
Pictures all taken. House should be online for Monday.
Roy

My heart sank.

And there it was. A reminder of all the reasons I wasn't one of the people splashing in the lake.

One, I didn't have a job here. But *two*, the house needed to be sold, like yesterday.

I glanced at them again. What if every weekend included a trip to the lake with friends? *Fuck.* I wanted that so bad.

The concept of it scared me, but I did want to know my uncle and Rhona.

I wanted to stay in this beautiful place.

I wanted to learn more about Mum and talk to her friends.

The want was so strong, it felt like need.

Brushing my hair back, I dialled Roy's number.

"Hey, Andie."

I hesitated. "Roy. Hi. I have an unusual question."

"Nothing is unusual to me anymore. Not when you've sold houses swingers used to live in."

That pulled me up short. "Seriously?"

"Carpeted bathrooms without windows. A secret bookcase door leading to a concrete room with a shower in the corner."

My brows climbed. That *did* kind of paint my question in neutral hues.

"What can I do for you?"

This was ridiculous. Absolutely bonkers. "I went away for a long weekend, but I'd like to stick around for a while. How present do I need to be for the open homes and sale?"

"That's your unusual question? People do that all the time. You already gave me a key for photos. No problem."

My mouth dried. "Really?"

"Sure. I'll go in twenty minutes prior and open windows and doors to get some air through, but otherwise, no issue."

Hiring Marie to clean would be another cost, but an empty house wasn't a big job… a fortnightly spruce would be fine. "Okay. Right. I… Can I get back to you to confirm? I'm unsure of my plans just yet."

"Fine by me. Hey, I'll send the house link through when it goes live."

I mumbled what I hoped was an appropriate response, hanging up.

Holy shit.

Of course, none of this was viable. I couldn't do this. Marie might not be able to clean regularly. I had barely any money. This…

This was *crazy.*

"Andie," Rhona bellowed from out of view.

Jolting, I grabbed my things and picked my way through the trees after her and the guy.

"Bye, Andie!" Cameron called.

I threw a smile back to where she stood waving beside Wade.

Rhona winked at me as I caught up to them.

"Thought you got lost." She hooked an arm around my neck, "Can't go losing my best and only cuz. Just wait until you try Dad's blueberry muffins, too. Oops, that was a surprise. He's giving them to you tomorrow morning."

A grin spread across my face.

I breathed in the surrounding pine scent, gaze snagging on the birds whipping overhead, and my heart squeezed in my chest.

I desperately wanted to make the biggest mistake of my life.

7

I glanced both ways down the crowded street, saxophone clutched tight. Dimples wasn't anywhere in sight, but I hurried just in case.

Locking the front door, I walked to my busking bench. Leaping on top, I chucked my old cap down.

My fingers flew over the keys in the familiar pattern of Louis Armstrong's "What a Wonderful World."

Keeping watch for blond-haired giants with dimples made sense, but this song was about as beautiful as they came. Closing my eyes, I poured out the angst of the day—which ironically led me to illegally busk after 5:00 p.m. again.

Rhona's one friend turned into a car filled with friends that needed to be dropped off. She'd promised petrol money, but I learned long ago not to rely on family members.

Illegal busking it was.

I smiled and bowed to the clapping crowd, holding out my cap. The coins rattled. *Hells yeah.*

The streets were packed again this evening. How the heck did *The Dens* pull such a crowd all the way out here? Were the drinks amazing? Did their hot staff put on a little show at midnight? Not that the scenery here didn't warrant the trip, but *this* many people came regularly… that was a freakin' business feat.

I scanned the packed street.

No sign of Dimples.

"Rehab" by Amy Winehouse. I let my music soar, swaying with the beat as a few people sang along. I blasted the last note, leaping it an octave so the shrill sound bounced off the surrounding cliff faces.

Grinning, I thanked those dropping money into my cap.

Huh, no Dimples. Maybe it was my lucky day—

"We meet again."

It was the voice.

I mean, the man *with* the voice.

My saxophone emitted a squeal in response to my tightening throat. I lowered the instrument, glancing back at the giant guy with honey eyes.

My heart thumped, the beat tripping.

I wasn't *scared* as such. I'd just never had a response to another person on this scale. Every hair on my body stood on end. My skin prickled, urging me to remove my jacket to cool down—even with the sun setting and a slight chill to the air.

My tongue unlocked. "How long have you been there?"

"How long have you been playing?"

I couldn't put my finger on the emotion behind his words. His greeting—*we meet again*—was delivered as a statement. Not with any anger over my rule flouting. Or sarcasm. Just a quiet, literal statement.

We meet again.

The second part was easy to translate. He'd watched me the entire time.

Stop overthinking shit.

Not taking any chances for a repeat of last night, I stood on my cap. His warm gaze dropped to my sandalled foot and a slight curve graced his lips.

Yeah, okay. His suit was expensive, and he didn't need my busking shrapnel.

Whatever.

Ignoring him, I set my lips to the sax. "Killing Me Softly" by Roberta Flack seemed appropriate. Except, *Killing me via Electric Fence* was more on point with what I felt.

The song wound around me like a heavy blanket but didn't block my absolute awareness of the male behind me. Like, at all.

He was doing what it usually took a few hundred people to achieve.

Finishing, I scowled over my shoulder. "Do you have to stand there like that? It's putting me off."

He tilted his head. "Tell me how I should stand. I'm happy to obey if you'll play again."

Damn. That was kind of charming. Except there wasn't any way this testosterone statue could stand that would put a wet blanket on my particular fire.

"Can I help you with something?" My crowd was losing interest.

"What will it take for you to work for me?" He was leaning against the fence.

I set my jaw. "I told you that—"

Cutting off, my mouth dropped. *Shit.* He'd offered me a job.

Again.

Only one thing stood between me and Deception Valley. Lack of income. Okay, understatement of the century. *So* many things stood in my way, but a job was the last major roadblock.

He stepped closer, and I gripped my sax with both hands like the instrument could provide a force field between us.

"What did you tell me?" Honey Eyes pressed. "I admit, our meeting last night is somewhat of a blur. You took me off guard, and all I can remember is your face. I don't usually forget anything."

Uhm, what?

Warmth stretched across my cheekbones, and I fidgeted. Men like him didn't speak like that. Assholery was the absolute drawback of alpha types. Men like *him* were confident. Big dick energy. Emotions were a foreign language.

Wrenching my gaze from his, I studied the chatting people

surrounding us. How weren't they reacting to this guy? Contrary to my issue, they kept a wide berth, focus averted from him.

I shifted, resisting the urge to sigh. An hour jog sounded perfect right about now—and I wasn't big on the pastime.

"Are you alright?"

He moved a hand to my elbow, and I yanked out of reach, nearly falling from the bench. His fingers curled, and his expression smoothed.

Whoa. Why did I do that?

Recovering my stance, I tried to appear relaxed.

I shook my head. "Fine. I'm fine. Thanks."

"And what did you tell me yesterday?" he probed gently.

Ugh, I hated acting like a moron. "That I was leaving on Monday, but that might not be the case anymore."

Air caught in his throat. I was *sure* of it.

"Why the change of heart?" he said, attention resting on my cap, shoes, jean jacket, and sax in turn.

Observant. To an unsettling degree.

I jumped down from the bench, snatching up my cap. "I'd be interested in exploring employment. How much are you offering and what hours?"

Playing saxophone in a bar was a fucking exciting prospect. Something that didn't feel real. A job I could *enjoy*.

There's no way it would pay enough.

"Maybe we could discuss details over dinner?" he asked, gesturing down the street.

Did he mean that in a *professional* way or *let's dance the horizontal dance* way? I took the safest route. "My boyfriend is expecting a call soon. Maybe another time."

His eyes flashed, and I blinked several times as the honey hue darkened toward black. He stepped back, and liquid honey flashed again.

Oh my god. I was losing it. Laughter bubbled in the back of my throat.

"A boyfriend. Will he join you in the valley?" His expression of polite enquiry was back. I didn't believe it for a second.

It was almost like he was forcing himself to remain calm—like me continuing to talk with him was of utmost importance.

But that was crazy.

The guy just had one seriously intense personality.

Ignoring his probing question, I looked out at the river, admiring the water pouring down in the three large waterfalls from high above.

A soft laugh left the muscled, suited man beside me. "No more personal questions. I can take a hint. None more than necessary if we're to work together."

"Thank you," I said, surprised when the words left my lips.

He maintained a professional distance, leaning against the poor fence again. "You'd need to play Thursday through Saturdays. Nights, of course. Let's say six until the DJ takes over—around nine-thirty. Sometimes, we have events on Sundays, but we won't require music on Monday and Tuesdays. I usually pay bands $100 an hour including set up time. Seeing as it's a regular gig for you, how about $50?"

That was double my hourly rate as a receptionist. Ten and a half hours guaranteed at $50, then there was tax.

... I could count on $400 a week. More than two hundred less than I'd earned in my full-time reception job. Of course, my costs were less now without Mum to feed and care for.

But how much would rent be? I'd need to talk with Herc or find somewhere else. Was food more expensive in Deception Valley? Petrol certainly was, and I also had that to consider.

Budget first. Accept job later.

"Is that your best pay rate?" I asked.

His eyes gleamed. "What's your proposal? There's wiggle room. Remember though, it is regular work."

"And regular entertainment for your establishment. Seems like that's hard for you to get out here," I countered, not offended. Business was business. I understood that blind charity didn't put food on the table. He wanted the best deal. I wanted the best deal. The best negotiator won—even better if they won without the other believing they'd made the larger concession.

The man's eyes roamed over me, and I didn't imagine the heat and interest there. *Yep*, the dinner offer wasn't the professional kind.

And *double* yep, this guy was the yummiest thing I'd seen in a while.

Not that it mattered. I was a taken woman and trust between partners was something I'd never shit on.

"My music fits the vibe you've got going on in The Dens." My gaze drifted to his powerful throat.

What the fuck? His *throat*? Throats weren't hot.

Except...

Stubble extended down past his chin and jaw a little, adding to that *barely contained rulebreaker* look he had going on. He definitely wasn't a natural suit wearer. The guy wore it like he could burst out of it any second.

Oh, yeah. I could totally have lumberjack dreams about this one.

"My thought exactly."

I cleared my throat. *Oh my god*, was I drooling? I licked my lips to check.

His brows lifted.

Shoot.

He was waiting for something... Which was...? Oh!

I blurted, "I'll get back to you on the figure, Mr...?"

"Alarick," he answered. "No Mister needed."

Old school, but not the weirdest name in this town.

Big dick Alarick.

My lips twitched.

He placed his hands in his pockets. "Something funny?"

Not to anyone else. "Nope. Should I come to the bar tomorrow night with my proposal, or is there a number to call?"

I'd have a day to research living costs. I'd need enough money to visit Logan too.

I slapped a hand over my mouth.

Logan!

"What's wrong?" The hand reached for my elbow again, and I gasped, evading it.

Alarick wrenched away as though burned.

"Please tell me what's wrong," he said, stepping closer.

I hadn't even thought about Logan in this. I mean, staying in the valley wasn't a viable option until three minutes ago, but *still*. Worst girlfriend of the year award.

Groaning, I backed away from Alarick. "Nothing. I just remembered something though. Thanks for the offer. I'll get back to you—" My heel caught on the bench leg and I barely prevented myself from sprawling over the pavement.

I panted, pushing my thick hair back.

Fucker was *grinning*.

My temper flared, narrowing my eyes, but his grin didn't abate.

Ugh, guys who could handle my temper were a turn-on.

"Goodnight, Alarick," I said, spinning on my throbbing heel.

"Goodnight...?"

He didn't know my name yet? Dimples either forgot it or neglected to pass it on.

Grinning, I ignored Honey Eyes yet again, disappearing into the crowd.

🐾🐾

"It's not finalised or anything. There are a few things to figure out." Smiling, I glanced to where my budget rested on the bed.

I could make things work with this job. The night hours left me free to get a second job too—full-time work if I wanted.

When the house sold, it should negate Mum's debt. I still had my student loans to pay off though, so I'd apply for another part-time job soon.

Voices bubbled in the background, and I heard Herc's footsteps and a muted thud before the sound faded. "Sorry, dinner time here. Now, do you need somewhere to stay? There are two rooms in the manor."

Herc's glee wasn't disguised in the slightest. Slight uneasiness thrummed through me at the renewed manor offer.

"Hold on. I'm running away with myself," he said. "There are visitors filling those next week. I can enquire about long-term rentals. Or if you prefer the apartment you're staying in, you're welcome to it."

Anticipation was a knot in my stomach. I *loved* this apartment. "I do like it. A lot. What's the rent?"

"Nonsense. It's on me."

I suppose Mum took care of the bills at some point in my life, but I couldn't recall the last time I relied on anyone else. "Thank you. I can't accept that."

"Please do. I'd feel better about missing the first twenty-one years of your life." He laughed sadly.

"My mind is made up. Thank you though."

"Stubbornness comes with the hair colour in our family."

His answer startled a laugh from me.

Truth.

Herc added, "How about a compromise? One month rent free. After that, you'll get the family 50 percent discount. Based on normal rates on that apartment, you'd pay eight hundred a month, utilities included."

I'd looked at accommodation prices in the valley earlier. Herc wasn't taking off more than the *family* discount. Eight hundred a month in rent was doable on what Alarick offered—totally doable if I wrangled him up to my offered pay rate tonight.

Except Herc's offer involved a *family* discount.

That had to have strings. Did I want to accept all the hidden family stuff tied to that?

Surely I could maintain a certain distance with living in town. "Sounds good to me."

"Don't mention it. Now, do you need a job? What's happening with things back home?"

His words rushed at me, and I started pacing the apartment.

Too much.

"All handled," I said after a beat. "I might have a job at The Dens, playing music."

He inhaled harshly.

"Herc?" I asked, stopping in my tracks.

Silence.

I pulled the phone away to stare at the screen. Still connected. "Hello?"

"Andie. Sorry. I lost you for a moment."

"Can you hear me now?"

"Fine, thanks. Did you say The Dens?"

"Yeah, I'm in talks with the owner. The job is perfect."

Leaning over the sill, I smiled at the people milling below. The solitude of the valley was unreal, but the energy of the crowd was electric and enticing, too, a natural magnet. I wondered if Cameron and Wade frequented the bar I'd play at. We could have a lot of fun.

I could have friends again maybe.

Herc spoke again, "If the deal falls through, get in touch. I'm happy to put the feelers out."

I opened my mouth to ask him to do it anyway.

Although playing sax and keeping my days free wouldn't be such a bad thing for a few weeks, especially with a rent-free month. I could explore the area and get to know people. Maybe just *chill*.

People my age did that, right?

Chilled.

Weird.

We spoke for a few minutes more, and I mentally checked *rent* off my list when the call ended. I'd already checked Marie's availability for cleaning. She'd pencilled me in fortnightly on Fridays and was awaiting confirmation.

The last call to make was the one I most dreaded. Which meant I'd make it over a drink. At a *bar*, no less because I was fancy as fuck —and because I didn't have to pay for petrol back to Queen's Way.

Looking in the mirror, I half turned to check my ass in the steel-blue dress, studying the front after. A chrome zip ran from the raised midline of the mid-thigh hem to the low-cut neckline.

Velvet—secondhand—hugging my curves in the right places. I couldn't recall the last time I'd worn it. Maybe out to dinner with Logan?

I partnered the man-killer dress with cream round-toe heels. If no one looked too closely, the chips and cracks in the colour would be missed.

Running a brush through my thick, wavy hair, I checked my make-up and glared at myself for good measure.

I shouldn't be making this effort. I could lie to myself and say I was dressing this nice to be well presented for the job discussion—or to match the people down on the street. Or for myself.

Yeah.

Alarick hadn't left my mind *once* since last night.

That made me angry because it felt like a betrayal.

I really needed to see Logan.

Plus, there was attraction, *then* there was whatever I felt around the owner of *The Dens*. The intensity between us was too high for casual, too high for steady, and just too fucking high across the board. After two failed relationships, I knew keeping my head in a relationship was paramount. Giving men power over me never worked out.

What Alarick made me feel? No way.

No way.

Love didn't always feel good or make the people *in* a relationship better. Anything with Alarick had 50 percent disaster written all over it.

I'd ogle the hot bastard from a distance.

Logan was the guy for me.

I scowled again and swiped my purse, checking my cards and phone were inside.

Locking up, I set off for *The Dens*, anticipation clenching tight within. This could be my life. Playing music three nights a week. For a *living*. Waking in this oasis and immersing myself in what the valley had to offer—lakes, cafes, drinks with friends.

Fuck. I wanted it so bad.

For the first time in a long time, there were so many possibilities on the horizon. That didn't make me as nauseous as it did a few days prior.

"Holy shit, Andie," I whispered to myself, executing a shuffle in my heels.

This *had* to happen.

Out of breath, I joined the line of partygoers seeking entrance to *The Dens*. The handsome bouncer caught my eye from the front, beckoning me.

Ugh, was he going to be a pain?

"You're here to see the boss?" he asked.

Extending an olive branch? "Yeah," I replied. "Listen, sorry about the other night. I was in a temper."

He drawled a smile, stamping a woman's hand and gesturing her inside. "Leroy has that effect on women."

"Dimples?"

"Cute. Mind if I borrow that?"

I grinned. "Go wild."

He lowered his head and dark hair flopped over his eyes. "In the interest of keeping the peace, you should know Leroy uses those dimples as a weapon."

Good to know. "Thanks."

"No problem. I'm Hairy."

He extended a hand, looking at me expectantly. A glint of humour shone in his eyes, and I cocked a brow. Guys played the same games as girls, and this establishment had bro code written all over it.

Hairy was finding out my name for Alarick.

I took his hand. "Nice to meet you, Hairy. Might see ya around."

Withholding a smirk, I strode into the thrumming club, heading for the bar.

The promise of an unforgettable night pulsed across the polished concrete floors, slithering up my spine like a lover's caress. Magnetic was an understatement. I didn't see how anyone could fail to respond to the blatant dare.

Slipping into a stool, I caught the attention of a male bartender. *Seriously, where is the sexy spring?*

He approached at a saunter. "What can I do for you, beautiful?"

My ego would be huge after a week. "I don't really know. Something fruity? Not too sweet though."

The guy leaned forward, face twisting. "Rhona?"

"*Not* Rhona," I answered. "Not a Thana."

The sneer disappeared as if snatched away.

Interesting. The people in this bar were the only ones not gushing over Mum's family. Even the cashiers at the supermarket had tripped over themselves to praise *the* Thanas.

The bartender dialled his smile to ten. "Well, *not* Rhona and *not* Thana. Do you like gin?"

No idea. "Sure."

"How does a lemon and raspberry gin cocktail sound, gorgeous?"

I cocked a brow at his over-the-top flirting. "Delicious. And could you let Alarick know I'm here?"

The bartender's smoulder vanished. "You're the saxophone player?"

Uhm.

"I wasn't aware that was associated with leprosy," I replied.

He flashed a grin. "It's not. I'll get him for you. Drinks are on the house for workers."

The bartender disappeared like I really did have leprosy, and I ignored the covert looks from the other staff as I dug out my phone.

Scrolling down to Logan's number, I dialled before I wimped out.

"Babe?"

"Hey, Lo. Got a minute?"

"Sure, just finished work."

"Busy day?"

"You know it, sexy."

Logan was a junior litigator and the job came with huge hours.

Licking my lips, I squeezed my eyes shut. "I have something to say that's going to come as a surprise."

His voice was tight. "You're pregnant."

"What? Jesus, no!"

"Thank fuck," he said, blowing out a breath.

I could second that. "It's nothing like that. Actually, some really good things have happened here. And. Well. I've decided to stay in Deception Valley—for a while."

My breath lodged in my chest at the heavy quiet.

"What the fuck? Are you serious? For how long?"

I grimaced. That's why I'd left this call until last. "For the foreseeable future. It feels right here. I can't explain it. Everything is so beautiful. The people are welcoming and, well, you know about my uncle and cousin. I want what this place—"

"What about *us*?"

Yikes. He was pissed, and I couldn't blame him. This move was selfish, especially when we were meant to be a team.

But I'd never acted selfishly in my life.

My eyes wandered over the bottles lining the back of the bar. "That's what we need to discuss."

"You're ending things."

From pregnancy to breaking up. Talk about whiplash.

"No, that's not it. I wanted to talk with you about long distance. It's up to you, of course. I can understand why you may not want to do that."

"So you're *asking* if I want to break up with you?" he said sarcastically.

Alpha males. "I realise this is a shock, Logan. If you're too hurt right now to discuss it, we can talk tomorrow."

"A *discussion*, Andie. Are you for real? You've already made the damn decision. Long distance never works. You'll be nine hours away. Is there even an airport there?"

"We could make it work. You just need to be sure that you're willing to commit to the distance thing. It's not fair of me to assume."

His voice deepened. "This isn't on me. Tell me what *you* want. How am I meant to take your sudden choice to live nine hours away?"

Logan rarely reached this state. He had a loud and explosive kind of temper unless truly riled.

"I want to be with you, Lo. Maybe long distance won't work, but I want to give it a try. I'll miss you—you know I will, but this wouldn't be happening if I didn't feel I had to do this."

"You aren't acting like the person I know. Buying a car and disappearing to that hole in the ground. Forgetting to check in, then calling to tell me this. Is it your mother dying? Is that it?"

Hurt speared me at the unexpected mention of Mum. "Of course. On some level. I came here to find out more about her. That's a big part of why I'm staying—"

"I'm asking if you're handling the grief or if it's handling you."

That was a jab. Heat crept over my jaw. "What's that supposed to mean?"

"What I said."

"Don't make this about my mother, Logan. I understand you feel shitty. Be angry at me, but don't make nasty comments. You know that's too far."

"Nine *hours* is too far. And the question was genuine."

Like fuck it was. "How about if you ever lose one of your parents, you let me know how you're *handling* the fucking grief? If you'd like to talk about this like a grown-up, call tomorrow. Until then, rub your fucking earlobes."

I hung up, throwing the phone on the bar and gripping the black stone counter, wishing I could snap off a chunk and crumble it to dust. After that, I'd smash all the bottles behind the bar and get to work on the stools and furniture.

"Good evening."

That voice.

I'd sacrifice lambs to that voice.

The tension drained from my shoulders, and I peeked up at Alarick. A grey suit tonight. I much preferred my lumberjack daydream—torn jeans and a singlet that revealed glistening muscles. Maybe a beanie.

Mmm.

His honey eyes fixed on my face, but not in a good way. It was like all my tension after the call with Logan had fled into him. He looked ready to smash a few things himself.

"Would you like to sit so my neck doesn't get stuck in this position forever?" I flipped my hair.

Bad Andie! Hair flipping was *bad*.

He took the seat next to me. "Allow me to say that you put every other woman in here to shame in that dress."

The guy got an A+ in the compliments department. I was used to —and pretty proficient—in dirty talk but turned out plain ol' charm had me floored, particularly because it wasn't greasy charm.

I also liked the way he sat with enough distance between us. I felt small sitting beside him, but he didn't use his size to intimidate.

The bartender placed my cocktail down, sliding an amber drink with ice in front of Alarick.

I sipped at my drink.

"It's so good," I exclaimed, eyes widening. What was this again? Lemon, raspberry and gin cocktail? This was my new drink. Such a twenty-year-old thing to do.

I smiled into the wide-brimmed glass.

The bartender rubbed the back of his shaved head. "Glad you like it, miss."

Miss?

This exchange was starting to feel like when one of my old friends called dibs on a guy and everyone else had to instantly friend zone them.

Had Alarick made me *off limits*?

I wasn't down with anyone calling dibs on me.

The bartender made scarce, and I took another sip.

"Can I get your name?" Did he purposely speak quietly to put people at ease? His voice should be twenty times the volume with the broad expanse of his chest. He must lower his voice on purpose—which was strangely attractive.

"Andie Booker." I shivered.

"Andie," he repeated.

I swallowed at the slightly dazed quality to his voice. "I've had time to think about your offer."

He blinked several times.

Was he okay?

"I'm worth one hundred dollars an hour." I looked him square in the eye. "I do appreciate the need to work my way up. Eighty dollars an hour with a wage review in three months, and another in a year—annually after that—works for me. I'm reliable and punctual and professional. You can expect me to be here and playing three nights a week and to keep the music fresh. Extended hours will depend on my availability, but I'm not afraid of work. I'd just like ample notice."

Alarick observed me. *Damn*, he was doing the "hot guy hold on the glass." Thumb and forefinger lightly resting around the brim.

Focus.

"Tell you what," he said. "Sixty dollars to start. If you prove over the course of a month that your music is increasing my revenue and numbers, we'll review your pay again then. Then every six months."

The deal was good, but just short of my end goal. "Sixty-five, Alarick, and you have a deal." I brushed my hair back.

He sucked in a breath and choked on his drink.

"You alright, boss?" It was the female bartender from two nights ago.

Alarick glared. "Fine, Mandy."

Ooh, there's the angry lumberjack. Now he just had to explode out of his suit.

Mandy fixed him with a shit-eating grin, eyes downcast in a demure manner no one could believe.

"What do you say, Alarick? Let's seal the deal."

Our gazes locked, and I became acutely aware my words contained a massive serving of sexual innuendo.

Kill me now.

"Agreed." His tone was all mild politeness.

I tried to conceal my inward quailing, lifting my drink to him. He took me in slowly, clinking his glass against mine.

"Andie," he murmured.

Swallowing the lemon and raspberry deliciousness, I cocked a brow. "Yeah?"

"What?"

I frowned. "You said my name."

Mandy cleared her throat. "You said her name, boss. Kind of mumbled it into your Johnnie Walker."

Alarick cut her a furious look, and I bit back my own smile. She played coy worker well, but Mandy had the run of him. They had a brother and younger sister vibe going on.

"I was going to ask you a question," he said, ignoring Mandy's wide grin. "Do you need help with anything else as you settle into the valley?"

Some wood. I don't have a fireplace, but I'll watch you cut it.

"All set, thanks." I crossed my ankles under the stool, swinging them gently. "I'm renting a place. Everything else is pretty much sorted."

"Pretty much or actually sorted?"

I shot him a look and didn't answer.

"You can say fuck off with just your eyes. Quite the talent." He returned to his drink.

My lips twitched, and I raised my cocktail, taking another drink.

"I'll say no more then. Drinks for workers are free, but please don't drink during work hours. Afterward is fine. You'll also accrue holiday and sick leave."

A huge and unexpected bonus. "I look forward to working here. When do I start?"

"Is tomorrow night too soon?"

Thinking of my sax locked up in the apartment, I said, "It's never too soon to play music."

His mouth opened as he stared.

I cleared my throat and glanced at Mandy.

"Uh, boss? Hairy needs help at the door with something."

Alarick snapped his attention to her. "Hairy?

"Hairy," she said slowly.

"*Hairy*."

"At the door," she said.

Alarick nearly fell over trying to stand. "Yes. The door. Miss Booker, Andie, have a lovely evening."

He straightened and met my gaze.

Okay. I looked good tonight, sexy even, but this sculpture of a lumberjack just acted like I was the most beautiful creation in the universe.

I nodded. "I did have one more question. You mentioned I won't be needed on Mondays and Tuesdays. I'm assuming the same for Wednesday?"

"We're closed on Wednesday nights," he said after a beat. "We play laser tag against one of the other families in town."

Dipping his head, Alarick left the bar. My mouth dried.

This was the second family? The enemy family of the Thanas. *Shit!* No wonder Herc went quiet when I mentioned a job at *The Dens*.

Groaning, I gulped at my drink, only to find it empty.

Another appeared in front of me.

"Sounds like you need it," Mandy murmured.

Did I ever.

I passed her the empty, swiping the new drink, but another realisation smacked me between the eyes. Twisting in my seat, I scanned the four bouncers in sight, then the six bartenders—two of them male. All of them large. All muscled—the doorman, Hairy, and Dimples included. Any of them could be the bastard who pushed me into the pit.

"I *have* to know what you're thinking right now."

I spun back to find Mandy leaning across the bar, propped on her elbows. The platinum blonde had the coolest upper arm tattoo, a band with a wolf face centrepiece. Athletic model *ripped* too. I'd never pulled off the athlete look—too much boobs and ass. When I wore activewear, people assumed my destination was brunch or the mall.

"There are a lot of big guys working here," I replied.

Is one of you the bastard who scared me?

Not that I truly held a grudge. Maybe a small one... Nothing a kick in the nuts wouldn't fix.

She shrugged. "The Luthers tend toward the large side."

"Is that a family name?"

Thanas vs. Luthers.

She wiped the countertop. "Kind of. More like a... branch or group, I guess."

"And, quick question. Do all of your guys look that way?"

"Hot? Depends what you like."

In my experience, the mention of alphas made people think of black leather and whips. That's not what the attraction was for me. I referred to alpha *personalities*. I liked men who could match and counter my own strength. I didn't want to walk all over someone. Others might find that attractive—but not me.

That's where things got difficult.

I simultaneously needed someone who could stand up to me while not trampling my heart. In my experience, the stronger two peoples' wills, the harder it was to strike that perfect symbiotic balance.

I'd never found it. Then again, I wasn't sure that flow of give and take even existed outside of movies and books.

"I like a confident guy," I told her. "One who knows his mind but isn't a dick."

Mandy scanned the room. "Good luck finding that with any alpha in this room."

Ha. Unexpected response. "I'm usually into alpha guys actually."

My words appeared to amuse her. "They're charismatic and sexy, I'll give you that. Powerful too. But if you don't want a player, avoid them like the plague."

Was Alarick a player? His compliments were genuine, but they fell from his full lips so easily. That had to be a bad sign.

I peeked over my shoulder to where he was in deep conversation with Hairy.

"Alarick isn't an alpha."

I jerked. "Oh, not interested. I'm with someone. I was just analysing the... aesthetic of the people working here."

Her blue eyes sparkled. "Uh-huh."

I tapped a finger against the countertop. "Alarick seems pretty alpha-ish to me though."

Almost detached in a mysterious way, I could help but note how unobtrusively he managed his staff. And yet they all deferred to his quiet, restrained manner. Alarick never outlined the rules of working here during our talk, yet I completely understood his expectations.

I hesitated to call his actions kind... more like *calculated.*

In other words, I was thinking about him too much. Looking was free, yes, but this was going a step too far for my own moral comfort.

Mandy leaned in. "Alarick isn't an alpha, Andie," she whispered so softly that I had to lean in to hear. "He's a sigma."

What the heck was a sigma?

I licked my lips. "What does that mean?"

Her eyes slid to the door. "A lot of things. But all *you* need to know is that when a sigma sees something he wants, he takes it."

8

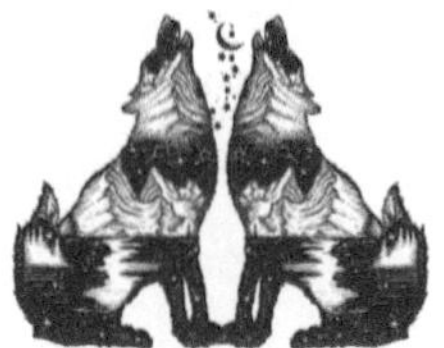

Standing beside Herc, I watched Rhona inspect the apartment. She'd already visited once, but this predatory behaviour had to be the norm—Herc's face only displayed slight sheepishness, like he'd given up trying to curb her behaviour a long time ago.

"Not in the bags," I said. "I told you last time."

She dropped the top of my suitcase, casting me a baleful look.

Herc muttered, "Sorry about that."

"People who bake me blueberry muffins don't need to be sorry."

The muffins were still warm and sat in a basket on the small dining table.

He lifted a shoulder. "People tell me they're good. I hope you like them."

My sweet tooth was a fearsome creature. Liking them was almost assured.

"I've been meaning to say," I stole a glance at him, "I didn't realise the Luthers were the team you play laser tag against. I hope working for them doesn't make things uncomfortable for you."

Because I rang my boss in Queen's Way this morning to quit my reception job.

Herc smiled. "I appreciate you asking, but it doesn't."

"That laser tag feud is intense."

His expression was serious. "You could say that. But you haven't grown up around it, and my biases aren't your own."

True. "Part of me wants to be more involved in this game. I'm half scared and half curious."

He shook his head as Rhona looked in the top drawers of the bedside tables. "See how you settle in. Laser tag isn't for everyone."

Was that a brush off? Seemed like one. *Dang.* Herc not wanting me on his team kind of hurt. Then again, did I really want to play?

"Dad said your mum died recently," Rhona said, flopping back on my bed. "How did she die?"

Herc shot me a look. "*Rhona.*"

"Bone cancer," I replied calmly. "Any other questions?"

She rolled to face me. "Yeah, this can't be all your stuff."

"It's not."

Rhona's eyes gleamed. "Are you poor?"

She wanted to test the boundaries with me? Why? She wasn't like this last time. The only change between now and then was that I'd decided to stay.

Did she feel threatened or think I was here for their wealth? There was a restrained anger to her that I felt deep in my soul.

"Dirt poor," I chirped. "Especially since I had to drive your friends around two days ago. Time to pay up."

Rhona frowned. "I planned to pay you."

Plans don't pay bills. "Glad to hear it. What does your mum do?"

Herc stilled, and Rhona sat.

"My mother is dead," she said coolly.

Oops.

Still. This wasn't a battle I wanted to lose. "How did she die?"

Rhona scowled. "None of your business."

"You just asked me the same question. Don't tell me you're the kind who can give but not take."

Fury painted her features, and I recognised it well. If her temper was anything like mine, the fallout would be all-consuming but quick.

"I like to visualise smashing things when I'm mad, if that helps. Please don't actually break anything." I turned back to Herc.

His eyes darted between us, slightly widened. The sight nearly made me laugh.

"Oh, I wanted to grab the number of Mum's friends off you, if that's okay?" I asked.

"Sure. That's..." Herc snuck another look at his daughter.

"Great." I reached for a blueberry muffin and bit down. "Holy moly. Seriously good. You'll have to give me the recipe."

"It was one of your grandmother's. Ragna never made them?"

I lowered the muffin. "Mum wasn't a baker."

"She used to bake all the time," he said sadly.

I stared at the muffin in my hand, and it came rushing back—the last name, the deception, the entire *life* that she'd had here and that she'd hidden so well.

I had to know more.

"I'd love to learn as much as I can about Mum." I peered into his steady blue gaze.

Rhona snorted, and I glanced to where she still sat, probably seething.

"That's funny to you? Don't you have the same curiosity about your mother?" I asked.

Her brows arched. "I know everything about my mother."

"That must be nice. Why is it funny that I don't know much about mine? Doesn't that make you sad on my behalf?"

There weren't many who could handle soft confrontation, and I could thank my mother for that lesson.

Her face blanked.

That's what I thought. She didn't have an answer.

I had issues, but they didn't manifest in the same way. To everyone else, she may seem like a bitch, but to me, she seemed deeply unhappy.

In that, we were the same.

"I don't have any other cousins and no siblings," I told her. "I'd like to spend time with you, and I hope that's returned. If so, I'd prefer that time be pleasant, but you're welcome to set whatever tone you like."

When I returned my attention to Herc, he seemed a little lost.

He jerked as she stormed out and slammed the door. Was he pissed I gave Rhona the linguistic smackdown? Rhona could take or leave my offer. I wouldn't cry myself to sleep. Though I really hoped she took it.

When he faced me again, his mild expression had morphed to sharp focus.

Interesting.

"Are you serious about joining our laser tag team?" He walked to the window.

The casualness of his question didn't jive with the intensity of his posture. "Uh, yeah. I guess so."

"You know there's far more to it than normal laser tag," he continued, watching the busy street below.

"You should know that I've never played laser tag in my life." I wasn't uncoordinated, but I'd never fired a gun, wrestled, or made anything other than a snare. Should I mention my Girl Guide sash?

"Laser tag is one part of it. The game extends to real life too. If we bring you into this... I don't want to say there's no going back, but you should know the Luthers you work with may not take kindly to your participation."

If the situation were reversed, I was willing to bet the Thanas wouldn't take it kindly either. If someone couldn't like me because I played a game for the other side, they could get screwed.

Though if I got sacked, that *would* be a problem.

Hmm.

"No one pulls shit outside of the game though, right? I mean, that's the whole point of playing laser tag, to confine the family feud to a Wednesday night."

Maybe this wasn't for me...

"Absolutely. There are penalties for those who act outside the grids too. I just don't want you to take the game lightly. It's a very serious thing for those who play it. Once, it was a serious thing for your mother too."

That caught my attention. "It was?"

"My sister was our star player."

My mother, running through the forest trapping people and kicking ass? I could totally imagine that. My smile faded. Only because of the way she used to yell and shout while gambling.

Her addiction tainted so many memories. My heart squeezed to breaking point. "Please tell me you have photos."

"Plenty." He assured me.

Could I do that too? "Is there someone who'd show me how to play?"

I understood what Herc was saying. Playing was a heavy commitment. I remembered the intense energy of the masked players in the forest. And the experience with Flannel Man had shown me the game could be scary.

I also got what he didn't say—don't waste our time, but I could leave the game at any time. Plus, the players I saw ranged from mid-teens to at least sixty.

My unlucky experience aside, the game couldn't be *that* dangerous.

Herc grimaced. "Actually, there's a training programme."

Whoa.

"I'll let you think about it. Know this though. If you enter the game, you'll learn things about yourself and the world. While that may seem overwhelming, I *can* promise that you'll join a community who will have your back."

Yeah, that concept was almost off-putting. The idea of *me*, Andie Charise Booker, joining a community made me want to run for the hills. Not because I didn't know myself. Because I *did.* This girl operated best alone.

Of course, I needed people. Just enough to not feel lost and alone. Maybe this game, these people, could provide that *enough*.

More to the point, this was an opportunity to know Mum better, and I didn't really need to consider my options past that.

But habit was a bitch.

Buying Ella F would most likely remain my sole spontaneous choice for another twenty-one years. "Okay, I will. One question."

Herc turned from the window. "Anything."

"What changed your mind just now?" I didn't imagine that brush-off earlier.

His gaze flicked to the door. "Rhona's my heir. That's an odd concept outside of these parts, but here that's laden with responsibility. I've never seen someone stand up to my daughter and win. She needs that presence, whether she likes it or not. Since her mother's death, I've struggled to reach her. Once, I might have pushed, but my past with Ragna taught me the stupidity of that approach. Sometimes, our loved ones don't need *us*. They need someone else. You may be that person for Rhona." His voice softened. "I hope she may be that person for you, too. There's more strength when we stick together."

I checked out my outfit. A broad smile curved my lips, even torn between nerves and exhilaration as I was. I dabbed eyeshadow on, making sure my emerald eyes would be stark to all that glimpsed them.

For my first night of work at *The Dens,* I'd settled on another secondhand score. The strapless, crimson dress clung to me until mid-thigh. Anything less and I worried the audience would get more of a show than they bargained for. I'd rarely been on stage in my life—not since high school when I'd done a few solos in the annual concerts.

Gold spaghetti-strap heels decorated my feet—three inches, I wasn't superwoman—a match for my eyeshadow and tassel earrings. A high and sleek ponytail completed the look after an hour spent straightening the mass of hair. Unfortunately, playing saxophone with hair down was a pain in the hole.

I sashayed before the mirror, taking a deep breath. "Okay, Andie. You have one month to wow the crowd."

I wanted seventy bucks an hour, and Alarick clearly outlined the criteria for a pay rise.

5:40 p.m.

I took out my sax, running through some scales and a song. I spent the day learning a new piece and couldn't wait to unleash it tonight.

Cleaning out the bell and mouthpiece, I opted to hang the sax around my neck and carry my case and purse.

Nerves twisted in my gut as I left the apartment. Mum would have loved this. She would have watched me every night, glaring daggers at anyone who didn't clap.

I bent my head to hide my grin from those milling around me.

Reaching the club, I strode to the front of the queue. "Hey, Hairy."

The towering man was the tall and lean muscle type, unlike Leroy and Alarick. Seriously, why the hell was he called *Hairy*? His face, and what I could see of his chest, were as smooth as my legs after meticulous shaving. Was it an ironic thing?

"Evening, gorgeous," he murmured.

"Good crowd tonight?" I'd never played for drunk people. I hoped they didn't invade my personal space.

Hairy caught my eye. "Don't you worry about the crowd. The bouncers will keep an extra eye out for you. You're going to kill it out there. I heard you playing the other day."

My shoulders relaxed at his words. "From all the way up here?"

I guess sound carried. The valley was a natural amphitheatre.

"You got this, Andie." He drew back the cordon, and I slipped inside, moving to the bar. Mandy was on duty.

"Hey, sexy," she greeted, mixing a line of drinks. My eyes nearly crossed with her rapid movements. She made mixing look like a dance.

A row of middle-aged guys sat before her, not bothering to hide their adoration. Couldn't blame them, she was all classy rock goddess

—short skirt, midriff off-the-shoulder top, and an array of tattoos and jewellery.

"How's the crowd tonight?" I asked her too.

Sue me, I was nervous.

"Before or after you showed up in that dress?" She slid me a water with a slice of lemon bobbing on top.

I peered down. "Too much?"

"Fucking perfect, I'd say." She seemed amused.

"Thanks. Where should I set up?"

"Boss wants you to start in here, and head into the back room later. He was going to show you around before you started, but he must be held up somewhere."

She snickered, but I was too wound up for joking around.

I followed her pointing finger. Across the plush floor filled with leather couches, low tables, and pendant lights, rested a small circle gold stage. Right in the middle of the club. Or this part of the club, apparently.

The stage matched my outfit. *Cute.*

If my music sucked, I could start stripping on it.

I pulled my shoulders back, moving toward the low stage. There was a lull in the conversation of those close by as I stepped onto the gold platform—in my gold shoes. I'd get over the matching thing one day.

A black stool sat in the middle.

Unlike a corner stage, there was nothing to hide behind. I was on display from all angles. The ear and eye candy of the entire bar. The phrase *unnerving as fuck* came to mind. But my sax was here, and it wouldn't fail me.

I set my glass of water on the stool, placing my case beside it as I wet my reed again on autopilot.

Act like you know what you're doing.

This was going to be such a high if I could channel my nerves into something constructive.

I smiled at the nearest table. "How are you all doing tonight?"

They chorused their answer in a wordless wave of approval.

"I think that was good," I replied with a wink.

They laughed, and I felt my insides unclench a teensy amount.

Here goes.

Setting my top teeth in place on the mouthpiece, I drew air into my lower ribs. A new song by Duffy was my intended opening piece, but I'd officially chickened out. Something tried and true sounded better right now until I conquered the nerves.

Warmth pulsed deep as I eased into the swooping dive of Nina Simone's "Feeling Good". I caught my throat tightening as conversation ceased to exist in the bar. Countering it, I loosened my body and settled into the classic piece. Playing this song was akin to sliding over silk sheets, but the euphoric composition meant so much more. No matter who covered it, the song spoke of freedom.

Entering the second verse, my fingers flew through the familiar sequence and I swayed my hips, Nina's hypnotic voice playing in my head.

The last note was powerful, and I pulled in a large breath, holding the note strong and ending in a growl that caused an outbreak of appreciative murmurs.

I opened my eyes, smiling at the rampant applause.

Phew.

Now to repeat that for three and a half hours.

I launched into work, only stopping for sips of the water that magically topped up when I had my eyes closed. Luckily, I was an on-the-spot dancer because I liked to play with my eyes closed and falling off the stage would be fatally embarrassing.

The patrons didn't press in on my space, and the volume in the bar steadily increased as the night wound on. Was their respectfulness due to the bouncers watching my back or the strange undercurrent riding the club? There weren't any rules plastered around the place. The vibe was seductive and enticing, but there was that subtle edge that spoke for what may happen to those who caused trouble.

It added a darkness that only added to the sultry atmosphere.

Was that Alarick's doing or the bouncers? Had to be the bouncers because I hadn't seen hide nor hair of my boss tonight.

I checked my phone.

Shit. Only thirty minutes left. My reception job dragged at half speed. This must be what a job of passion felt like.

What if every night was like this?

Maybe I'd give that new song a whirl after all. I'd need to get used to playing songs that I hadn't practiced for months. I was proficient enough to embellish my way out of mistakes.

"Excuse me," a woman in a severely cut navy blue dress called over the noise.

She reeked of money, and though she'd used manners, I had no doubt she expected my full attention.

"Yes, ma'am?" I asked.

She held a chute of champagne, but it was hard to spot through the dazzling light reflecting off her priceless rings and bracelets. "Are you here every night, darling?"

"Thursday through Saturday, every week."

The woman smiled. "Good. I like the addition. I'll be back."

Oh, cool. I'd live off her drop of praise until she gave me my next fix. "I'm glad to hear that, ma'am. Have a pleasant evening."

She held up a stack of red disks. "I will."

I froze, watching her leave. Those were... *casino chips.*

"Andie?"

Breaking out of my stupor, I looked at Dimples. Leroy, was it? "Yeah?"

"There's a guy at the bar. Says he knows you? He seems hopping mad."

Huh? I scanned the bar and swore under my breath. *Fuck.*

Logan was here.

"Want me to get rid of him?" Leroy asked.

Ugh, Logan's posture was rigid. Definitely pissed. He'd probably spent the entire drive down working himself into a rage.

I pressed my lips together. "Nah, that's okay. Sorry for the trouble though. You can tell Alarick it won't happen again."

"Tell me what?"

My eyes fluttered closed, just as they did when I played. I slanted a look over my shoulder. We were on eye level with me on stage and in heels.

"My boyfriend is here," I said, jerking my head. "He's hurt after our phone call last night, but this is a one-off. I assure you."

A deep bass filled the air, and I twisted to find the sound.

Those close by could hear it too.

What the heck?

Leroy gripped Alarick's arm.

The sound abruptly cut off.

"What was that?" I asked.

Alarick's head was bowed, and with an angry snarl, he tore away, heading for the staff door

I glanced at Dimples. "Was that anything to do with me?"

"Yep."

What? "Is it my playing? I kind of need this job."

He grinned. "It's his time of the month, so to speak."

I relaxed. "Good. Mandy said I was meant to move into another room halfway through my set, but time got away from me."

"Alarick decided to leave you where you were for tonight. He does want to show you around once you're done. Give you the tour."

I'd noticed people disappearing through curtains at the back of the establishment in a steady stream. "No problem. And it's nice to meet you. Leroy, right?"

He crossed his arms, drawing my attention to his biceps. "Back at you. I wish I could say I'm sorry for stealing your cap, but if it landed you on this stage, I can't bring myself to regret it."

What did Mandy say? Alphas were charismatic players? A hundred percent yes. "Noted," I replied drily. "I'll stop referring to you as Dimples in my head."

Leroy's gaze narrowed. "You started that?"

"Hmm, what?"

He snorted. "We'll get along just fine. Listen, I usually manage the back room, but I'm covering for another manager tonight. Let's call it a night. You played beautifully, and judging by the way people are spending, you'll be a great addition to The Dens."

Fucking hoped so.

"Good to hear. If I can have a few minutes to deal with my boyfriend, I'll be ready for the tour with Alarick."

"But will *he?*"

"What?"

"I'll get the boss."

Not what he said, but I had another problem on my hands.

Leroy left, and my hands shook as I dissembled my sax, twisting off the mouthpiece and tilting it so my saliva didn't drip out—the gross part of wind instruments.

How *dare* Logan come here and cause a scene. I'd promised Alarick professionalism, and within hours of starting, Logan caused drama.

Zipping my case, I grabbed the water, and smiled at those praising my playing as I strode toward the bar.

The seats either side of Logan were empty. Couldn't blame the patrons—he radiated rage, though freakin' handsome in a white shirt and black trousers.

I set my case and water on the bar, rolling my shoulders to relieve the ache. "Logan."

He finished his drink, placing the glass down with too much force. "Andie."

"Any particular reason you thought storming into my place of work was appropriate?"

His temper didn't scare me.

He stood, and I tilted my gaze up, unafraid. *Yeah*, that shit didn't scare me either.

"I just drove nine hours to talk things over. I get to your place and you're not in on a Saturday night. Then I hear you playing, come in here, and see a room filled with horny men watching you play music in that scrap of a dress."

There were so many insults in that remark that I simply ignored them all. "Would I burst into your workplace like this, Logan?"

His gaze narrowed.

Jesus, what did I say about emotion being a foreign language?

I folded my arms. "Is it possible you're still angry after our phone call last night?"

"Why wouldn't I be?"

"Lower your voice. This is my workplace," I said, drawing to my full height. I dug through my purse. "Here are my keys. I'll be back at the apartment in an hour. We'll talk there."

His face hardened. "You're telling me to go away after I came all the way to see you?"

So dramatic. "You know what I would have loved, Lo? Is to see you again after our time apart. I don't appreciate the way you're behaving. It has ruined that surprise for me. I'm aware that you're upset. You don't need to be a dick."

His fingers closed tight around the keys, but he sighed, running a hand through his hair. "Fuck, okay. I messed this up. The way they were staring at you though. How the hell is this going to work?"

I pressed my body against his and looped my hands around his neck. "It works if we want it to. That's how."

His gaze hooded. "Want?"

Logan pressed a hand into the small of my back, and I smirked at the rigid outline of his erection against my stomach.

"Been a few days?" I moved my hips, biting his lower lip.

"You could say that." He captured my mouth in a bruising kiss, three quarters arousal and a quarter anger—not a mix I minded by any stretch of the imagination.

I broke away. "I'll see you in an hour."

"Will the wait be worth my while?"

I trailed a finger over my collarbone, raking my gaze over his body. "I'm surprised you have to ask."

He reached for me, and I evaded his arms, snagging my case as I set off to find Alarick.

A bouncer stood in front of the staff door.

"Hey, I'm Andie. Is Alarick around? He's giving me a tour."

The bouncer didn't get a chance to answer. The door at his back opened to reveal the devil himself. He'd returned to his usual quiet demeanour, and I decided not to question him about what happened earlier. I hated people up in my business.

Alarick stopped in front of me. "Sorry about earlier. I received some bad news."

Well, that was a lie. But whatever. "Not a problem. Leroy said you wanted to give me a tour."

His eyes shifted to the bar before fixing on me.

"Yes, but I wanted to say your playing was absolutely exquisite. The sound you create matches the vision you present."

Heat crept into my cheeks. The bouncer was staring studiously ahead.

"Thanks." *Did he just call me absolutely exquisite?*

"This way, please."

We walked toward the back and his hand splayed across my lower back twice as we navigated between the couches and thick crowd, leaving a scalding warmth behind.

I shifted farther from Alarick, holding my case handle in both hands.

"Can I take that for you? It looks heavy?"

"More cumbersome than anything." My shoulders were sore, but this was my baby.

"I'm sure I can manage. You keep rolling your shoulders."

That level of observation stunned me into looking up. "Part of playing. Nothing I'm unused to."

"Even so, I can carry it for you."

I tightened my grip. "I'm fine, thanks."

Alarick paused, jaw clenching. "I didn't mean to offend you."

"I just like to hold it."

His honey eyes were *so much*. I might not like the way they turned me inside out, but I could marvel at the dangerous chemistry between us.

Remind me to never get drunk at The Dens.

I tore my focus from him with no small amount of effort and studied the space we'd entered.

Tellers lined the walls on either side. People queued, waiting their turn with a member of staff behind the counter. Some held suitcases. Others carrier bags.

Some clutched stacks of colourful disks.

My mouth dried. Casino chips *again.*

"What is this place?" I asked hoarsely, cold dread filling me.

"This is where people exchange their chips for money," Alarick answered, watching me closely.

My legs took over as I surged forward, bursting through to the next room.

The next *huge* room.

Filled with a green I'd hated since seven years old.

The money green covered the roulette and craps tables, the blackjack and poker tables, lending a uniformity to the crowded space that highlighted the flashing, gleaming pokie machines at the back.

Spend money you don't have. Forsake those you love. Give control to your disease.

My sax fell from my grip.

The *Dens.*

Not a word to describe an exclusive bar or club.

This place was a *gambling* den.

9

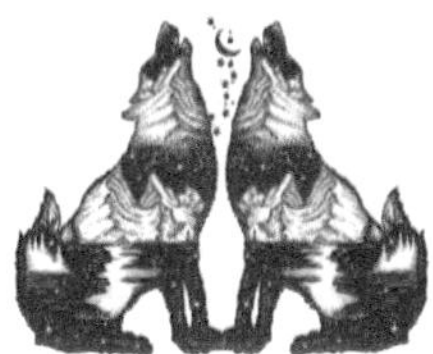

I burst from *The Dens* into the cool night air. A fucking *casino*. That's where I worked? After all my mother's pain and the shitstorm it landed me in?

No fucking way!

A large hand wrapped around my upper arm as I reached the other side of the street. Alarick drew me to a halt but didn't spin me around. He merely stood there as, with my back to his chest, I struggled to control my breathing.

A tear slipped down my cheek and I dashed it away.

"I assume you didn't know the purpose of our establishment?" he asked softly.

Another tear. I brushed it off angrily.

"No." I turned to him. "I thought it was a bar."

"That was my error." He sounded nearly heartbroken on my behalf. I wasn't mad at him—beyond the fact I found casinos and everything about them and the people who ran them vile in every way. If I'd known this about Alarick, we never would have gotten past the busking conversation.

I put more distance between us. "It caught me off guard is all."

Damn his eyes. They missed nothing. Not the extra space. Not my wet lashes.

I didn't want him to see me like this. I scooted farther away, and he didn't make a move to reach me.

My breath came easier.

"You don't like casinos?"

Understatement of the century. "How long has this been here?"

"A year. Why?"

No reason. I just wanted him to stop looking at me for one second. "I need to go."

His chest rose and fell, and he took a step toward me.

"I'm not going to hurt you," Alarick said low, hands raised.

Ugh, I was taking everything out on him.

On my boss.

Though he wouldn't be that for much longer.

I stared at the ground, "I can't work for you, Alarick. I loved playing tonight, but I won't have anything to do with casinos."

For a moment, I'd felt like I had it all. That's what made this extra shitty.

"Could you say goodbye to Mandy, Hairy, and Leroy for me?" My heart leaped into my throat as his gaze darkened.

"Will you stay in the valley?"

The desperate ring in his words reminded me of the last time I mentioned leaving. He didn't even know me then—and really, he didn't know me now.

I wrinkled my brows. "I don't know. I probably need to go back."

Maybe I could beg for my old job back. *One fucking day.* If I'd waited a *single* day to make that call, I wouldn't be in this mess.

Fuck!

"To your boyfriend?"

"That's none of your business." My hands curled to fists.

The whole thing between us toed a line I didn't want to walk. Alarick had to back off.

My anger didn't intimidate him. "What if I want it to be my business?"

Whoa. He could not be reading the signs I was flashing at him right now because one read *Casino Owners are Filth* and the other read *Fuck off*. "That is inappropriate. I'm with someone and you're my boss."

"What if you only play in the bar and not the back room?"

I nearly stumbled with the change of subject. He closed the gap between us, and I slammed against the wall, hands spread by my sides.

"Hear me out. You'd have nothing to do with the casino side of the business," Alarick pressed. "Music in the bar. Nothing more. Nothing less."

I glared upward. "It's not the point. I know that crap is there."

"I'm not asking you to forget the casino. I'm asking you to compromise. We need you. I thought you needed us too."

We were breathing hard.

With his head bent down, we were all but nose to nose. All I could see was honey. All I could smell was him, musk... something earthier.

No part of this—me against the wall, him in my face, our gasping bodies—made sense.

Why did he want me here so badly? And why did I want to stay?

Logan.

I lowered my chin, snapping the tension.

Alarick placed space between us this time. "I've frightened you."

Not in the way he meant. His proximity was nothing. What I'd felt on the other hand...

"I'm sorry to disappoint you." I swallowed hard. "You never intended this to happen. I never would have accepted the job if..." *I knew you were destroying families.*

To my reasoning, he should be anyway between pissed off and sympathetic, but a quick peek told me the casino owner seemed lost.

This was so messed up.

"Take tonight to think about it," he urged, searching my gaze. "Trust me, regret lasts a lifetime. One night. Think things over."

I straightened.

A night to think things over wouldn't change my mind. But habit sure was a bitch. "I will."

I cast one last look over the beautiful casino owner before weaving away in a daze.

How did this amazing night upend so fast? I'd felt invincible four hours ago.

I didn't feel invincible now.

Tears stung my eyes, and I couldn't summon the energy to worry about the people gawking and muttering.

Ugh, Logan was in the apartment. Seeing him was about the last thing I wanted right now.

Removing my heels, I walked along the river until the bitter turn of my life had blunted. By the time I knocked on the apartment door, the hour I'd promised was well and truly over.

Logan swung the door open. "About time, babe."

He was shirtless, trousers open at the top. That was irresistible to me on a good day, let alone a bad day.

Maybe this night could end okay.

"Hello yourself," I replied huskily.

A slow smile spread across my face as I dropped my heels at the door, sashaying inside. Back to him, I swept my ponytail aside and pushed the stretchy strapless dress down to my hips, unclipping my bra.

Cupping my breasts, I glanced over my shoulder.

He'd taken his erection in hand, grey eyes molten as he watched my little show.

I worked my hair tie out, letting my auburn hair slither free. A soft moan left my lips—totally planned, the sound drove him crazy.

Pushing the dress to the ground, I pivoted, stepping out of the red garment. Only my thong remained, black and simple. I refused to buy underwear secondhand, so it had to be cheap.

"Andie," Logan breathed. "Come here."

"Mmm?"

With a growl, he lurched forward and yanked me against his hard frame. My head tipped back. This was our strength.

Sex.

No talking.

Just mindless, incredible se—

"We need to talk." He pulled back.

This isn't happening.

I groaned, thumping my forehead against his chest. "Right this moment?"

"You're easier to convince when you're horny."

True. A grumble left me. "Make it quick."

I padded to a suitcase and kicked it open, pulling out a midriff sweater. If I wasn't working toward orgasm, Logan couldn't see my boobs.

"That's mean," he said in a deep voice.

I didn't deny it, grabbing a blueberry muffin. "Shoot."

"I want to try long distance. I'm not happy about it. I'm still pretty fucked off about your decision, really. But I love you, Andie, and I want to try."

Wow.

The love bomb.

He'd never told me that... word... before.

"I love you," he said again.

I forced a smile around my mouthful of blueberry muffin. "Oh. Since when?"

The words sounded just as lame out loud, and I winced, flushing.

Logan laughed. "The first time I tell a woman I love her, and she doesn't say it back. Shit, Andie."

I pulled a face. "Sorry. That's a new one for me."

He sauntered closer, kissing my forehead. "I'm not done convincing you, babe, so don't worry. You're not going anywhere."

Okay, cool. Great. But now he'd dropped the love bomb, and I was suddenly thinking how much I only *liked* him.

Even after a year.

People usually loved each other after a year, right?

"Are you okay?" he asked.

I tipped my head back, scowling at the ceiling. Why'd he have to go and ruin things? "Just found out something shitty about work. It's a casino."

That's why people flocked to Deception Valley. Not to some random bar in the middle of nowhere with really good drinks and hot staff. Not because of exceptional marketing. Outsiders came to *gamble.*

I understood better than most how far that allure could pull a person.

"Ah," he said, taking a seat across from me.

"Ah what?" Logan didn't know anything about my mother's past.

His face worked. "Ragna's problem."

Problem?

Heat crept up my neck into my jaw. "What problem?"

"I came to pick you up early one day and saw an app open on her phone when she went to the bathroom."

Clenching my jaw, I said, "When was this?"

He lifted a shoulder. "Just after we first started dating."

Nearly a *year* ago? I burst to my feet. "Why didn't you say anything?"

She'd eased back into gambling, betting more and more money in the last six months of her life. I could have *hundreds of thousands of dollars* less debt right now.

"Whoa, Andie. It wasn't my place."

I rounded on him. "Not your place? Not even to mention it?"

"I didn't think anything of it." He stood slowly. "I only remembered because someone mentioned the reason for the house sale."

Ice spread through my chest. I would drive back to Queen's Way and throat punch whoever was spreading fucking rumours. "*And why is that exactly?*"

Logan blanched, backing up. "Is it true? Because that's a fucking shitty thing for her to dump on you, if so."

I stalked after him. "What did you say to them?"

"That I had no idea. That I'd ask you. Why are you going off at me for this?"

He'd *ask me?* And then what? Go back and report to the town? Where was the fucking loyalty?

I laughed, gripping my hair tight. There was so much wrong between us. Why had I only realised it now?

"Baby—"

"No," I said, raising my hands. "I've changed my mind about long distance. A clean break is best. You're right. It never would have worked."

"Are you fucking kidding me? You are not breaking up with me. This has nothing to do with us. It's about your mother!"

I marched to the door, swinging it wide. "We're not right for each other. This wasn't much more than sex. You can get that with anyone, but there's someone out there who can really make you happy."

"Don't you think I tried to make it more?" he exploded. "You're like fucking *ice* sometimes. How is this meant to be anything more when you won't let me in? You don't open up. You treat me like a glorified booty call."

That was... pretty true.

"I'm sorry you feel that way," I said, wrestling with the heat flooding my face. "I enjoyed our time together."

Yikes. Wrong thing to say.

His face twisted. "A year of my life wasted, and you *enjoyed* it? That makes it all fucking better. You can't seriously be kicking me out tonight. Where am I meant to stay?"

Maybe that was mean. *Oops*, didn't care. "In your car. It's not so bad. Bye, Logan."

A siren wailed overhead, the shrill sound blasting through my ears. Jumping, I spun, searching for the sound.

An alarm?

Logan bowled past me, snatching up his bag and shirt. I stumbled out into the hall, and he slammed the door shut, storming down the stairs. My jaw dropped as people started streaming from their apartments.

Spinning, I twisted the handle.

Mothershitter!

He'd locked me out of my apartment.

I was dressed in a thong and midriff sweater! "You piece of shit!"

The sound was lost to the shrieking alarm.

"Uh, miss?"

I faced a red-faced older man, biting back my temper. Wasn't his fault I was pissed.

He seemed determined to look only at my face. "We, uh, need to gather across the road by the river. Fire alarm procedure..."

As though my be-thonged ass *was* the fire, he hurried away.

I rubbed at my face.

This day couldn't get any worse.

10

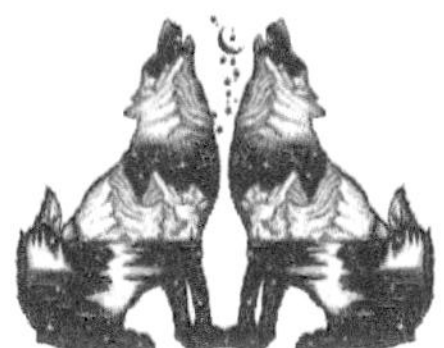

I was *that* person. I'd never really been *that* person.

Now, however, I had a two-metre span around me. No one wanted to be too close to thong girl.

Lights flashed against the night sky, dragging attention with the waning moon behind thick clouds and the valley pitched in darkness. In another situation, I might have found the old school fire engine that screeched to a halt in front of the apartment building adorable. But I'd just watched Logan screech his way out of Deception Valley five minutes ago in his fancy Audi, so adoration was out of reach.

Firefighters poured into the building. Judging by the lack of smoke and flame, I wasn't too worried.

Which was a good thing because my saxophone was in the building.

I paused at the thought. Did I have that when I left *The Dens*?

Shit.

Awesome. Fucking great.

"Hey, beautiful. Heard the sirens."

Leroy. I cast him a flat look, arms folded. "Yeah. Alarm went off."

Suited up, he took the spot beside me. Shouldn't he still be at work?

"Not that I'm complaining about the view, but would you like my jacket?"

I almost cried—the theme for the night. I couldn't help sniffling. "Yes, please."

The black suit jacket was warm as he dropped it around my shoulders.

"Anything you want to talk about?"

"How much time have you got?"

"In all honesty, not that long. You'd need to keep it quick."

Laughing, I bumped his shoulder. "Not a talker."

"Yep, picked that up. You look like more of a puncher."

His instincts were on point. Though the few times my temper resulted in that, I'd felt terrible for weeks after. "It's the hair. Sometimes I lose control."

"Tell me about it," he said, amusement plain in his warm voice.

I frowned. "What?"

A firefighter approached the crowd, pulling off his white helmet.

"Looks like you'll be inside soon," Leroy said. "Keep the jacket for now. Mandy said she found your saxophone, so just drop the jacket off when you come for that."

I'd intended to never enter *The Dens* again. "Sure. Thanks."

"No problem. And I'm sorry about the whole mix-up with the casino. Alarick was upset after your conversation. He thinks you may feel tricked. But anyway, if it helps to change your mind, The Dens is more than a casino. We're a family. From what I saw before your boyfriend turned up earlier, you'd fit right in."

The firefighter stole my attention.

"Ladies and gentlemen, the building has been checked and cleared. The alarm was triggered by significant damage to the central alarm system of uncertain cause. If anyone witnessed anything, please come forward. Otherwise, we thank you for obeying evacuation procedure. You can rest assured the building will be monitored until the alarm system is back in place."

Significant damage. Who would do that?

Although, there were a tonne of drunk people around tonight.

The crowd dispersed—only a small portion filtering back into the apartment itself. The rest were curious onlookers who'd either stayed to see the fire engine or my ass.

I wrapped Leroy's jacket tight around me, but I wasn't sure it would help with the ice around my heart. "Thank you, Leroy. Look, please tell Alarick there's nothing to worry about. This has nothing to do with him and it's..."

I shrugged lamely.

Leroy bumped my chin up with his hand. "You've got it. Maybe go put pants on now."

🐾🐾

I locked the apartment door, back in possession of my keys thanks to the firefighters. *Fucking Logan.*

I glared through tired eyes at a smirking couple. They held their heads together as they swept past.

"*...thong...*," the woman muttered.

Ugh. I thumped my forehead against the wood when they disappeared down the stairs. People remembered who I was. The definite *down*side to dark auburn hair. Blondes and brunettes had it good.

I left the building, my white summer dress a direct contrast to my low mood. Sleep came thin and hardly at all after Logan started blowing up my phone with messages. When I finally *did* get to sleep, I woke to find the sheer white curtains on the street side flapping around.

Unfortunately, I couldn't afford to spend a day wallowing when no money was coming in and I had a four-hundred-and ten-thousand-dollar debt hanging over my head.

I leaned on the fence, closing my eyes to better listen to the pounding river water.

No job.

A month of free accommodation.

No boyfriend.

People I truly liked.

Queen's Way.

Rhona and Herc.

I rubbed my temples. That was the giant problem. I didn't want to go back, but in my situation, I had to find employment. Queen's Way had a population five times the size of this place—therefore, my old town was the responsible and logical choice.

My last port of call was Herc.

I drew out my phone, ignoring Logan's new messages as I dialled Mum's brother. Who lived in a massive manor with one million staff.

Jesus. I felt like such a dropkick.

"Andie. Morning."

I squeezed my eyes shut. "Hey, Herc. Do you have a minute?"

"Always. Is everything okay? I heard about the alarm situation last night. The repair crew are handling it now. Looks like a large animal took a chunk out of it."

That side-tracked me. "Really? What kind of animal?"

"Bear, I'd say. They can cause a bit of trouble. Can't say I've heard of one going for an alarm system."

Yeah, that seemed weirdly strategic. "It's not about the alarm. The job at The Dens fell through. I just wanted to call to see if you could put out those feelers you spoke about."

"I'm sorry to hear that," he said after a brief pause. "I hope it wasn't anything to do with the Thana name."

"No, nothing like that. Unemployment just puts me in a jam. I've started looking for work in Queen's Way again, but if you could ask around here, that'd be great."

"I'll do it immediately. I'm happy to extend the rent-free period of the apartment, too, of course. Is there any particular rush to be employed again? We'd hate to lose you to the big wide."

Was a near half-a-million-dollar debt worthy of rushing? I couldn't rely on the house sale—which could take months, during which time I'd lose more money on interest. "I appreciate you doing that. And yeah, it's necessary. I'm not in a position to stop earning."

To say the least.

"I hear you. Have you got enough money for food?"

Yet another reason to visit *The Dens*. I was owed pay for last night's shift. "Yeah, I'm set with that." For a while.

My insides were quailing right now. I loathed this vulnerability. No, *scrap that*. I hated *showing* vulnerability. Even to someone as unassuming and generous as Herc.

"I'm glad to hear it. Listen, don't worry on the job front. I'm aware of several jobs you'd be perfect for."

I pressed a hand to my cheek. "Really? That's great news."

"Really. But since I'm doing you a favour, can I ask one in return?"

I tensed. *Like what?* "Okay?"

"Come for lunch at the manor. I could really do with company today. A tenant, Wade, is heading into town in an hour and could pick you up?"

Wade from the lake? He'd seemed cool.

Herc's favour was a poorly veiled attempt to feed me, but the least I could do was say yes with what he was doing for me. Maybe spending a day in the apartment as I tried and failed not to read Logan's messages wasn't the most exciting prospect.

"I'd like that," I replied.

A bare minute after the conversation ended, Herc sent confirmation of pick up and Wade's number.

Wade texted me a second after.

Ha! I have your number.
You'll never be rid of me meow.

The word *meow* was followed by a heart-eyed cat emoji. I shoved my hair—still dead straight—behind my ear. My smile splattered on the pavement as Logan texted again.

I'm sorry, babe. Let's talk tonight.
I shouldn't have gone after your mum like that.

Yeah, and I shouldn't have leapt down his throat for it either. I had the sickening feeling that I used anger over Mum's debt and the rumours back in Queen's Way to shove Logan away. I switched off when he deployed the love bomb.

A whole year, and I'd dropped him like nothing.

Not that I was going back to him. What we'd shared was over, but shouldn't I feel horrible? The break-up was part of my low mood today, but not one of the major players. I felt far worse about losing the music job and learning what *The Dens* was.

What did that say about me?

I'd thought we were perfectly happy and going somewhere before last night.

Was I really an ice queen?

My stomach rumbled as I texted Logan back.

I'm sorry for some of the stuff I said, Lo.
The year with you was a lot of fun, but I'm moving on now.
Take care.

Too cold? *Ugh,* I didn't want to lead him on.

Send.

I had forty-five minutes until Wade picked me up. *Dammit.* My excuses to delay the inevitable had run dry.

I inhaled, trying to push away the embarrassment from my emotionally charged conversation with Alarick last night. He had to be at least five years older than me, and that gap seemed bigger today.

Too soon, I stood under the massive sign. *The Dens.* How the hell did I never put two and two together?

An A-frame sign occupied half the foot path, but Hairy wasn't present at the door.

I clutched my small over-the-shoulder purse tight, Leroy's jacket in my other hand. Hesitation filled me, and I gritted my teeth. The place was a casino, not a den of wild animals. Not even strategic, alarm-destroying bears.

My lips twitched.

Squaring my shoulders, I entered *The Dens.*

Please don't be here. Please don't be here.

Mandy wasn't working. The male bartender from two nights before was here.

"That Leroy's, sweetheart?"

Peering left, I smiled at Hairy. "How did you know?"

A black suit jacket was a black suit jacket.

"He stinks." He waggled his dark brows. "Your sax is in the office. Alarick thought you may want your pay for last night too."

I blew out a breath. "I do. Is he around?"

"Not today. Just leave the jacket on the desk in there, would ya?"

Phew. One look at those honey eyes would send me cartwheeling into emotional territory. "Sure. I hope to see you around."

The distinctly un-hairy male shot me a look. "You're not leaving for the big wide?"

"Uncertain."

Hairy's expression softened. "We hope you stay, but if not, please say goodbye before you go."

That made me feel bad that I hadn't wanted to come here at all. The staff really did feel like a family. What a shame they ran a business that ran other families into the ground.

It was a moral ground I couldn't relinquish.

I snuck a sad peek at my gold stripper stage, crossing the floor.

A bouncer didn't block the staff quarter this morning, and I entered into a dark hall. Offices branched off either side. I squinted into each, working down until I reached the end—and largest—office.

My sax case sat on the black desk, visible through the windows framing the dark door.

I pushed inside.

A forest green leather couch ran wall to wall. Nature paintings covered the walls. The polished desk took up most of the space, and a large chair sat behind, two simple chairs in front. Computer screens occupied the desk along with neat piles of paper.

This had to be Alarick's office.

I scanned the empty hall and moved to the closest painting—a high angle of a tree. Rich and lifelike, the depiction couldn't compare to actually standing at the base of such a massive tree in person.

Going back to Queen's Way would be a life of me staring at a painting instead of seeing the real thing.

My chest tightened painfully.

"Andie."

Every muscle in my back tensed to snapping point, and I gasped, whirling. "Alarick. You scared me."

He wasn't in a suit today. Jeans and a fitted black T-shirt. *Oh my god*; he'd shoved a black beanie over his shoulder-length dark brown hair.

"I returned for my sax," I said lamely. "Hairy said you weren't here. I had to drop off Leroy's jacket."

"I forgot something."

Silence fell hard as we watched each other.

Remembering I had the power of movement, I placed Leroy's now crumpled jacket on the desk. "So—"

"I heard the alarm in your building was triggered last night," Alarick said, crossing his large arms.

He was blocking the exit.

"Yeah, bears tampered with the system. Probably on purpose," I mumbled, resting my hands on my sax case.

How the hell did I forget my sax? That had *never* happened.

I wouldn't have thought it possible.

"Won't you look at me?" Alarick said in a rough voice. Not angry. Almost like his chest was a concrete mixer. I shivered, not liking the marked change from his usual smooth-as-jazz tones.

Through my lashes, I met his honey gaze, managing a second of contact before my throat squeezed. *Yep*, knew they'd undo me today.

An envelope sat on the desk beside the case. "Thank you for the pay."

"You've decided then?"

My skin prickled as he walked behind me. "The Dens isn't the place for me, Alarick."

"Respectfully, I disagree," he countered in the same harsh voice. "You do belong here, but it's your choice to make, no matter how much I wish I could change your mind. I can't... I won't keep you here."

I turned then.

I couldn't *not*.

"What do you mean by that?" My whispered words circled us, cutting us off from the world and—*damn it all*—I craned my neck to meet those dreadful, beautiful eyes.

"Isn't it obvious?" His eyes roamed, resting on my lips.

"This doesn't make sense." Nothing past this being the last time I saw him—would *let* myself see him—made sense.

I couldn't leave without something more. Something to remember.

Just a simple touch.

I lifted a hand to his chest, but in a blur, Alarick intercepted the contact, pressing his warm, calloused palm against mine.

The roaring crescendo of a train blaring filled my senses, and air whooshed from my lungs in a blast, heartbeat ripping through my ears, as I was *thrown* flat on my back.

I rolled, choking for air.

Alarick cursed and drop to my side, and I managed to drag in a strangled breath.

"What was that?" Eyes huge, I panted on the ground. "Why did that—? What just happened?"

He didn't immediately answer. "Has that ever happened before?"

"A drop attack? Never. My mum used to have them from low blood pressure."

But that wasn't strictly true. I had a drop attack near Alarick the other day.

"You need to see a doctor, Andie."

I groaned, rubbing the back of my head.

He helped me sit up, and I froze at his touch, sagging somewhat when it became clear I wouldn't end up in a heap again.

Why had that happened twice in his presence? Did he short-circuit my brain? It couldn't be *him*. I mean, obviously, that was impossible. And he'd touched me at least once before without anything happening.

"I'm overheating," I moaned, lifting my hair off the back of my neck.

The summer dress was on the shorter side and low cut. It wasn't like I was rugged up, but that confinement was suddenly too much.

Warm was a fucking understatement.

I was *boiling.*

"What's happening?" My breath came quick.

I dropped my head back, hands bunching at my stomach. That felt good, so I swept them lower, pinning Alarick with a look no man could misinterpret.

My hair tumbled around my shoulders and breasts; the slithers elicited a gasp from my parted lips.

Alarick watched me hungrily, unmoving except for the rise and fall of his muscular chest under his black tee.

Rising high on my knees, I crawled until we were face to face. Cupping his jaw, I arched, breasts straining against the material confining them.

The scalding heat *consumed* me. I needed this man.

"Andie," he snarled.

I pressed my lips against the taut muscles of his throat. "Touch me, Alarick."

His arm circled my back, clamping my body against his.

That was it.

He kissed up my arched neck, and I couldn't process the feel of him through the shivering intensity. My hands scrambled to force him closer, but Alarick lifted me bodily, fitting me over his left thigh.

My hips gyrated against the coarse denim. My left knee rested against his erection, brushing against him in time with my rocking movement.

"*Fuck,*" he hissed, head dropping.

I shoved his head back and trailed hot kisses along his jaw. His chest filled with a gravelled growl, spurring me. A fire built. I had no desire to see it end.

I ground against his thigh, using the friction to *delicious* effect.

His hands were fucking everywhere.

Heat focalised. I became nothing. His hands clamped either side of my hips as he took over, grinding me against his muscled thigh as I gripped his shoulders.

Frantic breaths.

Desperate, mind-numbing pleasure.

Alarick drew back to watch me as the molten fire low in my stomach shrunk to a nearly painful pinprick.

"Let me see you, *beautiful bird,*" he whispered.

His wish commanded me.

I choked on air, body shaking as I crested the most intense orgasm of my life. Useless for anything, I just let Alarick continue to rock me. My head thumped on his shoulder as the pleasure filling me went on without end.

My body had checked out.

I was a slave to the steady push and pull of his hands.

Alarick pressed his open mouth against my bare shoulder, teeth resting on the skin there. His hold tightened, and his shout was muffled as a wetness seeped through his jeans against my left knee.

I smiled dreamily as his entire body relaxed and our rocking eventually slowed. Not that the lack of friction stopped the incredible aftershocks rolling through me like an encore.

Holy fucking *shit*.

That was out of this world.

We didn't speak. Was he trying to process the impossibility of how good that felt too?

"That's a first," I said hoarsely.

It seemed like something people with promise rings might do, but *fuck me*, hot didn't begin to describe what just happened.

I tried to separate from him, but Alarick breathed hard against my shoulder. I leaned back, tipping his chin up, a lazy smirk at the ready.

The sight of his pitch-black eyes stopped me dead and cold.

No amount of blinking rid me of the sight. They were *black*.

Completely.

Not a speck of white showed around the edges.

"Alarick." I released his chin, pressing a hand to my cheek.

He straightened, and I froze as his irises returned to warm honey.

What the *fuck*?

"Andie, that was... I can't believe how incredible that felt."

Yeah, that was the last thing on my mind at this point.

He frowned, the last of his dreaming daze clearing. "What's the matter?"

Your eyes turned a different fucking colour. "Nothing," I stuttered, standing.

Was I in danger?

I gripped the edge of the desk to remain upright, tugging my dress down. Behind me, he rose.

Shit. Shit!

I had to get out of here.

I grabbed my case and the money, turning on unsteady legs.

"I'm not understanding something," the *thing* said. The huge thing that could easily overpower me. I couldn't hear anything from the bar. These rooms must be soundproof.

Mustering my courage, I croaked, "I'm late to meet someone."

"Your boyfriend," he said flatly.

"Yep." I latched onto the excuse. "He's outside. I don't know what happened just now."

Distaste screwed his features, but whatever, he could think I was a cheating cow. I cared less than zero.

His eyes turned pitch-black again.

Oh my god. That wasn't fucking normal.

He wasn't *human*.

He couldn't be.

"Andie, please don't leave like this," he said quickly. "It's my mistake. I heard he left town and assumed things were over."

He was *watching* me? Fresh terror chilled my veins.

I backed out of the room, clutching my case. "It's fine. I'm not angry. I need to go, Bye."

Slamming the door, I tried to keep my pace normal until I pushed through the staff door into the bar.

Hairy and Leroy waved, but I couldn't muster any kind of response.

Lips numb, body in survival mode, I stumbled into daylight.

11

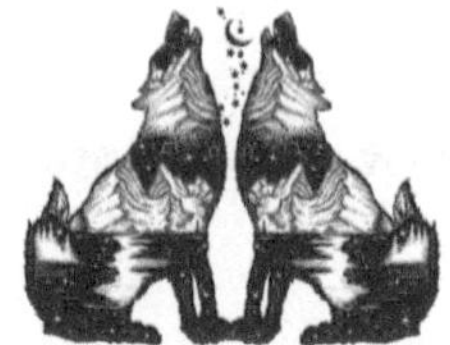

"Everyone, shut up for once! My niece is here. I don't want her to think we're animals." Herc's light-hearted greeting didn't touch me.

"Mr Thana," Wade said in a low, urgent voice.

The poor guy received monosyllabic answers the entire drive here.

Herc's grin faded.

I wrapped my arms around myself.

Fingers touched my lower back, and I jerked away as though burnt. Rhona inspected my lower back.

"What happened to your dress?" she asked in a dark voice.

"What?" I mumbled in a voice thick with unshed tears. I struggled to look at whatever caught her attention.

She rested a hand on my forearm. "I'll take a photo."

Those around the huge kitchen cottoned on to the fact all wasn't well with me. Their hushed silence was horrible.

Rhona tilted her phone screen so I could see.

Air hitched in my throat. The back of my dress was torn. Not in half. Four distinct tear marks were visible on either side.

Where Alarick gripped my hips.

"That's impossible," I whispered.

Rhona barked. "Wade."

They guided me to a seat, and Herc crouched before me. The murder etched across his features nearly shocked me from my discovery.

Alarick had fucking claws.

Claws.

"His eyes turned black." My shock cracked at last. "What are those? Claw marks?" The pitch of my voice climbed to hysterical territory.

A smaller hand gripped my shoulder, and I was so grateful to Rhona for grounding me in that moment.

"Andie," Herc said, gripping my hands tight. "What happened? What did you see?"

"A guy from The Dens," I babbled. "His eyes just changed colour. I got out as quickly as I could."

Herc released me, exchanging a look with Rhona over my head.

"What?" I shot at them. "What is it?"

Why was no one reacting to this news? People's eyes didn't just *change* colour. And what other plausible explanation was there for the back of my dress? Four thin lines either side.

"Tell me," I said harshly.

Herc returned his focus to my face, an inexplicable sadness crossing his features. "Leave us. Cameron and Wade, please stay."

I scooted out of the chair, pressing my back to the wall as the room emptied until only four people remained.

Herc watched me, not moving to restrain me in any way.

"What's going on?" I put the table between me and them. They weren't the threat, but I needed a safety net.

Hercules took a seat at the head of the long table while Cameron and Wade sat on the bench seat opposite me.

Rhona stood behind her father.

"Andie. *Niece.* There's an explanation, and I can help you, but I suggest you take a seat."

If this was about to get more fucked up, my legs wouldn't last.

I sat and looked at a pale Wade, sad Cameron, and feisty Rhona.

My eyes settled on the now calm Herc, but murder still glinted in those blue eyes, barely veiled.

"In my experience, there's no great way to say this," he said. "The next weeks of your life will be filled with uncertainty and fear. This situation isn't normal but know that your reaction *is*. None of this is your fault. We're here for you, Andie."

"Get on with it, Dad." Rhona rolled her eyes.

Herc leaned forward, and my chest tightened. He was about to say something that I couldn't unhear.

I knew it when Mum told me about her cancer.

I knew it now.

"This world contains creatures that look like us," he said. "But they are other."

Rhona butted in. "The fucker was a werewolf."

I stared at my cousin as pandemonium erupted in the kitchen.

"*Rhona,*" her father grated.

She flung her arms wide. "She's not an idiot."

"Everyone maybe chill out?" Cameron said nervously, rising.

Werewolves existed.

Alarick was a werewolf.

A werewolf made me orgasm.

What did the term mean beyond pitch-black eyes and claws? I could only think of the man changing into a wolf at the full moon.

My face slackened as another memory came to me. *Let me see you, beautiful bird.*

One person had called me bird before. A second after, they'd pushed me in a hole.

Alarick's voice was strange tonight. Gravelly and uneven, just like that first night in the forest.

I covered my mouth.

The shouting continued, and I met Wade's cool grey eyes.

Shock had rendered me incapable of thinking beyond single words—*who, what, where, when, how.*

Might as well start at the top.

"Who?" I whispered to Wade.

"The Dens. Those who work there. Hundreds more in the area. They operate in their pack on the south ranges of the valley. If a person is tall and really good-looking, you should tread carefully. Aside from me and you, of course."

Later, I might appreciate his attempt to lighten the mood. But monsters existed, and if those monsters had claws, they had something I didn't.

The others had ceased fire and resumed their seats. Rhona took the bench space on my other side, spitting eye fire at her father.

"Werewolves," I managed. Funny how my lips felt different forming that word now the species was a reality.

Somehow, in seconds, I'd become someone else—I'd climbed over an imaginary fence and found no option to return to the first grassy field.

Words failed me completely.

Herc leaned forward. "Andie, three hundred years ago, a caravan of newcomers entered this valley. Our tribe, the Ni Tiaki, guardians of the land, saw the newcomers were starving and hurt and welcomed them to rest in this area. Wolf activity skyrocketed soon after, but it wasn't until a hunter killed a wolf raiding his food stores that they discovered the truth. Imagine their shock when he changed from beast to man."

The hairs raised on my arms because black eyes and claws were more than enough for me. I couldn't imagine *seeing* a human become a beast and vice versa.

"By this time, the newcomers had lived in the area for many decades, but our ancestors took up arms then, desperate to protect their women and children from the monsters. The leader of the wolves met with our tribe alone, pleading the case of his pack. Had his wolves hurt any humans since arriving in the valley? If they could have some land to hunt freely without fear of encountering our own foragers and hunters, they wouldn't need to resort to stealing from our food stores. My ancestor was merciful. We were mere guardians of this land, not its rulers or owners. We had an affinity with all creatures that nature deemed fit to grace us with. The werewolves were one such creature. *Yes*, my ancestor said. And to her tribe, she ordered, *lay down your weapons*. That day she granted the pack their lands. *Not to own*, you must understand, but to reside upon. *But*, she said, *your pack must respect the very air of this valley and all between*. The trees had known our ancestors since the beginning of time and would witness the rise and fall of them over the ages. The water had bathed them as children and cleansed their weathered skin before death. The soil underfoot contained the bones of their ancestors and this, above all else, was their heart and soul. This was their *essence*. That was sacred. If the wolves could respect the land, they could be nature's guests here." Herc's blue eyes burned.

Cameron shifting reminded me others were in the room, but I couldn't budge my attention from Herc, captivated.

"What happened?" I pressed.

He exhaled. "What always happens? Greed. From our records, decades went by in this peaceful manner, but one day, the wolves made a show of force at the tribe's main camp upon which this manor is built. The pack was sick of the land being loaned. To them, this made their future uncertain. It wasn't enough. Now, they wished to own the land they occupied. By this time, our tribe had a new leader, the son of the woman who first granted the wolves space in this valley. He had the wisdom of his mother, and the essence of the land ran strong in his blood. *No*, he said. *And let me tell you why. This wondrous place does not belong to a blink in time, and that is what we are, you and I. Land ownership is a concept so small that the power of nature cannot even see it, let alone recognise such a thing. No, is my answer as guardian of this place. We can share in what the land gives, wolves and humans, but that is all.*"

Herc leaned back. "The wolves didn't accept this. A battle erupted right there, and many were lost on both sides. Because our ancestors were merciful but not stupid. For themselves, they would not fight. For the ground underfoot, to protect the burial grounds of those who had come before, for the essence that filled them, they would die a thousand times. They'd watched the wolves for their strengths and weakness, for their behaviours and tendencies. To see how they worked when in groups and when alone. Though the wolves were stronger, faster, and with far better senses, the tribe was prepared. The wolves retreated, not beaten, but with equal losses and the knowledge they'd underestimated the Ni Tiaki. And so it continued for far too long."

This story was somehow believable where I still struggled to grasp the term *werewolf*. "What did they do?"

"Our wise leader was killed in battle years later. His daughter inherited the mantle. Her soul cried for the trees who preferred rain to blood. Their roots were soaked with it. In her journal entries, she spoke of how, in her darkest dreams, blood rotted the buried bones of their ancestors, leaving a stench that their loved ones could smell in death. The death and anger left her cold, and she could not rest as things were." He took a breath. "To the wolves she went, alone and with child. *Stop*, she commanded the same pack leader who'd always ruled. *This is not how life should be. Stop with me, and our children will not live in fear.* He laughed in her face, giving his thoughtless reply. *Give us ownership of this land.* Still, the land was not hers to give, yet she refused to leave without a solution."

My mouth dried as it clicked. "The game."

I stared around the table and four serious faces looked back at me. "*Laser tag*. It's not laser tag."

"No," Herc replied, "Just yesterday I said that if you chose to join this game, it would change you forever. I told you the game formed our town. Our plight has existed longer than anyone here truly realises. By our records, over two hundred years, with some failed attempts at peace dotted throughout."

"You play the game to prevent bloodshed." I tried to assemble the puzzle pieces in my mind.

"Every Wednesday, we fight werewolves." His lips pressed together. "We fight to protect these lands and those within them."

This was insanity.

None of this could be real. I couldn't be sitting here, listening to the fabric of everything I knew unravel.

Yet I was.

Alarick wasn't a man.

Before my very eyes, he'd existed somewhere between his human disguise and a beast. He had the ability to turn into a creature that I didn't have adequate nightmares to visualise.

Did he recognise me from that night in the forest? Is that why he'd tried so hard to employ me after?

What the hell had he planned to do?

"You wanted to know why your mother left," Herc said, snatching my focus back. "The beasts damaged something inside of her that never healed again. My sister always did feel too much." His voice hitched.

That description fit her perfectly. All Mum's mistakes and pitfalls —they'd happened because life was always too much for her to handle. I'd often wondered if Dropkick leaving broke her, but apparently it happened a long time before him.

I closed my eyes.

"Each loss and defeat against them took her further from me," he said low. "Ragna shut off. Because of them, your mother ran from this valley to hide from the monsters in the night."

My mother lied to protect me from werewolves.

A strange calm filled me. The supernatural reason for her subterfuge soothed my heart on some level. Nothing possible would have been enough to explain away her lies.

But this was *done* to her.

Once, my mother was whole and happy.

The regrets of my life. The heartache and pain. They convalesced to a thrumming fury that filled my bones.

Locking my mother in her room when I was ten so she wouldn't visit the pokie machines.

Holding back her hair as she vomited after chemo.

Sitting at the bench at eleven, trying to understand the utility bills spread before me.

Cowering in the cupboard as people kicked and pounded at the front door for their money.

If not for the wolves, someone would have been around to help me. I wouldn't have been alone as my mother's last breath rattled in her sunken chest.

If not for them, I might have known a different version of my mother.

It was so much to feel. Lifting a hand to my chest, I pressed inwards to contain the mounting pressure there.

I had to know why.

I had to know what they did to her.

"I didn't want this life for you, niece," Herc said so quietly I almost missed his words. "Your strength nearly changed my mind, but I'd since resolved not to bring you in. My sister didn't want this for you, and I wanted to respect her wishes. To my great regret, a beast has revealed the truth and that path is now closed."

If Herc knew what transpired in that office, he'd *really* be murderous. The memory of grinding on Alarick's thigh—intertwining with him—made me want to vomit.

He'd used me. My resemblance to the Thanas and my ignorance of the game. He'd *used* me.

"I'll speak plainly, Andie." Herc broke the heavy silence. "The grids are slipping through our fingertips. We need your help."

"You can sleep here," Cameron said, her arm around my shoulders.

We'd climbed to the third level of the manor. People milled everywhere.

Not guests as Herc once told me.

They were part of this fight against the wolves. Every single one of them.

Wade pushed open a white door, and we entered a large bedroom equipped with four-poster bed, heavy drapes, and elegant furniture. Paintings of trees hung on the walls, and I shivered at the memory of Alarick's office.

Beautiful bird.

He'd known who I was without a doubt. He called me *little bird* in the forest.

Then he'd stalked me and drawn me in. To what? Trick me for a laugh? Or something more sinister?

A cold fury had built within me over the last few hours. Leroy stealing my cap. Alarick watching me busk before the second job offer. I had a sinking feeling that strategic bears didn't mess with the alarm system at the apartment building at all.

Which was why I'd accepted Herc's offer to stay at the manor.

And Alarick's plotting was just one of my worries. Looking back with a mind now opened to impossible things, I was *certain* something happened when he touched his palm to mine.

I didn't faint.

I was *thrown* from the werewolf. Then after, that unexplainable heat. When had I *ever* behaved like that with a virtual stranger? Riding his thigh like that. Throwing myself at him.

Those were the actions of someone else, not me.

Bile rose up my throat.

I sat on the bed; hands pressed into my cheeks. I hadn't felt this overwhelmed when Mum died.

That didn't possess this shock factor.

Cancer sometimes ended in death. Everyone knew that. When I blew into my saxophone, music poured out. When I inhaled, air entered my lungs. These were all things that people *knew*.

When I kissed a man, he clawed the back of my dress because he was a werewolf.

Nope.

That there. That was impossible.

Cameron and Wade watched me, hovering just inside the doorway.

"Thanks for..." I searched for an appropriate descriptor.

"Blowing your world apart?" Wade asked.

Cameron jabbed him with her elbow.

"It's true," he said. "You must remember how this felt and we grew up with it—kind of."

She flopped on the bed next to me. "What do you need, Andie? You need to know that we've got your back. So what's it gonna be? Crying yourself to sleep? Drinking yourself to oblivion? Making a wolf dart board?"

The last one *was* tempting. "No idea."

"What do you do when you lose the plot?" Wade leaned against the bedpost to my right.

Lose the plot? What a novelty. "I talk to inanimate objects sometimes. My car..."

"That's just general crazy," Cameron said. "Doesn't count."

I lifted a shoulder. "Really, no clue."

Wade exchanged a long look with Cameron. "Right. I'm not sure what to do with that. So how about a sleepover? Mattresses and popcorn."

It spoke for my current state that I was tempted. "I need to be by myself. Processing time or something. I guess my freak-outs happen alone."

I detected a contemplativeness in Wade's gaze that I wanted to know better.

"If you're sure," he eventually said.

"I am. But I'll see you guys tomorrow?"

Cameron rolled to standing without the grunt of effort I usually made. Come to mention it, everyone in this place that I'd seen were in serious shape, Wade included.

"Yeah," she said. "Herc wants to give you a tour of the grounds, remember?"

I must have looked shell-shocked. Wisely, Herc didn't unload everything on me today. We'd resume our chat tomorrow, and my orders were to think about joining them for as long as needed.

If I decided to *enter the grids*—as Herc put it—I needed to be absolutely sure. Joining the game was far more of a one-way street than he made out in the apartment.

My gut reaction was to yell *yes* at the top of my lungs. I felt this valley in my very soul. The sense of belonging and Herc's earlier words about *essence* struck a deep chord in me. Perhaps I wasn't raised here, but since nearly the first moment of arriving, I'd done everything possible to remain.

The choice warranted serious thought, however—that old bitch called Habit.

The game broke my mother. What's to say I'd fare better? Then there was the danger aspect. One, from playing the game itself. Two, Alarick's plans for me might not be over.

Though inclined to believe he'd used me to pass a petty jab at Herc, I couldn't rush into this decision. I owed myself that much. Some of my life had to be lived for *me*.

The door closed.

I stared around the large, empty room. *Ah, shit.* I didn't want to be alone.

Striding to the entrance, I ripped the door open.

My heart sank. *Dammit.* They were gone.

A flash of auburn caught my eye.

"Rhona," I blurted.

She paused, halfway into a room at the far end of the hall. "Lost it yet?"

"Can't be sure. Would I know?"

"Usually. I smashed up the kitchen. Dad got drunk for a week. We're pretty okay with breakdowns of all shapes and sizes at the manor. Stress is an ongoing thing to manage once you join the game."

Good to know.

I sighed. "Maybe I should process what I know so far, but I'm a whole picture kind of person."

She gestured inside her room. "Dad's treating you like a wimp. Come in, cuz."

Cuz.

I shut my door. Rhona would tell me like it was. That's what I needed. Facts and answers. How else could I make an informed decision?

She kicked the door shut after me. "What you wanna know? How to kill the fuckers?"

Consider me surprised I could still laugh. “Maybe later. Your father said—”

“Your uncle?” She cut me off.

I considered that. “Nah, feels strange. Herc explained how the tribe reached this point. How does *this* even work. How is the town unaware werewolves exist? What are the rules?”

She stripped off, and I gawked at her rigid abs. “Will I need to get ripped like Rambo too?”

“Kind of naturally happens,” she replied. “I’m not a natural athlete, but our diet here, and the whole sprinting around for several hours each week on top of training... Yeah, you’ll look the same in no time. You’re in good shape already. Shouldn’t be too painful.”

The hills in town nearly defeated me.

Her room was surprisingly warm given her prickly nature. I studied the pictures of her and Herc, and others taken with friends. An old dollhouse sat in a corner, but not a speck of dust coated the roof. A patch-covered teddy rested on her bedroom vanity.

Black sheets on the bed were mostly covered by a hole-ridden quilt

It was like I was seeing Rhona’s heart.

This room felt much better than mine.

I lowered into a plush lounge chair in the far corner. My body was so sore. Was it the adrenaline fallout or emotional exhaustion?

“I’m ready,” I said.

“I see that. You’re appallingly together.”

A second laugh. *Go me.*

She sat cross-legged on the floor. “Dad usually does this talk, so bear with me a second.”

I studied her emerald eyes and thick dark auburn hair. *So similar.* Though where I might push my hair behind my ear while thinking, she scowled. Where I might play music to relax, she’d probably punch someone.

“Here’s what’s what.” She leaned back against the wooden bed frame. “Old people call the game something else, but young people call it Grids because of the layout.” Her eyes darted over the old rug.

"After the most recent war sixty years ago, both sides acknowledged only one team could prevail or the fighting would never stop. The game changed then. Only one side can now emerge the victor. The winner must exhibit the utmost care for this land, and they must conquer all battlefields."

"One small question though. Does anyone die?"

She broke off. "Only accidents. The last death was twenty-two years ago. Grandmother Charise."

I sucked in a breath. "*Werewolves* killed her?"

"They say not. Her neck was broken which is pretty hard to do yourself, really."

I closed my eyes against that visual. She'd meant so much to my mother.

"Trapping, capturing, and shooting are fair game." Rhona ticked off her fingers. "Though you should be aware the darts we shoot are tranquilisers, not lasers."

They *were* real guns.

Well, more real than a laser gun.

She snorted. "Should I go on or do you need tequila?"

"Gin. But no, not yet."

"Knew you were made of the good stuff. There are five battlefields —or grids—in the game. We play in one grid each week, and each grid is a different resource. The winner of the match gains the resources of that grid and all associated profit until it's won from them."

Whoa.

My mouth hung ajar. "That's... far more complicated than I expected."

She dipped her head. "We've never brought in someone who didn't at least grow up in Deception Valley. I feel for ya while also wanting to see how much you can take before cracking."

Bitch. My lips twitched. "Off topic. What happened the other day in my apartment? You seemed upset with me, and I had no idea why."

She observed me with equal solemnity. "First, understand that I'm a bastard. This little chat is an outlier from which you should *not* draw conclusions. Secondly, I don't like making friends that I may need to say goodbye to."

I hugged my knees. "I don't like making friends who could say goodbye to me." And the same applied to lovers and family members.

The opposite issue.

We both found other places to look.

"Someone mentioned Timber that night in the forest. Is that one of the grids and resources?" I asked.

"Correct."

"I'm not seeing how a grid profits the winner."

"Businesses," she grunted. "For Timber—sustainable logging. Construction. Furniture making. There's a high-ropes course and biking tracks in there as tourist attractions. Each grid win comes with the handover of all its companies and current contracts for however long the pack or tribe manages to keep it."

"What are the other grids?"

She checked off her fingers. "Sandstone, Water, Clay, and Iron. The battlefield changes our game strategy drastically. Imagine what we might do in Water compared to Sandstone for example. And don't even get me started on Clay."

I smiled at her so hard my teeth hurt.

Rhona cocked a brow. "There it is. You're gone. When Dad asks, I didn't tell you shit."

My body shook.

"I'll get some gin, cuz." She patted my arm.

12

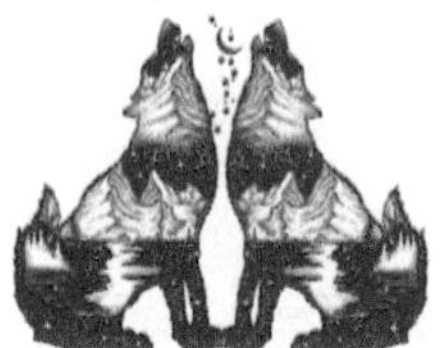

"We look the same, but I sure as fuck hope we don't smell the same."

Groaning, I rolled, clutching my head.

Rhona's voice was amused. "I was impressed you drank the entire bottle without vomiting. Though you may regret that move this morning."

I cracked open an eye.

Fresh-faced, she grinned.

"Stop smiling. Your teeth are too bright." They hurt my head.

Her grin grew. "That's a new one. Guess what though? Bet you feel too horrible to be scared of werewolves."

My bad mood dropped further.

"Maybe not." She tapped her bottom lip.

A knock sounded, and the door cracked open. "Rhona?"

"I'm not having sex, Dad. Which you know because you checked the hallway camera footage before coming here."

He pushed the door open and lingered sheepishly in the frame.

I squinted at him. "Morning."

He arched both brows. "Not a good one, I gather. How are you feeling other than extremely hungover?"

"Nothing." Nausea and a headache didn't leave room to question the existence of monsters. If a werewolf crossed in front of me, I'd watch them tootle past. Maybe half-heartedly kick an empty gin bottle their way.

Herc crossed his arms. "I could give you the drinking lecture Rhona received, but you're far more put-together."

"Hey!"

"Revenge is sweet." He winked at his daughter over my head. "So are the pancakes cooking as we speak. Breakfast, then tour of the grounds."

Rhona piped up, "I can't. I'm going out with—"

"—*both* of you," he called.

She flopped back. "Ugh."

"Please don't flop," I said in panic, curling around my tumultuous stomach.

"I love not being the hungover one."

"I liked you last night."

"That was an outlier occasion, remember."

So was me drinking that much. "What happened after I played with your doll's house?"

"Yeah, Dad clearly hasn't heard yet."

Carefully, I opened both eyes. "That means what exactly?"

Rhona smirked, rolling out of bed. "Shower's down the hall. Towels are in there. You can borrow my clothes."

"That means what?"

"It's nice to know you have a sense of humour." She grabbed a robe by the door. "Oh, and I was thinking—I had time because it took hours to fall asleep to the melody of your snoring. We could be twins, and we are *definitely* using that to fuck with everyone here. Amiright?"

I inched to an upright position. Gin was the devil. "Did I smash something?"

"I mean, gin makes me cry. *That* wasn't your problem." She wriggled her fingers in a delicate wave, disappearing.

I brought my hands around her imaginary throat and choked her. I'd never felt sick after drinking.

Never again.

Fishing around, I searched for my phone.

I found it inside my bra along with grass streaks and black marks on my white summer dress.

Logan.

You're a fucking bitch, you know that?

Cool. That was awesome to wake up to. I blocked his number and deleted the messages.

Unknown.

Andie.
I'm not sure what happened yesterday to upset you.
Let's talk about it.
When you're ready, you know where to find me.

My hands shook.

Alarick.

Standing, I ripped open Rhona's drawers, pulling out a loose top and leggings. I stormed to the middle of the hall and glared at the line of people waiting for a shower.

The front girl blanched. "You can go ahead of me, Rhona."

Rhona chose that moment to exit one of the shower stalls lining the wall.

Herc was right. Revenge was sweet.

"Get out of my way, Andie," I snapped. "You'll need to be sharper than that if you expect to survive here."

She stared at me, and I bit back laughter, pushing into the stall she'd vacated.

"Don't worry," someone whispered outside. "Rhona gets like that sometimes. Everyone else is really nice, I promise."

I grinned, stepping under the warm spray of water. I'd totally pay for that later.

Worth it.

Dressed in the borrowed clothing after, sans underwear, I surveyed the bounce of my boobs as I walked.

It was possible... my braless state was extremely noticeable.

Oh well, better than the clothes Alarick touched me in—which I'd burn later.

Wandering down the stairs, my nose led me the rest of the way.

Pancakes. Bacon.

Conversation didn't skip a beat as I entered the kitchen, and I marvelled at the happy bubble of conversation. *Hundreds* of years fighting a supernatural species the world knew nothing about. What did that even *feel* like?

No wonder they were such a tight unit.

"She's mine." Hands wrenched me onto the bench.

I pressed a hand over my mouth. "I will literally vomit on you."

Wade gasped. "Bitchhole. You got drunk without me."

"Yeah, it just happened."

"No. *Nuh-uh*. One-night stands just happen. Surprise erections when you're twelve just *happen*."

I peeked up.

"*Oh*. Now that look is hard to resist." He brought his face close to mine. "Stop it. It's adorable. I can't resist that bullshit. Okay, you're forgiven."

I grinned.

Cameron hauled me upright, and I found myself facing a plate heaped with greasy goodness.

"Are you vegan or stuff? I didn't think to ask." Cameron asked, staring at my plate of carnivorous pickings.

In answer, I picked up a slice of bacon and shoved it in my mouth.

She winked, and the pair dug into their food on either side of me.

I searched for Rhona and Herc, then studied the other occupants.

The three of us were amongst the youngest in the room, though I recalled seeing younger players in Timber.

Timber. My insides trembled. There was so much I didn't know, yet what I *did* know was inconceivable.

A once-a-week battle for a resource.

Against *werewolves.*

"Who are all these people?" I whispered.

"The important folk," Wade said loudly. "To be clear... though I'm important, Cameron and I usually aren't here. Herc thought you may want company today and it gets me off work."

"Same," Cameron said around a mouthful of miscellaneous.

Fair enough. "How many are in your team? I saw hundreds of you the other night."

"Yeah, we have one thousand players."

One thousand. Wade offered me more bacon and I opened my mouth on autopilot, chewing the piece he shoved inside.

"Does that mean there are one thousand wolves here?" My voice cracked.

Cameron answered, "They have just over seven hundred and fifty in their pack. Seven hundred in their Grids team."

Their pack.

One thousand and seven hundred played the game. That left over nine thousand in Deception Valley who I assumed were unaware a supernatural race existed.

"Where do you all live?" The manor was huge, but not *that* huge.

"We live in houses. Did you expect underground bunkers? But to give you a visual, the Thanas and stewards live on the north side of the valley. Furry fuckers occupy the south."

I did expect bunkers or some kind of guarded village. "How do you know the... furry fuckers won't attack?"

"They'd lose points." Wade ate a chocolate croissant in two bites, and I couldn't fail to be impressed.

"Teams gain penalty points for acting outside Grids. Five penalty points means loss of a grid—so neither team fucks with that. It could be the difference between winning and losing."

"When does a side win the game?" I asked, appetite gone. I grabbed a glass of orange juice instead.

Cameron nudged a piece of toast my way. "You really should eat up."

I nibbled at the edge.

"A side wins when they have possession of all five grids," she said. "Currently, the wolves have three grids. We have two. The wolves have a new leader, and we're still learning how he thinks."

"One side's never won all five grids?"

Wade shook his head. "This game is fierce, Andie."

"Your attention, please," Herc called.

I twisted on the bench. Rhona stood beside her father, hip cocked as she regarded me.

I smirked and saw her lips twitch.

Yep, the lookalike thing could be a lot of fun.

"I apologise for the interruption last night," Herc said. "There was an incident involving my niece that required my attention. Team meetings are postponed until this afternoon. In the meantime, you know what to do. The Luthers announced the next grid last night—"

"Every Sunday night, the previous winner announces the next battlefield," Cameron hushed.

"—We're in Sandstone, and I don't have to tell you this grid has always been a particular strength of ours."

"*So was Timber*," Wade muttered.

"This week, we need to roll out more backlist manoeuvres than ever before. We *cannot* afford to let this grid fall into their hands. Your best effort—that's what I'm asking for. You give it each week, and I'm asking for it again." Herc scanned the quiet room. Then his gaze fell on me. "Andie? Ready?"

Nope.

I rose, stepping over the bench.

An older male entered and hurriedly whispered in Herc's ear.

Rhona's grin grew.

Crap. I had a sinking feeling this might be—

Herc's gaze lifted to mine.

Shit.

I watched through bloodshot eyes as Wade snapped a few pictures of the erotically positioned practice dummies. There were at least twenty scenes arranged in a long row like some sultry display at a sex museum.

The grass patches on my white dress had been the warning sign. Rhona and I left the manor at some point last night.

I had zero memory of the training room we stood in.

Cameron was red-faced trying to contain laughter. Rhona's grin was wider than the Cheshire cat's.

Herc's face—studiously blank.

"Now, *that's* inventive," Wade said.

Three dummies were involved in the scene. All of them had spears for penises.

Wade snapped a photo of the orgy next to it that involved two females—I guessed from the lack of penis spears—and one male. "That's material for alone time."

"Took you an hour to set it all up," Rhona said.

I winced. "I don't remember."

The old man who'd whispered in Herc's ear glared at Wade, storming from the open-air shack. *Shack* was a poor description. I could see this wide, railed room on some brochure for a yoga retreat in Bali. The giant cupboards pulled across the room and contained any number of weapons and training props that somewhat dispelled the peaceful yoga illusion.

Nets, ropes, daggers, guns, freakin' crossbows.

This was the reality check I'd needed.

"I'll put everything away." My cheeks heated.

I mean, yes, fucking funny. But also, Herc.

Awkward.

"While that's what we usually ask after such, uh, events," Herc said, frowning at a vertical 69 down the end of the row. "I believe Cameron and Wade can do the honours today."

Laughter exploded from Cameron's mouth, and she failed to smother the whoops.

I snorted, coughing at Herc's wry look.

“Certainly the most creative incident I’ve seen,” he said. “And it didn’t cost us anything in repairs. Let’s move on.”

Gladly.

We walked to the far end of the training pavilion. I took in the large pillows and mats.

“Doesn’t it get cold training here in winter?” I leaned over the rail, spotting three surrounding pavilions.

Herc lifted a shoulder. “The game is outside. Tolerance to elements is needed. In times gone by, tribe elders would make young warriors stand in the river for ten minutes before they whipped the person with reeds. That was thought to toughen their skin to withstand harsh conditions.”

Uh...

He laughed at my expression. “That stopped long ago. Though I’m curious, would you prefer to train inside?”

They’d cleared only the trees necessary to build the pavilions and other buildings I could see. Otherwise, forest surrounded us. Birds chirped, darting between branches. Blue sky was visible high above, and I could imagine winter here—snow weighing branches while birds puffing their feathers to keep warm.

Autumn would be breathtaking too.

“No,” I answered him. “Not when this exists.”

This valley was magical.

It needed to be protected.

Herc crossed his arms. “I’m sure you have questions about the game. There’s a lot, so feel free to stop me at any time.”

He launched into an explanation I’d already heard, but I appreciated the repeat while in a more lucid state of mind.

“Training is daily at dawn,” he said next. “It’s not as intense as you may imagine. The werewolves have us physically beat even in two-legged form. Our focus needs to be, and has been for a long time, in strategy. Trapping strategies. Group strategies. Grid-specific strategies. Counter-wolf strategies. That’s why training isn’t our main focus. Otherwise, on a Tuesday night, everyone gathers to receive the game plan for the following day. As you heard at breakfast, the next grid is Sandstone."

The complexity of this was other level.

How could this exist without the world knowing the truth?

"This team has your back, Andie."

I felt his gaze boring into the side of my face.

Herc continued. "It's unusual for anyone to be hurt, and extremely rare for severe injuries or death to occur, but I won't lie and say it's never happened."

"How many?" I asked.

His jaw tightened. "On the battlefield? Two. To my memory."

"Who were they?"

"Your grandfather and grandmother."

That was something different. "The last name Thana is a dangerous pastime."

He shot me a curious look, mouth opening and closing. "I came to the same conclusion after my mother's death. Their deaths were ruled accidental, but I knew the Luthers were involved. That's why our players wear masks in the grid. I won't deny the risk of you being mistaken for Rhona."

I cast a look at my cousin. She wasn't paying any attention to our conversation. Perhaps it was one she'd heard many times. Her boredom consoled me.

Maybe one day, this would feel completely normal as it did to her.

"We need numbers," Herc said. "But this is your life. I may want to see you stay in the valley for selfish reasons, but you need to think this over."

I licked my lips. There were so many uncertainties—the danger, the unknown, *werewolves*. I had to consider the alternative as well. If I didn't play, I probably couldn't stay in the valley.

Not knowing what I did. And not without protection against Alarick.

My last tie to Mum would be severed.

The fresh ties to Herc and Rhona, as much as the ties unsettled me, they'd disappear too.

Rhona leaned against the railing, her shoulder touching mine. I made no move to establish more space as the self-professed bastard leant me support.

"Tell her the rest," Rhona said.

Herc ran a hand through his red hair.

"What is it?" I straightened

Mum's brother blew out a breath. "I had an idea last night. For the first time in our history, the wolf pack has a new leader."

The game was *hundreds* of years old. *Oh my god.* "They live a while."

"Immortal."

Oh, cool. Never-dying enemies. Super. "Right."

He took up a sedate pace, a deep frown marring his face. "This leader is different. The father preferred brute force and used physical strength against us, as one might expect. His offspring is doing the unexpected. Last week in Timber, we were blindsided with a group strategy unlike any I've seen before."

"How long has this guy been in charge?" I asked.

"Around eighteen months."

The casino was a year old.

Dread seized me. "What's his name?"

They looked at me quizzically. Rhona answered, "Sascha Greyson."

Thank fuck.

Dry-humping the pack leader would have been a fucking mess. "Never heard of her."

"*Him.* You haven't heard the name? He frequents The Dens," Herc said.

I wracked my mind. "Nope. Haven't met a Sascha." I always remembered *boy-girl* names, given my own.

"Your position at the casino worried me, I'll admit. However, it *does* open an avenue we've never had access to. The wolves are strategizing now and winning. We must adapt, too or risk losing.

I met his gaze. "You want me to spy."

"They've granted you access despite your resemblance to Rhona."

Or because of it. "I introduced myself as Andie Booker."

"Even so," he said. "You'd need to be an idiot to miss that you're a Thana."

I blinked.

Herc called me a Thana.

"But," he stressed, "whatever angle they're playing, whether they think that you're there on my behalf or not, we can use your position to our advantage. Having a steward in pack territory is of far greater benefit to us than to them. You mentioned that the job there fell through. Can I ask why?"

I clamped my mouth shut.

The silence extended.

He opened his mouth.

"Dad," Rhona muttered. "Cuz, did you end the employment or did they?"

I brushed my hair behind my ear. "I did."

They smiled.

I thought of the text from Alarick. He'd given me a definite way to wiggle back in, if I so chose. And maybe that meant he wasn't done with his plans for me, but I wasn't ignorant any longer.

His plans for me were at an end because I said so.

My lips curved.

Working at a casino to support myself?

Hell no.

Spying at a casino to figure out why Mum left the valley while doing my best to fuck over the werewolf who'd used me?

Hell yes.

And if the Luthers lost Grids because of me, their filthy casino would be shut down too.

Win-fucking-win.

13

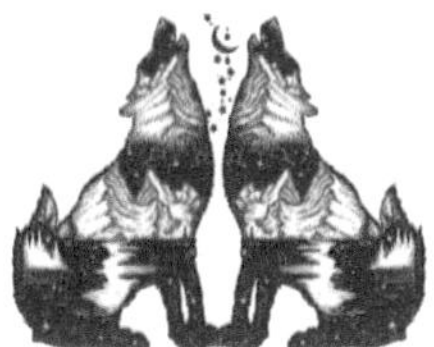

I counted the lengths of my inhales and exhales, ramrod straight in the passenger seat of the silver Bentley.

"Nervous?" Rhona guided the car out of the manor gates.

Understatement.

Rhona slid me a side-long look as we drove up the north side of the valley toward town. "You can still back out."

"No, I'm in." The choice was simple in the end. A wall of uncertainty or a lifetime of regret.

I chose uncertainty.

I had too many regrets as it was.

"Good." She lowered her voice. "Now, Werewolf 101. There's a lot to think about, but the main thing is to never, *never* forget their senses. Smell is the strongest. You've stayed at the manor for two days and used our soap. You're wearing my clothes. Before you set foot in The Dens, you need to wash your hair, use your own products, and dress in your own stuff. If you don't, they'll take one sniff and figure out the truth."

Shit. I didn't consider what powers they might have. "Okay. What else can they do?"

"In their two-legged form, their smell isn't as accurate, but they can smell strong emotion. Joy. Anger. Fear. Adrenaline. Sweat."

I thumped my head back. "How am I meant to manage that?"

"Yeah, this is new for us, too. Is there something you could use to cover your reaction in there?"

Did I have a logical reason to be afraid of Alarick? I'd run from our last meeting, spewing babble about cheating on Logan. "Yep."

At worst, I could pretend to read a fake emergency text.

Fuck. Shoving my foot in the door would be harder than expected. "In wolf form, they can smell other emotions?"

"Yes. And truth from lie. In meetings, a Luther is always in four-legged form."

Don't lie to werewolves. I'd file that next to *don't be that close to a wolf in the first place.*

"Hearing is their next strongest sense. In close quarters, they'll hear your heartbeat. If you have a reason to be afraid, it should cover your heightened pulse, but just keep that in mind."

My lips numbed as the stone buildings of town appeared over the rise. I couldn't do this.

"Remember, Andie. They can't hurt you. If they do, they'll be penalised."

Don't hurt me, werewolf. I don't want to give you a penalty point, but I will.

"That makes me feel tonnes better. What else?"

"Their sight isn't so much of an issue for detecting a lie," Rhona said as we drove alongside the riverfront buildings. "They *can* see super fucking well. Don't steal from the till."

I shot her a wry look. "I'll try my best. Just how good is their hearing?"

She gripped the wheel, checking the rear-view mirror. "In wolf form, kilometres, we think. In two-legged form, maybe one hundred metres, but it depends on the strength of the individual werewolf."

This was about to blow my mind for the second time and there was no time to get drunk and arrange dummies in erotic positions before my spying debut. "Unless there's something super important to know, that's probably enough. What's the goal today?"

Rhona parked around the corner to my apartment. I'd expected someone less conspicuous to drop me off, but Herc said there wasn't any point completely hiding my connection to them with the family resemblance.

I just had to keep my head.

Literally and figuratively.

"Focus on getting your job back," she said. "Then we can—"

"Nope. I want to know the whole plan."

She swivelled in the driver seat, checking the area. Tuesday morning and Deception Valley was a virtual ghost town in comparison to the last four days. "Okay, they guard the details of their nature super closely. We have fuck-all information about their hierarchy, what makes one wolf more powerful than another, and the exact limitations of their advantages over us. If you can gather intel on their plans for the next grid, that would be huge. I doubt they'll let you in that deep, but in short, we know who the main players in the pack are, but we need more. Dig up as much as you can. Even a tiny detail could be useful. And we need to know more about that fucker, Sascha Greyson."

I released a pent-up breath. "Right. That helps. I'll keep an eye out for him. And do my best to burn their casino to the ground."

"Psycho. Nice."

I grabbed the paper bag containing my clothes. "Not a casino fan."

My cousin watched me.

Holy shit. Calling her cousin didn't feel strange. In my head anyway. I felt more conversational ease with Wade and Cameron, but Rhona grounded me in tough moments.

I gripped the door handle. "My mum was a gambling addict."

"No shit."

I glanced back.

Her expression was grim. "Let me know if you need help burning the shithole down, cuz."

A small smile graced my lips. "You got it, cuz."

🐾🐾

Would the werewolves notice if I was *extra* clean?

I might smell like myself and have dressed in my clothes—high-waisted black jean shorts and a burnt orange cord bandeau—but the fact remained that I had several layers less skin after showering. My hair was mostly dry and starting to bounce into waves. I'd slathered bronzing moisturiser over my body. I challenged the fuckers to smell anything through the coconut scent.

Black sunglasses completed the look because they'd offered a little barrier between me and werewolf eyes.

Jesus. My legs weren't happy about the hill after dawn training. Puffing, I arrived at *The Dens* and bent over, heart racing to keep me from death.

"You alright there?" an amused voice asked.

Hairy.

The world was having a massive joke at my expense. Hairy. A perfectly normal name for a fucking werewolf.

My heart thundered from the exercise. Best to do this now while I had the cover. I clutched my side, steeling myself as I straightened.

This was happening.

I *had* to do this.

Looking at the werewolf, I no longer saw a hot guy. I saw a monster in human skin. I could understand why Rhona and Herc referred to this form as two-legged. Knowing what I knew—that this guy shifted or morphed into a beast—I couldn't think of him as human.

I couldn't even think of him as a wolf.

"It's a killer," I replied between breaths.

He glanced past me. "I'll be honest, I didn't expect to see you back after you ran out on Sunday."

His face could turn into a snout. His teeth to fangs. His fingers to claws.

The usual easiness wasn't emanating from him. Was I acting weird? Then again, I literally ran from here two days ago, ignoring his wave on the way out.

A vice tightened around my lungs. "About that. Is Alarick around?"

Hairy picked up a keg from the curb, grunting with the effort.

Two days ago, I would have believed the act. "Do you need a hand?"

He grunted again. "I'm fine. You're in luck. Alarick is in his office."

The soundproof *away from the public eye* office. "Thanks. And sorry about the other day. I had a meltdown. A few things have been happening."

Hairy averted his eyes. "Sure. No problem."

Hmm. I had some distance to recover there. But the Luthers could suspect all they wanted. I had one goal—get my job back.

I strode after Hairy.

Mandy waved from the bar, and I unlocked enough to return the gesture. My pulse pounded, and I made sure to keep my breathing heavy, clutching my side as I adjusted to being inside a space with paranormal monsters.

I could do this.

Lifting my chin, I crossed the room, ignoring the gold stage I'd once stood on in total ignorance. The pounding in my ears faded as I pushed into the dark hallway.

Alarick was visible through the window at the far end, typing at his desk.

I wiped my clammy palms on my shorts, recalling Rhona's words about adrenaline.

Think about the forest. River water, pine needles, and sunshine. I inhaled, more than aware he could likely hear the sound from inside.

I knocked on the door.

"Come in."

Alarick lifted his head as I entered.

"Andie."

Heat flushed my cheeks, and I averted my eyes. "Alarick."

"I was hoping to see you again. I feared you might have left the valley."

Because he'd watched my apartment the last two days? If that was the case, I *really* couldn't conceal where I'd been.

I forced myself to take the seat closest to him. He leaned back in his office chair, and my gaze dropped to his dark jeans. He followed my look, and our eyes met after.

Fresh blood poured into my face.

Fear wasn't the predominant emotion anymore. Disgust and shame sounded about right.

"Things got out of control last time I was here," I said to my hands. "I stayed with my uncle and cousin for a couple of nights to decide what I wanted to do."

He rested a hand on the desk.

What did that mean?

"I assume Rhona and Hercules Thana are your relations?"

Bringing that into the open was the right move. He wasn't surprised one bit. Which meant he hired me knowing that too.

That boded well for him accepting me back here again.

"They said you'd know them. From laser tag." I looked him square in the eye.

Honey eyes. So unusual.

Irises that belonged to a wolf.

Alarick's smile stretched wide. "You could say that."

He'd never been particularly forthcoming aside from compliments and in our business dealings. I knew so little about this guy. He wore jeans when he wasn't on shift. Every worker in the casino obeyed him without question.

His intense mystery had intrigued me as much as it drove me away, so I couldn't appear overeager now.

"The only way I can stay in the valley is if I have a job," I said. "The other night, when I found out this was a casino, I let my personal life cloud my judgement."

The werewolf interlocked his hands on the desk.

I brushed my hair back. "I feel a kinship with this valley. There's nothing left for me in Queen's Way. But to stay here, I need a job."

"Why don't you like casinos, Miss Booker?" Alarick asked.

Did he have to watch me so intensely?

I frowned. "Does that have anything to do with getting my job back?"

"It does if you have a gambling addiction I need to know about. Despite what you think of me, addiction isn't something we enable here."

Sure it wasn't. "I don't have a gambling problem."

"When I offered you a compromise on Saturday night, why didn't you take it then?"

I pulled my gaze from his unsettling focus.

"I'll put it another way," he said low. "Why, when you dislike casinos and your uncle owns many businesses in the valley that could employ you, would you choose to return here? Particularly after what happened between us in this office and your reaction afterward?"

His manner was unobtrusive, mild even, but the wolf was turning over rocks in search of my secrets. When I had nothing for Alarick to discover, his calculation wasn't a problem.

"I lied to you." I clasped my hands together like his.

His brows rose. "When?"

"Logan and I broke up on Saturday night. I wasn't with him when I came here and we... well, when I rode your leg until we both came."

His eyes flared and air hitched in his throat.

Got ya.

Mandy told me I only really needed to know one thing about sigmas. Looking back on the conversation, she'd absolutely been describing werewolf hierarchy, and I wished I'd quizzed her more, yet she *did* let slip one crucial bit of information.

When a sigma sees something he wants, he takes it.

Alarick wanted me.

I didn't know exactly what for. Assumedly, it had to do with fucking the tribe over. But whatever the plan was, dealing with me got him off in a twisted way. He enjoyed having control over me because he knew it would enrage his opponent.

"I wanted you to know that," I stared at my hands, "because afterward, it wasn't fair of me to pile my personal issues on you."

"I'm not sure you could ever be accused of that."

Was that an insult or compliment? "In saying that, I just got out of a long-term relationship, and rebounds aren't a great idea."

He stiffened. Didn't like being reduced to a rebound?

Snort.

"What we did felt incredible. I'm sure you can feel the intensity between us, too, but a term of me returning to work is that our relationship remains platonic. I feel out of control around you. Like I'm capable of doing anything you ask. It worries me that you wouldn't hire me back for my music but because you see me as a piece of ass to use and take whenever you want."

Yep, I had a diploma in dirty talk. Couldn't say I ever used it in this messed-up way, but the effect was undeniable.

Alarick jolted in his chair. Gaze on my lips, he blinked several times, hands disappearing under the desk as he moved slightly.

My guess? He just adjusted his boner.

He cleared his throat. "I assure you that isn't the case. Your music is unlike anything I've ever heard."

"Even so," I said demurely, lowering my lashes.

The only thing hotter than a woman a man could touch whenever he wanted? An untouchable woman—and the reason for revealing more skin for this meeting.

I'd drive him so mad with this twisted perversion of his, he'd be blind to my movements against him. Or at least willing to excuse them for a sultry smile or hot look.

"Of course," Alarick said hoarsely. "Will you let me know if your stance changes?"

I smiled shyly. "I can do that."

"That brings us to your employment."

It was like I hadn't just painted a picture of him using my body whenever he wanted.

"You didn't answer my other question."

I folded my arms. "Look. I'm not a fan of personal questions. I thought you'd received that loud and clear a while ago. Do I *need* to answer that question?"

Alarick tilted his head. "Yes."

My eyes narrowed, and a gleam entered his honey eyes.

Maybe the fact werewolves existed, and I sat across from one, should simplify the human pains of my life, but this *still* wasn't an easy thing to do. Splaying my ribs open to infiltrate the pack made it a fraction more palatable. But, actually, anything the werewolves knew about me could be used as ammunition later.

The clenching of my jaw wasn't an act. "Then listen good. I'll say this once. The information isn't to leave this room."

His darkening gaze was a stabbing reminder of what he could become.

What he *was*.

"One week ago, I discovered my uncle and cousin existed—" I let him savour that titbit. "—but in my experience, people don't give a shit. That's why working for Herc is out of the question. If our relationship turns to shit, I can't be financially reliant on him."

I'd never, not *ever* muttered those words aloud. The clawing in my chest wanted out.

"Give me the job or don't. If that explanation isn't enough, you aren't getting more." Standing, I glanced at the exit.

"Thank you." Alarick remained seated as I edged toward escape. "Words like that aren't easy. You've shown me how much you want this job."

Uneasiness stirred in my gut. That comment could be interpreted two ways. "Only if you can keep your distance. Even if I have trouble keeping my hands off you. And I never have to enter this office again. Those are my conditions."

"Done. We saw a 2 percent increase in spending on top of our best-ever Saturday night here. How does seventy dollars an hour sound?"

Like you just showed me how much you want me to have this job.

Alarick really, really wanted me here.

If he *at all* suspected I was here on behalf of the tribe, why agree? Was it his sigma nature or something else entirely?

Did Alarick know something I didn't?

"That sounds perfect." I pulled up my big woman pants and extended my hand to the werewolf.

He held it tight. "I believe in full transparency, Miss Booker. This is a business, and consistency is a driving force of any successful venture. This is your second chance, and I don't offer chances beyond that. Play like you did on Saturday without interruption by a disgruntled ex, and we won't have a problem."

Nostrils flaring, Alarick released my hand, and I curled my fingers against my bared midriff.

"That's fair," I said in a steady voice. "There won't be any problems."

He nodded, as though no other answer could have been given and returned his attention to the computer screen. "We'll see you on Thursday evening at six."

I turned on my heel, clinging to control. Because I—quite literally—wasn't out of the wolf's den yet.

"And, Andie?"

Stomach churning, I paused in the doorway. "Yeah?"

Alarick fixed me with an inscrutable honey look. "Welcome back to The Dens."

14

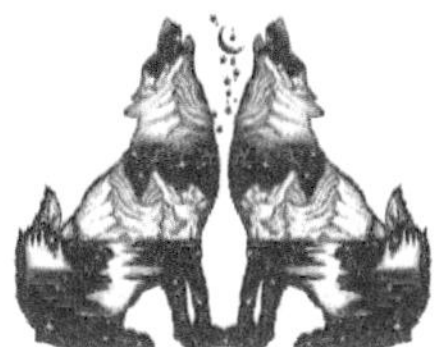

The temptation to drive straight to the manor was *real.*

And entirely stupid.

I walked back to the apartment, trying to contain the emotional fallout of the conversation with Alarick.

I had to act normally, but as necessary as that was, the coiled energy in me wanted no part of it.

I flung open the apartment bay windows. The bathroom sat to the right of the front door, the bedroom to the left. Really, aside from a door cutting off the bathroom, the entire apartment flowed from entrance into the kitchen, dining, lounge, and through a wide arch into the large bedroom.

Leaning on the glass table, I spread my fingers wide.

You did it.

I shot a text to Rhona and Herc.

I'm in.

Terrifying summed up what just happened, yet with the first meeting over, maybe the terror aspect would fade.

I set "Something Like Olivia" by John Mayer to play and turned to my suitcases.

Time to move in for realsies.

The excitement of moving to the valley had taken a massive hit, and my anticipation had shifted to determination since, but life didn't wait patiently for feelings. I was an old hand at faking it until making it—who knew that forced training would come in useful.

Pulling clothes from the cases, I arranged the garments in the drawers and on the rail wardrobe. The methodical work helped rid my body of the last tension from meeting with Alarick.

Afterward, I sat at the dining table, jotting down a supermarket list. The house stuff was back in Queen's Way, which sucked because I had apartment set-up costs to cover now. Pantry staples, a mop and vacuum, ironing board and iron. Maybe I should ask if the manor had spares of stuff because spreading these costs over six months would be hard, and cleaning items were necessary.

I studied the list and put an asterisk next to the items I needed today.

The envelope from Alarick contained one hundred and eighty-two dollars after tax. I had five hundred dollars left from my savings that I'd refused to break into. I laid out the cash and counted out one hundred dollars for an emergency fund. Two hundred for rent. Fifty to cover Marie's cleaning, and fifty for petrol. That left two hundred and eighty-two dollars.

Hesitating, I put another one hundred into a savings pile.

I'd spend the money from Alarick on groceries and the items on my list.

A Fleetwood Mac song had just started when my phone rang.

"Roy, how are you?" I answered.

"Good, but look. I drove past the house to put out the For Sale sign. You have some smashed windows. I walked around the back to check the whole house. It's two at the front. Nothing inside is damaged."

Mothershitter. I could guess who'd done that. "Which windows?"

"The lounge windows."

The biggest ones. *Logan, you complete and utter bastard.* "I don't suppose you could cover them up somehow?"

"Already on it. I had some old house signs in the boot, but that won't stop squatters who really want to get in. And... well, there's an open home on Thursday too. People don't like to think they're moving into an unsafe area."

I dropped my head into my hands, rubbing my forehead. "I'll see that they're fixed by then. Thanks for letting me know, Roy."

"You got it."

I had to sell the house and fast. The interest was crazy and in mere months, the house sale wouldn't cover the debt. "Any early bites?"

"Nothing yet, but the house went up yesterday. The market is slow right now, but the house has a lot of potential. We just need to find that one person who loves it."

Which meant *blah, blah, I have nothing.*

"Fingers crossed," I said, gaze heavy on the cash laid out on the table.

"We'll hope for a result soon," he said happily.

Hanging up, I strangled my phone. After mentally smashing the apartment, I released a breath.

My house insurance excess was one hundred bucks and, from past experience, I could guarantee the premium would increase by a ridiculous percentage after the claim. I emptied my savings into the pile with Marie's cleaning fee, and emptied the emergency fund onto the pile too.

"Bitchhole," I said to the money.

If Logan broke the window once, this could be an ongoing problem, and that was something I couldn't afford. Would he really kick me like this while knowing finances were tight?

Depended how much he hated me right now.

Judging by the last message... a lot.

I pulled up the cutlery insert in the kitchen drawer and placed the rent and petrol money inside before replacing the insert on top. I wanted as minimal money in the bank as possible until the house was sold, and Mum's debt cleared.

I snatched up my purse and shoved the rest of the cash in along with my phone, then grabbed my largest backpack for groceries. Poor Ella F. I couldn't drive if not absolutely necessary.

The teller in the tiny hole-in-the-wall bank didn't comment as I deposited the cash. I immediately paid Marie online, and then called the insurance company, paying the excess over the phone.

Would I like to pay the difference in premium now?

Yes. Clearing bills when money was available was the way to go. Cash may not be around in one month. My shoulders relaxed as the call ended. They'd send a glass repair contractor tomorrow.

Crossing the road, I found an empty bench seat facing the river and scrolled through my contacts.

Shit. I needed some good news today.

Jiani. I'd never met her. She was once Mum's best friend—according to Herc.

She'd just returned from a trip to Bluff City.

Exhaling slowly, I pressed the green button. Herc said her two closest friends were hurt by Mum leaving. This could very easily make my day worse.

Maybe I should hang up.

"Hello, Jiani speaking."

Her voice was clipped and no-nonsense—kind of militant. The complete opposite to Mum's light, carefree tones.

I took the dive. "Jiani, hi. It's Andie here—Ragna's daughter. Herc gave me your number."

A pause. "Andie. Nice to meet you. Herc said that you wanted to learn more about your mother."

Did I ever. "Is now a good time for you? I can call back."

"As good as it'll ever be. I won't deny that hearing Ragna's daughter was in the valley dredged up a lot of painful memories."

"I can imagine, and I'm sorry for that. You know she recently passed?"

Another pause. "I heard. So young."

"When she died, I discovered the Thanas—and that Mum was born here. She never mentioned Deception Valley. I only heard stories about her parents. So, really, I'd love if you can tell me anything at all."

She blew out a breath. "I lost my mother five years ago. Our parents' pasts aren't something we appreciate until too late, but I'm unsure where to begin if I'm honest."

I closed my eyes. "How about your strongest memory of her?"

"Oh, that's easy. She and Murphy were never apart. People say young folk don't know what love is, but those two sure did. Five years old, and I swear to this day that they loved each other even then. Most of my happiest memories of her include that lovely man."

I'd frozen at some point during the speech. *Dropkick.*

"Andie?"

"Sorry," my voice shook, "I didn't know him."

"So terrible, the rock-climbing accident. It was a shock to the entire tribe. I always wondered how Ragna survived the loss of him."

I *hated* my father. In times when hope and love were hard to find, the thought of showing Dropkick we could make it without him was all that kept me going. "I find it hard to talk about... Murphy. He left us when I was three." If a parent could leave, anyone could leave—that was the lesson I held to this day. I was always jealous of children who'd never learned parents weren't the same as everyone else.

"Impossible," Jiani answered.

I blinked at her vehemence. "That's what happened. Mum told me that he had demons he couldn't ignore. They became too much for him. He left us and wouldn't be back."

The woman scoffed. "You were around three? Well, Murphy died a few years after Ragna left. Maybe he didn't intend to leave you. Maybe he just couldn't get back."

Her words *rocked* my very soul.

I had no idea which date Dropkick walked out the door. If the date of him leaving and the date of his death were close, then...

I couldn't contemplate that possibility.

My entire being resisted the concept.

He'd always been Dropkick to me. If he wasn't, what would he then be?

"There was never *anyone* more in love than Ragna and Murphy," Jiani said. "Your mother had a soft heart—though you wouldn't know it when she played Victratum, and your father guarded her heart fiercely. He was her protector. Her champion. Having known him for over two decades before Ragna left, I can say that he was reliable to a fault. Ragna was the flighty one, and we loved her for it, but Murphy was the rock."

My throat burned and my insides began to shake. "Herc said that when Mum left, they didn't think Murphy was with her."

"You'd have to be an imbecile to think otherwise. He left to deliver logs to Bluff City and Ragna upped and left the day after. They were *never* apart, Andie. I can't emphasize that enough. Their parents gave up when they were seventeen and let them sleep in one room. Anyone could see they were forever."

"Why didn't Herc think Mum left with him?" I mused aloud.

"When people hurt us, we believe what we need to." Jiani sighed heavily. "Me included."

"You never heard from Mum again after she left?" I listened to the thick silence on the other end.

"Not ever. And I say that with more regret than bitterness. She was my best friend. Whatever she went through to make her leave... I wish she'd let me help her."

My heart thumped. "You think something drove her away?"

"I know it. Herc may not have noticed—poor thing had a lot on his plate in those days—but her closest friends did. She was always the life of the party, but then she didn't want to come out. She and Murphy had their heads together constantly. People chalked the circles beneath her eyes to Charise's death. That hit Ragna hard, no doubt. Yet she *spoke* about her mother and what happened. And when Ragna was really in trouble or in pain, she clamped up. If you ask me, something else drove her away from the valley."

"Like what?" I whispered.

"If you ever find the answer, Andie, then I'd love to know too."

🐾🐾

"Hey, girl!" Mandy popped up in front of me.

Just about to enter the supermarket, I managed to smile back. "H-Hey. You off for the day?"

"Nah, finally got away for lunch. I need to grab groceries."

Let me guess. Raw meat.

"I was about to do the same. Gotta set up the new apartment." I wasn't sure what to do with Jiani's views on Murphy and Mum yet, but they'd rattled me well and truly. I'd assumed Grids wore Mum down over time—that's what Herc believed too—but Jiani seemed to think an incident caused her to leave.

That made the potential answer far more sinister. My gut told me that the wolves were involved.

How could they not be?

Mandy shot me a sparkling look. "Alarick is on cloud nine that you're coming back. I guess you two worked stuff out, huh?"

"Uh, well, I'm working at The Dens again, but I told Alarick he'd need to keep his distance."

She grinned. "All boys or just Alarick?"

I pursed my lips. "Will my answer get back to him?"

I hoped so.

"I'm offended. Girl code!"

"All guys, but especially Alarick. Working at The Dens could be awesome, and I don't want to jeopardise that."

The lie rolled off my tongue.

Mandy grabbed a basket, and I opted for a trolley.

"Fair enough," said the female werewolf. "My relationship just ended as well."

This could reveal something about their kind. Alarick's interest in me indicated humans did things for their libido, too, but how did wolf unions work in general? Did they normally stick to each other? "Anyone I know?"

"Leroy."

My brows shot up. Dimples. "No way. Are there hard feelings?"

"Nah, nothing like that. Neither of us are the type to get attached."

I scanned the display, selecting a bag of the cheapest fruit—apples. "Leroy is the player type, I'm guessing. An alpha. You had to know going in things might not work."

She grabbed a melon.

"He is definitely an alpha. The more sensitive types are my go-to, but I thought I'd change things up this time."

From what an internet search told me, the strongest female and male in a pack usually hitched up. There was a female alpha who ruled the other females and a male alpha who ruled the other males.

"Can't say I've ever been into a sensitive type." Bananas were way too expensive. *Dammit.*

"Betas are where it's at for me." She lifted a shoulder.

What's a beta?

This is the kind of shit Herc wanted to know. "You know all the guy types. Is it just the sensitivity thing that you prefer?"

We moved to the vegetable section. This was a shopping date now, apparently. My eyes fell on her upper arm and the wolf band tattoo there. If werewolves were immortal, Mandy could have played Grids against Mum.

Mandy could have been involved in any incident. I had to look past their faces and remember their age and experience. She could be three hundred years old.

"It's the whole lover-and-best-friend mix." She tossed tomatoes and coriander in her basket without looking.

Could she smell what they were?

Mandy smiled. "And they're great with kids. Just stable, I guess."

Interesting. Did that apply to their overall hierarchy too? I could see how an overabundance of alphas would be detrimental—too many chefs spoil the broth and all that.

"Surely not *all* beta guys are exactly the same though," I said, scanning prices before selecting items.

"No, of course not. That would be too easy. And boring. You've got to find just the right one."

I grabbed crushed garlic. “It’d be nice if finding the right guy was a *little* easier though.”

“Tell me about it. You don’t seem super upset about the break-up, but I’m sorry your ex wasn’t everything you hoped he’d be. That’s shitty, no matter what. I’m here for ice cream and to ply you with free cocktails whenever you need it.”

I was sure she was. “Thanks. I may need to take you up on that sometime if the fucker doesn’t stop smashing windows.”

Her jaw dropped. “What a dick.”

Yep.

She snagged a box of pens at the end of the row, dropping them in the basket. I focused on her basket. Was she here for groceries at all?

“Let’s see that list,” the bartender said, beckoning. “We’ll get through it quicker together.”

I passed over my shopping list, half intrigued.

The werewolf absently added paperclips to her mix as she read.

Melon. Tomatoes. Coriander. Pens. Paperclips.

This was a set up.

She was here for Alarick.

Which meant he was gathering intel... in the form of my shopping list.

“You don’t overdo it on the snacks and treats,” she said. “Oatmeal cookies is hardly break-up food.”

I pushed the trolley ahead of me. “Corrie’s Chocolate Chip Chocos are my favourite.”

Mandy caught up. “Your *absolute* favourite?”

Scanning the shelves, I located a dustpan. “Yeah. Since I was a kid.”

My purse buzzed.

I dug it out as Mandy walked off down the next aisle, my list in hand.

Rhona.

Good for a call?

"Cheapest stuff, please," I called after Mandy. If I went over budget, I'd have to leave stuff at checkout. Not the first time. Probably not the last.

But it wasn't my favourite form of humiliation.

I texted back.

Nope. Grocery shopping with a new friend.

She sent a wolf emoji back, followed by:

You'll tag along with Dad tomorrow night.
Be ready at 7:30 for pick up.
*And Dad says good work. *eye roll**

I sent her a thumbs-up, nerves twisting in my gut. Obviously, I was nowhere near ready to go into Grids alone. I was glad Herc would be with me tomorrow night.

"Hey, cleaning products are expensive." Mandy interrupted my thoughts, "Nothing is on special."

"That's okay," I mumbled. *Dammit.* Herc must have a cleaner because aside from dishwashing and laundry products, there wasn't any cleaning stuff in the apartment.

"I have a recipe for a natural cleaner that I use. It would save you a few dollars if you want to grab the individual items to make it?"

That would be nice if she wasn't here to weasel into my good books.

I smiled. "Sure. That would be great."

15

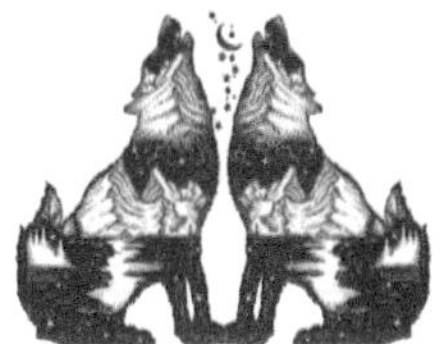

7:15 p.m.

Fifteen minutes to go.

Drawing on my first experience of Grids, I dressed in black jeans and a black tank, coiling my hair in a tight bun atop my head.

What was I meant to do about the colour? A mask wouldn't cover that.

Deliberating, I grabbed a beanie.

And what about my smell?

My phone buzzed.

Herc.

Here.

Typical parent texting.

My heart twisted painfully, and I stopped on the spot, closing my eyes until it passed. "I'll find out what happened to you, Mum."

There *had* to be a trail.

And I'd find it.

Goosebumps erupted over my bare skin that had nothing to do with the temperature, and I slung a dark leather jacket over my shoulders. Cool air brushed over my cheeks as I exited the apartment building.

"Jump in, kiddo," Herc hollered through the open window of the silver Bentley.

Kiddo.

I slid into the passenger seat.

"Kiddo was a weird thing to say. Sorry." He grimaced my way.

Despite my ample nerves, a grin escaped. "Agreed."

He peeled away from the curb and executed a U-turn. "I'll get the hang of the niece thing eventually. How are you feeling?"

I took stock. "Nervous. Relieved this part of the day has arrived."

"Always drags."

Tell me about it. "So where is the Sandstone grid?"

"About forty minutes out of town. We'll arrive once the game is running. The head team thought it best to keep your cover solid. The last of the wolves would have left town at least an hour ago."

"Smart," I murmured, tracking our route as we left the stone buildings behind. This was the road to the lake Rhona took me to.

Herc guided us around the sharp bends at a sedate pace—as though the loss of the grid tonight wouldn't be disastrous to the tribe. The pressure must be immense, but I couldn't detect a trace of it. He hid emotions well—and lied well. Before he confessed everything a few days ago, I'd completely believed his explanation about Mum. I mean, the lie was understandable given the supernatural happenings here, but there was a lot more to Herc than he showed.

I guessed a life on a pedestal would do that to a person.

"How are you feeling?" I asked.

He cast me an amused look. "A leader feels confidence no matter the situation. Morale is a very real thing."

"Sure, I get that."

"But you're a leader, too, so I'll admit that I'm seconds away from soiling myself."

I snorted. "Gross. Can't blame you."

"On that note, I brought you a uniform," he said. "We don't wear personal clothing in the grid. Uniforms and protective gear are washed in wolfsbane each week. Luthers can't scent us or recognise individual scents then. All our weapons and trapping devices are sanitised with wolfsbane too."

Whoa. Crazy. "Okay."

"We grow massive crops of wolfsbane under the manor."

"That sounds like a fancy way of saying you grow weed under your house."

He chuckled. "That's what Rhona says. How did your first trainings go?"

The instructor—the old man who I appalled with my erotic dummy displays—gave me a personal programme to complete at the apartment. I had to wear a strap around my ribs that synced to my phone and sent him data.

He said it was for progress. I was of the opinion Gerry distrusted my reliability because of my poor fitness level.

I'd visit the manor to train twice a week—and not at dawn. I'd go during normal *niece visiting* hours.

#spylife

"My body was so sore last night I couldn't sleep," I replied to Herc as we turned right toward the north valley ranges and away from the lake.

"You'll be glad for the power and endurance in the grid. There's nothing worse than a Luther breathing down your neck and finding you don't have anything left in the tank. On that note," he reached into the glovebox and chucked me two muesli bars, "tonight is just an intro for you, but the adrenaline will wear you out."

I opened the paper wrapping. "Homemade?"

"We try to limit plastic use. Kind of comes with steward life."

About that. "The game is Thanas versus Luthers, but on your side, those who aren't Thanas call themselves stewards?"

"Correct. We're stewards of the land. The tribe leaders have always been Thanas."

I nodded, chewing.

"Congratulations on winning your job back," Herc said, focusing on the hairpin turns as we climbed the range. "Whatever you may think, that wasn't something everyone—not even our veterans—could do. Thank you for putting yourself in that situation. If you're uncomfortable or feel at risk, I want you to leave at *any* time."

The only pressure I'd felt to return there was self-inflicted. I may empathise with the tribe—the wolves were trying to rip away their home. That wasn't fair, and yes, I felt an intense connection to this beautiful area, but my reasons for returning were mostly to do with my mother. "Thanks. I'll remember that. I found out a couple of things. Rhona said any little thing could help?"

"We want it *all*. We've scraped together a lot over the years, but there are large gaps in our knowledge."

"I researched wolf hierarchy after talking with a bartender there. She spoke about alphas once and about betas yesterday. At the casino, alphas are in charge of the major roles." I thought of Leroy. I wasn't sure Hairy was an alpha. He had a different physical build and seemed far more sensitive to others' feelings. He could be a beta perhaps.

Herc was quiet, then said, "The casino almost offers a slice of their hierarchy to study."

I hadn't looked at it that way, but he was right. "This Luther mentioned that betas offer stable presence. I wondered if that extended to their role in the pack."

"Interesting. Luthers have a clear pack ranking, but our knowledge of those exact roles is patchy."

"And sigmas," I added.

"What?" Herc stole a glance at me as the road flattened along the top.

"Alarick is a sigma. He works at The Dens. He's the casino manager or something. They call him boss, anyway."

"A *sigma*?" Herc shook his head. "That's a new one for me. You said his name is Alarick? I'm unaware of an Alarick in the pack. Did the bartender say more about him?"

I can tell you how many abs he has. "She said that he takes what he wants. From my interactions with him, I can say that he's calculative. Intense. Quietly authoritative is probably how I'd describe him."

Herc didn't answer.

After a while, I craned to look out the window. *Whoa.*

A serious drop to certain death sat on my left. I was glad Herc grew up with these roads.

"Can you find out more about sigmas?" he asked.

"I'll do my best," I answered. "Is that useful?"

"Possibly. It's new anyway, and that could offer a different approach. The pack is purposefully misleading us and has for some time. For instance, you mentioned seeing the Luthers' black eyes and we saw the claw marks on your dress, but you didn't see the Luther shift. We had no idea Luthers could partially shift. Is that true of the entire pack or just a particular gender? Does it require a certain strength and control? Maybe only a certain tier—betas or deltas—are capable of doing so."

Shit. Right, I saw what he meant. "If an opportunity comes up, I'll dig deeper. I work Thursday through Saturday."

Silence fell again.

I broke it. "What is this place?"

He straightened. "Sorry. It's hard to switch off the strategy side of my brain. A giant lake used to sit on top of this northern range. Just around here."

Jagged mountain tips buckled to a concave surface below our position on top of the ridge road. Like an ancient desert pushed up by giants, a random assortment of whites, creams, tans, and reds streaked the basin within the forest.

I'd be a speck on the quarry floor.

"The dried lakebed and surrounding cliffs are a sandstone quarry," Herc said. "That's where we're playing tonight."

"What businesses are associated with this grid?" Fear was sinking its claws into me.

"This is high-quartz Sandstone. Mature. We use it in construction. Paving. Housewares. Fountains."

Most of that meant nothing to me. It would take years to understand all this. "The businesses are local?"

He slowed and took a small dirt road. "Yes. This town survives on exports to the surrounding regions though. Bluff City is the largest of them. Ragna used to be the sales rep for that area after Dad died."

My mum? A sales rep. "I never knew that."

Herc didn't answer.

I spoke again. "I spoke to Jiani."

"Oh yeah?"

"Do you know when Murphy died?"

He clicked his tongue. "I'd need to look it up in our public records. Sometime in the spring around eighteen years ago."

When I was three.

"Why's that?" he asked.

"Jiani seemed to think Murphy would never leave Mum. She believes that his death prevented him returning to us. I'm not sure if I believe that. Mum seemed to think he'd left us for good. But I can't remember exactly how old I was at the time to check."

"Right. Well, I can tell you that Murphy stayed in the valley for a week. He wouldn't speak about Ragna. I asked many times where and how she was, but he refused to answer. He didn't mention you either, obviously."

Did Murphy drive here straight from Queen's Way? Did he intend to come back?

"He didn't say anything else?"

Was he Murphy or Dropkick?

Herc shot me an apologetic glance. "I recall being frustrated when he wouldn't give me details. We hadn't heard from Ragna for years. By then, we'd put two and two together that Murphy was with her. When he turned up, I thought my sister might want to come back too."

That would be a bitter pill to swallow.

"Murphy's family are stewards and still in the area," Herc said.

Really? "How many?"

"Two sisters, a brother, and his father. And his mother too."

Oh my god. I had a grandfather, a great grandmother, two aunties, and another uncle. My breaths turned shallow.

"If you like, I can arrange a meeting? Things between our

families deteriorated after Ragna left. She was the flightier of the two and they blamed her for taking Murphy away. But I'm happy to try."

I'd gained two relatives in the last two weeks. Five more was too much right now. "Maybe down the track. If they won't be offended? It's just a lot to take in."

I wasn't sure where I stood on the Dropkick Murphy front yet. Until then, getting to know his family was an overwhelming concept.

Shifting on the seat, I said, "Do you think something else happened to Mum to make her leave?"

"I wondered at times," Herc answered, a wrinkle between his brows. "What could drive her away though? She loved this valley more than almost anyone else. Her friends seemed to think there might have been an accident. For myself, I saw Ragna's mounting exhaustion. I saw the battle was wearing on her. It sometimes happens to people who throw everything they have into Grids. I think my sister just got tired of it all and didn't know how to face us about leaving. So she ran."

I absorbed that as we drove past a long line of cars on either side of the road. I had the number for another of Mum's friends. Maybe she could tell me more about Murphy and Mum.

Herc stopped the car by a sign that read, *Thana Reserve.*

"Isn't it awkward for both sides to drive up here and park? Do we just ignore each other until the game starts?"

He grinned. "Our side has a one-hour head start on the grids to counter the wolf's speed."

"Oh. Handy."

He passed me a bag out of the boot. "It is. Not their best negotiation. In this grid, specifically, the head start is a major advantage. We're able to claim higher cliff ground and essentially pick them off. Though we haven't played in Sandstone for a long time. The wolves usually pick Timber or Iron. Timber because it's the most even playing field. Iron because it yields the best profit of all the grids."

I wouldn't have suspected Herc's nervousness if he didn't admit the truth earlier. His blue eyes were firm, posture relaxed, and his chin tilted.

My teeth were rattling in my head.

Reaching forward, I squeezed his forearm. "We have this in the bag."

He winked. "I know. We should hurry. Go change, but here—"

I caught a small spray bottle.

"—spray your hands with that before dressing and cover any visible skin with it after."

"What about my hair?" I asked, clutching the spray bottle.

"Wolves are colour blind."

"*No shit?*"

Herc smiled. "Yes shit. Make sure to cover your skin with the spray. And put on the mask too."

Maybe I'd empty the whole damn bottle over my head while I was at it.

All the better to keep Alarick away.

I looked like a giant, saggy ball sac. Where were the badass black outfits from last week?

Herc snorted at my expression. "And that's why no one likes Sandstone."

"You don't look so bad." His uniform didn't have a tight condom hood or the white linen mask with built in bug safety lenses.

Seriously. A tight cream Lycra underlayer was flattering in approximately zero ways. Linen strips were stitched on top in an array of whites, reds, and tans. Cleated mountain shoes matched the cream Lycra.

I felt like a display of what happened when dogs ate white chocolate and socks.

"The leader should always be easy to see," he said, eyes watering.

"This better not be a new recruit prank."

His lips twitched. "The other stewards probably wish it was. Follow me."

I walked in his wake. "The game is going, right?"

"We're half an hour in. In another thirty minutes, the Luthers will enter the grid. But most have been here for hours."

"Really? Why?"

We worked down a steep slope through thinned trees.

"Because they're wolves. Google won't tell you everything about their kind. Some things you can only know from experience. Then there's the differences between wolves and *were*wolves, which are ample. For instance, most people have a visual of a wolf pack taking down a moose or deer or Belle's father from *Beauty and the Beast*."

My eyes flew to his back.

How the hell did he know I was thinking that?

Herc stopped at the bottom and waited for me to catch up. "The reality is somewhat different. Wolves are incredibly intelligent. It would be remiss of me to call Luthers anything but. Wolves in nature are very suspicious, and Luthers are no less. Both species expect traps. A hunter may pile meat in the middle of a clearing in the hopes of shooting a wolf. But a pack will eat other prey, or not at all, as they stalk and circle the pile for weeks—*months* even—before making a move. Then overnight, the meat will disappear."

"They're cautious."

The last of the trees cleared.

We'd reached the dried lakebed now, but from here the texture of the quarry was easier to note. High overhead, sandstone had been sliced away to form great tiers which casted us in shadow on the ground level. They'd sliced downward, too, and a huge pit yawned to my left. Another we walked past was deeper still. The quarry was like a giant uncompleted game of 3-D Tetris.

Stacks of sandstone were piled at intervals, and I tried to bury the uneasy feeling a werewolf could be behind any of them.

Herc spoke again. "Their caution is a strength and a weakness. The game is two hours long. The Luthers are on the grid for one of those. Their wariness has helped them survive the ages, but *inaction* does not help them in the game. Their tendency to assess for days and weeks is something to overcome. It's unnatural for them."

Humans had the opposite issue.

"How are we doing?" Herc asked.

I squealed when some sandstone moved.

Fuck, it was a person!

I did *not* expect the camouflage to be that effective.

"Everyone is in position. We managed to lay five new traps." The wrinkled, grey-haired woman held out a screen to him.

He took the tablet. "Pascal, have you met my niece, Andie?"

The woman extended her hand, but her mind was clearly elsewhere as we shook.

"Pascal is our marshal," Herc said. "Each side has one. At the end of the game, the two marshals walk the grid together and tally the points—one point for a trapping or shooting. The player must still be confined in the trap, physically held by an opponent, or unconscious from a tranquiliser dart when the end cannon sounds. One point is lost for each Luther that shifts to wolf form during the game and for any Luther who enters the grid early. Two points are lost for causing serious and sustained injury. Loss of grid for murder."

Chills raced down my spine.

This was eerie as hell. Cliffs rose up at least fifty metres overhead, but a tonne of stewards could be watching me. I couldn't see a single person.

"Why would a wolf shift if they lose a point?" I asked. "And how do you track that?"

Pascal murmured. "We have heat sensors throughout the grids. In wolf form, their heat signature is off the charts. They can't shift without us finding out. Plus, they have an almost uncontrollable urge to howl in that form, which gives them away."

"Do heat sensors pick up partial shifts?"

She glanced at Herc, then me. "No, but technically that wouldn't be against the rules. We have a team analysing small surges registered by the sensors to see if we can track it, however. The information would be useful."

"In answer to your first question," Herc passed the tablet back to Pascal, "Luthers can't always control the shift. Heightened emotion, particular negative emotions—fear, anger, grief, hate—loosen their control. We did push that aspect for a while, but in wolf form, they're unpredictable and deadly. Triggering that wasn't worth the potential consequences."

"Ten minutes," Pascal announced.

"We'll move to a higher vantage point for the game," Herc said. He jiggled a white rope I hadn't even noticed as we passed by a cliff.

Craning my neck, I followed the rope up the sheer stone face. Rock climbing ropes?

Would I learn to do that at some point?

Yuck. I didn't do well with heights one bit. Not in a frightened way. My vision went loopy.

Machinery was lined up around the corner of a tier. We filed onto a cherry picker, and I clutched the rail as Pascal directed the tray upward.

"Do you have a map of all the traps?" I closed my eyes as the ground rolled and surged.

"Recruits are required to memorise maps to the best of their ability through an app and a virtual reality programme. We used to wear watches that buzzed when a trap was near, but the wolves caught onto that after a while. They could hear it."

"I'm assuming they can't hear us now?" This all seemed like pretty crucial information to bandy about.

Cracking an eyelid, I caught his smile.

"Werewolves are sensitive to a particular frequency. They struggle to hear through it. We have frequency generators running right now. Though we encourage everyone to keep things vague while in the grid just in case."

This must have taken decades for them to piece together.

We stepped onto the top tier and Pascal beelined for a tower that extended higher still. A square viewing platform sat on a tall metal framing with stairs circling up through the middle. Kind of like an observation hide.

Herc climbed with me close behind.

I focused on the rail, clutching it tight.

"We alter the traps after the wolves are tricked the first time," he said, not puffing in the slightest. "Changing the location of the trigger —that type of thing. But Luthers do love to use our traps against us, so that can be an issue."

We reached the top of the observation tower, and I leaned on the balustrade to recover.

"There's a lot to learn," I muttered between pants.

I hated not being in possession of all the facts. I may be here for Mum, but Herc and Rhona's opinions meant something to me at this point. I didn't want to enter the grid and be a liability.

"Don't sweat it. Thousands of people have wrapped their heads around this in the past."

"So if I fail, it would truly be a first?"

Pascal laughed lightly, binoculars raised and focused on the opposite end of the valley to where we entered. "They're at the ready, Herc."

"Can I see?" I asked.

Herc unclipped his own binoculars, and I played with the dials, surveying the far end of the quarry.

My stomach lurched when I found them.

Fuck.

No matter how many times the lesson was hammered home, I couldn't wrap my head around this werewolf thing. There they stood in two-legged form, in three long rows that spanned the length of the quarry.

"The white is a new addition," Pascal murmured.

White chalk streaked their savage faces. I couldn't imagine the streaks would have much of a camouflage effect, but if their intention was to be terrifying, mission accomplished.

I scanned the rows until I found him.

He stood in the middle, near the front, talking with Luthers either side. Alarick had to be important. That seemed like an important-ish position, at least. I held my breath, tightening my grip on the binoculars as I noted the tense set of his shoulders and the clenching of his jaw.

He looked *terrifying* with the white chalk swiped over his face and through the ends of his shoulder-length hair.

I hope someone shot him in the neck with a dart. Teach him to touch me like that.

He lifted his head and looked directly at me. I froze before recalling he couldn't see me.

... *Could* he?

That was a really, *really* direct stare.

Alarick smiled and turned to listen to Leroy on his right. My gut flipped. That smile better not have been for me.

Boom.

Biting down on a yelp, I quickly passed the binoculars back to Herc.

"The Luthers aren't running in tonight," he said.

The wolves moved into the grid as a unit, sticking to the cover of walls and cliffs. Groups peeled off at intervals, stopping at uniform distances. The pack traversed across the lakebed toward this tower, and my breathing shallowed.

That was just a coincidence, right?

How the heck was Herc not pacing the shit out of this tower?

"This is how they entered Timber last week," Herc said, leaning on the rail.

Their unity was eerie.

A flag went up—red.

"One for us," Pascal said, tapping on her tablet. "Trap 113. Gets 'em every time."

My eyes widened. How many damn traps were there?

"They can hardly leave the cover of the cliffs," Herc said with grim satisfaction. "We place traps there. Stillness. That's crucial here, Andie. And to maintain high ground. From high up, we have the best vantage point for shooting. Their guns have less range uphill, they're limited by the extending tiers, and we're physically stronger when fighting from above. The wolves have tried any number of techniques to gain that ground in the past."

I squinted as *thwacks* rang through the quarry.

Herc groaned. "They cut the climbing ropes on the bottom tier. We have to set them up each time we're here."

Smart though. That had to put a massive dent in the Thanas's hour head start in Sandstone. And cost them dollars in replacing equipment.

Another red flag. And another.

"Two of the new traps," Pascal reported.

"Excellent," Herc murmured.

Was that three points to us?

A clatter echoed through the quarry, and I tensed, squinting at the wolves. They were holding something.

"They've brought net guns again," Herc said, gripping his walkie-talkie. "Knives at the ready. Nets incoming. Over."

He finished, and there was a rustle on the cliff faces before a series of deep booms thundered in rapid succession.

I jumped as nets exploded through the air.

Movement *exploded.*

Werewolves sprang for the cliffs, and only my grip on the balustrade stopped me backing away double time. They didn't need ropes. The monsters ran, leaping higher than humanly possible.

I gasped as they punched their hands into the Sandstone, surging upward in an unnatural, beastly tidal wave.

Stewards who'd fallen victim to nets were frantically trying to free themselves. Some were struggling. I itched to snatch the binoculars from Herc.

"They've reinforced the nets," he whispered. "Knives aren't working."

That couldn't be good.

Pop. Pop. Pop.

The frontline of the beasts reeled back. I pressed a hand to my cheek as one wolf ripped a dart from his neck. Snarling as he continued upward, but his scrambling climb turned sluggish, and his head lolled without warning. I covered my mouth as he toppled backward, crashing *all* the way down.

"Unless their heads are removed or they sustain fatal injury, they won't die," Pascal said conversationally.

I turned my still-widened eyes on her. I had a feeling they'd never return to normal.

Herc pressed his lips to the walkie-talkie. "Initiate phase two." Releasing the button, he shot me a look. "Communication over the talkies needs to be vague. We change the frequency each week, but they figure it out soon enough."

There was *so much more* going on down there than I could fathom.

The Luthers gathered in small clusters, crouching over something. I studied the protective rings around the clusters.

"Something is going on down there, Herc."

A surging rumble tore my sight from them.

From the mid-levels, stewards released nets filled with small boulders. The boulders rolled, crashing over the tiers. I jerked bodily as a female werewolf was caught square in the face. She was *out* for the count.

I relaxed as another female caught her.

"She'll heal in a matter of hours. Don't feel sorry for them, Andie, and don't underestimate their kind. Not ever. They will tear you apart the second you do."

Either side of the quarry, werewolves scaled the cliffs, regaining momentum as the last of the boulders thundered to the bottom. I grimaced as a Luther reached a steward trapped in a net and shot her point-blank.

Herc was right. I had to eradicate my instinctive reactions. The werewolves didn't register on any scale I possessed and underestimating them would land me with a dart in the face or worse.

"There's a chance she'll wake up in time," Pascal said. "If a steward can get to her, they'll administer a sedative reversal."

"We can't free them from the nets though?"

"Yes, but in this exposed setting, moving to help her isn't

advisable. Usually, it's not a great idea anyway. Some wolves will lurk around trapped stewards in the hopes of trapping a second."

The clustered groups of Luthers were moving back. "What's happening down there?"

Herc shifted his focus. "Some surprise."

A high-pitched whirring whined beneath the snarls and thud of wolves punching into the sandstone.

What *was* that?

Drones shot into the sky. A hair-raising howl went up, and the climbing werewolves rolled behind stacks of sandstone. Those on the opposite cliffs disappeared entirely from view.

"Fuck," Herc hissed, snatching for his walkie-talkie. "Take cover!"

High in the sky, and just below our position in the hide, the drones whined, spinning rapidly. I gasped as darts flew from them in every direction.

Oh, *shit!*

The drones emptied, their spin halting as their operators called them back to the ground.

The first stewards began to fall, the ropes connecting them to the cliffs preventing a fall to certain death.

Blue flags rose.

One, two, three...

Within minutes there were ten—with more going up every few seconds. Beside me, Herc was still.

"The howl," he said. "I've never heard them howl in two-legged form."

Pascal hunched over her screen. "No unusual activity from the heat sensors."

Herc's expression was grim as he gripped the rail.

The tribe couldn't afford to lose Sandstone. That would put them at one grid to the werewolf's four. I was just entering this battle and losing made me feel *sick* to my stomach. I couldn't imagine what Herc felt like right now.

"We'll have to do it," he said, straightening.

Pascal was hard at work, but she lowered her tablet at his words. "You're sure?"

His face was hard—almost as savage as the wolves faces below, and I tried to imagine my joyful, broken mother with the same expression. I tried to imagine her clinging to the rockface, remaining as still as possible before opening fire on a werewolf.

I just couldn't.

But she'd done that. For *years*. More than a decade before she left.

Did I ever really know my mum?

Herc picked up the walkie-talkie.

All the werewolves were climbing now. Heart in throat, I watched as they flooded over the lower level, up, up, *up* to the middle terraces.

Herc exhaled. "Operation Charise. Initiate."

At once, his stewards moved in a synchronised wave on the cliffs that rivalled the fluid nature of the werewolves' actions.

Note: Learn the operations. Just one more thing to add to the list.

"Cover your ears, Andie," Herc said, drawing a remote from his vest.

What was that for?

I obeyed. Pascal did the same.

That wasn't for a bomb, right? It seemed kind of like a bomb remote.

Herc spoke into his walkie-talkie. "North clear?"

He pressed a finger to his ear, and I noticed the black bud in there for the first time.

"South clear?" he asked next.

I scanned the south border of the quarry, watching as the last steward scrambled over the top of the cliff and into the forest.

The werewolves knew something was up. Some slowed before another howl had them pick up their pace to reach the top.

I hoped Herc knew what he was doing. Relinquishing that top tier made no sense. We'd be weaker anywhere else.

Herc nodded to the voices in his ear and spoke into the walkie-talkie again. "Cleared. Operation Charise initiating in three, two..."

He pushed the black button on the remote, and I shouted as a series of *coughs* puffed from the top cliff faces. Earth-deep groans rolled over each other as the entire ground shook with jaw-rattling intensity.

The middle tier of the quarry disintegrated, and a heavy chunk slid downward *slow*, faster, until an avalanche of sandstone hurtled to the bottom.

In horror, I watched the werewolves scramble for cover, their yells and screams barely audible over the awful crashing below.

"Penalty. Three. Four! Illegal shifts," Pascal shouted frantically.

I jerked my focus from the scene as any wolf below the middle tier was buried in stone. Above the avalanche level, four wolves stood with their hackles raised. I shivered, glad beyond measure I wasn't close to fully appreciate their size.

The last of the boulders thudded to a heavy, decisive stop and a sickening silence blanketed the quarry.

Herc spoke smoothly into his walkie-talkie as though he hadn't just buried nearly seven hundred wolves alive. "Open fire. Over."

The stewards appeared in short measure, taking out the Luthers perched on the top tier peering down at the carnage.

All except one.

As werewolves around him dropped like flies, one two-legged Luther dodged the darts flying toward him, climbing the last cliff face with blurring speed.

He alone made it to the top, proceeding to shoot two stewards.

"Who *is* he?" I asked, unable to tear my eyes from the one-man army.

Herc sighed. "Sascha Greyson. Here."

I accepted the binoculars, honing on the werewolf—who now wrapped a steward in a net, batting away the man's punches with ease.

The guy was *huge*.

Dressed in a black singlet and dark jeans, his muscles bulged as he threw a charging steward aside, unloading a dart into their rolling form.

Sinking to a crouch, the two-legged creature spun to face three stewards running toward him.

My mouth dried as I stared at the man's—the *werewolf's*—face.

Lowering the binoculars, I met Herc's steady blue gaze. "That's not Sascha Greyson. That's Alarick."

16

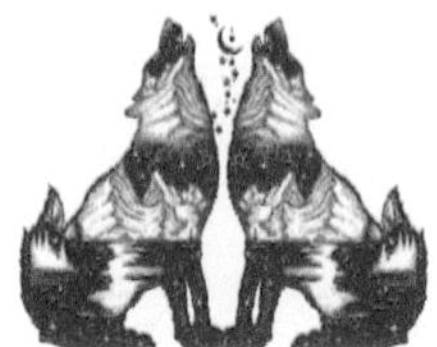

I punched the pad, setting my teeth.

"You seem... angry," Rhona noted, nearly stumbling back with the force of my hit.

I grunted. *Correct.*

The name switch shouldn't bother me. The Alarick and Sascha thing. But it did—more so, since I learned Alarick was the *fake* alias.

Why did he lie? I wasn't even a threat back then—unless he counted my similarity to Rhona as reason enough.

"Just tired," I told her as the timer went off.

Gerry, the old trainer, nodded, moving to where Wade and Cameron sparred at a far higher level. I winced as Wade smashed his fist downward, just missing the intended target as Cameron shifted her head to the left.

Rhona pulled off my gloves, and I tossed my liners in the laundry basket, groaning as I shook out my arms.

Ouch.

That earned me a grin from Rhona. "You're gonna be sore after that."

No kidding. Angry punching was only a good idea if a person had actual arm muscles.

We walked to a large red oak, and I leaned against the trunk, accepting water from her.

"What were your thoughts on last night?" she asked, sitting straight-backed and alert.

Uh. That this was far more of a war than I realised.

"We won," I answered. "The violence of the game was a shock. That could take me a while to stomach."

"We can't pull Operation Charise again," Rhona said. "That was a one-off. If the Luthers win and pick Sandstone again, we'll need something else to keep them at bay. Something good."

That I agreed with—simply for knowing *Sascha Greyson.*

Kind of.

I scowled.

Rhona slid me a twinkling look. "Let's try a switch on Dad."

"He'll see through it." We might have inherited our appearance from Grandmother Charise, but our personalities were as different as night and day.

"Usually, yes. But when you were hungover pissed off the other day, you had everyone convinced. And for whatever reason, you're just as pissed off today. This could work."

I tilted my head as she stood, dusting off her exercise tights.

"You're not always angry," I told her, accepting a hand up.

She looped an arm around my shoulders. "Don't lie to me."

Not a lie.

Saying the words aloud would drive her away though. We were hardened shells. Hers was painted in defensiveness, and mine in emotional distance.

What a pair.

She stopped us in the manor entrance, glancing around.

Our clothing was similar enough. Black exercise tights. I had a white T-shirt on. Hers was light grey. Rhona yanked out her hair tie, studying my sweaty hair do as she quickly braided the thick length of her hair over her shoulder.

I shook out my braid and threw my tresses into a replica of her messy bun.

She sprayed the contents of her water bottle over her head. "You're really sweaty."

I snorted, stealing her towel to dab at my face and arms. I couldn't recall my forearms sweating before, but there it was.

Rhona studied me. "Scowl a bit more."

I bared my teeth, growling.

She rolled her eyes, and I took it back a few notches, curling my lip. Folding my arms, I cocked a hip.

She made a choked sound. "That's pretty impressive."

I bit my lip, jutting my chest out. "Hey, Foley. Want a lift home? My cousin has a car."

Rhona widened her eyes, brushing her braid behind her shoulder. "Werewolves exist? B-But that's *impossible.*"

"Please tell me that's not what I looked like." *Mortifying.*

"He had *claws*!" she shrieked.

I burst into laughter, and she joined me as we strode into the manor, the length of our strides a perfect match.

"Shh, there's Dad," she hushed. "Let's test it out."

Curling my lip, I nearly lost my composure at her doe-eyed look.

I did *not* do that.

Herc's smile was broad as he looked between us. His eyes misted slightly. Seeing us together must be strange for him without my mother here and all.

"Good training?" he asked.

I shrugged a shoulder while Rhona grimaced, saying, "I may never feel my arms again."

"She was angry. Punched too hard," I glanced away, feigning disinterest.

"Angry? Why?" Herc asked her.

"Just tired," Rhona said, moving back a step and fanning her lashes downward.

My jaw dropped.

Herc's face softened. "Of course. If it's anything you want to talk about, you know where my office is." He turned to me. "Rhona—"

"I have plans to go out with my friends," I whined.

Two can play at this game.

His brows drew together. "Consider them cancelled. Something has come up."

I sighed dramatically and caught Rhona's glare.

"Andie," he said, turning again. "I pulled out boxes of your mother's things—journals and pictures. You're welcome to look through it all and keep what you wish. It's all in my office."

That shut me up.

"Thank you." Rhona beamed. "If you guys have stuff to do, I'll take a look now."

She was out of there in seconds.

Dammit.

I fell into step beside Herc.

Herc lowered his voice, speaking fast. "The Luthers are contesting Operation Charise. They've sent through a list of pack members with serious and sustained injuries."

Oh, shit. "How many points will we lose?"

"If all of the injuries are ruled valid, they'll win the grid."

Fuck.

This was a Rhona job, not an Andie job.

I opened my mouth as Herc pushed into a long conference room. Quiet hellos greeted us.

I counted ten people.

Clenching my jaw, I nodded curtly at those in the room and took the seat beside Herc in the middle of the long table.

Oh my god. I had to say something. Rhona's absence could make a serious difference to the outcome of this.

I opened my mouth again.

"We don't leave this discussion without Sandstone," Herc said solemnly. "The pack leader can't expect the win, but he'll take it if we don't counter his claims."

Sascha would be on this call? Like magic, channelling Rhona suddenly wasn't hard.

The screen turned blue, a phone symbol in the middle as we listened in silence to the ring. Four stewards sat to my left, another four on the other side of Herc.

One ring.

Two rings.

...Five rings.

Herc shot me a flat look. “Every time.”

“Mr Thana,” Sascha Greyson’s voice slid into the room. The screen flickered to show his face.

The Luthers weren’t seated. They stood in a row with their leader in the centre. I recognised Leroy and Hairy. Mandy was there too.

Good to know.

Glaring at the leader wasn’t any trouble even as his gaze focused on me for a long beat.

“Mr Greyson,” Herc said in bored tones. “We understand you called this meeting to discuss several so-called injuries on pack members.”

“The injuries are severe and sustained,” Sascha replied. “Per the rules of Victratum, points must be deducted to more accurately reflect the result.”

Victratum had to be the formal name of this game.

Herc chuckled. “Are you so desperate for the win?”

“Some may say collapsing a mountain side on another team was desperate.”

Guess the niceties were over. I couldn’t detect any anger in either man’s voice. What was the aim here? To poke and prod at the other side?

“The manoeuvre was well within the rules of the game.” Herc combated. “We named it Operation Charise after my mother. You may remember her?”

The werewolf dipped his head once. “I recall she met with a grievous incident in Clay.”

My grandmother died twenty-two years ago, so that didn’t really give me an indication of his age. To play the game, and recall what happened to my grandmother, he would have already been in his teens at least, but that was going by human standards. Maybe Luthers matured in a few years.

His honey gaze flicked my way again. *Asshole.*

"Grievous incident," Herc repeated. "Indeed. Today, we're talking of your own grievous incidents. Proceed."

Smart. I remembered the business lectures on persuasion—something we tackled for a month during my negotiation paper. Creating a personal note was one of the first steps—as was using guilt to prove a point.

My eyebrow muscles complain at the prolonged scowl. This anger business was harder than it seemed.

"Of course. Let's begin. I'm sure you're as busy as I am." The werewolf smiled before turning to Leroy on his immediate left. "Please carry Hairy in."

His gaze returned to me a third time. He couldn't possibly know it was me, but my thudding heart didn't acknowledge that.

I glowered. "Is there something on my face, Luther?"

Sascha. The name suited his eyes so much better than Alarick ever did.

"Rhona," he replied a second too late. "Always a pleasure."

I cocked a brow. "Wish I could say the same."

A pale Hairy was carted into view, and Pascal stood from our table approaching the screen.

Everyone's focus shifted to the panting werewolf, but mine stayed on the casino owner.

No.

The *leader* of the Luthers.

The werewolf I grinded against until we both came. Who'd lied to me about everything, including his name.

In silence, I followed Herc into his office.

"Oh, Andie didn't grab her stuff." He moved to the boxes filling half the desk and picked up a journal.

I fixed on it.

Rhona could have at least collected these before running off for the day.

"You're old enough now to begin leadership training with me."

"What?" I blurted.

He lifted a brow. "*Excuse me*. One day you'll lead this tribe, Rhona. It's time we prepared you for that role."

Ugh. This was the worst day to switch with Rhona.

Herc sat in the leather seat. "Can't say I planned to spend three hours talking to Luthers today. What did you think?"

The werewolves presented ten cases. Seven were ruled *valid* by the marshals. Our twenty-point victory had whittled to six. We'd kept Sandstone, but there were several times I thought we'd lose it.

I took the seat opposite him. "Sascha Greyson was showing you the risk of pulling that operation again."

"Correct. Well done."

Oops. I should step up my Rhona-ness. "I hate talking to those assholes."

"You must learn to deal with them. Grudges worked out in conferences are grudges that don't enter the grid. It's for the safety of our stewards."

I wouldn't exactly call what just transpired *working out grudges*. "Do you think they'll act out in Clay?"

"Almost definitely, if they're following their usual pattern."

Great.

"You're a natural leader," Herc said next.

These were words for Rhona, and I tried to hide my discomfort.

"Representing our family and leading the stewards," he continued, "is about management and leadership. You must have the ability to convince any steward to enter the grid and work in the best interest of this tribe and this land. If they're fearful, you must undo that fear. If they're arrogant, you must humble them. If they are strong-willed, you must walk the line of discipline and offering choice. Simultaneously, you must inspire those around you. By your actions and example alone, even the strongest stewards will push to emulate you. Your strength is indisputable,

Rhona. *That* is something you've shown every steward since fifteen."

Rhona was a literal badass, and I couldn't argue with that. But if I was honest, the rest didn't describe her at all.

"Your weaknesses lay in the management of people," he said.

I nodded.

Herc extracted an old workbook from the top desk drawer. "My father gave me this a year before his death. I hated working through it. Until I stood in front of the Luthers and our stewards at the reading of his will. *Then* I'd never been more grateful to know *something* of how to lead."

He pushed the book to me along with a pen and paper. "Page one, exercise one."

I opened the book and read aloud, "Your peer isn't completing their job to an acceptable standard. How do you approach this issue?"

"Remember, *always*, that these lands contain the bones of our ancestors. That shapes your every decision. Your personal feelings and problems cannot cloud how you react or analyse a problem."

Business was business. I understood.

Taking up the pen, I thought for a moment before jotting down an answer. We'd covered employee and conflict management last year, but I was rusty. After the first two lines, my memory dredged up some finer points, so I added those.

I slid the paper back, almost nervous as Herc read my answer.

He stared. And stared some more.

Glancing at me, Herc cleared his throat. "Meet with the peer as soon as possible, taking quantifiable data of their poor performance. Clearly outline the result they need to reach. Brainstorm solutions with the peer. Consider external stresses and their motivation, and/or training level. Listen so they feel valued. Don't close the meeting until the peer clearly understands how to proceed."

A textbook answer.

Herc's lips twitched. "How long are you going to keep this up, Andie?"

My cheeks heated. *Snapped.*

I winced. "Was it obvious?"

He drew another slip of paper from the top drawer. "Rhona's answer to the same question... *Make them stand in freezing water and beat them with reeds, just like old times.*"

I pressed my lips together. "That's Plan B. You got me. Challenges are my weakness."

Give me a sudoku any day of the week.

He regarded me. "A weakness not many possess. Gerry tells me you train hard."

"I didn't know he spoke."

"Pascal reports you memorised 70 percent of the traps in Clay after your first virtual reality training this morning."

That many? Probably because I was so damn determined not to be a liability. I would have expected 20 or 30 percent.

I sat, unsure how to respond.

"Humility and integrity," Herc said, reaching to take the exercise book back. He slid it away, along with my answer and Rhona's. "Those qualities are just as important as physical strength, Andie. Don't forget it."

...*Okay?* "Where did my Rhona impersonation go wrong?"

Herc smiled. "I can tell you that looking at gruesome werewolf injuries doesn't make her flinch."

Ugh, I did do that.

He rested a hand on the boxes. "It's nice to see you two getting along. Makes me think about the childhood you both could have had if things were different with Ragna."

The thought plagued me, too, especially after talking with Jiani. So much could be different. I'd have Mum's *and* Murphy's family. A father who I could turn to. A mother who kicked ass and protected me.

What a dream.

A horrible, bitter dream.

"Life could have been easier..." I trailed off. Rising, I grabbed at the closest box. "Thanks for these. I really don't know what to say."

Herc rested a hand on my shoulder. "You don't need to say anything. I hope they give you whatever you're looking for."

An answer.

That's what I wanted.

What happened to my mother?

17

Good as fucking gold.

That's how the Luthers looked when I entered *The Dens* just before 6:00 p.m.

An entire cliff face *fell* on them, and not a single bruise showed. Though I noticed Hairy and one of the bouncers weren't in attendance. No wonder. Hairy's leg hung by a thread when I saw him during the video conference.

Bile rose in my throat all over again.

I gripped my sax, far calmer for clinging to it as I approached the bar. "Hey, Mandy."

She shot me a flat look. "Hi."

I frowned. "Are you okay?"

"Just tired. Want a water?"

Depends. Would she poison it? "Yeah, thanks. Big crowd tonight."

I was here last Thursday, but Leroy's thieving ways distracted me.

"There's a poker tournament on." She slid a water before me, adding two lemon slices like last time.

Poker. I wrinkled my nose. "Right. I'll see you after."

She was already moving away. *Interesting.* Was that disappointment, resentment, or fatigue?

Maybe the avalanches broke both her legs and Mandy spent all night recovering.

I shivered.

Thursdays might not be the best day to fish for information if the Luthers lost Grids.

Was *Sascha* here tonight?

I'd dressed to impress just in case, putting in extra effort because he'd pissed me off. Had he laughed each time I called him Alarick? It really, really annoyed me.

I'd selected my third sexiest dress for the occasion. Black stilettos and a coiled half-up and half-down hair style—*yep*, temptation never looked so good.

The silk forest-green dress clung from lower back to just below my knees, ensuring my steps were small. The neckline hung in lazy folds, but my back was bare for all to see, only criss-crossing satin straps holding the front of the dress in place.

I stepped onto the gold stage, setting my water on the black stool. I wet my reed. Tightening my neck strap, I tucked my chin to check the position.

Perfect.

The hairs raised on the back of my neck. Stilling, I scanned the bar, almost snapping onto Sascha Greyson's honey gaze. He lurked across the bar outside the staff door, leaning on the bar.

Last night, the white chalk made him look like some ancient Viking. He'd been near the forefront of that attack, and he alone made it to the top of the cliffs to fight.

I arched a brow at him.

You have a reason to be standoffish. He can't read into this exchange.

He nodded at me before talking to Leroy.

He'd sneak a peek sooner or later. I pivoted to take a sip of my drink, showing him every inch of my displayed skin while smiling at the closest patrons.

Closing my eyes, I began.

"Try Just a Little Bit Harder" by one of my all-time favourite artists, Janis Joplin. Vocal covers of this song never convinced me.

This song required the undiluted gravel that only Janis could provide.

After a few bars, my eyes flew open.

This was an absolutely *terrible* choice of song. The Luthers were buried alive last night, and I was playing a song telling them to put more effort in.

Shit. What were the odds no one knew the song?

I belted out the last few notes and dipped my head in thanks at the applause. Thank fuck I didn't play "Landslide" by Fleetwood Mac.

Maybe a little more thought on song choice was warranted...

"Warwick Avenue." Duffy.

Perfectly neutral.

The shift passed as quickly as the first. This werewolf bullshit hadn't affected my music at least, and that warmed my heart. Relaxing, my mind drifted to the boxes of Mum's stuff that I had a chance to dig through.

She started journaling at twelve years old.

Dad said I have to do this each day. A whole page. Whhhy?

Mum had kept her handwriting large to use as much of her one-page quota as possible with minimal words.

I swung my hair forward to hide my smile as the last note of "In the Air" by l.a.b. faded. Child Mum was pretty hilarious. She hadn't known about werewolves at that age, and the entries were about trips to the lake with Herc and baking with her mother. Her words were nonsensical for the most part.

Those nonsensical words were so important to me.

She was happy once—through and through. That soothed me on a level even my saxophone couldn't reach.

The words devastated in equal measure. I wish someone had protected that version of her, or that I could have safeguarded her joyful spirit somehow, to preserve her happiness in life.

Whatever I did for her wasn't enough.

Things could have been so different if I succeeded. Not just with her addiction. Maybe we would have had money to pay for all the cancer treatments insurance didn't cover.

Maybe she'd still be here now.

I checked my phone, spotting a missed call from Roy.

The open home was today! I completely forgot.

Hopefully he was still awake for a call after this last song.

Scanning the crowd, I absorbed the edgy excitement. The more alcohol that flowed, the louder they got—and my music contributed to that effect.

"Dance Monkey" by Tones and I.

A whoop went up from the younger members of the audience, and I winked at them. *Please don't let the gambling get its hooks into you.*

Turning on the spot to work the other half of the audience, I spotted Sascha at the bar again. His expression was grim as he sipped on Johnnie Walker.

None of the wolves had smiled tonight. *Definitely* not a night to dig for information.

Drawing the upbeat song to a close, I thanked the audience and took a quick bow to their applause before dismantling my sax.

Case and drink in hand, I wedged myself into the far corner of the bar beside a group of women trying to catch the attention of...

I squinted across the bar.

Sascha Greyson.

For fuck's sake. I pulled out my phone to text Roy back.

Free for a call in ten?

Mandy swiped up my empty glass. "Need another?"

"I'm good," I told her.

She walked off without another word. Mandy was plenty vocal during the video conference in defence of her pack. The injuries to loved ones had hit her hard. I was sure the whole pack was pissed. Mandy just wasn't as adept at hiding her emotions.

"Oh my god. *Shh,* he's coming!" the woman next to me screeched.

She repositioned herself on the stool, knocking me off *mine*.

A hand under my elbow steadied me.

The electric shock gave him away immediately.

Dang it. I looked up into honey eyes. This time, they didn't hold a flame to the fire-breathing glare from my neighbour.

"Your playing tonight was breathtaking," Sascha murmured. "What was the last song? I didn't recognise it."

Because you're old as shit.

I righted myself, pulling from his grip. "'Dance Monkey' by Tones and I. There are apps you can use to identify songs, you know."

The woman next to me flicked her blonde hair, sending Sascha a look I could only describe as *visionary reverse cowgirl.* Sascha leaned against the bar on my other side, ignoring her.

Let me guess. Females fawned over him all the time.

Vomit.

They wouldn't do that if they saw what I did last night. My breath quickened. I felt his eyes on me. Could he hear my heart?

Think fast.

I cleared my throat. "Do you guys have a printer I could use?"

Printers always ramped up the heartbeat. Jesus, Andie.

His quiet voice flowed through my blood like a lullaby, nothing like the hair-raising howl last night. "Of course. I can connect you now if you like. It's wireless."

"Thanks. I'll download the application."

I logged into the university website, cursing softly as I navigated the menu on my phone. My laptop may be a hunk of shit that took twenty minutes to do anything, but at least the screen was bigger.

"You're applying for more work in the valley."

Did he realise questions had question marks? "No. Applications for this semester close tomorrow."

He moved closer. "You study."

Straightening, I flicked him a look. "Is that surprising?"

His gaze landed on my saxophone case. "I should ask instead what you study."

"I'm in my last year of a business and communications degree."

"Business. What drew you to that?"

Oh, he *did* know how to ask questions.

"Controlling your own money is a very good idea." I clicked the download button next to the correct form.

Sascha shifted closer, demanding my attention.

What *was* it about him that made me so damn aware of his every twitch? Was it the sigma thing? The hairs on the back of my neck lifted when he entered the room. Earlier, I knew he was at the bar before seeing him.

"I have a business and communications degree," he said. "I finished several years ago."

I bit back a smile with effort. In the context of Grids, a degree in business made complete sense. An immortal must have ample time to complete extra studies too.

But... a wolf reading a book. With glasses on.

My shoulders shook. *Dang*. The punishing training this morning and this entire fiasco had left me loopy.

He inhaled deeply.

I stilled. *What the fuck?*

He was fucking sniffing me.

"What are your thoughts on this establishment?"

I scrunched my face. "Aside from it being a casino?"

"Yes. Aside from the fact you hate it."

My initial impression of *The Dens*? "Your branding is exceptional. Whatever marketing you invest in to bring these crowds so far out is, frankly, awe-inspiring. If transportation out here wasn't so difficult, the crowd would be insane. Though perhaps the location lends an exclusivity to The Dens that adds to the allure."

"What could be done to draw in more customers?" His eyes were glued to my face.

When did we get this close?

I joked. "How about an airport?"

Sascha froze.

What did I say? "If you want more ideas, you'll need to hire me as a consultant."

His mouth spread in a slow grin that only served as a reminder of the way I'd clutched him to me post orgasm, panting for air.

His nostrils flared.

Seriously. Was I just noticing all these wolf traits now or had he ramped them up?

Fidgeting, I checked my download. *Complete.* I opened my wi-fi settings, turning the screen toward him.

The werewolf tapped in the password before passing it back.

I sent the application form to *The Dens Printer.* Original. "Thanks for that."

"Leaving your application until the day before is cutting things fine."

The DJ started his set and I seized the opportunity to look there. "Tell me about it."

A table of raucous thirty-somethings quietened suddenly. I peeked over my shoulder to find Sascha's attention on them.

Just like that, they stopped shouting. Without *looking* or knowing the werewolf was there, they'd sensed and responded to his threat.

Impossible. And definitely the source of the dangerous undercurrent in the bar.

No wonder I could sense the guy when he walked into the room. That was a relief.

My phone vibrated. Roy. *Shoot.* "Excuse me, please."

Sascha's gaze snapped to my phone where the name was clearly visible.

I slipped off the stool.

My heel caught, and I reached for the bar, but Sascha intercepted the movement, cradling my elbow again.

I blurted, recovering my feet, "Downside to heels like this."

The words gave him permission to look at the black stilettos and he wasted no time doing just that. He inhaled, his grip slackening.

"Roy. Hi," I said, cupping my hand around the speaker as I walked away. "Sorry, I know it's late."

"This is the only time I get anything done. Don't have children, Andie. Live for all of us."

I checked over my shoulder. Sascha was gone. *Good.* I didn't want him to overhear. The DJ's music would probably cover me if I spoke quietly.

"How did things go?" *Please, please, please.*

He exhaled. "Well, we got an offer."

My heart sank. "Someone low-balled me."

"An investor. They normally don't show on the scene for a few months, but I'm legally obligated to present all offers, which the guy wasted no time in reminding me of, so for your information, he offered two-hundred and ninety."

That was *outrageous*. "Yeah. No."

"So I assumed. A couple viewed the property but felt the kitchen was on the small side. An older woman loved the house, but she couldn't maintain the garden."

I rubbed my forehead. "No one else walked through?"

"No, but I have another open home booked for this Sunday. Weekend viewings always bring in more."

Three days. "Okay. Thanks, Roy."

"I'll keep you updated."

I hung up.

Fuck. Two-hundred-and-ninety thousand dollars would *not* cut the loan repayment.

Spinning back to the bar, I yelped, whipping out a hand to prevent myself smashing into Sascha.

I pounded on his chest. "You scared me."

How much did you fucking hear?

"I apologise." He searched my face, eyes solemn and a complete contrast to—

"Your *grin* says otherwise," I grumbled, taking the application forms when he offered them, still grinning.

My chest rose as our gazes met.

Electricity thrummed under my skin, and I shivered, frowning. "Thanks for these. I'll see you tomorrow."

"Andie," he called.

I paused. "Yeah?"

"Your saxophone." He jerked his head to the bar.

Shit.

Shooting him a glare that dared him to laugh, I stalked past to grab my case *and* purse, spinning to leave again.

I blamed the call with Roy.

"Your first song tonight," Sascha *damn* Greyson said as I passed him.

I stopped. "What?"

"It was good advice," he said. "Thank you for the encouragement."

I watched as he strode away, and my stomach plummeted.

Shit.

Try Just a Little Bit Harder.

18

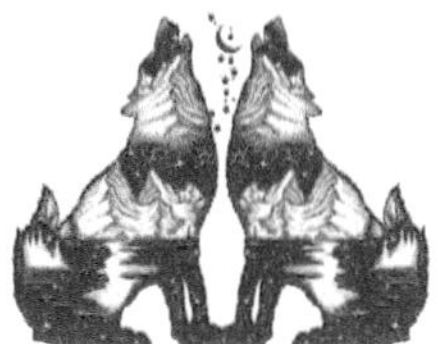

"Excuse me. Walter Nash?" I tapped the shrivelled man on the shoulder. Why couldn't I think of him as just *Walter* though?

He hobbled in a circle to face me. "Rhona!"

"Not Rhona," I said, smiling. "Do you remember me? I was looking for the Thanas a while back."

His eyes rounded. "I *do*. Kathy from Valley Designs said that Roger from the post office told her you're sticking around. That must mean things went well with Herc. Or was this place too beautiful to leave behind?"

No doubt he'd also heard of my thong escapade, too, but the old man was too nice to mention it. "A bit of both. Could you help me again? I'm trying to find a nice spot to swim."

I'd spotted Walter Nash from my windows as I tried to convince myself to leave the apartment. Facing werewolves in public was one thing, outside and alone… another thing entirely.

I couldn't let fear rule my life. Even if I really, *really* wanted to stay in my apartment all the time.

I wouldn't let Sascha Greyson control me.

"I'm the person to ask." He bobbed his head several times and grabbed my arm, hauling me down the street.

His grip was freakin' strong.

"See that sign?" He jabbed a gnarled finger.

The street post contained several brown signs—*post office, pharmacy, bank*. Below them were two green signs. One read *Lake Thana*. The other read *Deception River*. They pointed in opposite directions.

"Either of those'll set you right. Both roads are well sign posted. The river hole is one of the most beautiful places in the valley, or my name isn't Walter Nash," he said emphatically.

Lake Thana was where Rhona took me.

I slid into Ella F after, throwing my heavy tote bag onto the passenger seat. She hummed to life.

"Thank you," I told her. Car troubles would truly be the cherry on top.

I rolled down Main Street, stopping for the tourists cramming the streets. I hesitated at the street post and turned left over the bridge, following the sign for *Deception River*. I'd never been out this way.

The river that split the valley clean in half flowed beneath the gorgeous stone bridge, and I made a note to come back at sunset with my phone to snap more pictures.

Turning right at the other end of the bridge, I drove slowly, enjoying the winding river road and red oaks.

Tension drained from my shoulders.

Yep, I made the right choice getting outdoors.

Moving to the valley couldn't just be about the game. Grids was important to me, and so was fostering the connection I'd felt when arriving here. For me, and because Mum had loved this place so much.

The way was well sign posted. Walter Nash hadn't led me astray.

"Walter," I said aloud, holding my breath. "*Nash.*"

Calling him Walter was like calling Bradley Cooper by just *Bradley*. Except Walter Nash wasn't a movie star.

Or was he?

I grinned.

Around the next curve, rows of cars appeared, lining the road. Guess I'd found the watering hole. "This is not what I had in mind."

Me. Sunglasses. Blueberry muffins. Sunshine. Denial that werewolves exist. Alone time. That's what my Saturday would involve.

I tapped my bottom lip and drove on. Others had the same idea—I spotted smaller clusters of cars farther down the road. I kept driving until all cars were left behind.

Driving around a bend, I spotted a dirt area off the road. Looked like cars pulled in there all the time. Directing Ella F off the road, I parked and pushed through the trees.

Yes!

A rippling and natural water slide ran into a deep and calm pool. A narrow sandy beach lined the shore, bathed in sunshine.

Trees surrounded the oasis. *Check.*

Not a single person. *Check.*

This was me for the day.

Returning to the car, I heaved my bag out, locking Ella F.

A short forest walk, and I kicked off my flip-flops to sink my toes into the warm sand.

A sigh escaped my parted lips. Spreading out my towel, I groaned at the aches and pains in my body. I probably shouldn't swim today. I couldn't be sure of staying above water in this sorry state. Gerry was a mean bastard and angry punching received a D minus.

"Only happy punching from now on," I told the trees.

Tearing off my summery yellow dress, I slathered on sunscreen and set out my water bottle and phone.

Groaning again, I adjusted my navy sunbathing bikini and flopped on my back. The rippling river was the best kind of meditation track. Downriver a distance, a louder pounding and slap of water provided a soothing bass.

Beautiful.

I closed my eyes.

The sun soaked into me within minutes, permeating my bones. The warmth weighed like a heavy blanket, and with the state of my body, drifting in and out of sleep was far too easy.

I rotated like a rotisserie chicken, settling my cheek against the old beach towel.

A deep sense of rightness filled me at the mix of river water, pine trees, and sunshine. A deeper scent carried through the air, but I didn't know what tree caused it. Kind of like a musk.

I'd have to ask Walter Nash.

Mum might have sunbathed in this exact spot once. Now, I was here. In another twenty years, someone else could do the same. The Thanas were right; this valley didn't belong to anyone. No one *needed* to own this land.

How could it possibly belong to feeble creatures like us?

I rolled again.

How did Mum ever leave this place? Had she known this kind of beauty wasn't normal outside of the valley? At one point, this place meant everything to her, and she'd never said a word about Queen's Way to make me feel she loved it at all. She'd once requested her ashes be spread on this land. What was it that overrode her connection to Deception Valley in the end?

Was pregnancy the driving factor? Or protecting me from the werewolves? Stewards had children here all the time, so it didn't seem like enough despite my initial assumption. Surely there were other werewolves in the world too—and fuck knew what else. Wasn't there safety in numbers and what you knew?

She'd gone off with only Murphy for company, but I couldn't help feeling she still belonged here. Even in death.

Maybe when I knew more of Mum's past, I'd be comfortable spreading her ashes in the valley.

My phone buzzed and I fumbled for the damn thing, reading the message from Herc.

Murphy died October 9th.

I rattled off a quick *thank you*, lying back again.

October 9th. Three weeks after my third birthday. All I could remember was his face as he left and the toy truck in my hand. Was that truck a birthday present?

No idea.

I might be content to preserve him as Dropkick in my memory forever, except Mum's journals were filled with mentions of him—even at age twelve.

Jiani was right. Even back then, Mum knew she loved him.

The thought of changing my mindset about Murphy was, frankly, terrifying. Without me ever intending to, I'd built my life around him leaving. My fears, my drive, my expectations for others staying power… *everything* was tied to his betrayal.

That maybe never happened.

Scrolling through my contacts, I tapped on the number of Mum's second friend.

"Hello?"

"Nairee? It's Andie here. Ragna's daughter."

The woman gasped. "I'm so glad you called."

Wow, so different to Jiani. I could see Mum gossiping and laughing with this lady as opposed to seeking her advice.

"Nice to meet you," I mumbled. "I was hoping to ask you some questions about Mum."

"Of course. Ragna was one of my treasured friends. She might have left, but I remember our time together so fondly."

"I'm glad to hear it. Mum hurt a lot of people by leaving."

"Perhaps, yes. But Ragna was never one to hurt others if she didn't have to. I believe she had her reasons."

Same as Jiani. Though Nairee was a lot more forgiving. "You don't know why she left?"

"Unfortunately not. Jiani said that you spoke, and I've got to say we've always agreed on that something more happened to our friend. Further than that, I can't say."

Dammit.

"But there is something I've kept to myself for a long time," she whispered. "Ragna swore me to secrecy, but I feel she'd want you to find closure. She, well, Ragna called me after Murphy's death."

I sat. "What for?"

"She wanted to know if Murphy was safe. I had to pass on the bad news." Her voice cracked. "It was one of the worst moments of my life. They loved each other *so much*. I felt like I'd cut off her limbs by telling her. Haunts me to this day."

Mum knew that Murphy died. *Mum knew Murphy had died.*

I croaked. "How long after his death was this?"

"The day after. Her choice of words always got me. Is he *safe*? It's like she already knew the truth and just needed confirmation."

"Did she say anything else?"

"Before I told her, she said that Murphy was meant to be home by now. That he'd only come to Deception Valley for a week."

My heart splattered on the ground. "He only left to visit the valley."

"What's that, dear?"

He was Murphy, not Dropkick.

I closed my eyes. "Sorry, Nairee. Something's just come up. Do you mind if I give you a call another time?"

"Oh. Not a problem, Andie. Just whenever you want to talk, dear."

I hung up and stared at the water.

She never told me my father died. She'd let me think he'd left us, abandoned us.

Why did she hurt me like that?

Lie to me like that?

I dug the heels of my palms into my eyes, recalling Mum's exact words. *He had demons he couldn't ignore. He left and won't be back.*

In essence, that wasn't *un*true. Murphy did leave and didn't come back. But *Jesus*, she'd let me fill in the gaps with the most horrible assumptions.

At least her words gave me a clue now.

He had demons he couldn't ignore.

Those demons led him back to Deception Valley. By *demons*, did she mean the Luthers? Or something else?

Fuck. What a mess.

I didn't know how to face it. Any of it. I didn't even know how to think about Murphy now he wasn't Dropkick.

I'd always, *always* refused him the title of father.

My stomach rumbled, and that alone convinced my arms they should move. Riffling through the tote, I dug around for the paper bag. When life kicked a person in the vagina, at least there were blueberry muffins to save the day.

How many hints did I need to drop to Herc to get more?

A loud splash sounded downriver, and I lifted my head.

Fish?

A tiny scream sounded beyond the river curve, and silence fell.

Shit, was that a kid?

Another scream.

I froze for an instant before bursting to my feet, muffin forgotten as I took off down the narrow beach.

A third wailing cry.

It *was* a child. *Oh my god.*

I pumped my arms, sand flying as I sprinted. A pathetic howl arose, half gurgle as I leaped across boulders.

The pounding of the river was louder as I rounded the curve, searching frantically for the source.

There.

A puppy struggled against the far riverbed, intertwined in branches. It howled again, bobbing under.

Not a puppy.

A werewolf.

A baby werewolf.

A mournful howl rose far off in the distance, and the cub choked a weak response. I was already moving, scanning the river. The rapids here weren't a calming trickle. Shallow but fast moving.

"Fuck. Okay." Breath fast, I waded into the fierce river, immediately leaning against the shove of the water.

I waded through the white water, wincing as the rocks under the surface scraped at my ankle bones and shins.

"I'm coming. Hold on," I gasped.

A shrieking whine was the answer. Howls echoed through the surrounding forest. They barely registered as I cleared the rapids, blood pounding in my ears.

There was a tree under the water. The cub was caught in the bramble. Uneasiness stirred my gut as I studied the dark depths.

Anything could be under there. I could get stuck too.

The tiny werewolf bobbed. Three seconds passed and she didn't resurface.

Time's up.

I dove into the water, forcing my tired arms and legs to cut through the torrent. Branches brushed my legs, scraping along my body, spiking terror through my movements. I burst upward for air, struggling against the current as I clung to the thick trunk.

Where was she?

I worked down, shoving brambles aside.

My heart leaped as a small paw broke the surface. I ignored the wood digging into my stomach as I pushed over the trunk and grabbed at the cub, yanking her out.

Hooking my legs around the branch, I slapped her back.

"I've got you, baby," I choked between wheezing breaths. "You're okay. You're okay."

The cub vomited water and my shoulders relaxed though the tiny thing was nearly limp in my ruthless hold on the scruff of her neck.

She had to be exhausted.

The tree moved.

My eyes widened as the trunk started to roll, pushing me under.

Shouting, I threw the cub hard toward the riverbank. She tumbled across the mossy ground as water closed around me.

I shoved away from the trunk toward the bank but was dragged back by a grip on my ankle. Bubbles escaped me as I yanked my left leg.

It was caught.

Fuck.

The tree continued rolling until I was trapped against the rough riverbed. A thick branch crushed against my ribs.

My chest tightened.

I was fucking trapped!

Using my other foot, I kicked against whatever trapped my other leg, clawing at the limb crushing my side.

As my lungs burned for air, my eyes sought the light. The kicking of my legs grew weaker, my shoves and scratching feeble.

I'm dying.

Bubbles escaped my mouth, catching sunshine, and I noted the calming way my auburn hair floated in the water.

Like fire.

Pretty.

Heaviness overtook my body.

Smiling, I closed my eyes.

19

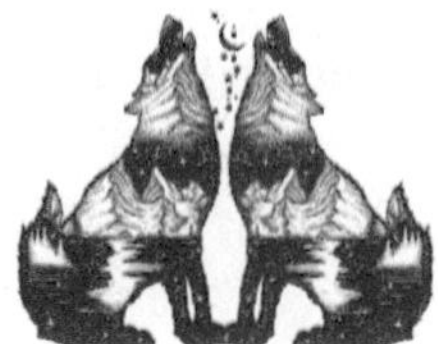

I shifted under a heavy blanket, moaning low. The pain in my body was at extreme levels.

I had to talk with Gerry—this wasn't sustainable long-term.

"Andie," an urgent voice said.

I smiled at the smoothness, sighing as the pain in my body eased somewhat.

"Wake up, Andie."

Say what now?

A large, calloused hand stroked my forehead and my eyes popped open.

I stared into a gaze that matched the voice and my heartbeat raced.

Not a speck of amusement softened his hard features. "There was an accident in the river. You're alive."

Pain ripped through my throat when I attempted to speak. Tears stung my eyes as I reached a hand up.

"Water," Sascha snapped, slinging an arm under my shoulders. I was a doll in his arms, unable to help or resist.

I sipped at the water he gently tipped into my mouth, closing my eyes. Was the cub safe? Was I safe here?

"What happened?"

Silence met my words.

I first looked at Sascha, swaying as I regarded the small crowd of Luthers gathered and watching in silence. I glanced down. "Am I on a kitchen bench?"

A yipping sounded, followed by a weary shout.

A young cub slid into the kitchen. I was already sliding off the bench to greet her. My legs had other plans, and I thumped into a cross-legged heap, reaching for the whining cub who leaped into my arms.

"You're okay, baby," I hushed to the trembling cub.

She whined again, and my heart broke in two.

"It was a scary thing, but we're both safe now."

The cub cocked its head.

"You don't believe me?" I asked. "I'm here, aren't I? And you're running around. We're as safe as can be."

Holding her close, I looked at Sascha as he crouched by our side.

"Aren't we?" I whispered to him.

Am I?

The game was officially up. I couldn't lie my way out of this and neither could he.

His fingers curled against the wood. "Always."

A simple yes or no would have sufficed.

I offered the cub to the woman I assumed was her mother—judging by the way she'd charged into the room. I smiled at the size of the cub's stomach, obvious as she hung in my grip.

Someone was very well fed.

"Thank you for saving my cub," the woman whispered, tears in her eyes. "He ran away. We couldn't find him until he howled."

Oh. A *he*. Confirming that revelation seemed rude. "I'm glad I was there."

A subtle shifting in the ranks.

Leroy, Hairy, and Mandy were relaxed. Some of the others weren't happy with my presence. Or did they think I staged the whole thing?

I yelped as Sascha scooped me up, placing me on the bench again.

"I can walk," I hissed.

"Can you?" he asked.

In all honesty? "Maybe not."

"What compelled you to enter the river like that?"

The danger under the words was palpable. It was the first time I'd felt that danger myself.

His tone was calm, but he was not.

"Sascha—" Leroy said low.

"He went under and didn't come up," I replied with equal calm. "There wasn't time to check for hazards."

Sascha's hands began to shake, and I jerked as his eyes flooded black.

"Andie, *back up*," Mandy said.

A roar ripped from the man before me, and I screamed, tears squeezing from my eyes as I clamped either side of my face.

Crack.

I didn't stop screaming as Sascha's face fractured, his teeth lengthening. He slapped a hand down either side of my hips, and the bench groaned. Mandy's warning registered, and I scrambled back, toppling over the other side of the bench as Sascha's back curved forward, accompanied by a sickening series of *pops* and *snaps.*

"Sascha, stop!" someone yelled.

A howl went up, and I rolled onto my back, fear choking me silent as a *monster* leaped over the kitchen bench.

The huge—*gigantic*—wolf stalked to me on all fours, padding steps heavy and precise. Standing over me, the wolf lowered its head to mine, and I choked back a sob, tears falling freely as its hot breath hit my face.

"Andie," Mandy hushed. "Don't move."

No fucking shit.

I screamed again as the dark brown wolf snarled, his fangs snapping an inch from my face. I turned my head from the savage honey eyes, waiting for death.

Instead, a rumble that was half growl and half whine met my ears. A paw the size of my head draped across my chest.

A *huff* and a *thud.* The wolf pressed his side against mine, his other paw above my head.

I was pinned in place, frozen beneath a monster.

The wolf rested his fucking massive head next to mine, a low warning growl rumbling from him.

I kept entirely still, staring at Mandy over his head for a clue of what to do.

"Just stay still," Hairy said.

Oh, cool. That didn't fucking occur to me.

I wheezed. His leg was heavy as shit. "Get. Him. Off."

The wolf shifted his paw over my mouth and face. *No way.* I tried to push it off, and my arms shook with the effort.

Leroy crouched. "He's just... reassuring himself. *I think.*"

Sascha's low growl got louder.

"You better be messing with me," I said, my voice muffled under the paw.

The wolf wasn't going anywhere. I sagged against the ground that would be cold except for the sauna of a beast next to me.

I shivered, and felt his tail twitch, coming to rest over my feet.

"Hey," I mumbled, nose twitching under the coarse texture of his foot pads—or whatever they were called. "You need to... un-fur yourself."

The paw slid off my face and I glared as the wolf lifted its head, lazily regarding me.

Did the black only show between forms?

"You're heavy." I grunted and tried to wiggle out.

He leaned his weight onto me until I stopped.

I licked my lips. "Please get off. I'm scared."

The wolf lowered its head again. Heat crept over my jaw, and I whacked his side eliciting a gasp from an onlooker.

"I didn't nearly drown to be crushed by a werewolf. Get the fuck off *now.*"

The wolf was up in a beat, snarling down at me. I shouted wordlessly in his face, shoving at his huge shoulders.

I crouched, facing off with him. "You have *not* had a worse day than me. So try it, Greyson! I will take you out."

A chuffing noise shook him.

"If that's laughter, I'm warning you this is not the time," I seethed, trying to stand.

Oh, dizzy.

Not good.

I sank forward, my grip on his fur now a clutch instead of a shove. Blood pounded in my ears as my head thumped forward against his snout.

Another gasp from those watching.

"*Her mouth is at his throat.*"

"I don't feel good," I slurred, listing.

Strong arms caught me before my head hit the ground. My head lolled and a whimper left my lips.

Lips pressed against my temple.

I regarded the man cradling me to his wide—and entirely naked —chest. Honey burned into me, and my eyelids felt unbearably heavy as a foreign warmth poured into me.

"You should show more fear around my wolf," Sascha whispered against my ear.

Drowning could make a gal feisty. "Some warning would have been nice."

He pressed his lips together. "Looks like the truth is out between us, little bird."

I'd show him a bird.

... When I could operate my body.

I woke.

The darkness of the cabin brought cold last moments in the river rushing back. Breathing in, I played the memory through from

sprinting down the beach to losing consciousness. Nothing good came from burying that shit.

At least I felt marginally less drowned, though my stomach was eating itself.

The door swung open, and Sascha strode in, a food tray in hand.

My chest seized, heart sputtering as I recalled the dark-brown beast.

"How long was I out?" I sat, staring at the furs covering the gigantic bed.

"An hour," he replied.

I wasn't in the same clothing. "Who changed me?"

"Mandy."

"Still not cool with that. Don't do it again."

"Don't drown yourself again, and we have a deal."

I thumped the bed with a fist. "That's exactly what I set out to do this morning; drown myself."

Sascha set the tray on a low table at the far end of the dark-wood cabin. The bifold doors were opened wide and light streamed in, displaying the stream outside and a curtain of trees. This room was a bedroom and lounge all in one.

I ignored how insanely picturesque the setting was.

Wincing, I shuffled to the edge of the bed. Wisely, wolfman didn't attempt to help.

"Is this your bed?" I grumbled.

"It is."

Great. "Does this tent-like excuse for a T-shirt belong to you?'

"It does."

I closed my eyes. "What's going on?"

Sascha crossed the room and rested a hand on my shoulder. "Please eat something first."

My glare was murderous. He cocked a brow, lips twitching.

"Eat," the werewolf said. "And we'll talk."

When he brushed my cheek, I batted his hand away.

A grin. Bastard.

Sascha Greyson, barefoot, shirtless, and clad in dark jeans, settled into one of the wicker chairs in front of the food tray.

My stomach growled again, and I caught his gleaming enquiry. *How are you going to play this?*

With my foot up his ass, that's how.

I inhaled, pushing aside how much of a screw up this was on my part. And now, Sascha wanted to talk. I'd watched Herc verbally spar with this guy for two hours on Thursday. I had no chance.

I was... dog food.

I snorted, testing my legs before forcing them to carry me to the empty chair.

"You'll feel stronger after eating," Sascha said.

"Twenty-one years of living has certainly showed me that." I studied the platter.

Bread. Cheese. I took some of each.

Oh. My. God.

Corrie's Chocolate Chip Chocos!

I dropped the bread and cheese, filling my hands with the cookies. I crammed one in my mouth, feeling the weight of Sascha's gaze on me.

Slowing my cookie massacre, I shuffled back in the wicker chair, curling my legs under me. The T-shirt covered most of my legs. I dropped the treats onto my lap.

"Eat as much as you want," Sascha said, breath hitching.

I shot him a suspicious look. "Why?"

His expression closed off. "Because you saved one of our cubs. We treasure our young. Food is a poor repayment, but it's all I can offer."

A dark undercurrent grated his words.

"Because I'm related to the Thanas?" I asked, biting into another choco.

Sascha fixed me with a veiled look. "Yes."

Did that decision come from him or the pack? And what *could* have been offered to me otherwise? Herc remarked that the casino offered a slice of werewolf hierarchy to study. I had to wonder if that was the case. In the kitchen before, the other Luthers behaved with complete deference to Sascha's wolf. They didn't dare approach.

In *two-legged* form, could the pack outvote Sascha? Did he need to move politically and pick his battles then?

Maybe we shouldn't assume there was just one set of rules for the Luthers.

Finishing the last choco, I reached for some bread and cheese. Sascha darted forward, holding out both. Shooting him a look, I selected different pieces.

His expression was unfathomable as he replaced both on the tray.

"You're not telling me everything." Something more was happening here. "Werewolf existence aside, what's with the other stuff?"

"Like?" He cocked his head, reminding me of the dark-brown wolf. My mind stalled as I recalled my terror when he shifted to that *thing* and stood over me.

Me.

No one else.

Me.

Leroy had said Sascha was reassuring himself, but why would he need to do that?

"Don't be obtuse," I said with a bite. "Twice, I had those drop attacks in your presence. Your eyes have turned black several times around me. Then before—"

"When did my eyes first turn black?" he interrupted, leaning forward.

Excluding the time that I wrote it off. "That day in your office."

I broke eye contact, nibbling at the cheese.

"I see. My mistake. I don't usually slip like that."

"Yeah, the guy who just made you orgasm is actually a werewolf. Oh, werewolves exist by the way. *That* was a shit day."

Sascha stilled. "You didn't know what I was prior to that?"

"Stop changing the subject."

His focus lingered on my lips. "You're very demanding."

"I thought I died in the river. Then a wolf erupted in my face. I'm not in the mood for games, Sascha. If you don't want to explain what's happening, that's fine. But I'd rather leave if that's the case."

The wicker chair barely accommodated him. The werewolf widened his thighs, running his thumb over his lower lip. "That's the first time you've used my name."

I shifted my gaze from that little show, tearing at the bread. "Probably because you *told* me another name. Trying to keep your stripper life from your personal life or something?"

He lifted a shoulder. "Essentially."

Good for him. "Last chance. Explain or I'm outta here."

Sascha's face worked. "My wolf is fixated on you," he said eventually.

"What does that mean?"

"I'm unsure. Werewolves don't usually go for humans. No one in my pack has any experience with such a thing."

That answered one of my questions about their kind. They tended to stick to relationships with each other. I wonder if the pack and Sascha viewed this *fixation* with the same disgust I did. "How did this happen?"

He surveyed me in silence.

I waited.

"I smelled you," Sascha said gruffly.

My brows shot into the stratosphere never to be seen again. "What?"

"The night in the forest. I thought you were a steward. Then *our scents met*. My wolf recognised you as a good match for—"

"For *what*?" I asked dangerously.

Credit to him, that tone would have scared hardened drug lords.

"Breeding." His lip curled.

Did he enjoy pissing me off? I was starting to think yes.

This officially just catapulted past the *scream and run* stage. I glanced at the door.

He spoke again. "If you were a wolf, you would have felt a similar drive toward me at that point."

"Just like that, huh?" *Arrogant much?*

"Yes."

Really? Was that a chemical werewolf thing?

I recalled the sudden change in his behaviour. He'd gone from trapping me, to offering his hand, to pleading in the space of ten seconds. "That's why you tried to free me from the trap."

The werewolf lowered his chin, gaze raking the bottom hem of the T-shirt I wore.

I couldn't linger. Not with this breeding shit on the table. "Just so you know, I thought you were a serial killer that night. You should work on your entrance with any scents you meet in the future."

Whatever *scents meeting* even meant. "In the bar that first time, did you already know who I was?"

"Your smell is unmistakeable. To me."

Like in a compost kind of way? I scratched my cheek. "Uh, okay. So, the first drop attack I had."

"Our eyes met for the first time."

I pressed my lips together, but his solemn expression didn't waver.

We weren't going to discuss how romcom that sounded?

Okay.

"You did react that time," Sascha said. "But not in the usual way. The female normally enters into a heat that ensnares the male."

I choked on a mouthful of bread. Swallowing hard, I thumped my chest. "What the fuck is a heat?"

Amusement. "Exactly what you'd imagine. The couple is usually mindless for a time."

Sex for days on end? That's what he meant? Those words weren't leaving the hole I called a mouth. "In your office when I had the second drop attack, what met then?"

"We touched for the first time."

I shook my head. "Not true. You'd touched me before and after without any problem."

"Keeping track, were you?"

My glare was answer enough.

"The touch has to be wilful on both sides. That was the first time you chose to touch *me*."

He'd intercepted the movement, pressing his palm to mine. I stared, waiting for the punchline. "You did that knowing I had no idea about this."

He held my gaze with unwavering regard. "In the interest of transparency, you should know that it's impossible to resist the breeding call. It must be obeyed."

Breeding call. *Nope*. No way.

"This girl ain't breeding," I said. "Unless you want your dick chopped off, *bury* that call double time."

I stood, brushing off the T-shirt.

"The heat is controlled by the female, Andie. The male is a slave to it, but sex doesn't occur without her permission. You, of course, weren't aware of the ins and outs of the heat that day in the office. That was my fault and I'm sorry for letting the situation spin out of control."

A big fucking mistake. My voice shook. "Where are my clothes?"

He followed after me. "You hadn't reacted with a heat after the first two meets. When you did on the third occasion, it took me by surprise. I'd never experienced one either. Before I recognised the signs, you'd ensnared me."

My cheeks flamed. The *heat* thing made me sound like an animal. "*My clothes*, Sascha."

"They're drying."

I whirled. "Where's my car?"

He watched, maintaining his distance. Knowing he did that to put me at ease only spurred my fury to new heights.

"I had two of my betas collect your belongings from the river. I'll tell you where your car is when we're done talking."

"This conversation is over."

"That would be unwise of you."

Wow, the breeding call did *not* make him smart. "Is that so?"

If I had claws, they'd be extending right... about... *now*.

His eyes narrowed and the Luther remained silent. I strode to the bedroom door, yanking it open.

"I can't fight the breeding call, Andie," Sascha spoke to my rigid back. "I have to continue with the meets. Believe me, doing so makes no sense for my situation either. I've tried and failed to keep it at bay. Believe me."

"*Try Just a Little Bit Harder.*" I hissed the reminder, stalking from the room.

He followed me, new urgency in his tone. "The capture meet is next. If you don't want to talk about what's happening, then consider this your warning. My wolf has started stalking you, and I have no idea when he'll make a move."

My head panged with the beginnings of a hellish headache.

This was all just *too much.* "Please, Sascha. Just stay away from me."

20

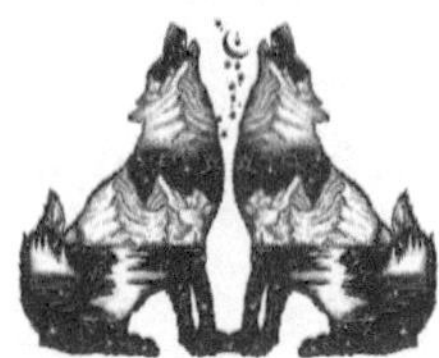

I startled awake at a quiet knock.

Stumbling from bed, I straightened my tank and pyjama shorts before peering through the peek hole.

Wade.

I yanked open the door, and he took me in.

"What the hell happened to you?"

Did I look like roadkill? That's what I felt like. "Drowned."

He laughed, then stopped at my expression. "Are you serious?"

"Yep. Didn't feel great."

He gripped my forearms. "Honey, are you okay?"

"I'm fine, but please don't call me honey." That reminded me of one thing and one thing only.

Wade's brows shot up. "Noted."

He walked me back and sat me down, moving to switch on the kettle before pulling out a small black device.

Pressing the side of the device, he set it in the middle of the table. "We're good to talk if we keep our voices low."

I craned to see. "What is that?"

"Frequency generator."

I want one.

Settling back, I pondered how much to tell Wade. The fact—*the huge fact*—remained that having any connection to Sascha Greyson looked terrible—a sexual connection was worse still. The thought of telling Herc that Sascha was experiencing a breeding call for me, that I'd gone into heat in *The Dens*, that Sascha's behaviour couldn't apparently be stopped… made me want to shrivel and die.

The Thanas hated the Luthers.

I'd just found Mum's brother and Rhona.

Did I need to tell anyone when this would dwindle to nothing in time? How many of these stupid meets could there be?

Calm enough after an eighteen-hour sleep, I could now admit that leaving without questioning Sascha thoroughly was unwise. He was right.

Asshole.

"Just so you know, every second you delay is taking a year off my life," Wade said.

Placing Wade in an awkward spot wasn't fair.

I'd edit. "A wolf cub got stuck in the brambles in the water. I heard howling from upriver and ran to help. I managed to free him, but the tree rolled and took me underwater."

His mouth bobbed. "Fuck, Andie. Who saved you?"

I frowned. *Good question.* "No idea. A werewolf, I guess."

Whom you didn't thank.

"I woke on their pack lands."

Wade slid a hot drink before me. "*The* pack lands."

I lifted a shoulder. "Is there more than one?"

Crossing the bridge had landed me on the south valley ranges. *Fuck you, hindsight.*

Walter Nash had a lot to answer for.

"*No one* has entered Luther pack lands. That place is trussed up tighter than Ana in *Fifty Shades of Grey*. What's it like?"

Cabins. Trees. A stream that wound through the cabins. I hadn't seen much—Ella F was parked right outside Sascha's cabin, and I burned out of there like someone who'd farted in a supermarket aisle. "Like a summer camp, maybe."

"Maybe?'

"I've never been to summer camp."

Wade eyed me. "We'll come back to that, and I expect a better description than *summer camp*. What did they do to you? You seem pretty okay?"

More than okay.

As I lay in bed trying to sleep last night, I'd recalled more of the blurring moments in the river. The stones scraping at my ankles. Yanking and clawing and being crushed.

Where were the scratches and bruises? My skin was unbroken and smooth.

Not a single scratch.

"One of the Luthers turned into a wolf in front of me," I found myself saying. "I thought I was going to die."

Rounding the table, Wade enveloped me in his arms.

"You were scared, baby girl," he hushed, rocking me.

Fat tears leaked out. "Yes."

I still was. Sascha was stalking me. He turned into a wolf. None of this made human sense.

Wade hushed me until the ringing of my phone interrupted us. Untangling myself, I sniffed, answering.

"Hello?"

"Andie, Roy here. Look, I've just arrived for the open home. The windows are smashed again."

I closed my eyes. "How long have we got until the open home?"

"Around three minutes. I've boarded the windows with sale signs and cleared up the glass. I'll make an excuse to the viewers, but this kind of thing doesn't look... well, safe."

"I understand. I think my ex is doing it. We broke up last Saturday."

Wade crossed his arms.

"Might I recommend that you call the police?" Roy said. "At least register the problem. They may be able to monitor the area sometimes."

"Good idea. I'll ring the insurance company again first thing tomorrow morning."

I hung up, dropping my head into my hands.

"Do I need to hurt someone for you?" Wade asked conversationally

He'd definitely kick Logan's stupid ass.

Ordering a hit on my ex was tempting, but I'd regret murdering him, or anyone, tomorrow. "I'm trying to sell Mum's house, but someone is smashing windows. I'm not sure it's Logan. But he was pissed, and he knows what a pain this would be for me. I'll try to call him. The police too. That should scare him off."

Wade reached across the table, taking my hand. "What about insurance payments?"

I met his grey gaze.

I missed work last night—but there were two days of pay owing to me. After paying another excess and the increased premium, I'd be left without a savings buffer *again.*

"It's covered," I said firmly.

A knock startled us. Wade grabbed for the frequency generator, clicking the side and sliding it out of sight.

I crossed to the door, swinging it wide.

Mistake.

"Hey, Andie." Leroy bowed slightly. He stilled, nostrils flaring. Over my head, the werewolf stared at Wade.

I blocked the doorway. "Leroy. How can I help you?"

If he didn't give me his jacket that one time, he'd have a door in his face already.

"Good to see you with pants on."

Ugh. Thong girl.

"What now?" Wade said at my back.

I could see how that comment could be misconstrued...

"Nothing like that," I called over my shoulder.

"She calls me Dimples."

At my flat look, Leroy's lips twitched. "Sascha wondered if you could play today. We have an event at midday and they specifically asked for you."

Sure they did. "I have plans."

I wasn't going back to *The Dens* ever.

Leroy searched my hard face. "I'll pass that on. Have a good day, Andie."

Wade turned on the frequency generator again. We waited until Leroy was out of sight through the bay windows to talk.

"You need to speak with Herc," Wade said. "Thanas haven't entered pack lands for over a century, and he'll have questions. Plus, based on what I just heard, this changes your position at The Dens, yeah?"

I lowered my head into my hands. "I screwed up."

"You saved a life. No matter what Grids is, children aren't part of our feud."

My shoulders eased. Acceptance of my actions did worry me a little—with the bad blood between the Thanas and Luthers.

"Fine," I said, blowing out a breath. "If you think it will help."

Dammit.

Herc would ask far more questions than Wade.

Hairy wrenched to a halt at my approach, bowing.

The bowing was new and had to stop. "Hey."

His mouth lifted in a crooked smile. "This is all out in the open now, and you're still going with *hey*?"

What else was I meant to say?

"I thought you weren't coming," he said.

So did I.

Herc convinced me otherwise. If the Luthers still wanted me inside, we should use the advantage. Of course, Herc didn't fully understand *why* Sascha would still allow me inside. He'd puzzled over the wolf's reasoning for a good, long while as I grimaced on the other end.

"A woman is allowed to change her mind," I shot back.

"Hercules Thana sent you, didn't he?" Hairy whispered conspiratorially.

I studied the werewolf. "You're going to enjoy this, aren't you?"

"Correct. And now we can be properly introduced. I'm Hairy, Beta Luther and proud doorman. You are?"

I filed that information away. "Late."

He bowed again and drew back the cordon.

Leroy shot me a look when I entered but didn't say anything as I strode toward him and Mandy at the bar.

"You're lucky I need money." I placed my case on the bar.

"Hercules Thana told you to come back, didn't he?" Leroy asked.

Ugh. "Yeah, but you're lucky I need money."

"For the ex-boyfriend who's smashing windows?" Mandy asked, sliding over a water.

"You're smiling at me again." I took the glass.

"I was pissed after being buried alive."

I lifted a shoulder. "Can't blame ya. Looked painful."

The werewolves regarded me.

"I'm Leroy, Alpha Luther and manager of The Dens." He didn't bother holding out his hand, opting to bow *again*.

Mandy bowed next. "I'm Mandy, Delta Luther and head bartender."

Now that *was* interesting because Hairy, Mandy, and Leroy were usually glued to Sascha's side along with two others. *Sigma, alpha, beta, delta, gamma, and omega.* Did Sascha keep a wolf of each status in his head team on purpose?

Did that help to keep the peace? Or did each wolf view problems in a different way that helped Sascha make objective decisions?

Dang. Herc was right. I needed to be here.

"What's with the introductions?" I asked. "And stop bowing. It's weird."

They smirked.

Leroy replied, "Our noble leader wants the pack to extend you a warm welcome now, well, now we've stopped dancing around each other. You're going through breeding meets with our leader. It is customary for the pack to bow."

What? To my ovaries?

Custom could kiss my ass.

Shaking my head, I hooked my sax case and water, leaving them grinning at the bar.

I greeted the patrons.

Looked like a snobby party. I caught sight of a *50th Birthday* balloon. Best liven it up for the bored members of the family who seemed to number over half.

Adjusting the neck of my sax, I leaped into "Mustang Sally" by Mack Rice. I'd just get this shift over with. A couple of hours, and I'd be free until next Thursday, and it'd mean more cash for me.

Opening my eyes when the song ended, I jumped at Leroy right before me.

"'Mustang Sally,'" he murmured, consulting the screen of his phone.

He jotted the song title on the bottom of a notepad.

Ending the song with a hasty embellishment, I snatched the book. "What's this?"

"Every song you've ever played," the wolf answered, bowing.

I ran my eyes over the list. He wasn't wrong.

Leroy slid his phone away. "It's much easier now we know there's an app for it—thanks for that. Sascha had me asking guests before."

My eyes narrowed. "What's this for?"

"Sascha thinks studying your songs is the best way to know you better than you know yourself. You're kind of cagey, no offense." Leroy plucked the list from my slackened grip.

"That's what the stalking thing means?" I whispered. *Know you better than you know yourself.*

My chest tightened at the thought. I didn't want anyone looking at me, let alone that closely.

Leroy sent me a curious look—like I was the weird one. "It's up to the individual male to set the tone. Some physically stalk. Others mentally. And others... both."

Sascha Greyson. That *mothershitter*. I jabbed a finger at the list. "How long has this gone on for?"

He pursed his lips. "When did you arrive?"

I groaned. "I don't want to know this shit."

Untrue. I just wanted it to end.

The blond werewolf smirked. "That's why Sascha told us to stop hiding what we were doing. He wants you to know that he's stalking you. Guess the extra challenge makes stalking more intense for him."

Staring for a second, I brought my sax to my lips and blasted the first notes of "Bad Moon Rising" by Creedence Clearwater Revival in his face.

The werewolf reeled back, and I had a moment of complete satisfaction before he extended his phone again.

Leroy read the song title and his eyes narrowed.

Interpret those fucking lyrics, Greyson.

Was the stalky wolf fucker watching from the shadows? My neck hairs hadn't risen, so maybe he really wasn't around.

Leroy retreated as my set extended, but I had no doubt he was lurking somewhere, creeping for his damn boss. I kept my songs as disjointed as possible, kind of hard when I'd purposefully learned these songs because the lyrics meant something to me.

Between the end of this shift and Thursday night, I'd have an entirely new set list revolving around the theme of *fuck off.*

Finishing my favourite Vance Joy song, I turned for a sip of water, freezing at the plate next to it.

Corrie's Chocolate Chocos.

I glared toward the bar. Mandy waved, bowing as she smirked.

These same cookies were on the tray of food Sascha brought me this morning. *Bastard!*

I gritted my teeth, a telltale heat creeping over my jaw.

Leroy didn't specify the length of the shift, but he gave me a nod about two hours in when the first partygoers started to leave. I withheld the urge to slam my sax into the case, attaching the shoulder strap so I could carry the untouched cookie plate and glass.

Striding to the bar, I slammed both down, and turned away.

Hairy fell into step beside me, clipboard in hand. “Wine or beer?”

I ignored him.

“Don’t worry about that one. Hiking or swimming?”

He grinned at my murderous glare as we reached the entrance of *The Dens*. The wolf stopped at the door, and I stormed down the street, my hair about to set alight.

“Books or movies?” Hairy hollered.

I was going to kill Sascha Greyson.

21

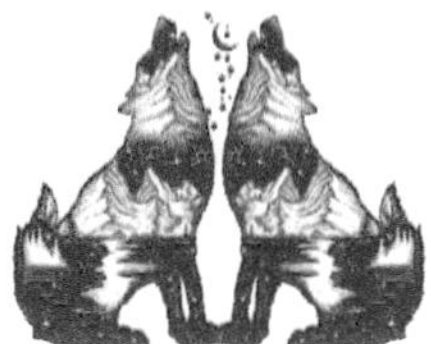

Monday never felt so normal and good.

I turned the page of Mum's *I'm 14* journal. I'd burned through ages twelve and thirteen.

> *I got my period three days ago. So that sucks.*
> *Dad and Herc leave the room whenever I talk about it though.*
> *This could come in handy...*

Snorting, I set the journal on the bed and opened the Clay app on my phone.

Yeah, the tribe had a password protected app for each grid—a game to learn where the traps were. Because a virtual reality simulation wasn't enough. Pascal said stewards recruited at fifteen responded best to game-like training. The head team released the new traps into the app each Wednesday morning, so everyone had a few hours to learn where they'd be put in that night's grid.

I entered a new game on Clay, wrinkle between my brows as I made my way through the grid. This one was a quarry, too, but the terrain wasn't as sheer and dramatic as the Sandstone playing field. More like rolling hills with steps cut out.

Rhona said it got slippery as hell. Which would usually make our traps really important.

Unfortunately for us, the Luthers had controlled Clay for decades and liked to go through after each battle and dismantle traps we'd set up. Timber had the largest number of traps at two hundred and fifty.

In comparison, Clay had fifty.

Our hour head start was spent checking those traps were functional and adding what we could.

I tapped on the last trap and waited for the app to calculate my score.

100%

I smirked, perching on the edge of the bed and mentally ran through the three manoeuvres learned that morning. I'd practiced them for two hours with Cameron after shooting practice.

Making my bed, I put away Mum's journals and cleaned the kitchen, stretching as I went to relieve the aches from... well, the origin was uncertain at this point.

Determined to extend my normal morning into a normal day, I called the insurance company to confirm the windows were fixed, then called the police.

It spoke for my life that I considered *these* tasks normal. May as well speak to Logan while I was at it.

Drawing out my phone, I unblocked his number, holding my thumb over the dial button.

"Open up," Rhona yelled from the other side of the front door.

I yanked it open. "You gave me a heart attack."

"We're going to look at dead people. Want to come?"

What?

Not waiting for an answer, Rhona strode away.

"Will I need anything?" I shouted.

She didn't answer, and I rushed inside to grab my keys, slamming the door behind me.

She was opening the passenger door when I caught up.

Squeezing around her, I dove inside, taking her spot.

Ha!

"Good morning?" Herc said from the driver seat, brow raised.

Smirking at Rhona, I locked the door.

She narrowed her eyes, sliding into the back of the silver Bentley. "Real mature."

"So what's this about seeing dead people?" I asked. "That's not true, right?"

Even if it was, I'd take this over calling Logan—though *dead people* did blur the parameters of my normal day.

Herc frowned at Rhona in the rear-view mirror. "That's disrespectful."

A *whatever* was her reply.

He shook his head. "I'm showing Rhona around our ancestral burial grounds today, and I thought you may like to join us. We can visit your grandmother and grandfather—and many more of our relations. We can trace back ten generations—and further still from rudimentary drawings and artwork that depicts where the leaders lay through the valley. Though some burial grounds are nameless."

I clipped my belt. "That sounds really cool actually. Thanks for thinking of me."

"You're a Thana," Herc replied solemnly.

My chest filled with a warmth I almost believed.

Almost.

"How about a leadership question to pass the time?" he said.

I laughed as Rhona groaned dramatically in the back seat.

"Please no," she muttered.

Herc led us down the road to Lake Thana. "The Luthers introduced a new strategy during the last grid. You need to plan a counterattack, form fresh strategies, organise urgent repairs and replacements for equipment, monitor the state of your stewards, and still have time for your family. How do you manage your time?"

I settled back. *That's impossible for one person.*

"There are teams for all that," Rhona said, staring out the window.

"Yes. How do you utilise and manage those teams?"

"They know their jobs," she answered. "Next question."

"Andie?"

I was a pro at time management after the free course Mum put me through. "When are all family members free? I'd set time aside daily for them first. From there, an order of equipment may need to include weapons or materials for new strategies. The top strategies will need to be decided on first, and I'd then order whatever is needed to allow for delivery time. I'd delegate members from the head team to join the current teams to continue developing our new strategies." I couldn't recall what the teams were. "At the end of each day, head team members will report to me and we'd decide on the direction for the next day. As this continued, I'd use my days to visit our grids and stewards. Perhaps it would be beneficial to appoint several stewards as go-to people. Other stewards could take matters to them first."

Had I forgotten anything. *Oh.* "On Monday and Tuesday, I'd finalise plans with the head team. Presentation to the tribe would be on a Tuesday evening."

I tapped my mouth. "Yes, that's what I'd do. Delegation. Prioritising."

Rhona piped up first. "Gross. You like these questions."

Growing up, school was a reprieve for me. I loved it. If funds had allowed, I would have started college early.

Herc pursed his lips. "Well thought-out, Andie."

Really? I bit back a pleased smile.

"Question two," he announced.

Rhona slid down the back seat and pretended to die.

"You have a plan. But for it to work, you need the help of other stewards that you aren't very familiar with. The plan requires resources they have—that you don't. Do you abandon the plan or ask for help?"

"Ask for help," I said.

Rhona continued dying on the back seat.

Herc slid me a look. "It has come to my attention that your ex-boyfriend is smashing windows at a house you're trying to sell."

Dammit, Wade. I was reasonably sure Rhona didn't know.

She stopped dying. "What?"

I sighed. "Yeah. Pretty sure he's the culprit."

"This boyfriend, what does he do for a living?"

"He's a lawyer."

Herc's scary glare arrived. "Then he understands the law. Several of our stewards are lawyers, Andie. You need only ask."

I shook my head but stopped, remembering his *leadership* question. "To be clear, my answer just now was for a business question not a personal question."

"If you need help, is there a difference? What do you lose by asking?"

Emotional distance. Give people an inch and they'd take a mile. Soon, they'd ask for favours in return, and I had nothing to offer them.

"I have a plan for Logan," I muttered.

"Put him in a freezing river and whip him with reeds," Rhona burst out.

Yikes. "That's Plan C, cuz. I've called the police. I'll call Logan tonight."

"And if the windows are smashed again?" Herc guided us off the main north road.

I set my jaw. "Then you may hear from me."

May.

He nodded. "Any time of the day or night just give the word. Our lawyers will smother him."

His words were meant to be reassuring, I supposed, but *letting* him assume that role was so foreign.

I tried to swallow down panicked edginess cloying my throat.

Herc parked between two trees. "Rhona, please go on ahead."

She cast me a long look before obeying. Couldn't blame her. He'd used his no-shit voice.

Herc faced me. "I don't mean to make you uncomfortable. You're my niece and one of my stewards. That means that I'll protect you. A woman should be able to stand on her own two feet, and I'm not seeking to take that away from you, Andie. But you can lean on me and Rhona. On the other stewards too. You'll be stronger for it, not weaker. And you don't need to give anything that you don't want to."

I grabbed the door handle. "Okay, thanks."

"To be part of a crowd but keep yourself apart is a lonely existence. Take it from someone who once thought he had to live like that to be a leader. Take a risk on us. You may be surprised."

"Roger that," I answered, one leg out the door.

"One more thing before you escape." Amusement coloured his voice. "I can see that you loved Ragna dearly. I want you to know that for stewards of this land, our loved ones never leave. Their hearts pulse in the soil and trees. Their souls clean the air we breathe. In *this* place, for our tribe, death does not separate family and friends. Andie, you will never be alone. Not ever."

The words slipped out. "Is that what I feel when I'm out in the trees?" *My mother?*

Herc's throat worked. "Yes. That's your *family*. Your tribe."

You will never be alone. Not ever.

I couldn't count all the times Mum said the same thing to me, but I'd stopped believing her after the cancer diagnosis. Everyone left, and I'd accepted that somewhere along the line.

So why did I so desperately want to believe my uncle?

Sighing, I relaxed my grip on the door. "I found out more about Murphy."

"Like what?"

"Apparently he wasn't the dropkick I thought he was. Mum called Nairee soon after the rock-climbing incident."

Herc stared for a beat. "She did?"

I nodded. "Don't say anything to Jiani, please. It would hurt her feelings to know Mum didn't call her too. Murphy didn't leave me and Mum. He came back here for some reason—to face something in his past. Mum seemed to believe he might be in trouble when she spoke to Nairee."

"Did she say from who?"

"Nope. Nairee just got that vibe."

Mum barely spoke about Murphy throughout my life. I'd squeezed the same abandonment explanation from her every few years until my mid-teens, but I never asked more because I could see how much she hated him.

Everything, the journals and her friends, refuted that and displayed how much she *loved* him. So why did she never pay him the respect of speaking well about him in death? To his *daughter*, no less.

Her anger had to do with why he returned to Deception Valley. There was no other explanation. What I wanted to know was if Murphy's reason for returning here, and his and Mum's reason for *leaving* the valley, were one and the same.

"Do you know anything about Murphy's incident?"

Herc grimaced. "I was there that day. A group of us were climbing, so yes. He didn't anchor properly, and his rope was faulty, they said. He fell to his death."

"He never mentioned anything about coming back to us?"

"As I said, he was cagey with any details about Ragna. It's something that I've held against him to this day. More so since you walked into our lives. If I'd known you existed, I would have searched for you without fail." His voice cracked, and he looked out the window.

My throat tightened. I really wish Herc had found us.

"You know." I licked my lips. "Maybe I will meet with Murphy's family."

He looked at me. "Want me to set it up?"

I hesitated, a *yes* on my lips. I swallowed it back. "Perhaps when I've finished Mum's journals."

"Just give me the word and it's done."

My shoulders eased. "Thank you."

I reached for the handle.

"One more thing," Herc said, opening his door.

"Yeah?" I glanced back.

"Gerry tells me you're ready to enter the grid with a mentor. You're up for Clay on Wednesday."

22

A clipboard slapped down on the table nearly oversetting my coffee—a *free* coffee because I name-dropped the Thanas.

I glared at Hairy, snatching Mum's journal out of harm's way. "Do you mind?"

"Books over movies," he muttered, checking off an answer. "Is that a sudoku book there? Interesting, interesting. Have time for a few questions?"

"Sascha sent you to do his dirty work again." I covered the completed sudoku with my coffee cup and returned to reading the journal. I was up to *I'm 15*. She'd really ramped up the Murphy mentions.

> *I did something today. With someone.*
> *But I'm pretty sure Herc sneaks in to read these, so I'm not saying what.*
> *Butt out, Herc!*

Was it gross to read about whatever my parents had done as teens? I was so desperate for any information on them at this point, the sexual details flew straight over my head.

A camera clicked.

I lifted my head. "Did you just take a photo of me?"

"Yeah. For your files." Hairy bowed.

Files.

Plural.

"But," the Luther said conversationally, "Sascha is doing the real grunt work. He's not a lazy male. You'll find him to be a very hard worker. Great genes. We're just honing on the finer details. This man knows how to delegate his time to focus on the important things in life."

Was this now a sales pitch?

I glanced around. "Is Sascha watching this?"

"Does stalking mean something different where you're from?"

Very funny. There went my attempt to relax before Clay tonight. "Yeah, I'm not answering your questions. You're pissing me off. Tell Sascha to stop or I'll doubt the quality of his genetics."

"He can't stop. We all heard him tell you that. Would you say you're reasonable in day-to-day decisions?"

Why me? Actually. "I'm not denying what he said. I only have his word for it, of course. To me, it seems his control is lacking. Not a desirable trait for any female looking to breed."

Hairy's flippancy dissolved. "Sascha has the best control of us all."

My smile was extra sweet. "Then he can figure out how to stop stalking me."

Never thought I'd say that sentence.

"Impossible," Hairy said, consulting his board. "Favourite season?"

I threw a bun at him. "Go away."

The werewolf caught the bun and took a bite, peering around the café. Only locals filled it today.

Hairy drawled a smile, and I tensed.

"It's a simple question, Andie," he said loudly. "The other night, did you prefer anal sex or—"

I lunged over the table and slapped a hand over his mouth. "Don't you dare." I'd already name-dropped the Thanas. Even if Walter

Nash hadn't been in here spreading the word about me, they knew who I was.

His dark eyes danced.

"Answer my questions," the wolf said.

"Get fucked."

He called out. "Not the *beads*, you say? What about the dild—"

This time my slap was more of a punch. My cheeks burned as the other patrons paused their conversations.

"I'll answer *five* questions," I hissed.

Hairy waved cheerfully at the occupants of the other tables and they returned to their coffees.

"Make it quick," I said. "And to be clear, this is a one-off. Next time, I'll just walk out."

His teeth gleamed. "First question. You should know that at this proximity, I can smell a lie."

He could? That's not what the tribe thought. They thought that was confined to a Luther's four-legged form.

"What's your favourite movie?" The werewolf leaned in.

I lied. "*Mary Poppins*. The new version."

His eyes narrowed. "I told you not to lie."

Ha. "*The Matrix*."

He clicked his tongue. "Question two. Favourite colour?"

"Brass."

"Lie," the werewolf stated.

"Not a lie," I said.

Hairy frowned. "That was truth though. Weird. I'll put a question mark next to that one."

Maybe there were limitations to their truth-nostrils. My favourite colour really was brass.

"Question three. Bath or shower?"

"Shower. No one has time for baths."

The werewolf jotted down my answer, and the strangeness of this encounter hit me square between the eyes. A werewolf was taking a survey from me—to pass on to my supernatural stalker—and I was participating. "Sascha isn't really following me around, right?"

Hairy grinned. "Whatever helps you sleep at night. Though you may wake up with things missing."

My mouth dried. I couldn't find my pyjamas or bed throw the other day. I'd woken to the curtains flapping around though I recalled shutting the windows. "That's crossing the line. I'm serious."

"So is he. Male Luthers never joke about meets. This is the most important thing he may ever do—an interview to his dream job. He's showing you why you should pick him."

Breeding with me was Sascha's dream job. "What do you mean?"

He cocked his head, eyes sliding left as he concentrated, and I gasped.

"You're *listening* to him right now!"

Hairy's dark eyes gleamed. "Question four. Favourite subject in school?"

"Economics."

"Thank you for your honesty," he said solemnly.

I snorted despite myself. "You're such a brat."

This gal needed more coffee in her for this. I gulped back the rest. Hairy snatched the cup, sniffing.

"Cinnamon latte."

"That's five," I quipped, grabbing my purse.

"Good try, auburn. I didn't ask a question."

"Don't call me that." I bit back a sigh when he jotted *that* down too. "I have a question for you though. Who pulled me from the river?"

"You really need to ask? Sascha is the strongest wolf in the pack. And he had incentive to run really, really fast. He's intelligent too. Did I mention hardworking?" He cocked his head, concentrating again. He nodded twice. "And extremely good-looking."

"I prefer ugly, lazy, stupid, slow, and weak males."

"Since when?"

"Since right now."

"Question five," Hairy announced. "Would you class yourself as a mummy's girl or a daddy's girl?"

The smile slipped from my face, and his was quick to follow.

"I'm not answering that. Ask a different question."

He hesitated. "No. That's question five."

"Ask another or this is over."

"Are you a mummy's girl, Andie? Or a daddy's girl?"

I sent my chair skittering over the ground. Leaving the werewolf sitting alone, I hurried from the café.

Hunkering against the chilly wind today, I sidestepped a bowing Mandy on the way down, and then a bowing Leroy.

Bursting into my apartment, I slammed the door shut, sliding down the other side. My breaths were harsh and uneven, and the bastards could probably hear.

Damn werewolf caught me unawares. Maybe the stress of the last two weeks was getting to me.

Sniffing hard, I rattled a text off to Wade.

Where can I get a frequency generator?

My phone rang.

Speedy.

"Hey, Wade," I stood to find a tissue.

"Who the fuck is Wade?"

I wrenched the phone back, staring at the name. Logan. *Fuck,* I forgot to block him again.

I put the call on speaker—wolves be dammed.

"None of your business," I replied.

"Imagine my surprise when I returned home from work last night and found my house windows smashed. *All* of them."

My eyes widened. *Oh, shit.* "Who did that?"

"Don't play dumb," he seethed. "I know it was you."

It really wasn't, but his wording interested me. "Why would you think that?"

Silence.

Yep. Logan was my little window-smasher. *Piece of shit.* "I don't know who broke your windows, Logan. I've had the same issue at my house though. I called the police and they promised to monitor the area. You may want to do the same."

His scoff made me wonder how I ever found him attractive, but hate brought out the worst in people. This wasn't *really* Logan—though his petty acts now made me glad I dodged the bullet of staying with him.

"You can expect a civil suit for property damage in your inbox tomorrow," Logan stated.

The line went dead.

I resisted the strong urge to hurl my phone across the room. I'd told two people about the broken windows. Mandy and Wade.

Wade told Herc, and we'd discussed the matter already.

Which left Mandy and whomever she told. Which I strongly suspected was...

I slapped my hands down on the kitchen table and marched to the bay windows. Flinging them wide, I hollered, "Sascha Greyson. Get in here *right now.*"

I'd wring his damn neck.

Knock knock.

Wrenching open the door, I scowled at a delivery man.

He paled. "I h-have a delivery for Andie Booker?"

I snatched the pen and signed for the package, tearing it open with my teeth as I slammed the door in his face.

A frequency generator. *Whoa, Wade.* That was impossibly efficient.

"You called, Miss Booker?"

Shrieking, I whirled to find Sascha sitting on the window seat. "Jesus. Couldn't you use the door?"

His honey eyes were sombre. "Yes."

I planted myself before him. "Is that the first time you've come in that way?"

"Like this, yes."

Which meant no. He probably just held his tongue differently. "I want my pyjamas and throw back."

His expression smoothed. "Is that why you screamed my name down the street?"

Did anyone see him scale the damn wall?

I scowled. "Did you, or did you not, smash a bunch of windows at my ex's place?"

Sascha's brows climbed. "That would be impossible."

I hadn't seen him since yesterday morning. If he drove there and back, it *wasn't* impossible. "Did you send one of your wolves to do it?"

"That would be impossible," he repeated.

"I'm not joking."

Sascha rose slowly. "Hairy upset you. I apologize."

"That's not what this is about." I crossed my arms.

He circled behind me. "Are you sure?"

I didn't answer, refusing to turn in a circle to keep him in sight.

"I'd never intentionally make you sad."

My chest rose. "I'm asking you to be honest, Sascha. Did you have anything to do with what happened to Logan's house?"

The werewolf stopped behind me. "Yes."

"He's filing a civil suit against me."

"It has been handled."

What? "I don't need or want you to handle my problems! *Back off.*"

I put distance between us.

Sascha closed it. "I'll handle your problems. Because I want to."

I scooted around the bed to the windows. "*No.*"

"So feisty," he murmured around a smile.

My heels hit the window seat and I sat *hard*. Sascha blurred to stand before me. I stared at the outline of his abs under the tight white T-shirt before he lowered to a crouch, hands either side of my hips.

"Your jealous ex problem is solved," he told me.

I shivered as his smooth voice curled my hussy toes. "Not jealous. Bitter."

"*Jealous.* I've received more than a few letters from him. That night of our tour, he was watching us until we went into the backroom. Then he left."

That was news to me.

"You were aware he was still there and watching us?" I croaked. I tried to remember if Sascha touched me in that time. I seemed to recall his hand on my lower back a few times—nothing bad.

Though if he knew Logan was watching, the Luther touched me on purpose.

He grinned lazily, and I forced my gaze from his mouth.

"It was in my interest for the relationship to end," he said.

The werewolf was too close for comfort. "I don't like being handled. In fact, I hate it."

"I will protect you regardless." He straightened, and I scooted from the window.

I followed him to the front door. "Call off your wolves, Sascha. The questions and bowing stop. Now."

Sascha paused. "What will you give me for the boon?"

"This isn't a game."

"No. Not a game. Never a game." He contemplated me. "Why don't we look at it like... business?"

Business was business. I could do that. "Okay. I'll answer one question each day for you until Sunday."

"Three questions."

"Two."

"Two deep questions."

I shook my head. "*No* deep questions."

"Then the deal is off." He opened the door, and I stopped it with my foot.

I glowered into amused eyes.

Whatever. He let me stop the door. I didn't care.

"You can ask one deep question each day that I can choose to answer or not. Or two easy ones."

He extended his hand. "Deal. A non-answer is an answer anyway."

Dammit. "The pack is not to bother me at all."

The werewolf stepped closer, and I backed away double time, causing him to grin.

"Here's my *deep* question for the day, little bird." His voice vibrated low in my stomach.

Eye contact never led to good things with this fucker, and I could never forget that he was a werewolf and dangerous. I fanned my lashes down.

The Luther leaned closer. "What will you do when you realise outrunning me is pointless? Guessing the answer haunts the best of my dreams."

Frozen in place, I didn't answer. Fear. Confusion. Anger. My mind couldn't settle on just one emotion.

His stubble grazed my cheek. "Be careful in the grid tonight."

23

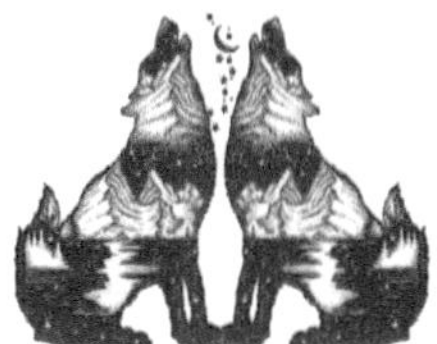

The door of the white van slid open, and one of Ed Sheeran's rap songs blasted out. Rhona sat behind the wheel and stewards our age filled the vehicle.

I brushed my hair behind my ear. "Hi."

The shouted greetings hit me in a wordless wall. Cameron clapped me on the shoulder as Wade dragged me into the van.

Rhona met my gaze in the rear-view mirror. "It's Andie's first game, everyone. Give her a cheer."

I grinned as fresh shouts surged in the van. Rhona pulled away from my apartment, turning left across the bridge toward Deception River. *Now* I knew that led to the wolves' turf. Though I couldn't regret being there, really, when it had saved a child's life.

"Nervous?" Wade whispered.

Cameron draped an arm over my shoulders. "Of course she is. But Wade said you had a wolf shift in front of you the other day. That's about the scariest thing out there, so you're all set."

Did it matter that I hadn't managed to land a single dart in the test dummy yet though? Aside from the time I accidentally pulled the trigger while turning to speak to Gerry. *That* earned me fifty burpees.

I grimaced. "I really don't feel ready."

"I won't lie," she said. "Recruits usually train for a year before they start mentorship in the grid."

"*What?*"

Cameron grimaced. "They're fifteen though. And the wait is more so they're sixteen when we put them in there. Then the adults don't feel so bad."

One *year*.

What the hell, Herc?

"You'll tag along with Rhona." Wade nudged me. "Don't tell her I said so, but she's kind of the best at this."

"I thought she was pepper," I replied.

"Exactly. Who wants pepper in their face?"

Cameron shook her head. "In all seriousness, you'll be fine out there. No one expects much from you."

I choked on a snort. Either side of me, the pair grinned.

Low expectations *were* a relief. I was a fake Thana, and I didn't compare to Rhona's badassery.

People wouldn't compare us, would they?

Shrieks rolled through the van as Rhona pelted down a bumpy dirt road. I clung to Cameron, laughing as Wade was thrown against the window.

Brakes screeched as Rhona skidded the van to a halt not far from where Herc stood with the head team. Impressed was a gross overstatement of his reaction.

I schooled my features to what I hoped was an appropriately serious expression as we piled out.

"Rhona, come here please," Herc called.

She shot me a grin, walking off.

Cameron passed over a bag, and we walked with the other females into the trees. I opened the bag with no small amount of dread after the Sandstone ball-sac fiasco. Black garments. The same ones the stewards wore in Timber.

Phew.

I stripped, drawing on the black cargo pants, black T-shirt, and the protective vest. I doubled over, grunting through an attempt to shove my foot inside a thick sock.

"Boots before the vest," Pascal said, stopping at my side.

"That probably makes sense." I ripped off the vest, bending to slide on the socks and boots that laced up my shins.

Pascal held out my vest, adjusting the Velcro straps down the front. She studied me. "You'll do just fine today, Andie."

I'd only spent a couple of hours with the woman, and the marshal was always pretty focused, but I kind of liked her. Or at least found her intriguing.

She turned, calling at the others for quiet. "Today we're joined by a Thana—"

Ugh.

"—One we didn't know existed. This is a moment to celebrate!"

I fought back the smile that spread at the resulting whoops and cheers, but the damn thing forced its way out.

My face warmed. "Thanks, everyone. I hope to get through this without shooting myself in the foot."

Women flanked me after, wishing me luck as we returned to the parking lot where the male stewards waited. Rhona approached, scowling.

I gripped her shoulder. "Are you sulking because you got told off, cuz?"

She glared at me. "Yes."

We both laughed.

I checked my watch. *7:50 p.m.*

Ten minutes.

Oh my god. I'm about to fight werewolves.

"You good on the manoeuvres?" Rhona waved me forward as Herc led the stewards through the trees and downhill. We were the West team. The people here made up one fourth of the stewards.

"Yes."

"Traps?"

"Yes."

"Good. Tonight, we'll make a new trap, then scope out other traps.

Most of the time, the Luthers fuck with them. After that, we'll find a good spot to hunker down."

"Which is?"

"Depends. It rained last night, and things will be extra slippery and dangerous. We'll see what's available."

I held my breath, nodding.

Our horde reached the edge of the Clay quarry, and Herc moved back through the stewards, talking and touching shoulders here and there. Just as in Timber, the mood of the crowd altered. The chatter died as a palpable tension permeated the air.

Butterflies erupted in my stomach. I couldn't believe this was happening, but a small part of my mind was distracted by Sascha.

He knew this was my debut, but he wouldn't do anything to me in the grid, right? That would be idiotic.

What will you do when you realise outrunning me is pointless?

Was that a figurative thing? Or—my stomach churned—was that what he literally planned for me tonight?

Shit.

Rhona bumped my shoulder. "Don't worry, cuz. I'm there with you every step of the way."

Herc reached us. "Andie, all set?"

"Sure. Let me at them."

He cracked a smile at my wooden reply. "Last week was intense. Clay isn't as bad."

"*Because we always lose,*" Rhona muttered.

"Rhona," Herc scolded low and fast. "You know better than that."

A few people around us definitely heard her comment.

"I'm ready to do my best." This was just like an exam. A challenge. A puzzle of 3D proportions.

I *liked* this shit.

Maybe.

Herc tilted his chin. "Go get 'em, werewolf killer."

"That's worse than kiddo."

His lips twitched. "I'll see you both after."

Rhona dragged me over to a group of people who had muscles as defined as hers.

"This is our working unit." She bumped fists with them, and I did the same, missing twice.

"Here," she said. "Put this in."

I accepted the earbud, shoving it in my ear. She checked the position, then inserted her own, testing her walkie-talkie. Everyone had one but me.

She checked over everyone's gear. "There are four teams—North, West, East, and South. Each team is made up of units. I front this unit, and I'm also the leader of the West team. The unit leaders in West report to me, and I communicate with the three other team leaders and Dad. Your job is to report to me."

Units made up the teams. Talk to Rhona. "Okay."

"She's the best," one of the guys announced.

The guy from the lake. *Foley*. I waggled my brows at Rhona.

"We wear helmets in this grid," she said, lobbing a helmet into my gut.

Oof.

Glaring, I put it on, attaching the strap under my chin.

Rhona flicked down the attached bug glasses. "Just like the lenses in the mask, they'll naturally adjust to the lessening light."

The team leaned in, stretching out their hands. I hastily added mine.

"This grid is ours. On three," Rhona shouted.

I dutifully mumbled the chant.

Shouts from the surrounding units were followed by the tell-tale *boom* of the starting cannon.

"We're out," Rhona said.

Heart pounding, I ran onto the rolling clay quarry. *Crap*, they ran really fast. Perhaps today would just be about not dropping my lungs out my ass.

I'd started wheezing when Rhona stopped.

"Billy and Laura. Lay foundations," she ordered. "Foley and Jordyn, start on the frequency generators."

She turned, not laughing at my wheezing gasps.

"It's important to never give away details of what we're doing," Rhona instructed. "Be vague always. Over the walkies, and any time you speak. Even with generators up."

Foley and Jordyn placed clay-coloured generators at intervals. I guessed every unit in each team was doing the same thing.

"The only thing they can't touch on the grid are heat sensors," Rhona said. "Everything else is fair game between times."

I'd memorized the new traps for this grid this morning, and as the crouched pair strung a trip wire between two mounds of slick clay, I mentally added the cans on each end. The cans were filled with liquid wolfsbane.

Many traps in Clay were one-offs because the wolves tended to dismantle them anyway. The stewards called these *Drain Traps* because they stripped the wolves' senses and made them easier targets.

Rhona tapped Laura on the shoulder and beckoned me in. She passed me one of the cans, and I studied my end of the tripwire, looping the end of the trip wire through the bottom of the can. The trap was battery operated and when a wolf triggered the tripwire, the can detonated. I set it down carefully, sprinkling clay over the top. I searched my cargo pockets and found my wolfsbane, spraying the area to cover my presence.

"Well done." My cousin checked over the trap.

Thank you, Gerry. Maybe I'd cut that silent bastard some slack.

"Here's where we split into pairs," she said as the others peeled off, running in different directions. "Foley will join us today too."

I set my mind to keeping up with the pair as we visited established trap sites. Out of the three assigned to our trio, only one remained intact.

Rhona gripped my arm when I moved closer.

"Stay still."

I froze in a crouch. "What?"

"They sometimes alter traps."

Foley squinted at the ground, and I closed my eyes, trying to orientate myself from my memories of the app and virtual reality. My eyes popped open. This was a *Delay Trap*. In front of us, a flip board disguised a deep hole. The tripwire on the bottom triggered nets over the hole. Any tugging on the net locked the flip board in place. The wolves were strong enough to escape most traps. Delay traps held the wolf until a steward could get in position to take out the target.

This trap didn't look different to me.

Foley left, and returned in short measure with a stick, which he waved over the flip board.

Pop. Pop. Pop.

Rhona jerked me back as darts exploded across the board.

"Fuck," Foley said, sprawled on the ground. "Motion detectors. That's new."

Rhona waved her gun through the middle again. No more darts erupted. "Let's run checks."

She guided me through the trap maintenance and Foley smashed the detectors. We checked the tripwire mechanism and reset it, climbing out of the hole.

A howl went up.

Sascha.

"Ten minutes," Foley said.

Rhona grinned. "Time to hole up."

Foley left us, and I faced my cousin. I held my tranquiliser gun against my thigh. *Wait*, Gerry said not to do that.

I cradled it again.

"Ready for the fun part?" she asked.

Nope.

I jogged after her, breaths as quiet as I could keep them. We reached a small rise with wide cuts that formed large and uneven steps to the top. Rhona pulled herself up onto the first ledge and stretched a hand down to help me up. Wedging a foot against the slippery wall, I made it.

"Roll around," Rhona said low.

She covered herself in clay and I did the same, smearing some on my black helmet. I was going to have clay in places I didn't know existed after tonight.

"Cleats on."

In my pocket were spikes that screwed into the bottom of my boots. I scraped off the goop already accumulated there and twisted the metal points in place.

Boom.

Sascha howled again as the cannon boomed, and my heart leaped into my throat. They were coming.

And the bastard was yowling to scare me.

Rhona beckoned me after her, and we walked to a mound of clay on the ledge. Copying her, I set my back against the mound. She patted the air, and I crouched. She left me then, moving around the other side.

I hoped.

Fuck. Was she gone?

Okay.

I ran over the operation of my gun a few times, inhales quickening at the pounding in the distance. The Luthers were running.

Another howl.

I gritted my teeth.

Was Rhona still here? I really wished she was in sight.

My exhale shook. *It's simple, Andie. Shoot or trap.*

The pounding footsteps in the near distance cut off, and my breath followed. I shifted in the crouch, not daring to breathe.

Herc's voice crackled through my earpiece. "*Four hundred West.*"

Four hundred! That was over half their force. In this area.

"*South. Mobilise West.*"

Rhona reappeared around the mound and pointed upward. I nodded. Higher ground was dangerous, but with those numbers saturating our current territory, we had no choice.

I hauled myself over the next step after her.

Pop.

Rolling, I stared up at the grinning Rhona, mouth dropping at the drunkenly weaving werewolf below.

She shot him!

I didn't even hear the fucker.

Another werewolf crept around the mound, and on all fours, I fumbled for my gun.

Pop. Pop.

The werewolf dodged both of Rhona's shots, glaring at us. Her eyes landed on me. Throwing back her head, she howled.

Shit!

"Time to move." Rhona fired another shot at the howling wolf. Her aim was true. I hadn't managed to remove the damn safety yet.

Low to the ground, she slithered over the top ledge. Feet pounded toward us from afar, and I wasted no fucking time joining her.

The other side of the rise was much like where we'd come from. We slithered down to the middle level, and Rhona jerked me back against the wall, finger to her lips.

Seriously? She was still grinning.

I removed the safety in advance—*sorry, Gerry*—and clamped my lips together at furious whispers above our position.

One was female. Two low tones... but different. Two males.

I trusted my ears.

Catching Rhona's eyes, I held up three fingers.

Two wolves leaped down onto the shelf, backs to us. I clutched my weapon, waiting for them to turn.

Pop. Pop went Rhona's gun.

Right, waiting was fucking idiotic.

Clay crumbled on my head from above and I jerked the gun upward, jumping and squeezing. The wolf tumbled over me, thudding heavily at my feet.

Oh my god. I shot one.

I stared at him.

"Down," Rhona hissed as a dart embedded in the clay by my head.

She yanked me to the ground.

"I only got one of them."

A howl rose from below. The female was still on her feet.

Herc's voice crackled in my ear. "*Luthers converging on 15 West. Immediate reinforcement.*"

I didn't need to know where 15 West was to know that was our position.

Fucking. Sascha.

I shifted, my legs aching. Rhona's eyes widened. Shoving me aside, she grunted.

Yanking a dart from her neck, she fired twice before collapsing to her knees. The female werewolf who'd crept up on us followed suit, falling heavily.

I stared between their unconscious forms for a second.

Antidote.

Antidote!

Fingers numb, I searched my cargos. Too many damn pockets. I found the vial, and unscrewed it, stealing furtive looks around. Pouring the contents into Rhona's mouth, I dragged her against the back of the ledge, shoving clay over her body. Only her face was exposed.

Another howl rang out from the other side of the rise. They were coming for me.

I crept along the ledge, keeping low.

Clay crumbled above, and I tensed, leaning back. I almost fell on my butt when I encountered thin air.

A crevice.

Oh my god.

Squeezing into the deep crack, I crouched in a puddle behind a jutting part of the clay wall and lifted my gun.

"She can't have gone far."

Male.

He walked past my hiding spot. I'd never been gladder for frequency generators in my life. They'd hear me in a heartbeat. Literally.

"I'll head down," a second male said. "Cover me."

I squinted, watching as he ran and launched into the air with impossible speed. The first male stopped directly in front of my crevice.

Shit, I had to do this.

Lifting my gun, I squeezed the trigger.

It embedded in the wall inside the crack.

Mothershitter.

I shot again.

Wall.

You're kidding me. I shook the thing.

"Technical issues?"

The wolf stuck his head in, and I took in his blond hair. *Leroy.*

I shot a third time, my aim true, but he dodged back.

"Found her, boss," he called.

Not fucking happening, buddy.

I peered back into the crevice. How far did this thing go back? … I'd take my chances.

My bug lenses adjusted to the dark, but I fumbled anyway, slipping over the clay floor.

"*Little bird.*"

The gravelly version of Sascha's voice echoed to me.

"That's fucking creepy." I snapped.

Laughter.

Whatever. Laugh it up. Sascha couldn't fit in here. Though that wouldn't stop him digging in.

If I got in deep enough, I could wait him out.

There was light up ahead. My breath hitched.

Maybe there was another entrance.

The walls tightened to a sliver, and I forced my thoughts from being buried alive as I edge sideways through the gap. Rain had collected in here, and I pushed through the knee-high water, part of me expected to fall through the squishy floor at any moment.

The light wasn't another entrance. Just a hole. The gap was small, but the clay here was super soft.

I clipped my gun to my vest and pulled in handfuls of the goop until I had space to pop my head out.

I was halfway up a slope. The incline above and below was slick and uninterrupted for a good thirty metres. This was a massive slide.

Two Luthers loped at an easy run through the space below, and the area tugged at my memory. Different vantage point aside, I was reasonably certain this was where we checked the flip board trap.

Scanning the space, I located the two mounds framing the mechanism.

Yep, this was it.

The two werewolves seemed too relaxed. They hadn't sensed me. And, honestly, they were probably pretty safe considering my shooting ability. But this was the game. I should do my best to take them out.

Unclipping my gun, I aimed to the far right of the Luthers.

Pop.

The miss was inevitable. I'd counted on it. The pair darted left for cover. I shot to their far right again, watching as they dove behind the mounds.

Bang! Bang!

The cans exploded, wolfsbane spraying into the air. The two wolfs dropped, and I gasped before recalling the next part. I had to finish them off.

Ah, shit.

Holding down the trigger, I released waves of bullets until landing a dart—or two—in each wolf. That took an embarrassing number of shots.

Reloading my gun, I shoved the empty chamber in a cargo pocket.

I froze at voices overhead.

"Tate and Charlie are down."

Leroy.

"The area is clear, administer the antidote."

Sascha.

Seconds later, Leroy slid past my hiding spot. I popped up and unleashed a wave of darts.

He rolled to the bottom, flopping to a halt, and I ducked into the hole, cramming myself back through the tight sliver and knee-deep water. Water erupted around me, and I burst through to the other side as the light was snuffed out.

"*Little bird*, here you are. Does this tunnel have more exits or are you trapped now?"

"Fuck you, Sascha."

"I can only hope."

I shoved my gun between the two walls and held down the trigger.

I expected him to laugh.

Light flooded in, and I lowered the gun as a rhythmic thudding reached my ears. My jaw dropped.

No way.

I waited several minutes, because *no way.* Creeping forward, I approached the hole, gun at the ready. When claws didn't skewer me, I popped my head up, peering down.

Oh my god!

I fucking *hit* him.

Laughter bubbled up my throat. "That'll teach you, cocky bastard."

And he'd landed on top of Leroy. Even better.

A howl went up as darts thudded near my head.

I threw myself back.

I couldn't let them deliver the antidote to Sascha. This was personal.

Waving my gun through the hole, I bobbed down as more darts thudded into the clay. I piled up the clay to make the hole smaller again. Removing my protective vest, I framed my head in the vest's arm hole, pulling it low over my eyes without obstructing my vision. Unless I copped a dart in the cheekbone, I was good to go.

Setting my gun on the edge first and wedging my vest-shrouded head in the space after, I opened fire on the three wolves sprinting to Leroy and Sascha.

They were *fast*, like a Usain Bolt that didn't slow. My spray of bullets caught them, and I smirked as their legs buckled.

Another storm of darts embedded into the vest surrounding my face. At least if I went down, they only received one point.

Who was shooting at me?

I scanned a smaller rise around fifty meters away and to my right. *Yep*. I didn't have a single hope of hitting them at that distance.

Far below, Sascha groaned, rolling onto his back. *What?* He couldn't be burning off the sedative already.

I shot the clay slope four times before hitting him again. Would that be enough? Pursing my lips, I fired again, grinning as a second dart lodged in his kneecap.

This was kind of fun.

24

The manor was going *off*. Music pounded. The half-screamed conversations were nearly as loud. Groups danced on the huge patio. Splashing and shrieks sounded from the pool.

We hadn't won, not even close.

"We can safely label that one of the best debuts we've seen in Victratum history," Herc said. He hadn't stopped grinning.

Turned out a debut was a big deal—even more so for a Thana. This was *my* party. When I shot Sascha, this party catapulted to epic proportions. Most of the younger stewards were in attendance.

A person would think we'd just won Grids.

A woman named Valerie leaned over Herc. "Was your strategy inspired by the Vietnamese's defences in 1968, Andie? Củ Chi?"

Say what?

Herc's glinting gaze flicked to me. "Just natural smarts. Must run in the family. She only trained for a week too."

Luck summarised my debut. I found a crack and happened to fit in it.

"Do you want a drink, Herc?" Valerie asked. Or purred, more like.

When she moved off, I slid him a look. "She's into you."

"Valerie's nice." He lifted a shoulder. "She's not my wife."

"She passed two years ago?"

He nodded. "Multiple Sclerosis. Savannah was her name. She was an extraordinary woman. Maybe I'll love again in time, but for now I just miss her."

"Long-term illnesses and diseases take their toll," I muttered, watching Wade bopping his butt out on the patio. Cameron caught my eye and beckoned.

Nope. Dancing wasn't my jam. I belonged in the band.

"It does. Found anything good in those journals?"

I spied Foley trailing after Rhona like a lost puppy. *Ick*. "Just the ramblings of a young woman. I'm nearly to age sixteen."

Mum had found a good hiding spot for her journal and wasn't holding back details. Like any teenager, she was all about sex and the forbidden. Believing Murphy was anything other than incredible was impossible after reading her words.

When Herc first told me about Murphy's death, I'd almost celebrated. Now, I wanted to grieve a father I never knew—eighteen *years* after his death. Except what if I started believing he *was* the father every child dreamed of only to discover later that he was a dropkick?

I wasn't sure my heart could take it.

"The year we lost our father," Herc murmured.

I hadn't come to that part. "Herc? I'd like to meet my father's family. Could you talk to them?"

Herc took my hand. "You're sure?"

I almost laughed. "Not at all. But Murphy came back for a reason. I need to know what that was?"

"What if no one knows?"

My stomach lurched.

"I'm not saying that's the case. I'm just saying he might not have confided in anyone. I don't want to see you chasing answers that aren't there."

This could get unhealthy in other words. "I won't let it become an addiction. I swear."

"Then," he said, "introducing you would be my honour. Leave it with me."

We sat for a while, snorting at the drunken antics of the stewards.

"Do you wonder what life without Grids would be like?" I asked.

Herc shrugged. "This game has been my entire life. I found out about the Luthers very young. There was an incident out in the forest, and I saw a Luther shift."

"How old?"

"Five."

Shit.

"I didn't have the same blissful ignorance of the other steward children. This really has been my life. Speaking for the others... we've fought for so long that I doubt we'd know what peace looked like. I'd garden more. Tend to our burial sites. Put more focus into the people living in this valley."

Pretty much what he already did, but more. I supposed a person had to live the life they wanted despite the game.

Herc looked at me. "Do you regret joining the fight?"

Maybe I'd had second thoughts before entering the grid tonight, but the game had stirred my blood and interest. If there was a fever to catch, I'd caught it. "Not at all."

Something changed with the visit to my grandparents' graves on Monday, and I couldn't deny that this game had deepened in importance to me. Herc had said our loved ones never left the valley. That's what this place felt like to me—a warm hug or a long-awaited reunion.

This wasn't just about finding answers anymore.

I cared about this tribe and our connection to this land.

"I'm happy to hear that," Herc replied. "And now, I'll simply wish you good luck."

"Huh?"

Strong arms hauled me upward.

"Stop hanging out with old people," Wade complained.

"Thanks," Herc said drily.

Cameron shoved a drink in my hands. "Gin, right?"

I took a cautious sip, expecting my body to revolt. Heat slid through me. "Apparently so."

"Then let's introduce you to everyone."

I was dragged out onto the patio. Wade shoved a shot in my hand, and I sniffed it.

"To Andie!" Cameron roared to a crowd of people I couldn't place. "Debut extraordinaire. Though she used over two hundred darts to take down six wolves."

Truth.

I raised my glass to the sea of laughing faces, knocking back the jelly shot.

Gross.

Wade grimaced. "Rhona made these. Hey, Andie? Have you thought about how awkward work will be tomorrow, now you've darted the pack leader?"

I lowered my gin cocktail.

Cameron wacked Wade, but the warmth of the shot had ramped my body temperature higher. It was hard to worry about Sascha's reaction—especially when I enjoyed shooting him so very much.

He'd set his wolves on me, *hunted* me through the grids. I had zero regrets on knocking him out after all his stalker *little bird* bullshit. And part of me was just stoked to have made it through the full game conscious.

I smirked into my gin. "Worth it."

"Cheers to that, baby girl."

After another round of shots, I spotted Rhona beside Foley and the others from our unit. I joined them near the spa pool.

"Good work today, red," one of the guys said.

Billy, was it?

I brushed my hair back. "A fluke. Don't tell anyone."

Rhona's emerald gaze locked on mine as the unit chattered happily around us. "Thank you for the antidote."

"Thanks for taking a dart for me," I replied.

She didn't need to. Really, it made more sense to use me as a human shield. She was by far the more talented player.

"What are cousins for?" she murmured, taking a sip of beer.

"Burying you in clay?"

"I call that a smart idea. And using the tunnel too."

Total fluke, but whatever. "Is it wise to be drinking after taking a dart and drinking the antidote?"

Rhona took another swig of her beer in reply.

"Your strategy could change the game," Laura cut in, nudging me. "Seriously."

I glanced at her. Was Herc thinking of using tunnels?

"One week of training. You shot the leader, and you might have just changed Clay for us," Laura continued.

That's what everyone thought? I'd call that a serious overexaggerating of what was mostly sliding on my ass and blindly shooting.

Rhona clinked her beer against my glass. "Last time, I had to watch you get drunk. This time, we drink together."

The unit cheered, and I cheered with them. I entered the grid tonight with these people. We ran together. *Worked* together. Rhona took a damn tranquiliser for me.

Herc's words about tribe and family...

Damn if they didn't sink in a little deeper.

"Wade." I answered the phone.

"Baby girl. How's the head?"

I'd remembered why I didn't party much. My organs were wimpy. "It's been a long day,"

Now I had to work. My reception at *The Dens* tonight was uncertain to say the least, and maybe my bravado from last night had worn off some.

How angry was Sascha over being shot five times?

"Gerry found the dummies a few hours ago."

I held the phone with my shoulder as I adjusted my sax case and purse over my shoulder. "How did we ever convince ourselves he'd believe it was someone else?"

"That's what alcohol does," Wade said sagely. "I couldn't get rid of the messages you scratched into the balustrade, but luckily he didn't notice."

"What message?"

"Thong girl was here."

For fuck's sake.

"The other one said *Habit: A bitch since ages ago*. That was my personal favourite."

I rubbed a hand over my face. "What did Gerry say?"

"I apologised to him and the upstanding fellow in the horrific gang-bang situation. After taking some more pictures, of course. It'll be fine."

"You have a sex problem, Wade."

"You *nearly* had a sex problem last night."

I stopped. "Billy? What's wrong with him? His muscles gleam."

"He's the biggest player out. You're so lucky I stopped you two sucking face."

"I have a thing for players. Let drunk Andie do what she wants."

"No way. I'm saving you from yourself."

I frowned. "You're not into me, are you?"

I didn't get that vibe.

"Nah, you don't make my dick twitch."

"Thanks for the visual... Really though? Not at all?"

"Not even a tickle, baby girl. You can check one time."

I laughed. "That sounds like a line to get your dick touched."

"Just offering proof of my lack of attraction. I bet your nipples never get hard around me."

"I'm leaving this conversation."

He laughed. "We've achieved platonic symbiosis, a nearly unheard-of phenomenon. It only works with Cameron because she's a lesbian. Our best friendship is a miracle event."

"Promoting yourself to best friend." I slowed my steps, spotting Hairy ahead. "Look, I gotta run."

"Be good," he said.

"Or be good at it," I murmured.

Hairy beckoned me forward. I tried my best to ignore the werewolf as I walked to the entrance.

"I'm sorry, Andie."

I folded my arms, looking at him.

"I pushed too far and hurt your feelings. I was out of line. I got you these to say sorry. Mandy said you liked them."

He reached under his table and drew out a packet of *Corrie's Chocolate Chocos.* The tourists in line *aww'd.*

That was kind of sweet. *Damn apologetic werewolves.* I took the cookies. "Thank you."

"Do you forgive me?"

I had firsthand experience with the charming ability of wolves. He wasn't an alpha, but Hairy knew how to wield the sensitive sexy angle. "I'll put you on probation."

His eyes narrowed.

I opened the cordon, entering *The Dens.*

Leroy flanked me immediately. "Boss wants to see you in his office."

"No," I replied, heading for the bar.

"Don't make me drag you in there," he said.

I squinted up at him. "Where exactly did I shoot you last night?"

Instead of scowling, the wolf smiled, snatching my sax case off my shoulder.

"Leroy," I hissed, hurrying after him—as fast as my sleeve dress would allow.

He disappeared into the staff quarters, and I burst in after him.

"Come back," I was *far* too sore for this.

Glaring, I moved past Leroy into the office. My sax case rested on the desk, and I ignored the man sitting there.

My saxophone was okay.

I faced Leroy, ignoring his wide grin. "Please don't ever touch my saxophone again. It's very important to me."

His smile faded. The werewolf nodded. "Okay."

"Thank you." I spun on my heel as he closed the door.

Sascha took me in. Honey all but dripped over the missing panels at either side of my torso as his gaze skated the bared skin. I'd picked up my fair share of bruises last night and this was my most concealing dress. Wedges, hoop earrings, and a wavy ponytail completed the look.

"You're breathtaking." Sascha Greyson rounded the desk and extended his hand.

"What's that for?" I glowered at his massive palm.

"I've never been taken out in Grids. Well played."

In that case. I took his hand. Mistake. He gently tugged me towards him.

"It's right that you'd be cunning and strong to match me," Sascha murmured, his thumb stroking my wrist and eliciting a body-wracking shiver.

He considered me shooting him a *good* thing. This was more breeding-call bullshit. He was thinking about my genetics.

Jesus.

I freed my hand from his grip, curling my fingers against my stomach. "You realise I shot you five times."

"I counted eight."

"If I shoot eight darts into your balls next time, will you leave me alone?"

Sascha threw back his head and laughed.

I turned for my case, but the werewolf spun me back, circling an arm around my waist.

Warmth melted me from the inside out. *Oh my god.* What was that? "Let me go."

"If you really want that, I will," Sascha said low. "Or you could admit that your hangover is disappearing and accept the help."

I blinked. "Is that really happening?"

"You tell me."

My slight headache *was* ebbing, drawing back from my temples and the base of my neck. I sucked in a breath. "How is that possible? Magic?"

Maybe this crap had one perk.

"No more magic than I am. For breeding pairs, feeling better when touching, hearing, seeing, and smelling each other just is."

"That's a pretty lame explanation." *God,* this felt incredible.

He held my gaze. "Our knowledge of pack origins is poor at best. Much was lost when my father brought us here."

"Were you around to personally witness that?" I pressed closer to him as the slight churning in my stomach faded.

"What will you give me if I tell you?" He drew me closer still.

"I'm only here because you're curing my hangover, Sascha. Down, boy."

"This feels right. You can't deny it."

"Because of the meets," I replied. "This is no indication of how I might have felt if magic wasn't involved. Or Luther juju."

"Perhaps. Perhaps not."

His body was hot against mine, heat searing everywhere we touched. He was enjoying this.

A lot, judging by what I could feel.

I placed my hand against his chest and stepped back. He caught my wrist and my eyes flew to his.

Sascha inhaled. "When you're turned on, I want to rip your dress off as much as I want to look at you in it. It's the most exquisite torture."

My breath hitched. "I'm not turned on."

He stalked forward. "A wolf's nose never lies. I've catalogued your scents. Lies, half-lies, concealment, joy, and grief."

There were smells for all that?

"Is that because you're a sigma?" My back hit the wall.

His arms caged me in, and his head dipped. I arched my neck to the side, and a deep purring chuff echoed through him.

"Not a sigma, Andie," he growled. "*The* sigma. Rules do not apply to me."

Sascha disappeared, and I nearly staggered forward at the slight cold.

"Tell that to Herc," he said, riffling through papers on the desk. "Maybe in exchange you could tell me something though?"

I scoffed to cover how truly shaken I was and returned to the desk to snatch up my case. "How about you just solve our problem and get your wolf under control?"

"He grows more demanding with each passing second. Especially when you smell this way. So ready."

My mouth dried. "You're scaring me, Sascha. I want you to stop."

His jaw clenched. The Luther dropped his gaze to the desk. "I know, little bird. I'm scared too."

I moved around the desk. "Then, please, just stop."

The werewolf lifted his head, and I wished he wasn't so fucking handsome. He was a monster. But he walked and talked, and my mind couldn't always hold onto that truth.

"Even with the world against us," Sascha said to me. "Even with such impossible odds. This can only move in one direction."

He blurred, cupping the base of my head and forcing my head back.

"Then what are we going to do?" I whispered in defeat, throat bared. "How can we outsmart this?"

Sascha rested his forehead against mine and even with my hangover long gone, the contact felt so good that I shoved away the shouted warnings of my heart.

His lips moved to my ear. "I don't want to outsmart anything. In case it wasn't clear, Andie Booker, my wolf wants you. And I trust my wolf implicitly. You are a match for me. You will be mine."

His grip in my hair was borderline painful.

The werewolf studied me intensely. "More than anything I've wanted in ninety-five years."

Ninety-five years old.

Jackpot.

The wolf eased his hold, massaging the base of my skull gently before freeing his hand from my ponytail. "There's just one last question I need answered, and then my wolf will be ready."

I became aware that my legs trembled. My breaths were shallow and fast. My lips moist.

I had nothing. No witty quip. No furious remark.

"Get to work," Sascha said gruffly, returning to his seat. "And you can be sure I won't underestimate you in Victratum again, little bird. You're a worthy foe."

I mustered as much dignity as possible, grabbing my sax case.

"Before you go, I haven't asked you my deep question for the day." He hummed.

I almost asked what he meant before recalling our conversation yesterday. I stiffened, dread seeping through every part of me.

"What is it?" I said, a definite bite in my voice.

Sascha inhaled deeply, searching my face for a time. "Tell you what. Let's call a truce today."

25

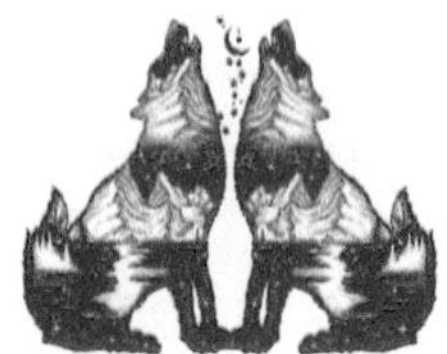

I rolled down the window as Uncle Herc drove.

"Ninety-five years old," he said.

A frequency generator sat between us, something I'd only recently noted the stewards had in their cars. I'd have to remember to take the one Wade sent out with me.

"Yep. And he said he's *the* sigma. That status mustn't be a common thing."

"Online searches should be taken with a grain of salt, but from what I can find, sigmas are usually lone wolves."

"Then how is he leading a pack?"

Herc focused on the road out to the timber mill where Rhona waited. Hanging out with them beat sitting around all day. I'd trained, cleaned the apartment, completed my pre-readings for the first lectures next week, *and* done the grocery shop.

I missed Mum.

She filled the empty spots just by living in the same house. I'd thought that people weren't for me, but I'd lost my person a month ago, and a void remained that, instead of closing, seemed to stretch wider as time went on. I'd coped so well in those first two weeks—but looking back, I didn't have *time* to be upset. I ran from Queen's Way, discovered my family here, got a job, broke up with Logan, found out about werewolves, started training, nearly drowned.

I hadn't *stopped* once.

And I didn't like the feeling I now had.

"We need more on him," Herc said. "I become more uneasy each day you work there. The Luthers flocked to the West on Wednesday. They've never done that before."

"Yeah. But it worked." They'd systematically flushed out each team. *West, South, East, and North.*

"It could be that. But why did Sascha end up so close to you? A fluke or by design?"

Ah, shit. "I was with Rhona when the wolves saw us and howled. One howled again on a second sighting of us. When we split up, they stopped howling. Leroy found me in the tunnel."

"The big blond? Greyson's second-in-command."

Is he? "What do you think it could be?"

"Perhaps it's Rhona they're after. Or both of you. Which is highly concerning, but my gut tells me whatever his reasoning, it has to do with offering you a job at The Dens. Or getting even with you for what you're doing—he can't attack you outside of the game after all."

Herc was far too smart. It made hugging Sascha two nights ago all the more stupid and irresponsible. Headache Andie had a lot to answer for. She fell for the hangover cure gimmick.

Billy the player sounded like a far safer option. He could work out a few kinks and remind me other men could bring comfort too. Human comfort.

A blur of brown caught my eye through the trees as Herc turned the car into the timber mill. My chest tightened.

Another flash of brown. That better not be—

A huge form leaped between the trees.

I faced forward, breathing thinly. *That. Fucker.*

Sascha was here.

"Here we are," Herc said. "This timber mill has been around for over a century."

For once, his words flew in one ear and out the other. "Is Rhona here already?"

My uncle frowned. "I can't see her car. She shouldn't be far away."

I fell into step with him a moment later. My back was tense as I resisted the urge to search for the wolf. Because I knew one thing for a *fact.*

The bastard let me see him.

He was toying with me. Again. He got a kick out of knowing I was aware of his presence. Why tell me about the capture meet at all, if not? Or that he'd *catalogued my scents*?

What the fuck did that even mean?

It meant Sascha Greyson wanted me to feel vulnerable.

To my memory, only one of us had ended up with a tranquiliser dart in the kneecap so far. Yet his grip in my hair. His forehead pressed to mine. *Honey.* My shaking legs.

All of that told me I should be worried.

There's one last question I need answered. Then my wolf will be ready. He hadn't asked his Thursday or Friday question since our meeting.

What was the last question? The thought had kept me up until the early hours ever since—in addition to the expectation Sascha would burst through my bay windows at any second.

We stopped outside a small office that read *Reception*.

Herc popped his head in. "Hey, Missy. Has Rhona been in?"

The rosy-cheeked and very pregnant woman beamed. "She left not long ago. Said she had a top-secret strategy meeting to attend."

I pressed my trembling lips together.

Herc thanked her and shut the door, pulling out his phone. "*Rhona.*"

"I'm sure she just got caught up."

My uncle shot me a wry look, shoving the phone in his jacket pocket. "I appreciate the loyalty that makes you say so, but Rhona has a worrying habit of doing this."

"Worrying?"

"She's not taking this seriously enough. My father and mother were gone by my mid-twenties. Even after losing her mother, Rhona doesn't understand that I could be gone tomorrow, and this will all land on her."

"She's serious when it counts." I frowned. "The stewards respect her ability in Grids."

Herc held up his finger. "Exactly. In the Grids."

I remained mute, trying to remember how far werewolves could hear. This wasn't a conversation for Sascha.

"I'll speak to her tonight for all the good it will do," he said. "I can still show you how things work here though. Unless that's a boring uncle thing to do."

"Not at all. I'm interested," I replied truthfully. "I've been curious about the business side of the game."

"Unsurprising with your chosen area of study."

We walked side by side past reception.

"I start again on Monday," I told him.

"I'm glad to hear that. I'm proud of you, Andie. Very proud."

I waited for the *hugging mall Santa* feeling. I really did. Any second now I'd be smacked with that *pants three sizes too small* squeeze.

It never came.

"Thank you," I said slowly.

He cocked a brow. "No need to sound so surprised."

"It's not that."

I understood that people could be proud of one another. It's just that somehow… inexplicably… I *believed* he was proud of me.

"You were a natural out there," he said.

We strode through tall stacks of milled timber. Was Sascha crouched on top of one?

I shivered. "Not really. I got lucky."

"You showed creativity. And thought on your feet. If there's enough time around your studies, I'd like you to shadow my team leaders during meetings from now on. You're a clear-headed thinker and like a puzzle. I predict that you'll land yourself as a member of a strategy team in no time."

Those people did *not* mess around. "It feels like there's a lot to learn before that."

"You have no trouble absorbing material. Information can always be rote learned. The ability to reason and reflect outside of your emotions is rarer, and the speed with which you're able to do so at your age is promising. In time, with dedication and application, you'll make the head team, I'm certain."

He had to be messing with me. That was *ludicrous.*

"You don't believe me," he said, chuckling. "You'll see. I protect one thousand stewards and you, my niece, are a gem on the gold pile."

How was I meant to respond? Did he really think of me that way?

"Now, hold onto your seat. I'm taking you to see where the logs first arrive."

I followed him, mind spinning. Herc was planning for me to be in his life for years to come. He expected me to enter his head team one day.

He valued me.

My family wanted me here.

Someone wanted me. And I believed they wanted me.

Inhaling deeply, I focused on his words, determined to commit them to memory.

Some of my clothes were missing. They'd disappeared as I slept after my third shift at *The Dens.* Jeans, a sweater, the forest green silk number, and some of my fucking underwear.

I flung open the bay windows, the demon's name on my lips.

"Hey, baby girl!"

Stumbling forward, I choked back my furious roar. "H-Hi, Wade."

"It'd be cute if you called me baby boy," he called up.

"Not happening. What brings you all this way?"

An elderly woman stepped around him, shooting a look between us.

"We're Romeo and Juliet," Wade called after her.

I waited until the woman was gone. "Did Romeo ever tell Juliet she didn't make his dick twitch? I can't remember."

"Scholars are undecided."

He was full of shit. And I really liked him for it. "You coming up or what?"

"Or what. It's a new moon. We gather at the manor on the new moon for obvious reasons. I came to get you."

I waited.

He eyed me. "Which you apparently don't know. Okay. Grab comfy clothes, and if you have a pillow and blanket you like, bring them along. I'll fill you in on the ride."

Better than sitting in the apartment fuming about stolen underwear.

I changed into old sweats and a holey sweater that read *Queen's Way Little League*. I stole it from a secondhand bin at fifteen. Thick socks. Scrunchie and ponytail. I smacked some moisturiser on, grabbing my pillow and queen blanket. Mostly because there was a damn werewolf thief in town who didn't have boundaries.

"You own casual. Sexy as hell. If I was into you at all," Wade told me as I tossed my stuff in his black Jeep.

I slid into the passenger seat. "Do you find Rhona attractive?"

"Oh, totally."

My jaw dropped. "That's so insulting! We look the same."

"Guess your personality is the issue."

Laughter burst from me. "You're such an asshole."

He darted in to press a kiss to my cheek. "You have a personality that my balls recognise I can't do without."

I wrinkled my nose. "Ten percent sweet. Ninety percent gross."

He ripped out of the park and I clutched the *oh shit* handle.

"Wade!"

"Turn on the frequency generator, would ya?" he asked, not slowing in the slightest.

"I'd need to release this handle to do that. And that will only happen if you slow down."

Wade braked ever so slightly.

I pressed the button on the generator in the console, waiting for the light to flash green.

Wade punched into the phone settings on the console and called Cameron.

"What?" she answered.

"No one explained the new moon thing to Andie," he answered.

Cameron cursed. "Sometimes I feel like I'm surrounded by fucking idiots."

"Her period is due next week," Wade whispered.

"I heard that, you dick."

I grinned out the window, searching for dark brown fur. "What happens at a new moon then?"

"You know how werewolves usually turn at the full moon in movies and stuff?" Cameron said.

No. "Sure."

Wade took the turn for the manor, screeching around the corner. "From what we've figured, it's the opposite. Sunlight gives wolves power. They're strongest and most in control during the day. At night, their control varies according to how much sunlight is reflected off the moon. At the full moon, they're safe and predictable. Then their control ebbs with the waning and waxing moons, growing strong again at the half-moons. During a new moon, when no sunlight is reflected to Earth, Luthers are most volatile. You'll never see them off pack lands around that time."

Whoa. "Why does sunlight help them?"

I naturally associated wolves—and monsters in general—with darkness.

Cameron's voice crackled through the speakers. "No idea. But when it happens, we get a week off Grids and meet at the manor for Tribe Night. So yay."

Wade snorted. "Don't call it that. Old people get offended. Plus, it's called Ancestor Appreciation night."

"Don't say that, Andie. *Everyone* will get pissed." Cameron butted in.

I glanced out the window again. Was there some way to low-key ask Sascha about the sun thing? He didn't know much about pack origins, apparently, but it was worth a try. "I'm not going to call this anything. You two are trouble."

Cameron was waiting at the manor gates when Wade pulled up. She jumped in, waving at the replacement guard I remembered from the first night.

When we reached the manor, I gaped at the sea of stewards covering every inch of the lawn. "I've never seen everyone together."

There were so *many*. Only the younger stewards and those without children came to the party on Wednesday.

"It's cool when everyone gets together. Usually just happens on tribe nights and the Deception Valley ball." Wade scoffed.

I smirked. "You don't like the ball?"

"I *want* to like it. It just currently sucks."

I grabbed my pillow and blanket from the boot, scanning the ground. "I don't think we're going to fit anywhere."

"Rhona's waving us down," Cameron said. "Best seats in the house."

We picked through the crowd, and I nodded to all the greetings. They knew my name—which wasn't the hardest thing in the world with my resemblance to Rhona, but still. I recognized some faces and recalled a few names, but if I'd met the others, I'd forgotten them.

"Girl, you're a freakin' legend," Cameron whispered. "People haven't stopped talking about Clay last week."

"All the better to disappoint them in the next grid."

Billy had an empty spot beside him, and I took a step to claim the space, but was jostled aside by Wade who dove into the gap. Cameron and I exchanged an amused look.

Wade really didn't want me with Billy.

I arranged my blanket beside Rhona, who immediately dragged it to cover her legs. Guess it was her blanket now.

"What's new?" she asked.

"I start the last year of my degree tomorrow."

She smiled. "You'll blitz it. I'm thinking of starting a degree actually."

Everyone shut up.

"What will you do?" I asked.

"I was thinking of physical education or something."

Foley snorted. "Babe, you'd kill kids if you trained them."

The group laughed.

"That's a great idea," I said to her. "You love fitness stuff and you could teach at the schools here or even train stewards."

"As long as I'm not in her classes," Billy said.

I turned. "You'd be lucky to be trained by someone like Rhona."

He gawked at me. "I know. I was just—"

I faced my cousin again, ignoring Wade's smug smirk. "Anywhere in particular that you're looking?"

She shrugged a shoulder. "Just a stupid idea really."

I glared at Foley, who swallowed and faced forward.

A mic screeched. Herc took the small stage in front of us. Three drums sat in front of seats at the back.

I glanced around. What happened at these things? I had *Tribe Night* and *Ancestor Appreciation Night* as clues.

That involved drums, clearly.

"Good evening, all," Herc spoke into the mic, "I'd like to start by announcing the next grid will be Sandstone. This is, of course, in ten days' time due to the new moon."

I tucked Rhona's hand in mine and rested my chin on her shoulder. "Whatever you choose to do, you'll be fantastic at it."

She didn't move as three men sat behind the drums. Five women took up position in front of them.

Rhona still didn't move as the drums started a steady rhythm and the women danced, their sweeping movements telling stories, vivid even without words. Slow and fast they dipped and turned until I was ensnared in their beautiful tale.

Only then, did Rhona rest her head atop mine, interlacing our fingers.

26

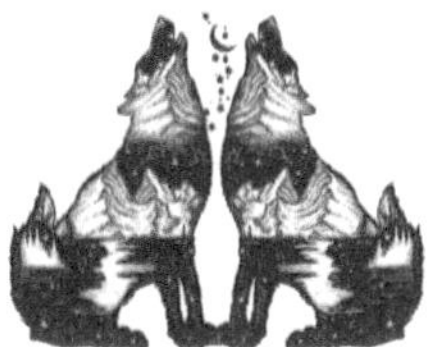

The run was unavoidable. Gerry could see when I'd completed training sessions and not. Unless I wanted to tell him that I couldn't go outside because a Luther wanted to breed with me, running it was.

I left the apartment safe in the knowledge the wolf in question hadn't gleaned a single thing more from me since last Thursday. In fact, four days had passed without a single werewolf sighting. Should I worry or was the new moon to blame? Wade said Luthers stuck to pack lands around this time, but I *also* recalled Herc's words about wolves stalking their prey for weeks or months before striking.

Walking to the end of town, I stretched my legs, lower back, and shoulders, slipping my phone into the back pocket of my shorts. After wheezing so much in the last grid, I was determined to work on my running so I could keep up with Rhona's unit.

I set into a pounding rhythm down the road to Lake Thana, dredging up that hammering excitement I felt entering Clay last week. My legs warmed, loosening, and I lengthened my stride.

Who knew running could be almost enjoyable?

I focused on my breath and the pumping movement of my arms, sticking to the shoulder of the road. The earthy scent of the trees cleared my senses, filling my lungs, and I smiled, pushing harder.

A car swerved next to me, disappearing around the bend.

Rounding the corner, I saw the person had pulled over. I'd been running well in the shoulder. They weren't pissed, were they?

I didn't slow my pace until the person got out of the car.

Oh, fuck.

Logan.

He shut the door of the car I should have recognised, leaning against the boot to await my approach.

I closed the distance at a walk, leaving ample space between us when I stopped. "Logan. What are you doing here?"

He'd driven nine hours. That was commitment. When we were together, he'd made the journey for sex. Now we were apart with numerous smashed windows and legalities between us. He didn't drive here to say anything good.

"Cute stunt with the civil lawsuit," he said, folding his arms.

I breathed hard, hands on my hips. "You drove all this way to tell me that?"

His gaze lingered on my bare legs, and I had a moment to regret selecting shorts over leggings.

"You look good, Andie. Really good."

"If you have a point to make, make it." Gerry would make me do demon burpees for stopping during the run.

Logan pushed off the car. "I keep replaying how things went so wrong, and I can't figure it out. What changed?"

That's what he drove nine hours to ask? *Yeah, right.*

Where was the sneering, angry dick who smashed windows and threatened me? That version of Logan couldn't be far away, but the question seemed genuine, so I'd play along for now.

I wiped my brow. "I did, I guess. Or my situation."

"We were happy once."

Was I? A mother with terminal cancer. Constant bills and calls to my boss to say I wouldn't be in. Looking back, I saw that Logan just *fit* into the little time I had. He had nice foliage and didn't require watering or sunshine.

Lucky for his ego, I wasn't a bitch either. "Yes, we were."

"We could be happy again."

The hell you say? "Logan, that would be off the table even without the smashed windows and ugliness since."

His face clouded. "I didn't smash anything. Your lawyers won't win. Call them off."

Ah. The real reason he'd come. "Not happening."

"You don't have the money to fight this, babe. All that shit about your mother's debt is true. You're trapped."

My hands balled to fists at his gloating smirk. I opened my mouth, but shut it as Logan jerked, looking over my head.

"Andie. Is everything alright?" a honey voice said.

My heart sank.

Please don't be here right now.

Sascha wasn't alone. Leroy and Hairy flanked him, Mandy and two other *Dens* bouncers called Grim and Lisa followed close on their heels.

"It's fine, Sascha," I said, jaw clenched.

"How did you know we were here?" Logan demanded, pushing past me. I stumbled back.

Sascha's mild manner dropped in a flash. "Logan, wasn't it? You just pushed Andie."

Logan's gaze narrowed as I moved between them again.

"You're the casino owner," he said. "The fucker moving in before we were over."

The werewolf smiled, his wolves fanning out. "Yes. I moved in on Andie the moment I saw her. I've enjoyed your little jealous letters."

If Logan knew those teeth became fangs, he would *not* be bristling for a fight right now.

I faced him. "Sascha has nothing to do with why we ended. I promise you. But it *is* over between us. If you came here to ask that I call the lawyers off, then we can discuss that, but everything else is off limits."

Logan lowered his head. "And I'll say it again. You don't have the money to fight me."

The wolves were silent at my back. I desperately wanted them to leave.

"What's the total figure, Andie?" His voice oozed glee. "Nearly half a million, I heard."

"Stop." Heat flooded my face.

Logan grinned, looking over my head. "Did Andie tell you that her mother had a little gambling problem? Well, not so little."

"*Stop it,* Logan." I grabbed his arm, but he shook me off.

"While Andie was slaving away to pay her mother's cancer bills, ol' Ragna was racking up *quite* the debt through online gambling."

I lowered my arms to my sides, the heat draining from my cheeks. "She didn't mean to."

He snorted. "Whatever helps you sleep at night. A month has passed since she died. Tell me, how much interest has piled on in that time? Soon, the house sale won't cover the repayment."

I'd gain another twenty-three thousand in debt over a year if the house didn't sell.

Logan leaned closer. "Do you hate the bitch, babe? Be honest."

I slapped him, embracing the burning sting in my palm. "Don't speak about my mother like that."

Logan clutched his face. "Assault." He laughed. "Thank you."

Heat seared into my back an instant before Sascha spoke, "Time to go."

Logan's face twisted. "Who's going to make me? Or would the six of you like to be slapped with a lawsuit too?"

"No problem," Sascha rumbled. "My lawyers are aiding Miss Booker and are particularly adept as you've found."

Logan stared at him before spearing me with a contemptuous glare. "You're sleeping with this guy, so he'll pay your lawyer fees?"

Fucking. Asshole.

I lifted my hand for round two. He wanted to sue me? For what? Hard to get money from someone who had none.

Sascha wrapped an arm around my waist and deposited me behind him.

"Please just leave," I whispered to him, knowing the wolf heard when his back tensed.

Everything I'd tried to hide from Deception Valley had been outed. Behind Sascha, I didn't meet the gazes of his wolves. Their eyes bore into me, and a lump rose up my throat.

I'd never, *never* felt so small.

I squeezed my eyes shut.

A car door slammed, and footsteps sounded behind me.

"He's gone. He won't come back."

That fucking voice drew tears to my eyes. Tears I didn't want him or anyone to see.

"It's okay, little bird." His hands wrapped around my upper arms.

It's not okay.

I yanked free, moving around Sascha without looking at him. "Thanks, but I could have handled it. See you at work."

Breaking into a run, I drew in ragged breaths, forcing my legs to move at a steady pace.

I managed two bends before I turned sharply and sprinted into the forest. Leaping over dead trees, I didn't react to the branches scraping at my cheeks as my lungs threatened to burst with my gasping sobs.

The forest floor gave way without warning, and I crashed to the ground, skidding down an embankment. I punched the earth, picking up a rock and standing to throw it as hard as possible before sprawling on my ass again.

Threading my hands through my hair, I curled my legs into my chest, bursting into gulping cries against my knees.

Logan had no right to do that. This beautiful place hadn't needed to know my mother was anything but perfect.

Now they did.

There wasn't a single place that Ragna could be remembered as she should have been.

I sucked in a breath, sniffing.

A hand rested on my back, and I froze as warmth wrapped around my bones.

Wiping my face, I peered at Sascha when he crouched beside me. My chest rose at his pitch-black eyes. Not a speck of honey showed.

Gravel churned in his voice. "Stop crying."

Whenever Sascha's eyes darkened or he gained that gravel quality to his voice, I'd learned his wolf was joining the conversation. I'd accidentally called his wolf Greyson once, but there really were two different entities inside of Sascha and it helped to give them each a name. Not that his wolf was grey at all. The name just suited the beast's solemnity and dangerous vibe.

Right now? I was speaking to Sascha's wolf.

I jumped at a crack, and twisted to see five wolves padding down into the ditch I was having my pity party in.

They flopped to the ground around me, closing their eyes.

Greyson hooked a finger under my chin. "Stop crying."

I hugged my knees again. "It doesn't work like that."

"It does if you give me all your problems."

"Not happening."

In a bare second, he had me cradled on his lap, his back to a large tree. I shoved at his arm, and a sinister growl erupted from him. The other wolves lifted their heads, taking interest.

Shit, he wasn't home right now.

Stilling, I sat tense on his lap, and his arms clamped around my body. We were still in the new moon. *Crap.*

"Warm vanilla," he murmured in a voice filled with gravel, stroking my hair. "That's what it smells like when you cry."

My exhale shook.

"You must hate me," he said in smooth tones.

Sascha was back. I relaxed but didn't attempt to move again just in case Greyson wasn't far away.

Sascha hesitated. "Your mother—"

"My mother is off limits." Straightening, I looked into his honey eyes.

More than one leaf was in my hair, and dirt covered my legs and arms. I could only assume my face was the same because the more he scrutinised me, the more he paled.

"The things Logan said. I don't ever want to speak about them again." With a narrowed gaze, I dared the werewolf to defy me.

Sascha considered me, then with purpose, tilted to expose his neck.

What the what? "Did you hear me?"

He breathed a sigh. "This is me telling you that I understand, Andie."

Oh.

Good then.

The werewolf resumed stroking my tangled hair, trailing his fingers lightly down my back. His other arm was still clamped around my waist. I wasn't going anywhere anytime soon. Fresh tears stung my eyes, and I tucked my head against his chest so he couldn't see.

"Sascha?" I said.

The purring chuff sounded in his chest. "Yes, little bird?"

"Are you more wolfy than usual right now?"

A chuffing came from one of the other wolves. *Yeah*, they weren't sleeping. Fakers.

Sascha's voice held a dream-like vagueness. "My wolf has greater control over me in this moment."

I wriggled as he reached a ticklish spot at my lower back. He paused and lightly stroked the same area. I wiggled, and he slid his hand higher.

"Will that be a problem?" I relaxed in his hold despite myself. The magic hangover thing was at play again. Dread seeped out of my very heart as I lingered in his arms.

I shouldn't be entertaining this. I shouldn't be in his arms. My family hated his pack. His pack hated us. My mother. Herc. Rhona.

The casino.

Grids.

Me.

His mouth moved against my hair. "I will never hurt you. It would kill me."

Was that a literal thing? If not, the creepy factor was too high for my comfort. Actually, either way. "That's part of the... breeding call?"

His whole body went rigid.

I swallowed hard. "Guess I shouldn't mention that?"

Sascha shook under me, and I placed my hands on his shoulders, chest tightening as his teeth lengthened.

His wolf looked out at me again.

"It makes sense now," Greyson said, menace rolling from him in droves. I could barely make out the words through the harsh clipped tone.

"What does?" I said hoarsely.

He opened his arms and, hands under my ass, set me gently on the ground beside him.

I wrapped my arms around my body. "What's happening?"

Greyson's lip curled. "I have my final answer."

27

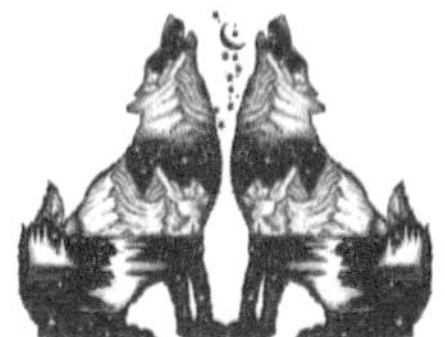

Pop. Pop. Pop.

Three fake darts embedded in the swinging practice dummy. The thing didn't move as fast as two-legged Luthers, but shooting at them was more accurate than the stationary dummies.

Another dummy bolted across. I named this one Sascha Greyson.

Pop. Pop.

One dart made it into his upper thigh. Not too far below where I'd aimed.

"You're improving." Rhona leaned against the stall door.

"How long have you been there?" I asked.

"A while. Gerry said you've been here for an hour morning and night the last two days."

Yup. Clay made me realise how crucial tranquiliser guns were, but I'd spent the two days since Sascha's wolf spoke with me filling these dummies with puncture wounds.

Rhona stood silently as I landed another few darts.

"I don't know who pissed you off," she said when I lowered the gun. "But keep it up."

I'd *keep it up* as long as it took to convince Greyson to back off. I'd run through our conversation several times and couldn't see exactly what question I answered in the forest.

So he got his answer when Logan was around.

Was his question to do with the mystery of my mother? Her cancer? Her debt? Or had he wanted to understand why I hated casinos?

Whatever the answer, Logan fucked me well and truly. Maybe I'd name the next dummy after him. Picking up the gun, I fired another five times.

Flicking the safety on, I set the gun on the barrier.

Rhona held out an envelope. "From Dad."

I took it. "Have you already read it?"

"Your new schedule. You've spent an hour with each of the strategy teams now. The head team believes you showed particular aptitude for counter-wolf strategies and Dad wants you to shadow the team until we play in Sandstone."

Whoa. Really?

I ripped into the envelope. The top paragraph pretty much reiterated what Rhona just said. Word for word. "Am I ready?"

She lifted a shoulder. "You either have it or you don't. And remember, you're six years older than our usual recruits—and a Thana."

I couldn't remember Rhona ever calling me a Thana. That usually came from Herc.

Phew, this roster would fill up my time. Lucky thing I didn't get that second job. With my study, I couldn't have managed everything.

Dawn training would be followed by a two-hour strategy meeting. Virtual reality training with Pascal came after. I had about 85 percent of the Sandstone traps memorised by now. The new moon break came at the ideal time, considering I'd never rock-climbed or abseiled before last week. By the time Wednesday came around, I'd be ready to go, or at least wouldn't accidentally hang myself.

Gerry had me on additional climbing training in the evenings, and I'd added shooting practice on top of that.

I could make my shifts Thursday through Saturday and the afternoons were mostly free for study.

This could work. I'd have no social life, but that wasn't anything new.

"How are things at The Dens?"

My eyes flew to hers. "The same."

Lie.

Despite Sascha's absence, Thursday and Friday night were fucking uncomfortable, especially after the scene with Logan and crying all over him.

I gritted my teeth.

"You're acting extra strange is all."

How much could I say? Were things at a point that I needed help? Maybe I should let someone in. A little. "Things are unsettled."

Her eyes became slits. "How so?"

How could any steward understand this breeding call business without passing judgement? I barely understood it. "You mean besides the obvious working for my enemy thing?"

Her lips twitched. "What are they doing?"

Offering their condolences on my mother's passing. Showering me with compliments and Corrie's Chocolate Chip Chocos. Smiling and patting me on the back. Hairy hugged me yesterday in front of the entry queue. "Things are just... noticeably tenser. Nothing I can't handle."

Her focus slid to the Logan dummy whose absent testicles had become dart pincushions.

Everyone's a critic.

"Logan showed up in town yesterday." I removed my safety glasses.

"Your window-smashing ex?"

I blew out a breath. "Yeah. He started shouting a whole heap of shit about Mum and the Luthers were around to hear it."

Rhona stilled. "Her gambling addiction?"

I met her gaze.

If the Luthers knew, it was only fair Rhona and Herc knew too. I didn't want the wolves to use my personal problems as ammunition against the Thanas or the tribe. "There's more. Mum left a debt against the house we co-own. The house sale should cover the repayment. The lawyers are on Logan's ass about smashing the windows, but I just *hate* that—"

I pressed my lips together. Putting everything into words was impossible. I had no idea what to feel about what Logan said. Or *more so,* who heard it.

Did I hate that people knew or the Luthers specifically? Sascha, if I wanted to be *more* specific.

"Do you need help?" Rhona asked in the lull.

I shook my head. "It's fine. Seriously. It's more the strange dynamic at The Dens that's unsettling me."

The Luthers could see inside me. They knew too much.

Including what brand of underwear I wore.

If Sascha's goal was to chip his way into the deepest, darkest, and most fearful parts of me, he was achieving it. For the first time since arriving, I wanted to leave Deception Valley. Finding out werewolves existed didn't send me over the edge, but this threatened to.

Rhona crossed her arms. "You need to stop working there. Any intel they get on you is intel they get on us as a whole. If things are out of control, it's time to leave."

Except I was learning so much about them.

My sessions with the strategy teams had shown *how* much. Tiny things added up. When I really stopped to think about my interactions with the Luthers, details kept rising—of Sascha's head team, the fact I hadn't seen the little cub in human form, and what changes in their voice meant. The social dynamic when I'd entered pack lands that time. Differences between their two-legged and four-legged form. And I'd discovered Grim was a gamma wolf while Lisa was an omega. With Hairy, Leroy, and Mandy, the five made up Sascha's head team. He had one wolf of each status. If Sascha had to politically form his head team to represent all factions of the pack, those could be cracks we could hammer on.

Not to mention that when I ran away from Sascha after Logan, there was certainly more than one hundred metres between us before I ran into the forest. Yet they'd found me without difficulty. Their senses in two-legged form were stronger than they'd let on.

I was steadily working through the history and strategy books Roderick gave me and could say with confidence that the *Ni Tiaki* hadn't discovered this much about wolves in the last hundred years. *No one else* was currently in a position to learn anything new about the Luthers.

Sandstone was coming for us again in five days, and any information was crucial. If not, I wouldn't have returned there on Thursday night. "I've got to stay. It's too important."

Rhona pressed her lips together. "That's your choice. Just... you're in their company more than any other steward. Please tell us if you're in trouble and don't be a one-woman army."

I cocked a brow. "I'll stop being a one-woman army if you will."

She pursed her lips. I would have believed her cocky act if she didn't swallow. "I can do a two-women army. No hugging allowed."

I hugged her.

"Just this once," she said, relaxing. Her arms wrapped around me and we stood in each other's embrace.

"That course you mentioned," I murmured. "What's happening with it?"

She didn't answer.

"If you need help searching for the right fit, let me know." I released her, picking up the schedule again. Rhona did best when she didn't feel targeted, so I focused all my attention on the paper.

I checked my phone—an hour remained until my shift at *The Dens.* Last shift of the week. I could do it.

"That'd be good," she murmured.

"Cool. How's tomorrow? Looks like I'll be swamped with this schedule during the week."

I couldn't wait to be busy again.

"Rhona."

We turned to find Foley striding toward us. I smirked and Rhona shot me a glare. The guy clearly did something for her. I just didn't see the draw.

"We're having drinks at the river," he said, slightly out of breath. He peered my way. "Want to come, Andie?"

To watch them suck face while I wasn't sucking face with anyone? "Sorry, got work."

"Oh, sure."

Foley grabbed Rhona's hand, and I mimed kissing my hand, earning another scowl.

But seriously. She could do better. Or was that weird protectiveness for my one and only cousin?

When I couldn't hear them anymore, I peered around the shooting stalls. Everyone was at dinner. As planned.

Dragging out my duffle, I scoped the area again and slid the tranquiliser gun inside along with two rounds of *real* darts.

Come at me, Sascha Greyson.

🐾🐾

I stormed down the street to *The Dens* in the barely there dress. Returning to my apartment to shower and change revealed one thing.

All of my dresses were gone except one.

"*You motherfucker*," I said, hoping the bastard heard somehow.

A woman decked out in gold jewellery gasped as she passed.

The dress was short to the point of indecency. I'd be up on a *stage*. Did he realise I didn't work at a strip joint? And that I already had a reputation as Thong Girl?

I didn't even wear this thing anymore. I bought it at sixteen when sex became the most important thought of the day and before my boobs were this size.

Perhaps the most annoying part was the collar that held up the front of the dress. He chose the dress purposely for that reason.

I just *knew* it.

I charged up the hill toward Hairy.

The beta drew back the cordon for an already-drunk group of mid-thirties males, whistling when he saw me.

"Where is he?" I demanded, placing my free hand on my hip.

His expression smoothed. "Of whom do you refer?"

I drew close, pointing a finger at his chest. "Where is Sascha Bastard Greyson?"

"His middle name is Alarick."

Really?

I jabbed my finger into hard muscle. "Tell me, Hairy. You owe me for making me cry that time."

"You made her cry?" an intoxicated woman at the head of the queue asked.

I nodded sadly. "He did."

Boos rose from the line, and I tilted my head at the werewolf. He stared at me for a beat, then swept his eyes upward. I followed his line of sight to the overhanging cover.

What... My mouth dropped.

Sascha was on the roof?

Hairy practically shoved me into *The Dens*, and I studied the low ceiling inside. Is that how Sascha followed me through town?

Oh my god.

"Big purse tonight." Mandy eyed my duffel as she slid my water over.

I wasn't leaving the gun at the apartment for Sascha to steal.

She leaned closer to the bag, sniffing. The tattooed blond grinned.

Snapped.

"Hey, could you hang around for a few minutes after your shift tonight?" she asked, pouring drinks for the women next to me.

"Why?"

She rang up the drink order, passing over the change. Mandy leaned across so we were face to face. "Sascha thought you might like to know a few things about what's coming."

"Then no." *Trap.*

She lowered her voice. "He'd like me to tell you how to deny the heat."

I paused, cheeks heating. *Dammit.* "That's all?"

"Yes, I promise. There's no way Sascha's furry side would choose The Dens for the capture meet."

"I thought it was something he couldn't deny—like it could happen anywhere."

"Oh no," she said easily. "That is, *Sascha* can't, but his other half can control the time and place."

I relaxed. "Then this isn't going to explode in Sandstone."

She lifted a shoulder. "I wouldn't exclude the possibility."

My mouth dried at the thought of Pascal and Herc's vantage point of the grid. That could *not* happen. "He can't shift in the grid. He'll lose a point for your side."

Mandy slid the women beside us a look, but they were more interested by the guys at the opposite end of the bar. "While Sascha may acknowledge Victratum, his wolf, being a sigma, does not. In fact, his wolf is more likely to flout rules in pursuit of the ultimate challenge. The pack accepts this as unavoidable."

Like a council decision?

"Sounds like you all sat down and had a good talk about it," I sarcastically replied.

"We did. It's a serious matter for us."

I *knew* the two-legged form came with all the usual human politics. With a wolfy spin. "The ruling of the pack can't be undone, right? I don't want anything to come back on me because of Sascha."

"The pack ruling is final. Which is why we take it seriously."

Interesting.

"That's fine, but Sascha could just change his mind," I probed. "He's your leader."

Mandy arched a brow. "No, he can't."

Dang. That answer didn't give me much, but I could assume the pack had the ability to outvote Sascha.

How many Luthers were involved in this decision-making

process? And how much power did Sascha's vote hold? "The pack won't be happy if he loses you guys points in the game."

She smiled. "Sascha won't be happy about it either, but there are only two meets controlled by a male's wolf. This is one of them. Don't expect him to make human considerations because Sascha is effectively a bystander in this. It is a chance for his wolf to prove his worth, and he will not share that privilege. Not even with the other half of his soul."

Chills trickled down my spine.

Greyson was terrifying. *Huge*.

My tranquiliser gun suddenly seemed really cute and pitiful.

"When will this happen?" I asked her in a low voice. My nights were spent tossing and turning. My days—looking over my shoulder. I could only balance so many things at once without spiralling.

I hated that feeling. That's when doors got kicked in.

And this capture thing could *not* happen in Sandstone. No way.

Mandy studied me. "Not even Sascha knows that. But I'll tell you that during the capture meet, a male wolf is after the ultimate challenge. Only in that way, can he prove to you that he is worthy."

Right. So in order to guess when Sascha would attack, I just had to understand what his wolf considered the ultimate challenge.

Awesome.

Too easy.

I grabbed my drink, sax case, and duffel.

"Have a good set," Mandy called.

She was enjoying this. All the wolves were. The pack had *accepted* their leader's breeding call operated outside of the game though. They couldn't be happy about that.

Sascha explained the breeding call to me as though it happened every now and then—maybe a few times a year. Or maybe I'd assumed it wasn't a rare thing from his casual tone.

How important was this occurrence to wolves?

Or was it so serious to them because I wasn't a Luther?

I rested the duffel beside the stool and went through the normal motions of set-up. I had a slightly sick feeling in my stomach. Nights playing music here would end soon. I'd genuinely miss the loss of this stage and the audience.

Scowling at Leroy, who'd already crept in with his phone extended to add more to his song list, I drew my lips in around the mouthpiece.

"Go Your Own Way." Fleetwood Mac.

Forgetting my woes—and the shortness of my apparel—wasn't easy as I worked through my set. In all honesty, I didn't expect to, given the last two shifts. One song never failed to ease my heart though. Except I didn't want to play it with Leroy around.

Seriously, if someone told me werewolves used drones and apps and offered platters of cookies, I would've laughed and edged away.

Bouncing with the music, I finished one song and flowed into another. Soon after, I drew that to a close too. The crowd was on a high tonight.

I ran my eyes over the closest members of the audience—all younger males tonight, probably hoping for an extra show from me.

They smiled, and I nodded politely.

Pretty sure they'd end up with wolf jaws around their noggins if I entertained the idea of a night with a male patron. There were more than enough hot guys at the manor to peruse. I just hadn't gotten a chance yet.

I should get onto that once Sascha got this crap out of his system.

"Hey, beautiful." A lean guy with a shaved head paused at the edge of the stage. "Can I buy you a drink after your set?"

Not my type. "Thanks, but I don't drink."

With you.

He slid a hand into his suit pocket ready to start a chinwag. *Groan.* I put the sax to my lips in a clear hint, but Grim rested a heavy hand on the guy's shoulder.

"Don't bother her," he said gruffly.

The man paled under his regard, and I smiled thanks to the gamma wolf, scanning for Leroy. I couldn't see him anywhere in the bar.

Maybe I'd sneak in my favourite song after all.

They'd never know.

Janis Joplin, here we come.

I closed my eyes, calling forth my mental forest. My shoulders eased, and I blew into my sax, easing into "Me and Bobby McGee."

My feel-good song.

The world faded as I built through the song which told the story of a couple hitching a ride cross-country. Dipping, I let my fingers fly across the keys, turning and swaying as I made the sax growl.

Yes.

Taking the volume low, I bent forward, feeling my hair slither over my back. I eased the intensity up a notch. And another. Building into a blasting crescendo, I moved my shoulders and spun on the spot.

Janis was the queen of letting loose. That's what drew me to her music, and when I played, I could do the same. I poured my woes and hopes into the saxophone, surging to the last bars, putting *everything* I had into the build.

Arching my back, I gave full throat to the powerful ending. Holding the note, I straightened, hair swinging forward, and swayed.

My sax squealed as I toppled backwards. *Fu—*

Air rushed from my lungs as strong arms caught me, cradling me much the same way I cradled my saxophone.

Breathing hard after giving the song my all, I blinked up at Sascha. His honey eyes were filled with something I hadn't seen before, but at least they weren't black.

He straightened, and I remembered the crowd for the first time. I gasped.

Oh my god. I just fell off stage.

"Andie Booker, everyone," Sascha called to the patrons struggling to get a look at us. "Playing so hard she falls off stage."

Loud laughter, and the incident was forgotten as everyone returned to their drinks and conversations.

Sascha set me on my feet, and I pressed a hand to my burning cheek.

"I don't normally drift."

"My fault," he said, gravel in his voice.

"How is it your fault?"

"I've never heard you play like that. When I entered the bar, you drifted toward me."

Setting my jaw, I didn't comment. Because truthfully, I really didn't *ever* move off the spot while playing and this shit between us was weird juju.

"Well, thanks for catching me," I grunted.

"You're done for the night."

"I have another forty-five minutes."

His gaze wasn't on me anymore. At Sascha's regard, the closest guys found other places to look than my ass.

Oh, brother. "You've got to be kidding me," I huffed. "*You* made me wear this. I'm going to kill you for that, by the way."

His lips tugged up in a slow grin. "I look forward to it."

Molten heat spread through my stomach.

"I thought the clothes you owned would fit," the Luther admitted, his attention on my breasts.

"Stop looking at my boobs, Sascha."

He shifted his focus to the bottom hem that skated high on my thighs, just covering the goods.

I gripped my sax. "That wasn't an invitation to look there either. I'm finishing my set. Unless I say otherwise, the men here are free to look their fill."

His eyes flooded black, and air hitched in my throat.

Stepping forward, I forced his head down. "Sascha, your eyes are black."

Said eyes hooded. "Say my name again."

Oh, jesus. We were not doing that. "Get control of yourself."

That was bad for *both* sides.

His hands found my hips, sliding over the breezy satin. His thumbs circled my hip bones, and my eyes flew to his as fresh heat pooled between my thighs.

He froze, nostrils flaring.

Humans didn't do that. "You need to chill. People will notice."

His lips twitched. "I'm nearly a century old, Andie Charise Booker. I'm not sure chilling applies to me at this point."

Fair enough. I wasn't sure the word ever applied to me.

"Your nipples are hard," he murmured.

I stilled in his arms. "They're not."

"I can feel them against my chest."

How did we get this close? "Your *eyes,* Sascha. Now."

"What do you know about predators, little bird? Because generally speaking, issuing orders isn't a great idea."

Oh.

The circling of his thumbs was agony. I shifted my hips, but he easily maintained the hold, continuing his torture.

My chest rose. "I don't know anything about predators, but I know calling a woman less than one quarter of your age *little bird* is weird."

"You don't see me as much older than you."

He couldn't possibly know that for sure.

His eyes were still hooded. Lips curved. "Or you wouldn't smell so turned-on. Do you know what turns me on? When you press your hand to your cheek. *Fucking irresistible.*"

His hands felt so good. "I'm thinking of someone else."

"Impossible."

That got my attention. "It's really not."

"You're engaged in... our breeding call."

Yeah, and Billy looked delish the other day. "I'm human, genius. Everything is in working order, I assure you."

His lazy grip was gone in an instant. Sascha clamped my hips against his upper thighs. And, *holy fuck.*

I wanted a re-run of that day in his office.

"Who?" he snarled in my ear.

The conversation wasn't moving this way. This wasn't a jealous lover's spat. "I'm just *saying* that it's possible. For me. Sorry if that punctures your ego. I have a feeling it will survive."

To hell with it. Black eyes or not, the guy was on his own.

The arm around my back had other plans.

"Let go of me, Sascha," I said calmly.

I recalled the crowd for the second time. This breeding call bullshit was strong.

Sharp pricks jabbed my back, and I jolted, staring at him in real alarm. "Those better not be claws, Greyson."

He began to shake.

Fuck!

I twisted as far as he'd allow, signalling Grim and Lisa. They exchanged a long look and didn't budge.

Seriously! Did they want a wolf in here?

Turning back to Sascha, I brushed my fingertips from his temple to jaw. Moving in, I lowered my voice to bedroom level—the feat was disturbingly easy to accomplish. "Your hands are on me right now, aren't they, Greyson? I'm in the dress you chose. Others are looking, but only you can feel my nipples against your chest right now. Do you feel them?"

Yeah, I'd agonise over these words later because they weren't meant to turn *me* on too.

A throbbing took up place between my thighs as I rose on tiptoe as he stopped shaking. I whispered in his ear, "You can smell how much I want you, can't you?"

Lowering, I peeked up at him through my lashes.

Honey.

Sascha's hold eased, and I dropped the act—or not so much—folding my arms.

He didn't say a word, and after a breath, it occurred he might be genuinely speechless at my dirty talking. Or maybe the blood that usually resided in his brain was otherwise situated.

"Don't bother coming by the apartment anymore," I told him. "I'm moving to the manor until *this* is over."

His eyes darkened, but he held onto the honey shade for the most part.

The DJ was waiting to set up, and we were drawing far too much attention with our tense bubble.

"Andie?"

I peered at Sascha.

His expression had never been more serious. “Don’t leave tonight without having that talk with Mandy.”

I clenched my jaw, remaining mute.

Sascha stepped forward, taking my hand. “Whatever you think of me, I never want to take anything you’re not willing to give. I couldn’t bear to look at you again if I hurt you. *Promise me*, please.”

My heart skipped a beat, and I pulled my hand free, dropping my gaze to the saxophone I’d completely forgotten about while crushing my body to his. “I promise.”

28

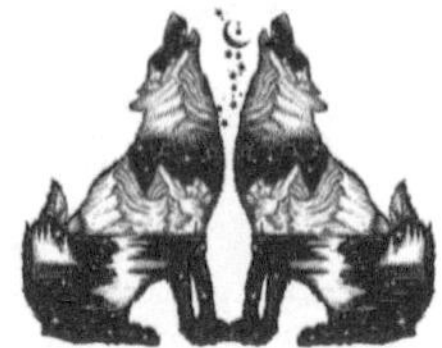

"Which side of the bed do you want?" Wade asked, far too excited about our sleepover.

I hooked the window latch tight, scanning the manor grounds before drawing the curtains closed. "Either is fine."

"Cool." He flopped onto the bed. "Not that I'm complaining, but why the sudden change?"

Wade didn't make a big deal when I called from *The Dens* and asked him to meet me there and follow me back to the manor. He'd barely peeped until now as I sat stewing over the things Mandy told me after my shift.

I walked to stand at the foot of the bed. "Shit is tense at The Dens. I need to talk to Herc before I say anything."

Grabbing my robe, I wrapped it tight around me, sliding into fuzzy slippers.

"Best hop to it," he said. "In case I'm asleep when you get back, I like to be little spoon."

My nerves churned as I padded down to Herc's office.

The light was on, and I knocked.

"Come in."

"Hey, Uncle Herc. You got a few minutes?"

He stared at me for a few beats. "Of course. Come in."

Did I interrupt something? "You sure?"

"Assuredly. Take a seat. Is something wrong?"

I blew out a breath. "Not really. I just wanted to pass on a few things that happened."

He rested both palms on the desk, blue eyes regarding me. I had a fresh moment of heartache at his resemblance to Mum.

"Does this have anything to do with your ex-boyfriend showing in town?"

Rhona beat me to it. That made this easier.

"Things are becoming tense at The Dens. I'd like advice on how to manage the situation. I feel like I'm balancing too much stuff."

He leaned back. "Give me the list. We can brainstorm solutions."

I studied my hands. "Did Rhona tell you about Mum's debt?"

My uncle tensed. "No. She didn't."

"Mum had a gambling problem. For as long as I can remember. She managed to beat it during my teens with help. I guess the cancer wore her resolve. She was gambling in secret. A lot. I found out after her death."

Herc's fists curled. "What did she do to you?"

My mouth dried. "What?"

He shook his head. "Forgive me. I..." Herc shoved his chair back, turning to the window.

Heat crept over my jaw. "I loved my mother."

"I don't doubt that. Truly I don't." He faced me. "Maybe when, *if*, you have children one day, you will see your childhood through different eyes."

"What are you saying?" I demanded.

Blue eyes rested on me again. "Something you aren't ready to hear, so let's bring this conversation back to something constructive. This debt, can I ask how much is owed?"

I struggled to rein in my temper and settled for digging my fingers into my thighs. "The sale of our house should cover the amount."

He didn't react, but that meant nothing when it came to Herc.

"I don't need help with that," I continued, "But until the house sells, it's an extra stress which is why I brought it up."

"Particularly when ex-boyfriends are smashing windows."

To say the least.

"Tell me," he said. "Rhona mentioned you'd sought lawyers."

Oh. Fuck.

Did I tell her that? Herc could *not* find out Sascha's lawyer wolves were handling Logan. Even if it wasn't at my request.

I kept my features schooled, stealing a page from his book. "She was worried and asking a lot of questions. I lied."

My uncle's focus didn't waver.

I sighed. "It's okay. Really. Logan has backed off, but I'll ask if I need help, remember?"

His face softened. "I'm glad to hear it."

That better not come back to bite me in the ass.

My chest loosened. "So that's one thing, and I'm accruing interest each day and there haven't been any solid offers on the house yet." Soon, I'd have to accept pittance for it, or the bank would seize the house anyway and chase me for any outstanding amount.

"That by itself is a lot to manage."

Was it? "Things are changing at work. To start, the wolves seemed amused, but after I entered Clay and shot Sascha, they're different."

Nicer.

He smirked. "I can imagine. What's happening?"

"It's more a feeling that they're planning something. I can't explain it."

"Does this feeling come from Sascha Greyson or other wolves?"

If I was careful, maybe I could mention more than initially intended. "All of them, but Sascha more regularly."

"How?"

"What?" I stalled for time.

"What gives you this feeling?"

Oh, you know, him mentioning my hard nipples. "The way they look at me. I think they're following me around outside of work. They overheard the conversation with Logan when he came to town."

Herc steepled his hands.

"I went for a run and six of them must have been following, because when Logan pulled over, they showed up."

My uncle scowled. "Have any of them touched you?"

My heart leaped into my mouth at his murderous expression. "What? No."

He didn't relent. "Have you felt anything strange in their presence?"

"Aside from fear? Anger, I guess. Frustration. But that's normal, right?"

Uncle Herc rested back. "Are they just using you as we're using them? I'm missing something here. I've known it for a while. Sascha Greyson is up to something and it involves you."

Did it ever.

"Is there *anything* else you can tell me?" he pressed.

I tried to still my leaping heart. Herc was asking really pointed questions—about touching and strange feelings. Did he know about the breeding call?

If so, his sentiment on the matter was more than plain, unless I was mistaking rampant disgust for extreme protectiveness.

I couldn't mention anything else on the Sascha front. "I learned more about sigmas tonight from a bartender. She said that the pack accepts a sigma will act out sometimes because they don't acknowledge rules. You spoke about sigmas being lone wolves. The way she spoke made it seem Sascha Greyson has almost forced himself into leading the pack, like it's not a natural thing for a sigma."

His eyes gleamed. "Fascinating. That's great information. That's all she said?"

No. "She didn't even say that much. Most of that is me theorising."

"Yes, but your observation skills are exemplary. You never need to be told twice. You pick up on cues and make connections so easily that I need to remind myself you've only been here for a few weeks. I trust your theories."

I smiled. "Thanks."

He perched on the desk. "Pretend we're in a counter-wolf

meeting, Andie. How would you use that information against the Luthers?"

This felt kind of like an interview; my natural competitiveness rose. "It shows another potential weakness in the pack. We could exploit rifts between wolves of different status, but also with Sascha's control over the pack. They surely won't accept endless rule breaking."

I stood, pacing. "I think it's a mix. In wolf form, they behave more as a typical wolf pack would in that they obey their leader absolutely. In two-legged form, Sascha is able to take human considerations into account. That could extend to hearing out other's opinions and making decisions as a team. If he was to stop doing that, what would happen?"

My uncle spoke from his perch. "Sascha Greyson's father was an alpha."

I glanced at him. "Really?"

"The sigma status is important."

"I agree."

We shared an excited grin.

Maybe there was still time to take Sascha down—enough so this breeding call situation would resolve somehow. I didn't mind being in his company or playing Grids—or even working at *The Dens.* I just needed the breeding bullshit gone.

I can figure this out.

I straightened.

"Looks like you've sorted out your own problem," Uncle Herc noted.

I brushed my hair back. "Perhaps. Talking through things helped."

"As for working at The Dens. How about you take a week off and reassess?"

"He was perfectly clear that inconsistency wouldn't be tolerated. The casino is important to him."

"The revenue or the venture itself?"

Both. Sascha was proud of the casino's success. I guess it was the stamp of his new leadership. I wrinkled my nose and considered the patrons in expensive suits and dresses and the regular flash and gleam of jewels. "It's crucial income for them."

My uncle dipped his head. "Correct—if their drones, motion sensors, and reinforced nets are evidence of a surge in income. Whatever he is, Sascha Greyson isn't stupid."

Only a stupid person would call him anything but keenly intelligent. Those eyes didn't miss a beat. Even several hours later, I couldn't be sure he didn't orchestrate the black eyes and claws earlier just to get me close.

Without knowing it, people just *did* what he wanted.

I set my jaw.

"Do you want to return to The Dens, Andie?"

Mulling over the question, I bit my lip. "It's important."

Herc watched me closely. "It is. Yet you must always consider your own safety. With that said, leadership sometimes means putting your feelings aside for the betterment of those around you. You're my niece, and you weren't raised in this valley, but you understand that being a Thana means protecting our stewards fiercely."

I wasn't born with this specific responsibility, but responsibility was something I learned at a young age. "Without dedication, the world quickly turns to chaos."

Families fell apart.

Debt collectors got nasty.

"What's that quote from?" Herc asked.

I shrugged. "Just a personal observation."

His face hardened, and I ran back over my words.

"Does that offend you?" I asked.

He rubbed both hands over his face. "I'm just trying to reconcile myself with... a lot of things, chief amongst them, your life to date."

My uncle reached across the desk, and I squeezed his hand, holding tight.

"You can always come to me, niece." His eyes drilled into mine. "Promise me you always will. Even if you're furious at me or upset or afraid. I missed twenty-one years and I can't stand the thought of losing any more time with you."

A lump rose in my throat, and for a brave second, a full confession lingered on the tip of my tongue.

"You can depend on me." He reached forward to hold my hand in both of his.

I blinked a few times. "I'm happy I met you."

"Not happier than me, dear one."

He released me, wiping at his face. "Now get to bed. Gerry is springing a surprise and very brutal training on the stewards at dawn."

I winced. "Good to know."

"Don't worry, you'll have recovered by Wednesday night."

Dread unfurled at the mention of Sandstone. I had a bad feeling that dread was a warning sign I shouldn't ignore.

I walked to the door. "Goodnight, Uncle Herc."

His quiet words followed me. "I'm honoured to be your uncle."

29

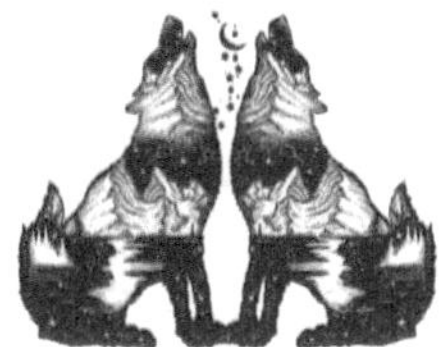

"Incredible. I don't even get morning wood around you."

I cracked an eyelid open to discover Wade too close. "Huh?"

"My body doesn't even *subconsciously* react to your bits. I really do find you absolutely unattractive."

Not the best words I'd woken to, but at least he hadn't snored or occupied too much of the bed. Grumbling, I couldn't help peeking down my singlet top to check if my nipples were hard.

"What's the verdict? Chimp tits?"

A laugh startled from me. "Excuse me?"

"Chimp tits. When a woman's nipples aren't hard."

"That's... I don't know what to say to that."

He hummed. "Right. I thought you might want reassurance of our platonic friendship considering the pillow wall you built between us overnight."

"I didn't."

"Well, it wasn't me. Four pillows stacked in a row between us—like you expected me to steal your five-years-gone virginity."

Eerily accurate on the virginity front. "I don't sleep-move. No idea how that happened." I flopped down again as Wade perched on the edge of the bed.

He crossed the room. “Where did this come from?”

I tensed, staring at the ceiling. “What is it?”

“There’s a record player here. And a record. It’s right in the middle of the room. Did you bring it in after seeing Herc?”

Anger curled around my heart. “What’s the record?”

He fumbled around. “Uh, Janis Joplin. Never heard of her.”

I balled my hands. Sascha Greyson was *inside* the manor last night.

Was he *insane*?

And the idiot got close enough to insert a fucking pillow wall between me and Wade.

“Maybe someone’s playing a prank,” I croaked.

Wade turned the record over in his hands. “The record is signed.”

I kicked off the bed covers, snatching it from him. “It is?”

“You know who did this!”

Oops. I lowered the record which was—indeed—signed. It must have cost a fortune.

Wade folded his arms. “Not talking? That’s fine. I’ll figure it out by myself.”

Shit. “There’s nothing to figure out.”

“Oo, Uncle Herc wouldn’t approve, huh? Juicy.” His brows slammed together. “As long as it’s not Billy.”

I turned to my duffel, dragging out exercise clothes. Dawn couldn’t be far off. “What have you got against Billy anyway?”

“He treated my younger sister like crap.”

“You have a sister?”

“Yes. You should never get one.” His fond tone contradicted that.

“Where does your family live?”

“There are cabins covering the entire north range from here and nearly to the lake. Our cabin is about a five-minute walk away. I usually stay with them. Just me, Mum, and Dad. Chrissie lives with her new boyfriend. For the moment.”

He was super protective. I bit back a smile.

We dressed and hunkered against the cool air, hurrying to the pavilion.

"Training will be brutal today," I muttered. "Herc said."

Wade groaned. "I don't like to know that shit in advance."

"Sorry."

He wrapped an arm around my shivering frame. "That's fine. We'll know each other soon enough. Little details don't matter. Far more important that we know we're soulmates from the get-go."

I snorted. "Is that what we are?"

"You don't feel it?"

"I thought it was gas."

Around fifty bleary-eyed stewards were already gathered. Wade and I joined Cameron, Rhona, and Foley.

Rhona's gaze shot between us.

"Nope," I chirped.

Her brow cleared.

"You still good for later on?" she asked.

Wade glanced between us. "What's happening later on?"

I ignored him. "Sure. After training?"

"Sounds good."

"What's happening later on?" Wade asked again as Gerry arrived.

I fell into step beside Rhona. "Any idea what's on the cards this morning?" Unlike Wade, I preferred to know.

"A mountain run and manoeuvres. That's all I've got."

Wade wedged between us. "*What's happening later on?*"

Gerry passed me two tablets. My vertigo medication.

"Looks like we're rock-climbing," I murmured, swallowing the meds.

Gerry blew a whistle, and Rhona took off at a jog behind him as he led us into the trees. I fell in behind her.

"I thought we were soulmates," Wade hissed at my back.

My lips trembled. "I didn't agree to that. Maybe I like the small details before life-long commitments." Especially given recent circumstances.

Conversation dwindled as Gerry led us further into the bush. For an older guy, he could move.

Jesus.

The climb was steady. The flat sections of the mountain trail felt fucking glorious. I was just happy when we reached the top an hour later that I hadn't stopped once—though I'd fallen back toward the middle of the group.

Ice bins filled with bottles awaited us at the top.

Rhona lobbed me one. "Nice stuff."

"It's getting easier," I panted, catching the bottle.

A lot easier. My body had never felt stronger.

I felt so capable.

One of the head team members called for silence. What was her name again? Trixie?

I gulped at my water.

"Stewards, it was here, nearly three hundred years ago, that our ancestors stood vigil over the land and spotted the Luthers entering these parts." She pointed behind us.

I turned with the others, chest filling at the first rays of sunlight bathing the narrow western gully that served as the entrance to Deception Valley.

"When we fight in Victratum, we fight to honour not only this land but those who have stood strong before us. We are just one link in a very long chain, but that chain anchors us always." Trixie regarded us solemnly and only ragged breaths disturbed the cool mountain air.

She held up a fist. "As you all stand here today, we make a pact. *The chain will not end with us.*"

Rhona moved closer until we were shoulder to shoulder. On the plateau, others moved to do the same. Wade rested a hand on my left shoulder, and Cameron did the same on my right. Laura from the Clay unit smiled at me as she flanked my other side. Soon, everyone touched.

Utter silence.

Trixie's voice was just above a whisper. "As our ancestors stood where you are right now and vowed to do the same, *protect* this land with your last breath, and in return, the land will fill your lungs until the end of time. The chain will not end with us."

I closed my eyes, focusing on the borrowed warmth seeping into me.

I was part of a chain now, and this chain wouldn't break—I wouldn't let it

Fumbling, I grabbed Rhona's hand in a tight hold.

The cookies were arranged around the bed and *on* the bed in a way one would usually associate with rose petals.

Honestly? I had to give him points for that one. Most of me was just glad Sascha was here during the training session and not up on the mountain. What I'd felt up there was too personal to share with anyone but my tribe.

Each cookie was on a plate, and I shook my head and picked them up, imagining a robber wolf with a rucksack full of porcelain plates sneaking onto the manor.

Thank fuck Rhona and I didn't do her course research in here.

I crouched by my duffel bag—hair wet after a much-needed shower. Where was my damn brush? Day two and I already hated living out of a bag again.

I had one of those glitter ones every girl owned at ten and usually replaced by twelve. My hand wrapped around a cool handle.

Frowning, I drew out a heavy comb. "What the hell?"

This belonged on some duchess movie. My jaw dropped. He'd been in my bag.

And he'd *left* the tranquiliser gun behind. *Cocky bastard.*

I dug around for my old hairbrush.

Gone.

Dammit.

Shoving a cookie in my mouth, I combed my hair, glowering at the wall. Rising, I checked the cupboards and leaned out of the window. I couldn't see the roof from here.

Dressing, I scoured the rest of the room for new objects.

A yellow tulip. My favourite flower. And how the heck he'd known that was mind-boggling.

New saxophone reeds. My preferred size.

Pine-scented candle.

A Sudoku book.

Black ankle boots that I looked at in the window of *Noni's Apparel* earlier that week. In my size.

Fuzzy pyjamas. Also my size.

My chest rose and fell as I stared at the final item. He'd taken a photo of me and Mum from the apartment and framed it.

The frame was carved from wood, an intricate design that made the photo appear to be cradled within an ancient tree.

My throat tightened.

Shoving aside the frame and a few other items, I scooped up the other items, flinging the windows wide. Checking the coast was clear, I threw everything out.

"Fuck you," I hissed to the tree line.

Yanking the curtains closed, I snatched up the duchess comb, Janis Joplin record, and photo frame, pushing them deep into my duffel bag where I could forget they existed—and that I hadn't thrown them out too.

Whatever game the werewolf was playing, he was winning. I couldn't be on the defensive anymore. I had to figure this out.

But no matter how I resisted, he wouldn't stop stalking me.

I lifted my head. A smile curved my lips.

No matter how I *resisted*.

Greyson wanted a challenge.

My smile widened to a grin. *Yep*, that wolf chose the wrong woman to fuck with.

I cleared the room of my stuff, making the bed. Herc said this was my assigned room for whenever I wanted it, so I didn't fuss too much.

Latching the windows, I strode through the manor and to my car, tossing the bag inside.

Back to my apartment it was.

The manor was a *challenge*.

I smirked, rolling down my window to belt out a song as I drove back into town. There couldn't be a *challenge* if I made no effort to hide.

Pulling into the bakery, I bought a batch of blueberry muffins and returned to the apartment, spending the next hour jotting down a *very* comprehensive list.

I copied over a vague version of my manor timetable onto paper too.

Rummaging through my suitcase, I drew out a black thong and two sexy bras. One showed my nipples. One didn't.

Hmm.

Tossing one back into the case, I yanked off my clothes and pulled on the skimpy underwear, slinging a loose off-the-shoulder dress over the top.

Waving at Walter Nash outside, I slid into Ella F and set off for pack lands.

Be bold, Andie Booker.

After crossing the bridge, I rolled down the window, shouting, "I'm heading to your pack lands, Greyson. Meet you there."

Was he around? I imagined his expression. This was the way to put a serious hole in his boner. For good.

I knew it.

Pulling over as the road tightened, I ripped off my dress, committing to the role.

"Thong girl don't take no prisoners," I whispered.

The pack lands didn't have a guarded gate like the manor, but a large male wolf stepped from the tree line as I crossed some invisible line.

"Andie," he grunted in surprise.

"Hey, Grim," I said cheerfully. "Just here to see Sascha."

The wolf opened his mouth, catching sight of my outfit. Or maybe my nipples. *Yeah*, I'd gone with that bra. I wouldn't want to cover my milk machines and have Sascha interpret that as a *challenge*.

The massive bouncer coloured and averted his gaze.

"Thanks, Grim."

I drove on. The odd cabin was visible through sparse trees on either side of the dirt road. After a further five minutes, the trees cleared to show large harvest fields pushing to the creek several hundred metres away.

The fields came to an end, and cabins filled the space after. Most of the pack must live in this area. I couldn't see the end of the raised houses around the curve of the stream through the trees.

I scowled at Sascha's home—one of the only dark-wood homes—closest to the water.

Parking outside his cabin, I grabbed my sack of props.

A male Luther exited his cabin.

"Hi there," I called. "Could you tell me where Sascha is, please?"

The man jerked to a halt.

I smiled encouragingly. *Thong girl doesn't feel discomfort.*

Tilting his head to listen, the Luther pointed a finger to a larger building off to the left.

"Thanks so much."

Striding in that direction, I braced for the best performance of my life. My courage—admittedly—did falter somewhat when I burst into a meeting bungalow of sorts filled to the brim with Luthers.

Gasps rang out, and I paused in the doorway, scanning for the bastard.

Sascha had a throne. Well, a huge, high-backed chair covered with a fur pelt with massive antlers.

Definitely a throne.

The fucker had to know I was here, and the shocked reaction of his pack was unmissable, but he ignored me, speaking with Leroy—also part of the act judging by how hard he *wasn't* looking my way.

No problem.

Greeting those I passed, I waved at gawking male Luthers on my right.

"Hi. Nice day out. Been busy?" *Oh my god.* This was a much better plan when a hundred people weren't here to witness it.

Leroy slipped first, sneaking a quick look. His eyes widened, and then Sascha Greyson was *mine.*

The werewolf turned, and his eyes flooded black.

Ha. No one could miss that. Visual boner.

Sascha blurred to his feet, and I stumbled at his speed before remembering this was my chance.

"Greyson. How are you?" I asked, aware that 100 percent of my ass was out.

His snarled breaths were music to my ears.

I held up the bag. "I was looking at your wonderful gifts today and realised I haven't done anything to help you out with all this breeding hoo-ha."

Leroy rose, glancing at a trembling Sascha. "Andie—"

"Let me rectify that." I dragged out the list. "Here's a list of my favourite things and preferences. You won't need to waste resources fishing them out anymore."

I held out the list, but Sascha continued to shake.

"Here, let me," I said. "You're out of sorts."

Lowering the bag, I tucked the rolled paper in the waistband of his jeans. "You'll need to take it out later when those pants come off, bad boy."

Walking back to the bag, I bent over giving him an unobstructed view of my ass.

I can't believe I'm doing this.

I cleared my throat, straightening. "You've been tracking me, and that must be really tiring, so here's my schedule. That way, you can just come out when you really need to. I'm happy to give you a call whenever I leave the apartment, too, if you like." I tucked the schedule in his pants with the list.

He stopped shaking and his claws retracted.

Greyson was leaving the scene.

I peeked up.

"You must be *hungry* after all that work," I purred.

I drew out the bag of blueberry muffins. "I've recently become fond of these and thought I'd share some with you. Maybe we could eat them just before we have sex. Maybe during. Are you available now?"

Leroy choked, turning away.

I shrugged a shoulder when Sascha didn't respond. "Just give me a call. Better yet, *just show up*. Doesn't matter if I'm sleeping or with other people. Just interrupt and give me the nod. Crook the finger. I'll drop my panties right then, right there. You get the idea."

Black drained from his gaze, leaving honey behind.

Gotcha.

This was a massive turn-off for his wolf.

I twirled my hair. "You seem busy right now. I came here ready to breed with you at all costs, but would you like a rain check?"

Muffled laughter sounded behind me.

Picking up my bag, I flicked a glance at the row of wolves either side of Sascha. They seemed split into two camps—baffled and amused. Or put another way, male and female.

Sascha opened his mouth.

Closed it.

"Okay, then, handsome. I hope to see you around." I raked his body with my gaze. "And remember, *any time, any place.* I've noted my favourite positions on the list too."

The males automatically looked at the rolled paper in Sascha's waistband.

A high-pitched yipping sounded behind me.

I crouched to catch the cub. "How's my favourite little man?"

He wriggled in my grip, whining.

"It's nice to see you too. I wasn't away that long."

The cub bounced to lick my face, and I stroked his back.

"I'm here to see Sascha. We're going to make you some little friends. Maybe a hundred."

The mother came running in, groaning when she caught sight of the cub. "*Axel.*"

The cub hid behind me and I flashed my ass at the still-silent Sascha as I scooped the little werewolf up, standing.

I held the cub at eye level. "Did you run away from your mother, Axel?"

He didn't make a sound, and I brought our faces closer. "Do you see that you worried her?"

He whined.

"I hear you. Your mother doesn't want to stop you having fun. You just need to tell her where you're going. If she says no, it's for a reason and because she loves you."

The cub lowered his gaze, and I passed him to the woman.

"How is he?" I asked as the cub licked her face.

She smiled. "A day later and you would never have known."

I squeezed her arm. "I'm glad."

Her gaze flickered over my shoulder.

Oh, yeah.

Tossing my hair, I smiled saucily at Sascha. Could werewolves turn to stone? I don't know what I expected, but it wasn't *no* reaction.

"Call me, honey bear." I blew a kiss.

Leroy lifted a hand and caught it.

Sascha glowered at his right-hand wolf.

Spinning on my heel, I sighed happily and strutted to the door. The women stood grinning to my right, though the male Luthers skittered back as though burned.

Mandy's grin was the largest. She held up her hand as I passed.

I slapped my palm against hers.

"I think I'm in love with you," she hushed.

Snorting would ruin my work. "I could only ever love Sascha Greyson. His dick or no dick."

Her laughter followed me out.

30

Roderick, the head team member I was shadowing, moved a large black statue that denoted a Luther team into position at the far end of the Sandstone mock-up board.

At this moment, the other strategy teams were finalising ideas to evade the Luther's drones and nets in the grid.

New manoeuvres rolled out this morning at dawn and would be practiced again tomorrow.

But my team sought to understand the wolves—their habits and tendencies, their strengths and weaknesses and hierarchy. We could then exploit those things.

I loved it.

Intense didn't *begin* to cover the energy in the room.

The fifteen men and women—all above thirty—considered the board covering the square table. So much hinged on the next grid and Operation Charise was no longer. What we'd come up with was good, but it centred on information I'd yielded from *The Dens*. The pressure of that was huge.

"Any final comments?" Roderick asked.

I leaned forward.

Our plan was research, really. We'd go for Sascha—to observe what effect this strategy had on his pack.

What no one knew was that Greyson might go for *me*. But with our attack centred on him this week, the tribe's plan would also act as my personal defence.

"That's a wrap then, people," he said. "Great work. We'll unleash things the Luthers have never seen before thanks to Andie."

I forced a smile as the team shot praise my way, some patting me on the back. They filed out and I studied the board. Was there anything we'd missed? What had the other teams decided upon?

I couldn't feel confident only knowing one piece of the plan.

"The trick is to let go of the outcome," Roderick murmured, collecting the papers and dismantling the board. "It's the hardest part."

"Yeah, I feel responsible for how this goes."

"It's a lot to handle. Over time, your resilience builds—after a few more rounds with the gin and dummies, you'll be fine."

Ugh, everyone knew about that.

The early-forties man laughed as I pulled a face. "Let it go, Andie. Trust me on that. You've done the work and put in the effort. Now trust in yourself and this team. Know that very little else is in your control."

The last part didn't jive whatsoever. "I'll work on that."

Roderick held up his full case. "I'm sure you will. Before I forget, here are the books you asked for."

He drew out two thick and bound files. "One is a more in-depth of the tribe's history. The work of our older stewards. The other contains the notable successes of past grid strategies."

I wanted to deepen my understanding of the tribe beyond what I'd already learned. I'd like to learn more about Mum's family, and I didn't want to let this team down—even if I was only Roderick's for a while.

"Thank you. This is great."

"Keep them," he said. "Those are your copies. It's nice for a younger person to take interest in tribe history. Our lead historian nearly fainted from joy when I told her."

"Sorry to interrupt." Herc popped his head in. "Rod, could I have a word with Andie, please?"

My pulse ramped up.

Roderick left with a nod to Herc.

"How are you getting on?" he asked, entering the room.

I smiled. "I really like this."

"So I've heard. I see you have a bit of light reading there?" He gestured at the books in my grip.

I shrugged a shoulder. "It's a strange feeling to come into this tribe. I feel like I belong here but lack the knowledge and experiences."

"I wish you could hear and see how our stewards view you. A fantastic debut in Clay. Extra trainings and shooting practice, not to mention your work in The Dens on the frontline. You're committed to learning everything you can. Don't think for a minute that any person here is unaware of your aptitude and dedication to Victratum."

I appreciated the reassurance after charging into pack lands in my thong. Especially because I hadn't heard hide nor hair from Sascha since. I was starting to think my plan really worked.

"I do have one question," he hesitated. "Gerry noticed a gun missing from our stores. I looked back through the footage and well..."

Ah, fuck.

A sinking feeling pitted in my stomach. "I took the gun when things became tense at work. Before our talk."

Herc perched on the square table. "I didn't realise things were bad enough that you felt you may need to physically defend yourself."

I really didn't want my uncle to think I was a thief. "I should have asked—"

"I'm pulling you from The Dens."

My jaw dropped. "What?"

"If you're grabbing a tranquiliser gun, you're more than worried. You're scared."

"It's important that I'm there. The stuff I'm learning is changing the way we approach the game."

"If there was a way to do that safely, I'd do it in a heartbeat. But I don't gamble with the lives of my stewards and certainly not my niece."

The use of the word *gamble* wasn't purposeful, perhaps, but it drew me up short. He didn't want to risk my safety.

He, unlike my mother, was putting *me* first.

I lowered my chin, trying to assemble the scattered direction of my thoughts.

"Sometimes, when we're in something, it becomes hard to make clear decisions," he said softly.

I sighed. "I'm not being objective, am I?"

"Can any one person be entirely objective?"

Sascha Greyson. "Guess not."

"Sometimes, we must trust in those around us to provide clarity. I admire your dedication to this tribe, Andie. It warms my heart and has lit a fire in the hearts of the Ni Tiaki. But as head steward, I'm drawing your time at The Dens to a close."

There wasn't any room for argument, and I didn't feel the need to do so anyway.

"I can deal with that."

"I'm glad," he said. "Now, I need a favour if you can handle another three hours of meetings today."

I grimaced. "Rhona isn't here?"

"Nowhere to be found. Could you pretend to be her, so my head team doesn't think my daughter has better things to do than her duty?"

I checked my laughter, perceiving Herc was upset. "As long as that won't stand on her toes."

"She has steel-capped boots. My daughter won't feel a thing."

I stumbled into my apartment, tired beyond comprehension. My nose twitched at the aromas filling the kitchen.

What?

Dinner bubbled on the oven top. The table was set. *Two* placemats. My pine-scented candle flickered there.

The last time I saw *that* was when I threw it from the manor window.

"Sascha, honey bear?" I called.

I tensed as he padded from the bedroom, *shirtless* and barefoot, ripped jeans slung low.

Blood rushed in my ears.

"Little bird," he said conversationally, crossing to the cooker. "How was your day?"

Slowly, I set my duffel by the door. "Long. My brain hurts."

"I know the feeling," he murmured as I circled behind him.

My stomach growled and the corner of his mouth crooked.

"It's nearly done."

I sniffed. "What is it?"

And why the fuck are you cooking me dinner?

My eyes wandered over his muscled back. Body fat was a foreign concept to this man. I swallowed.

Hard.

"Spaghetti bolognaise."

"My favourite." I sat at the dining table.

This was another game.

Greyson hadn't made up his mind about my thong stunt. And this was their test—cook me dinner half-naked.

What reaction was he after?

"I prefer men to cook for me naked," I probed. "Forgot to put that on the list."

"What can I say?" the Luther replied. "I'm shy."

Yeah, and I was the Queen of Cusco. Did he want me to feel uncertain? Was that it?

This couldn't be the capture meet... surely.

I ran through Mandy's instructions in case. I had to, *shit*, what was it? Maintain distance. Speak the formal words. Take up that weird position she made me practice.

"Can't say I have issues with shyness." I crossed my legs.

Amusement coloured his voice. "So I saw. My female pack members are quite enamoured of you after yesterday."

Because they were smart enough to realise what I was doing. Had they helped translate my actions for their male leader though? "Were *you* enamoured, honey bear?"

"I was enamoured the first moment I heard your voice. Sweet as chiming bells. A siren's call on a soft, summer breeze."

Uh... Pretty sure I screamed in his face.

He turned, honey eyes in place, but I wasn't fooled for a second.

Greyson was behind this.

I raked his chest with my gaze. "Well, serve dinner, hot stuff. Your woman is starving."

His eyes darkened ever so slightly before a wolfish smile graced his face. He set a glass of red wine in front of me. "Of course... lover."

I forced back laughter, fanning my lashes down. "I'm not sure about that one. People may think we're not forever."

"Mother of my children?"

I moaned. "*That's* more like it. Such a turn-on."

His lips twitched and he got to work. Soon, two plates of pasta and sauce, sprinkled with parmesan steamed before us.

Sascha sat gingerly, staring at the glass top in consternation. "This table is very breakable."

For someone with super strength. Probably, yes.

"How was your day?" I dug in, and my eyes rounded. "Whoa, this is really good."

"My mother's recipe. She looks forward to meeting you again."

I lowered my fork.

He met my gaze steadily.

Did your mum see my ass yesterday? I gathered the answer was yes. My tone was demure. "I hope my mother-in-law approves of me."

He choked on his pasta.

"Be careful, baby daddy." I shoved more pasta in my mouth.

He sipped at his beer, eyeing me.

Greyson was in the driver's seat, lurking under the surface. I *knew* it. The werewolf couldn't seriously believe I'd meant anything from yesterday, but the fact remained that I removed the challenge. My actions drained some of the mounting tension between us. Without it, Greyson couldn't be satisfied for the capture meet.

Ha!

I sipped at my wine, unbuttoning the top of my jeans.

He tracked the movement. "Better now?"

"I recommend you try it. Pasta isn't meant to be eaten in jeans."

Holding my gaze, he unfastened the top of his jeans. I took in the challenge in his eyes.

Is that why he'd come? For a game of chicken?

Game on.

Sascha leaned over. "I hope you're ready to be fucked, Andie Booker."

Christ.

My heart rate skyrocketed.

That fucking escalated.

He searched my face. "You've never been with a werewolf, but don't worry, I'll take care of you. You'll be ruined for human men when I'm done."

"Please ruin me," I managed to say.

He rounded the table.

Sascha Greyson was trying to re-establish the challenge.

He wanted to see how far I'd go, but I had an ace in my hand. This man wouldn't take anything I wasn't willing to give.

Sascha tilted my chin, and I didn't hesitate to stand, grazing my hands up his rigid abs on the way.

His stomach tightened under my touch, and I pressed my advantage, going for the kill. I kissed across his chest, softly biting his nipple.

He hissed, arms clamping down my wandering hands.

I peeked through my lashes. "Is this okay?"

His jaw clenched and after a beat, he eased his grip, hands sliding up my arms. Growling, he jerked me close, lifting me with a hand under my ass, his other arm tight around my waist.

I ground against his erection as he strode through the apartment with me in tow. Sascha inhaled sharply, his eyes never a brighter honey.

"Undress me," I panted on the bed.

Sascha paused briefly, then his hands moved to his jeans. His pants hit the floor.

Underwear apparently wasn't a necessity.

I took in the naked werewolf, ears buzzing. Dragging my gaze upward, I didn't say a word. His lips curled and he gripped my legs, thumbs circling my ankles as he worked his hands higher.

I rested back, arching. Guys loved that shit.

His fingers deftly flicked open the buttons of my shirt, but he left it unopened. Concealing my smirk, I did the honours, shrugging out of it and unclasping my black bra.

My breasts bounced free.

He stopped moving. Maybe breathing.

I didn't budge as Sascha closed the space, his mouth latching onto my nipple.

A soft cry left my lips and I cupped the back of his head, warmth flooding my body. My legs fell open, and a fierce snarl filled him. He drew back, no softness in his expression as his hands moved to the front of my jeans.

Our eyes locked in silent battle.

He wouldn't do it.

I was a Thana. He was a Luther. There were things we couldn't play with.

Sex.

We were pushing this too far.

I didn't move. Sascha's eyes darkened for the slightest moment. *Shit*. I was in this to win. I gripped his hand, directing it to my zipper. He drew it down with a slowness that bordered on painful.

It spoke for how he may do other things.

Tense, I lifted up as he removed my jeans.

"I'm going to make you fly, little bird." He dragged a thumb over my lips. "The town will hear your screams."

"That better be a promise." My fear spiked at the image he painted for me.

His expression faltered for the barest second before he pressed my thighs wide, breaking eye contact as he lowered his head. Sascha ran his nose over my black underwear and I choked on a gasp, clamping my knees around his head.

It was nothing for him to spread them again.

He looked at me.

I recovered. "I'm so sensitive. Don't stop."

He hooked a finger in the crotch of my underwear, and I became aware neither of us were breathing. His honey eyes held mine and I *burned*. He moved my underwear aside, head lowering again.

I could feel his breath on me. It felt incredible, like a promise.

Maybe I could do this and never say anything. Maybe—

"*Stop*," I blurted, squeezing my eyes shut.

Sascha was gone in an instant, and I closed my legs tight.

When I sat, his jeans were back on, but they didn't hide the evidence of his arousal.

Pitch-black eyes regarded me over a subtle smirk.

Fucking damn it!

I smiled sweetly. "I want our first time to be perfect."

Greyson's smirk widened. "My match is cunning."

I grabbed my shirt, shrugging into it. Where did I throw my bra? "No. Your match is just..."

He waited and I clambered off the bed in my underwear and shirt.

"The game is up," he said, voice guttural.

I nearly bolted from the bedroom back into the kitchen.

He stalked after me. "Yesterday was a clever ploy."

"Not a ploy," I gasped. We both knew the charade just imploded. "That should show you what lengths I'm willing to go to for this to stop."

"*This* doesn't stop until we are one."

Heat crept over my jaw. "You said I can say no."

The wolf smiled. "You can, but you won't. Not for much longer. Not in the end. All that stands between us is the world."

He'd said that twice now. "What do you mean?"

I choked as Greyson rushed me, but he merely rested a hand at the base of my throat, palm covering my collarbone.

His lips brushed my ear. "If it were just us, *lover*, then you would already be ours. Nothing will keep us from you for long. And one day, *one day,* you will fight the world to reach us too."

The gentle weight on my collarbone disappeared, and I sagged forward, gasping as the white sheer curtains surged outward.

He was gone.

31

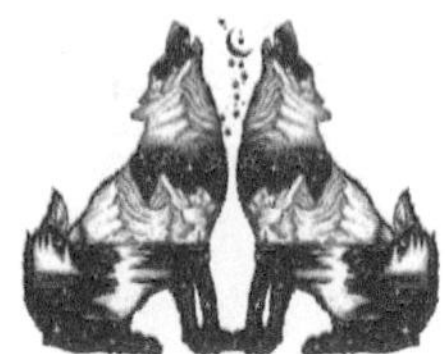

"Just a few notes?" Wade scrolled through the huge memo on my phone.

I snatched it back. "I don't want to forget important stuff."

The stewards gathered every Tuesday night for a grid rundown, but this was my first time at one. Two members of Herc's head team spent the last hour and a half running through the master plan, and I was determined not to miss a thing.

Grey eyes twinkled down at me. "A clear head is important too. Don't stay up all night pouring over this stuff. You need sleep, superwoman."

I blew out a breath. "I'll try."

Did the intensity of this game ever lessen? Because I'd expected nothing could be more nerve-wracking than entering Clay last week.

Wrong.

"You'll shadow Rhona," he reminded me.

My shoulders eased. *True.*

"Better, soulmate?"

"Perhaps." I'd be better when Greyson and Sascha fucked right off. I'd barely slept since he cooked me dinner and I lost *sex chicken*.

What had my life become?

Leaving Wade to find my family, I smiled at Laura and Billy, waving at Roderick and a few other members of the counter-wolf team.

"Andie?"

I glanced at an elderly woman. She leaned heavily on her cane but extended one hand to me.

"I'm Margaret Frey. One of the tribe's historians."

Taking her hand, I shook it. "Oh, nice to meet you. Thanks so much for the book. It's beautifully written. I've just reached Naatira's rule."

The historian's kind eyes lit up. "One of my favourites, and," she moved closer, "your mother always liked her too."

My smile faded. "You knew my mother?"

"I daresay that I did. Your father was my grandson."

My head jerked back. "You're my great-grandmother?"

She chuckled. "We can leave the *great* off, don't you think?"

I searched for something to say and came up blank. I mean, it made sense that Murphy's family would be at these gatherings and in the valley, but had I just been strutting under their noses? In hindsight, that seemed incredibly rude. "I'm sorry for not reaching out sooner."

"Thank you for saying so, but Herc told us you weren't ready to meet. I probably shouldn't have surprised you like this, but I'm old and I must seize opportunities before I expire."

I grinned, brushing my hair back. "It's fine, really. I asked Herc to set up a meeting between us not long ago."

Her gaze lingered on mine. "Indeed. Well, we look forward to hearing from him soon. My son and other grandchildren are wild to meet you."

"I'd love to hear more about my father and mother," I said shyly. I'd never had a great grandmother. Or a grandparent.

My family was growing, and that didn't make me want to run and hide as it once would have.

Margaret's eyes misted. "Your mother's love for this land was unmatched, and I was very sorry to see her and my grandson leave this place—and very glad to see their daughter return. I'd be happy to speak of them both. Perhaps, like your mother, you might feel the inkling to speak on tribe matters of the past and present too. You need only ask if you have any questions about our history."

"Thank you," I whispered around the lump in my throat.

Margaret dipped her head and limped away.

A hand rested on my shoulder.

"Hey, Uncle Herc," I said, watching my *great grandmother* limp away.

"That was Margaret Frey. Are you alright?"

She just gave me another connection to my mother. "She seems really nice."

"I've been meaning to contact them again. Sorry. I'll make sure to do that without delay."

"You've been busy saving the world. I forgive you."

"Then can I ask why you look so serious, niece of mine?"

"Just thinking about Mum."

"Ah."

I'd read her *I'm 17* journal, but she apparently gave up journaling after that. I had so many questions about her childhood and the years before she left Deception Valley. She'd breathed this land—and I wasn't only convinced of that from Herc and Margaret and Mum's friends. I'd *seen* that lost love in my mother, never knowing the cause.

Her occasional despondency.

Her love of nature.

More and more, I understood Mum's heart remained in this place when she left. A part of her died with that decision.

But whatever troubles she'd carried in life shouldn't follow her to death. That wasn't fair for anyone. I now felt secure in the knowledge that people here had loved her and still did. Her journals had proved just how much she loved this valley.

I had the power to free Mum of her decision to leave at last.

"Can I ask you something?" I asked.

"Anything," Uncle Herc answered.

Mustering my courage, I hugged him tight. He stiffened, but soon relaxed, hugging me back.

"I'd like to scatter some of Mum's ashes in the valley. Will you and Rhona come with me?" I listened to the hitch of his breath.

He drew back. Tears sparked his eyes. "It would be our honour."

Any tears I'd cried over my mother were from lack of closure, regret, and that unexplainable guilt that came hand in hand with terminal illness. Scattering Mum's ashes was something I didn't need to cry about though.

This felt right.

"This is a bad time."

"It's never a bad time." Herc cut me off. "Have you got her ashes with you?"

Since a certain werewolf started stealing my stuff? "Yes."

I'd moved her ashes into a zip-lock bag and stashed it in my sax case. Sascha wouldn't steal the saxophone I needed for work. Though after Mandy's *his wolf doesn't acknowledge rules* speech, there wasn't a chance in hell of me leaving my sax alone in the apartment either.

"How about we find Rhona and rest your mother where she belongs?" Herc said.

"I'd like that." Then maybe my heart would feel lighter at last.

Mine, and Herc's.

He guided me through the crowd, and Rhona took one look at my face before making her excuses to Foley and our unit.

She grabbed my hand when Herc explained what was happening.

"Do you have a place in mind?" he asked as we left the other stewards behind.

"If you know of a spot Mum loved, that would be great. I'd like to eventually put a headstone for her close to Grandmother Charise's."

Herc was silent, and I watched the struggle on his face. "Of course."

I grabbed my saxophone case from the car. "Okay, ready."

"She's in there?" Rhona asked, snorting.

Herc's brows rose when I nodded. Perhaps that seemed strange when a stalking werewolf was removed from the equation.

We followed Herc through the manor and out the back. We trekked an easy trail behind the training pavilions and cabins. Eventually, the trees parted to frame a meadow blanketed in the soft rays of last sunshine.

"Beautiful," I whispered.

Herc's voice was thick. "Ragna loved this meadow. She came here to read and write in her journal."

Mum wrote here? I closed my eyes, drawing forth her words. Her woes and complaints—the small and large excitements in her life. I could just imagine her here in the summer furiously jotting thoughts on paper.

I opened my eyes and watched Herc cross to a large red oak.

"Right here," he said. "Hours at a time. Whenever our parents couldn't find her, we'd search this spot. Ragna's Meadow, Mum called it."

The grass beyond the tree line sat knee-high, rustling in smooth waves. The meadow was straight out of *Bambi*—a movie I'd watched alongside my mother at least fifty times when young. That made this space special in a way unique to me too—which relieved an anxiety I hadn't realised was there.

"It's beautiful enough for my mother," I said at last.

"What was she like?" Rhona asked, hands shoved in her jacket as she stood by the red oak.

I couldn't trust myself to speak for a long beat. I forced away the burning in my eyes. Turned out this *was* a crying occasion. "She was..." *Broken.* "Joy. Fierce joy."

My voice cracked, and I knelt to open my saxophone. Passing the instrument to Rhona, I eased back the lining, pulling out the insert that kept the saxophone snug and safe. The plastic baggie was beneath, and I took it in my hands.

My mother was inside.

I had to say goodbye to the part of her that belonged in this meadow, but I didn't feel strong enough to part with all of her tonight.

"Just some," I told them. "I'd like to keep her close too."

Herc's voice was hoarse. "Whatever you need, Andie."

"Will you play first?" Rhona held up my sax. "Your music must have been important to Ragna if you kept her ashes in there. We've never heard you."

More to stave off the moment of farewell, I handed Mum's ashes to Herc, who hesitated before cradling the bag in both hands.

Slipping the neck strap over my head, I wet the reed, taking a breath that didn't fill me. Mum's funeral was a farce, really. She hadn't deserved to be alone for the goodbye or for things to be so damn silent.

Maybe I'd expected more at the time. To find acceptance or...

I had no idea what. But I didn't get it.

The song was a no-brainer. Mum always requested one in particular.

Standing beneath the red oak, I closed my eyes and played the sombre opening notes of "From Now On," a song from *The Greatest Showman*. Mum fell in love with the movie, and while I'd always felt more connected to "This is Me," Hugh Jackman brought tears to Mum's eyes with this number.

I imagined the choir behind me and the slap of drums as the song built in my chest and heart, the dramatic music flying from the bell of my sax. The song of regret and resolve soared through the meadow, filling the air as my mother filled my life.

She'd always be here. In this valley.

And with me.

Softening the final bars, I held the last note, lowering my sax. I didn't brush away my twin tracks of tears, and neither did Herc.

Rhona sniffed, rubbing at her face.

"A beautiful gift," Herc croaked. "And a beautiful gift for your mother."

I set the sax in the case and took the bag back. Opening the zip-lock, I drew forth my favourite memory of Mum.

Nothing specific. Nothing outlandish.

Just the moments we'd spent in the garden when she had cancer, talking about this and that.

Just her company.

Maybe cancer stole her away too early, but we'd appreciated each moment together after her diagnosis until the end. Not everyone could say the same. Long-term illnesses took so much, but they gave us that—a warning.

I sprinkled half of her ashes around the base of the tree in a circle and stood between my uncle and cousin.

Herc did his best to remain silent at first. I wrapped an arm around his shaking shoulders, squeezing tight.

Rhona stepped forward, looking at the red-leaf tree illuminated by the dying sun.

"I didn't know you, Aunt Ragna. But you gave us Andie, and I'll always be grateful to you for that. Be at peace."

Uncle Herc approached and bowed his head, not speaking aloud. It was fine. I'd had my moment in silence too.

Rhona lingered by my side when her father faced us, wiping his face.

"Thank you, Andie," he said. "That meant more than you know."

I could see that. "Don't feel guilty about the past. My mother made her choices and you made yours. Guilt and regret are so small in the scheme of things." Our lives were a grain of dirt on the forest floor. Almost insignificant.

He gazed at me, attention shifting to Rhona for an instant. He opened his mouth and started speaking, only to shake his head and stop.

Herc encompassed us both in his arms. "I love you both."

Releasing us, he left the meadow.

"My mother played the piano," Rhona said suddenly.

I took her hand. "I bet she played beautifully."

"No, it sounded fucking awful. But... I miss it. And her voice. Terrible too. I miss that most of all."

My cousin dropped her gaze, and I set my forehead to hers.

"Where do you see your mother now?" I whispered. "I see mine in the air. She was so free-spirited."

Rhona exhaled. “Mum anchored me and Dad. Made us better people. I don’t feel complete without her. She was my earth, I guess.

“It’s okay to miss someone who’s gone. You’re incredible, Rhona. Never forget it.”

“I’m not kind like she was.”

“If you’re fierce, it’s because you’re loyal and willing to give your all. Don’t lose yourself on the scale of someone else’s personality. Even an amazing person.”

She was quiet and we swayed, forehead to forehead until the sun disappeared.

“Sleepover tonight?” she asked quietly.

My cousin felt like an extension of myself sometimes. “Sleepover.”

I glanced back at the red oak.

I felt lighter.

32

"Will this thing make it up the hill?" Cameron asked over the whine of the engine.

Her question was valid.

"This *thing* has a name. Ella F will get us there," I said, inwardly quaking. That really didn't sound good.

Driving Wade, Cameron, and Rhona to Sandstone seemed like a good idea to calm myself before Grids, but the steep terrain had Ella F shook.

My passengers were silent as the Corolla crested each peak.

I snuck a look at Rhona. Dark circles smudged beneath her eyes, and I suspected mine were the same. Wade's advice on sleep was soundly ignored last night, but what I'd shared with my cousin seemed like something I'd remember for the rest of my life. We'd talked until the early hours about our mothers.

When I looked at her, I couldn't feel any walls between us. *This* was what it felt like to trust someone.

I trusted Rhona.

I became aware of Wade's laser focus.

"On your period?" he asked.

That's what contraceptive arm implants were for. "No."

"Good. Because wolves can smell it."

My jaw dropped. "For real?"

"Probably."

Cameron whacked his thigh as I navigated a tight hairpin turn. "You're a dick."

He smirked. "Just keeping it real."

"Will we arrive in time, cuz?" Rhona sounded as bored as always.

I patted Ella F. "Unsure."

She snorted, resuming her vigil out of the window.

I made the turn to Thana Reserve at last, ignoring Wade's sarcastic celebrations as my nerves returned a hundredfold. Greyson hadn't reared his head, and nothing was amiss in Rhona's room when I woke this morning.

My belongings were accounted for without any expensive, stalker additions.

Given the ending of our last meeting, his absence just made my stomach churn.

Parking behind a black Jeep, I shivered, remembering the way Sascha hooked my panties, drawing them aside. His mouth lowering. Those honey eyes—

"Who are you thinking about?" Cameron blurted.

My gaze flew to hers in the rear-view mirror. "What?"

She turned to Wade, fanning her face. "Andie's having a wet daydream."

"Probably about the guy who left a signed record and player in her room the other day."

Ugh, shit.

Rhona rose both brows.

"Nope. Not thinking about anyone." I threw open my door.

We grabbed our packs from the boot, and I ignored their digging questions as we joined the swelling mass of stewards. Unlike Clay and Timber, we only entered this grid from one side.

Changing into our cream latex and linen ball-sac uniforms, Rhona and I located our unit near the quarry frontline. My cousin ran through her checks on our protective vests and climbing harnesses, checking her own after.

"Anyone feel like a ninja turtle with these on?" Billy tapped on the white ballistic shield covering his back—a new addition after the drones.

The shield wasn't as restrictive as I'd expected. Running and climbing with it shouldn't be too hard.

"Why do the ninja turtles wear masks?" Foley asked. "The masks don't hide shit. They're walking and talking *turtles*. Picking them out of a line-up wouldn't be hard, you know?"

Ignoring the banter, I swept a hand over my ropes and carabiners and searched my pockets to locate smaller gear. The goal was to fumble *less* this week and run faster.

If I managed not to hang myself on the cliffs, that'd be awesome.

Dang. Vomiting was a very real future for me.

"Taken your vertigo meds?" Rhona asked.

"Yep." I breathed thinly, focusing on slow exhales as Herc called for quiet.

"*Sandstone*," he began, red hair visible over the masses. "We've controlled this grid for over fifty years. During that time, the wolves have thrown all manner of strategies our way. Many times, they've come close to overthrowing us, always falling short. This is such a time. For centuries, *stewards* have stood where you stand now, in *your very footsteps*. This is our time. We will protect this land and those contained within it. Today, we honour what our tribe stands for. Today, we fight for the right to protect this land—"

It never ceased to amaze me—that moment when the mood shifted from game to battle. I felt it within me today. This land was in my blood. These people too.

Roderick was right. The Luthers had their own agenda. My job was to focus on our plan. I had to trust this tribe—because the alternative was to act as an individual and screw our chances.

I couldn't let my uncle and cousin down.

Herc held up a fist. "—*Today,* we show our enemy that their best tricks aren't enough. This land flows in our blood!"

I shouted with the others.

Energy thrummed under my skin, unable to be contained. I fidgeted on the spot between Billy and Laura until Rhona beckoned me over.

"Any questions?" she asked.

I shook my head. "Nope. Just want to start."

"You'll be fine."

Glancing at her, I took in her earnest face. She didn't show that side of herself to many. "I trust you, Rhona."

She stilled.

"Completely."

Her voice trembled. "I won't let you down. And ditto—on the trust thing."

I squeezed her forearm gently. "I won't let you down either. Not ever."

"Not ever," Rhona echoed.

It was as much of a vow as I'd ever made to another person, and the air almost buzzed between us.

Boom.

Her grin was immediate, and I felt my lips spread in a grin of my own.

We were both crazy.

"Let's take the furry fuckers down," she shouted.

I sprinted behind her, pride touching my shoulders as I managed not to drop my lungs out my ass. My speed still needed work, but *better*. Much better.

Ascending and descending tiers extended either side as we ran across the flat middle strip of the ground level. After the last game here, most of the middle tiers were missing from each side—blown to smithereens. The rubble from the landslide had been cleared, so we settled into a rapid pace, dodging fifteen traps before we reached our position in the middle of the grid.

Our hour blurred by at a dangerous pace as we arranged a new trap. We covered two new quarry cuts with camouflaged cloth that mimicked our uniforms, disguising the edges with slabs of sandstone.

This week, the teams hadn't messed around and a new level of savagery had been unleashed. This was a *detaining trap*. A bear trap rested in the bottom of the pit, but this one couldn't be pried apart—not without the twin keys on Pascal's belt. The thought of Mandy or Hairy—or even Leroy stuck in the trap made me feel sick.

I shook off my unease, trying to remember the Luthers survived a literal *landslide* three weeks ago.

Herc said I had to get rid of my human qualms.

"Our turn," Rhona said as I returned from setting out frequency generators. "Masks on, everyone."

I slid mine on, and our unit ran at a fast clip toward the wolves' starting point. My heart hammered faster at the thought of Greyson watching from the tree line.

The cherry picker was waiting.

We usually rock-climbed all the way to the top. Each time, the Luthers destroyed our ropes. This idea would save some money while also giving those groups who had to run to the middle and end of the quarry more time to build new traps.

Filing out on the top tier, our unit spread in a line facing the cliff.

"Up we go," Rhona called. Turning to me, she checked my gear again, setting a frequency generator in a small crevice by our heads. "Remember, complete stillness when you're in position. You've got this, Andie."

I was involved in a shitstorm involving guns, werewolves, and ball-sac uniforms.

Anchoring my rope, I lined up with the vertical crack in the sandstone, tying myself in with a trace-eight knot. Gerry couldn't take credit for that.

Thank you, Girl Guides.

Most of the climbing nuts were in place from the last game. I checked my harness and hooked a carabiner on the first nut, giving it a sharp tug. Tying a figure-eight knot next, I set a foot into an indent, reaching to attach a carabiner to the next nut. *Tug. Knot. Reach. Clip. Repeat.* The rest of my unit were several meters above me, and I tried not to let that bother me as I secured a missing nut and another.

Stewards had climbed these rockfaces for longer than I'd been born and at least the holds were well developed and easy to find, especially with my long reach.

"Nice stuff," Rhona murmured when I reached my position, breathing hard.

I made it.

We'd staggered ourselves along this stone face. Rhona and I were positioned just below the top edge. Less than a metre above my head, the quarry tipped into a forest plateau.

There couldn't be long until the second cannon.

I quickly attached myself to two nuts on the left and two on the right and faced outward from the cliff. The rope drew taut along my stomach. Doing this was about the most nerve-wracking thing *ever*—even if the vertigo medication steadied my vision. Who wanted to look out into thin air?

Gross.

I tied off with shaking hands—grossly aware no one was moving but me. I relaxed my weight onto the belaying station.

Feeling for my white tranquiliser gun, I held it amidst the strips of red, white, and tan linen hanging from my uniform.

And *stilled.*

Hood on and hair covered, I closed my eyes, focusing on quietening my breath. Seriously, could Rhona hear me sucking in gulps? Or Laura, three metres to my left and two metres down?

Maybe it didn't matter if they did. I only had to fool one wolf.

His sense of smell shouldn't be a factor with the wolfsbane I'd sprayed over my uniform. That meant I had to keep my mouth shut so he couldn't recognise my *siren* voice. Hopefully the ball-sac garment and bug lenses made it harder for him to locate me—with the colour blindness factored in too.

Boom.

My heartbeat surged with the cannon.

Ninety minutes. I just had to get through the next ninety minutes. And when Grids finished, I'd set my mind to another plan to get rid of this breeding call crap.

Maybe I should try to tell Herc again.

I didn't trust his reaction before, but now—after spreading Mum's ashes—I couldn't imagine him turning his back on me for something out of my control.

Or anything at all.

I should ask him for help.

The Luthers didn't rush into the grids, so the pounding stampede from Clay was absent, replaced with the echoing whisper of seven hundred werewolves creeping fifty metres below.

Stay still.

I slitted my eyes and spotted the first werewolves against the far cliff face. In our section, the tiers were intact—which was why Rhona's kickass unit was assigned.

Herc's voice crackled in my ear. "*Prepare for Phase One.*"

This was a decoy. And research.

We took a recording of Sascha's howls in Clay.

I curled my fingers around my tranquiliser gun, determined not to waste darts or take five minutes to fire the damn thing.

I'd practiced drawing it all day, much to Wade's amusement.

The recorded howl blasted through the grid. I celebrated in silence as Luthers exploded up the cliffs, falling for the ruse.

"*Initiate Phase One,*" Herc crackled in my ear.

I unclipped my gun and set my sights on a wolf paused in confusion on the lip of the first tier. She was looking back in response to the *real* howl from her leader.

I darted her in the stomach, moving to the next.

Managing to land another shot before the wolves regained their lines, I grimaced at Sascha's next howl.

With the echo, pinpointing his position was impossible.

He could be anywhere.

I licked my lips.

Sascha howled again, and then they really began. My chest tightened at the ringing of claw scraping sandstone.

I waited for the first wolves to appear over the lowest ledge, breath shaking.

"Open fire."

I shot at a male, tracking him when he dodged and rolled. *Pop. Pop.* I caught him in the thigh and moved on, shooting until the first wave of Luthers reached the protection of the next cliff face and I lost sight of them.

The second wave came, appearing on the lowest edge.

Another recorded howl rang out and they paused on the edge to glance back. The stewards around me wasted no time picking off the confused werewolves and neither did I.

Roderick, you're my hero. The recordings were his idea.

"*Luthers gathering at the middle tier,*" Rhona's voice crackled in my ear.

They were?

Ah, fuck. I really hoped that was a coincidence.

"*They have shields.*" Herc said. "*Keep your aim low.*"

Bitchholes.

I relied on a large target to land my shots.

"*Prepare for Operation Happy Birthday,*" he added.

On the other side of Laura, Billy drew a grappling gun from the sling on the cliff beside him. I held my breath as he took aim.

A red dot appeared on the X on the opposite quarry cliffs. He fired, the *crack* exploding through the air.

Three more *cracks* followed shortly after.

Four ropes extended across the quarry like flying foxes. Excitement rose up my throat. That plan seemed impossible when I first heard it.

"*Drones incoming,*" Herc said.

I rolled to face the wall, curling my knees so my body was mostly covered by the white ballistic shield.

The drones whined overhead. and I gasped as darts rained on the hard plastic. *Ninja turtles for the win.*

The whining burr had barely finished when Herc roared in my ear.

"*Initiate Operation Happy Birthday.*"

Shit!

I rolled to face out again, awkwardly raising my gun as Billy fixed a balloon onto our flying fox. He sent it flying and our unit took aim.

I had no idea whose dart hit the balloon—likely not mine—but the balloon exploded, showering wolfsbane over the Luthers below.

No time to think.

I shot at Billy's next balloon and another before the first wave of Luthers appeared on the second tier. They had shields, but most were affected by the bane, rubbing at their faces and sneezing.

Breath harsh, I lined up one werewolf after the next, aiming for what I could see of their legs and shoulders. Snarls and the tell-tale *pop* of our guns filled the air, punctuated by the scraping of claw on stone.

Their shields slammed together, creating a ceiling on the ledge below. I stared at the wall of solid black.

Fuck.

I aimed for the cracks, gritting my teeth as darts *pinged* uselessly off their defences.

"*Prepare for Bar Hop,*" Herc said.

Smiling grimly, I waited for Laura and Rhona to extract and drop their canisters before I stopped firing to grab my own. Ripping the pin out, I dropped the canister on the Luthers. The can bounced twice before it rolled under their shield wall.

A series of sharp hisses rose as the canisters started their job. Shrieks and moans rang out as wolfsbane gas permeated their ranks.

A sinister *growl* burst from beneath me.

My heart dropped.

Oh my god.

That was him.

How the fuck did he find me so quickly?

As wolves fell to their knees, I fired, searching. *Where are you, you bastard?*

The Luthers hardly broke rank as the hissing continued, holding their shields high even as their legs gave way.

"*Initiate Bar Hop.*"

I watched the Luthers closely for signs. Our human ears were too weak to notice that Herc just deactivated the frequency generators in one quadrant of the quarry.

Almost as one, the wolves turned south to where I imagined a wave of noise just rose.

Confusion. That's what we'd hoped to create today until we could locate Sascha.

The wolves peered around as Herc moved through the quadrants at random, turning the generators on and off. It had to be hugely disorientating.

An eerie howl lifted the hairs on the back of my neck.

Sascha Greyson just revealed himself.

Rhona grinned at me, winking as she spoke into her walkie-talkie.

This was it.

There wasn't *any* way Sascha could stay conscious through what we were about to throw at him. But he wasn't a normal man, and Greyson ruled seven hundred and fifty other wolves because he was more powerful than them all.

I swallowed back the urge to turn tail and run. That was my last resort.

"*Prepare Operation Valley,*" Herc said.

Shit. Okay, this was my job. Well, it worked out that way, and I'd known it would be likely with Greyson stalking me.

Rhona and Laura covered my area as I reached into a knee pocket and drew out a red powder ball.

Holding out my arm, I relaxed my grip, watching the ball fall. Red powder exploded over Sascha's shield.

Herc roared, "*Initiate Operation Valley.*"

Laura and Rhona fired nets at our target. The surrounding wolves fell away as we pinned him to the ground. While the unit fired on the surrounding Luthers, I dropped another canister.

We couldn't kill Sascha, so while opening fire on him was tempting, the reality was that too much sedative would cause his death.

Rhona was the designated gunwoman. She took aim, firing twice, but Leroy intercepted the shots with his shield.

Dammit!

A terrible, menacing howl surged from below. I couldn't be the only one whose heart *seized*.

Shields covered Greyson, and the Luthers began to *stamp*.

In time.

Slow.

One foot after the other. *Hundreds of werewolves.*

I caught Rhona's veiled look, but my dread increased with the terrifying tempo. Snarling, Sascha broke free of the fucking *reinforced* and bane-soaked nets. His wolves stood back, drawing their shields away.

Rhona wasn't frozen in horror. She fired at him again. Claws extending in a flash—Sascha batted the darts away like flies.

Oh, fuck.

Should I shoot too?

Whoops and cheers swelled deeper with the stamping that shook the entire quarry, and I knew, I just fucking *knew* this was it.

This was the capture meet.

Sascha Greyson craned his head and regarded me with pitch-black eyes, slicing at the incoming darts without looking.

He shifted his eyes to Rhona.

Oh. Fuck.

He didn't know which of us was which.

I lifted my gun and opened fire on him too.

"You're going down, fucker," Rhona yelled.

I closed my eyes. *No.*

Opening them, I met Greyson's menacing smirk. Our gazes locked for a heavy instant.

He punched his claws into the sandstone fifteen metres below me.

Jumping, he punched into the cliff again. *Higher.*

This couldn't happen here! I—

Shit!

I rolled to face the cliff and worked at the knots. They pulled free easily, but I'd left my exit too late.

I listened to Greyson puncture his way toward me, pace slow and steady. Torturous.

He wanted me to know I was caught.

And I knew it without a doubt.

"Andie," Rhona whispered

"He's after me," I choked.

"Not on my watch." She spoke into her walkie. Nodding once, she peered downward. I released the fourth knot and reached high for the top ledge.

The rope attaching me to the last nut didn't give.

Confused, I stared at Greyson who held tight to my rope below, smirking.

I reached for my gun. Fucker only had two hands.

Ward these off, asshole.

"*Now*," Rhona's voice crackled.

A grappling hook slammed him in the shoulder. His body rocketed to the side as he roared. Some pain, but mostly *fury*. Greyson clung to my rope, and the extra weight tore my grip from the top ledge.

I fell, but my scream cut short as the top nut saved me.

Eyes wide, I fumbled for purchase. Gripping the cliff with one hand, I worked at the knot on my harness. There was nothing for it. I had to get the fuck out of here.

The stamping and roaring from the wolves hadn't abated. They screamed for their leader as he came for me.

The knot came free, and I gasped, toes curling in their holds. *Don't look down.*

I pulled myself upward, hooking a forearm over the top. Panting, I swung a leg up, rolling to safety.

Relative safety.

The horrible grating of claw puncturing sandstone began once more.

He was climbing. And he was injured.

Shoving to my feet, I ran into the forest, breathing hard. The harness jangled and I loosened it as I ran, stopping for a precious few seconds to get rid of it. I continued running from tree to tree, slowing as the noise from the quarry ebbed.

This cream uniform was fucking useless out here. Behind a pine tree, I quietly stripped to my black tank and shorts.

Crack.

I crouched, battling the urge to steal a peak.

"Andie," Greyson's gravelled voice wound through the trees.

Too close.

I looked to where my gun rested on my ball-sac uniform. I couldn't fight him with that shit.

In reality, I had *no* physical chance against this werewolf.

I just had my brain.

Biting my lip, I stepped out from behind the tree.

He stood two tree-lengths from me and made no move to close the gap. Blood covered his body, and I swallowed at the gaping wound on his shoulder.

Pitch-black eyes.

"Greyson," I said. "Here I am."

"*Mate*," he growled.

I locked my knees, knowing a retreat would egg the predator on. "What did you say?"

The wolf circled me. "My heart. My soul. My only. *My mate*."

My *only*.

No.

No way. That was a lot more fucking serious than *breeding call.*

"What?" My face numbed. "That's not what this is. This call happens all the time. You said—"

Greyson shook.

My insides curled and died. Shaking only meant one thing.

My brain wasn't cutting it!

I *bolted,* gasping at the *cracks* and *snarls* ripping behind me. Leaping over tree roots, I dodged through the forest as though my life depended on it.

Because it did.

A howl went up at my back.

He was coming. Stopping beside large rocks, I glanced around. A tree? I'd seen how far Luthers could jump.

I spotted a crack in the rocks and wedged into it. The idea served me well in Clay. Inside, I covered my mouth, squeezing my eyes shut. There weren't any frequency generators up here.

Nothing stirred the woods except the faint booms and shouts from the quarry that told me Grids continued. That didn't mean Rhona or the others wouldn't follow me out here.

Fuck.

Rhona would definitely come.

If she found me, she'd encounter a shifted Luther who viewed me as his one-and-only mate. He didn't kill me last time he changed, but by the skittish reactions of his pack that day in the kitchen, I got the feeling Greyson didn't mess around.

I could run all damn night, but I couldn't outrun this wolf.

And he'd known that all along.

What will you do when you realise outrunning me is futile?

I rested my forehead against the cold rock, balling my hands to fists.

Damn it all.

I'd face him. That's what I'd do.

Bracing myself, I left the safety of my crevice, peering through the forest. Where was he?

"Greyson," I called with a calmness I didn't feel.

Dirt crumbled on my head. Whirling, I stared at the huge dark-brown wolf resting on top of my hiding place.

Yawning, he rose to his full height and I swallowed hard at the massive creature. He leapt down and I shrieked, tripping over a rock to land on my ass.

The wolf limped to stand over me, honey eyes burning.

He lowered his head to mine and growled. Gasping for breath, I arched my neck, straining to get away from him.

I froze as he moved his teeth to my neck. Hot breath coated my skin, and I whimpered at the brush of teeth against my throat.

"Please don't," I whispered.

Greyson growled louder, taking my throat in his mouth.

I shuddered against the impulse to pull away. "Do it then, fucker."

His teeth cut into my skin, and I *really* stopped moving then. "What is it you want? Submission? Fine, you fucking win. You—" I broke off, feeling the truth of my next words to my very bones. "You caught me."

And the physical part of that capture affected me the *least.*

He released his hold and I fell heavy to the ground.

Greyson licked a long line up my neck. I shoved at his shoulders and he yelped, backing away.

Oops, his wound.

Cracks and *pops* sounded as the wolf shifted.

I hugged my legs to my chest, staring at my knees. When I lifted my head, Sascha crouched. Naked.

He wasn't smiling. The Luther looked about as grim as I felt.

"You are captured, *mate*," Sascha said in smooth tones.

I arched suddenly, cheeks flushing. Heat flooded my body, and I swept my hands down to my thighs, moaning at the feeling.

His words meant nothing. He needed to *touch* me.

Sascha.

I locked eyes with him, and he went predatorily still, nostrils flaring. Rising to my knees, I parted my lips, battling with the wave of lust consuming me.

My chest rose and fell fast, and a low cry tumbled from my lips.

I wanted him.

More than *anything*, I wanted this man. Inside me. On top of me. Beneath me.

I—

He stepped forward, and I panted, slapped with a molten wave that sent me sprawling to the ground.

I had to—

I clutched my head and rolled to put distance between us. *Distance.*

The position.

On my knees, I bowed my head, extending my hand, palms up to either side like some sorry version of Cleopatra.

What were the words? My legs shook with need.

I moaned the chant. "*Doore koh e baka.*"

Heat drained from my body in a rush, and my sigh of relief was half sob. I lowered my chin, panting hard.

It was over.

A warm hand tilted my face. Sascha crouched before me. Weary beyond measure, I didn't resist his touch, peering into his bright honey eyes.

"You're safe, mate."

"Don't call me that."

Sascha's eyes flickered.

Whatever my fears, I could appreciate that he hadn't asked for this either. I *believed* him on that front. There was no sane reason for Sascha to continue this farce unless he had no power to stop it.

I placed my hand over his where he still held my chin.

He shuddered at my touch.

"Thank you." I whispered.

"You're welcome," he murmured, searching my face. "Might I ask what for?"

Air lodged in my throat. "For showing me how to protect myself. I know you didn't ask for any of this either."

He seemed entranced by the feel of my skin as he traced my jaw. "I'll rest easier knowing you did so even as I yearn for another outcome in my heart."

My lashes fluttered closed. This was so messed up. "Is your shoulder okay?"

"It will be, little bird. Don't worry about that."

The blood covering his entire body said otherwise. And he wasn't using that arm to touch me.

"Let go of her, dog."

I jerked, spinning on my knees. "Uncle Herc!"

Sascha wrapped an arm around my middle, drawing me against him. I elbowed him, trying to establish distance.

This didn't look good. *Fuck!*

"There's something we must discuss, Hercules," Sascha clasped me to his front.

Herc trained his gun over my head. "Oh, I'm well aware of what *this* is."

I stilled. "You know?"

He didn't look at me. "I've heard of it before. Release her now, Luther. Or I shoot. I'd rather lose a grid than see this happen to her."

Lose a grid? What did he mean?

I studied his gun, stomach churning. The weapon was far smaller than our tranquiliser guns. "Uncle Herc. Is that a real gun?"

"Yes. *Release her.* Andie, come here."

"This isn't what it looks like," I said in desperation. "It's something that Sascha isn't in control of either, but if we move through these meets, and I say no, it will go away."

Herc met my gaze then, and it was like looking at a stranger. "Is that what he told you?"

I stiffened.

Sascha's grip was borderline painful. "She will always have a choice."

"Against monsters, there is no choice. You've shown my family that time and again." White fury filled the lines on his face, and I was far less scared of the werewolf at my back than my uncle in that moment.

"It's okay, little bird," Sascha whispered in my ear. "You're safe. Just stay back here for me."

With a rush of wind, he *moved.* The grip on my middle disappeared.

A gun fired, and Sascha jerked.

"No," I screamed, knees buckling.

Uncle Herc's gaze slid to me, and I read the confusion there before Sascha swiped, sending him flying backward into a tree.

He rolled, bringing the gun up again. I rushed forward, stopping short as my uncle trained the gun on *me*.

"What are you doing?" I lifted both hands.

"Your argument isn't with her, human," Sascha snarled, clutching his stomach wound.

Herc's voice shook. "This isn't one-sided."

My breaths were shallow and fast. "What do you mean?"

"You almost had me convinced." His eyes shifted to Sascha.

"I don't know what you're talking about." My voice climbed higher.

"Tell me, niece. I'm going to kill this beast. Will you stop me?"

He aimed at Sascha once more, and I couldn't help my panicked shriek.

My uncle smiled. "I thought not. But we can still fix you. *You* can live without him."

"That's a lie," Sascha growled.

"Oh, but it's not," he said grimly. "I've seen it."

He fired.

I moved to insert myself between them. *Ridiculous*. I couldn't beat a bullet. But every fibre of my being tried to.

Sascha blurred and a third shot rent the air before a sickening *crack* summoned a silence I'd only experienced once before. All sound from the forest fled, and a finality crawled out from the earth like a disjointed horror.

Just like the silence after Mum's death.

Sascha dropped Herc to the ground, and I stared at the abnormal angle of his neck.

A numbness seeped into my bones as a cannon boomed in the distance.

The black-eyed Luther glanced at me, face impassive.

"You killed him," I said, unable to tear my gaze from my uncle.

The werewolf staggered, dropping to a knee.

"You killed him," I repeated as footsteps pounded toward us through the forest. "You killed my uncle."

Leroy crashed through the trees, looking at me first before dropping to Sascha's side. He swore at Herc's body.

His body.

That unlocked me.

I staggered forward, tripping over a rock before I managed to crawl to my uncle's side. My eyes fixed on his head, reversed on his shoulders, part of it torn clean off the body.

My breath shuddered high in my throat as I reached—needlessly—to feel for a pulse.

"Uncle Herc?" I whispered.

Others gathered behind me. I didn't care.

"Where is she?"

I jerked. *Rhona.*

I died inside.

Rhona.

Wiping my face, I grabbed Herc's head. No child should see their parent ruined like this. Gagging at the sound, I twisted until he faced upward.

His blue eyes were wide and for a moment, they looked into mine, his disgust and accusation blasting into me in death.

I turned to face the silent Luthers. A wolf I didn't know tended to Sascha.

I didn't care.

Rhona burst into the clearing alone. She breathed a sigh of relief as she caught sight of me.

"Rhona," I said.

She stopped in her tracks, looking closer. "What's wrong? What happened?"

I'd never done this. I'd been in the *my mother has a long-term illness* position. Not this. Never *this.*

Crossing to Rhona, I blocked her view. Taking my cousin in my arms, I held her tight. "There was a fight."

She pushed away, gripping my forearms. "Andie, where's my father?"

Tears flowed down my cheeks. I forced the words out. "He's gone."

She stared past me, a low cry leaving her as she spotted his limp form.

Closing my eyes, I listened as my cousin began to scream.

33

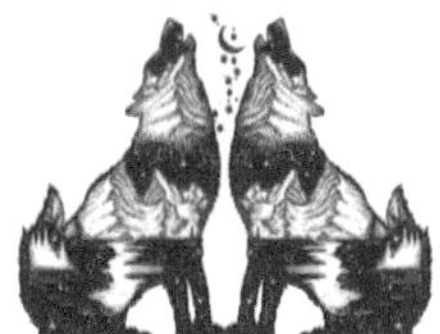

I sat beside my cousin in what used to be her father's office. It would be Rhona's now, when she took up the mantle.

The Luthers had agreed to a week off Grids for the tribe to grieve.

And for Sascha to heal, no doubt.

"The people in this valley loved your father," I said, watching dust trickle through the sunlight streaming inside.

She gripped my hand tighter. "They did."

Three days and Rhona hadn't spoken much. I couldn't blame her. She'd lost her sole remaining parent. She'd become an orphan.

All I felt was anger.

Anger at myself.

Anger at Sascha.

Anger that Rhona had started to heal, and the world dealt her this blow.

Herc's death was my fault. Maybe I didn't intend for this to happen, but I should have told him what was going on.

It was my idiocy that got us here. My determination not to accept help.

I'd never forgive myself.

And yet an idiot I still was—because I couldn't bear to tell Rhona the truth.

Not yet.

How could I ever say the words?

"Can you tell me what happened again?" she croaked.

Only I got to see her this way. Outside of four walls and a shut door, she was the same old Rhona.

It made me realise just how much of a mask her adopted persona was.

It made me realise that Herc was wrong about his daughter.

She *was* a leader.

I breathed in, running through a story I'd told at least ten times to her and the head team. "Sascha Greyson ran after me into the forest and I hid between two rocks. It was quiet for so long, I crept out. He was there—in wolf form. Then Uncle Herc arrived with a gun. He shot the Luther, and the wolf attacked. It all happened so fast, and then he was just gone."

I dropped my chin to my chest. "It's my fault."

She squeezed my hand tighter. "Whatever this was, it was *not* your fault. I should have protected you. You were my charge."

Herc had ordered Rhona to hold the lines when she tried to follow me.

"Dad *knew* that bastard had something planned for you. He had to. I've never known him to carry a real gun anywhere. Especially not onto the grid."

The head team had handled the negotiations in the wake of Herc's death. He'd brought an illegal weapon into the game. Sascha's injuries were serious and sustained which would usually mean a loss of points for *us*, but he'd killed Herc which meant the loss of a grid for them—a lucky thing, as they'd won Sandstone by three points.

The Luthers had argued that their leader was protecting himself. We'd argued that I'd needed Herc's protection from *him*.

I just couldn't believe a person had died and his life was being quantified like that.

"I'm going to kill him one day," Rhona whispered low. "I'll win the game first. Then I'll kill him with my bare hands."

If someone murdered my mother, I'd want vengeance. "Rhona. I can't play Grids anymore."

She faced me. "No."

"I'm a liability." The capture meet was over, but there were more meets coming, and I had no idea what they involved. This *thing* between me and Sascha Greyson wasn't over. He considered me his only mate.

Herc was right. I'd never have a choice in the end result.

With time, I could find an out. I *had* to find an out. But I couldn't bring more harm to my cousin or the stewards.

Rhona gripped my hand. "You're blaming yourself for something that was out of your control."

I squeezed my eyes closed.

"What you consider a liability could prove a *strength* for this tribe. If Sascha wants revenge for you spying in his stupid casino, we can use that to our advantage."

I met her gaze, so like my own. "I can't bear for anyone else to be hurt because of me."

Her lower lip trembled. "My father knew the risk of being a Thana. He knew that our reason for being here in this valley meant more than our lives."

I'd rather lose a grid than see this happen to her. What Herc saw and assumed about me and Sascha had disgusted him.

I was disgusting.

"Promise me that you won't leave me, Andie," Rhona said, voice cracking.

With my thumb, I brushed away her tears. "What did I tell you? I won't let you down. Not ever."

"I already let you down. And Dad."

"I can tell you categorically that you didn't let anyone down. *No one.* You obeyed your father's order. You think he'd have wanted you there in danger's way?"

"Maybe things would be different if I was there."

The hollowness of her voice crushed my chest. "What ifs will kill you. And you already know that." I took her hand. "The world hasn't been kind to us."

Rhona choked on a bitter laugh. "Orphans before twenty-two."

We were silent for a time, dressed in black. I assumed someone would collect us when it was time to go.

Uncle Herc's will would be read before all stewards and Luthers, which seemed unimaginably cruel. But what affected us, affected them too. Tradition wouldn't be denied.

"We can be kind to each other."

Roused from my stupor, I regarded my cousin, too tired to do much else. Guilt was a strong insomniac.

She did her best to smile. "The world hasn't been kind to us, but we can be kind to each other. You and I."

Oh, god. My shoulders shook as tears slipped from my traitorous eyes. "Yes," I whispered thickly. "We can. We will. I love you, cousin."

"I love you too."

I dried my cheeks at a knock on the door.

Eleanor popped her head in. "The car is ready."

"Thank you," Rhona answered in a strong voice that broke my heart a little more.

I had to be there for her now.

Standing, I extended my hand down. "Let's go."

"I'm not ready for this. I fucked around. They won't respect me."

"Look at me, Rhona Thana."

She obeyed.

"You *are* ready for this. These stewards have watched you in Grids for five years. You are the best of the best. Don't ever doubt yourself."

"Or what?"

"I'll raid the chocolate stash you keep in your doll's house."

She cracked a smile and took my hand.

I held it tight. "Let's go, cuz."

The silver Bentley waited for us. The manor was empty and quiet, the others already departed ahead of us. I slid into the driver seat, arranging the pleats of my scallop-neck, black dress.

I headed out to Lake Thana. There was a hill there, the official location for peaceful gatherings between Luthers and stewards.

The drive went too fast.

I gazed sadly at the dirt road that led to the steward's secret spot on the lake, continuing past it, and then past the pier that drew the tourists like flies.

"Turn here," she said.

This dirt road wound up a rise, and Lake Thana soon extended below us. Cars covered the flat top of the hill, lining the road on both sides.

Sascha would be here.

I'd have to look at him.

At a murderer.

I swallowed down bile.

"Andie?"

"Yeah?"

"If I try to kill him, can you stop me?" she asked.

My heart lurched. "Sure. Got any weapons that I should know about?"

A ghost of a smile touched her lips, but as I drew the car to a halt, the swelling crowd rendered us both silent.

The divide was obvious from the back. Stewards to the right. Luthers to the left.

I listened to Rhona's breath and looked at her. "Ready?"

She clenched her jaw and dipped her head.

I walked just behind my cousin through the middle of the two sides. Toward the front, someone had set up chairs like some kind of sadistic wedding.

A hushed quiet descended as we passed, and heat crept over my jaw at the Luthers' regard.

Where is the bastard?

It was impossible not to look for him.

My gaze skimmed over Mandy, Hairy, and Leroy, until I found the person who'd killed my uncle. He watched with shadowed eyes, standing slightly in front of his trusted pack members.

Fresh bile surged in my throat at the sight of him, and I tore my focus away.

Pascal beckoned to me, and I stood between her and a ceremonial-looking boulder that separated us from the Luthers. I'd expected to sit in the front row, but the head team faced our tribe like groomsmen in a wedding.

Rhona echoed Sascha's position on the other side, raising her chin as she regarded our people.

They were *her* people. They saw her poise and were proud.

My heart filled because, truly, she had nothing to worry about. And I'd do everything in my power to help her.

Pascal left my side and stood before the ceremonial boulder. A dark-haired werewolf joined her, but I knew not to disregard his youthful appearance. Sascha was nearly a century old. This guy could be ancient.

"Let a Luther shift, so all may be assured of the truth of these proceedings," Pascal spoke.

Mandy shifted, eliciting an alarmed murmur from the watching stewards.

She lay at Sascha's feet, alert.

"May all bear witness to the will and testament of a much-beloved leader, Hercules Bowen Thana. Son of Charise and Nicholas Thana. Sister of Ragna Booker. And beloved father."

She'd missed off uncle. The omission relieved me.

I didn't deserve recognition in his death. The Luthers looked at me, and I glared back until some lowered their eyes.

As Pascal set a carved wooden box on the boulder, the pack's marshal passed her a key.

She opened the box and extracted a scroll.

Rhona was pale, focused on Pascal. Otherwise, she had control over her need for revenge. Which was good because I was, by far, the worse fighter between us—even if she didn't have weapons.

Her eyes flicked to mine, and I nodded in encouragement.

Pascal unfurled the scroll, scanning the gathered crowd.

She turned to Sascha, and I forced myself to look at him, to get *used* to being in his presence. I couldn't let the Luther cloud my judgement ever again, and that meant learning to push everything aside to deal with him.

I'd spend my life ensuring he never won the game.

"Does the leader of the Luthers, Sascha Alarick Greyson, agree that the contents of this will and testament are final and binding?"

Sascha didn't return my condemning look. "I agree that the contents are final and binding."

There had to be a lot of red tape on what could be included in a leader's will because agreeing beforehand seemed careless.

Pascal faced the stewards. "Do the stewards, children of the Ni Tiaki tribe, agree that the contents of this will and testament are final and binding?"

I would follow Rhona without question. She understood the gravity of her role—no matter what Herc's reservations had been.

"*We agree,*" the stewards boomed as one.

Shit, missed it.

Pascal glanced at me. "Andie Charise Booker, do you also agree?"

I met her calm gaze. "I agree wholeheartedly."

Rhona threw me a quick smile that I returned.

Pascal stood side by side with the other marshal, their shoulders nearly touching as she raised the scroll to eye level and said, "With both sides bound to the words within, let it be known that Hercules Bowen Thana will be succeeded in Victratum by his eldest child, Andie Charise Thana."

I didn't register her words at first.

Gasps rocketed through seventeen hundred onlookers, replacing their leaden attentiveness.

I stared at Pascal, numb. Ears buzzing.

That's not right.

"Andie Charise Booker," Pascal repeated, extending the will to me.

I didn't reach for it, locked in place. Rhona snatched it away.

"There's been a mistake." But she didn't read the will. Rhona looked at me instead. "Is this true?"

"The box contains a birth certificate," the Luther marshal said, a paper in his hands. "Her father was Hercules Thana. Her mother was Savannah Thana."

My soul left me then.

It just *left*.

My cousin wasn't my cousin.

Rhona was my sister.

Oh, god. Herc was my father.

So many lies.

Mum wasn't my mum

She wasn't my mother.

I turned to stone—from the inside out. Steel coated my heart. My mind froze. My expression smoothed to a hardness I'd only seen in others.

I met Rhona's wide gaze. "I didn't know."

Her face crumpled. I took her hand to lay a gentle kiss on the back.

"If you need to leave, then go," I said softly. "I'll be with you soon."

Not needing more encouragement, my cousin—my *sister*—fled. The gaping stewards and Luthers parting like curtains in some dreadful theatre show.

Dispassionately, cut off, I noted smirks from several werewolves. Were they *enjoying* this?

Did they think Rhona and the tribe were easy targets now?

"Andie," Pascal hushed. "You agreed to be bound to the will."

I regarded her.

She'd known what the will said. Why else ensure I agreed in advance? My reply was icy. "I'm aware."

The woman lowered her gaze. "Then please step forward to claim your birthright."

My *birthright?*

What a fucking joke.

One person made me step forward.

Rhona.

I took the hit for both of us and left the row of shocked head team members to step forward.

Had they known?

Did everyone know but me?

I clung to the coarse hardness inside as I faced one thousand appalled stewards. I listened to the screech of tires as Rhona made her escape.

A spear was passed into my hand. A cape of feathers rested on my shoulders. With deft fingers, Pascal twisted my hair up, inserting an ornate jade pin to hold the thick mass in place. Roderick passed her a bowl and a floral oil was smeared on my forehead.

"Will you protect the stewards of Ni Tiaki with your final breath, Andie Thana?" Pascal said.

I had to get away. "I will."

"Will you lead us in Victratum to the best of your ability?"

My ability was about zero. "I will."

She faced our tribe. "Stewards, the blood of our ancestors runs strong in this woman. Through her, we will be protected. Through her, we will be led! All here today lay witness. Andie Charise Thana is head steward and leader of the Ni Tiaki."

I gazed back at the shaken tribe.

No one cheered. No one made a fucking sound. Wade and Cameron were white-faced in the second row.

"The leaders must meet in the spirit of Victratum," the other marshal boomed.

I managed one step, but Sascha crossed the ground between us. He stopped before me and I met his gaze, aware that anything less would be viewed as a weakness.

The shadow in his eyes was marked, and he flinched at whatever he saw on my face.

Good.

Forcing my lips upward, I extended a hand to him. "The best of luck to you, Luther."

Growls arose from his pack at the disgust I infused into the word.

Sascha took my hand, tilting his chin down so his hair swung forward.

I, alone, saw when his eyes turned pitch-black.

Greyson spoke softly, gravel riding his voice. "And to you, mate. Let the game truly begin."

MOON CLAIMED

SUPERNATURAL BATTLE: WEREWOLF DENS, #2

Grab Your Copy Today!

BOOKS BY KELLY ST. CLARE

Supernatural Battle

Vampire Towers (Paranormal urban romance)

Blood Trial

Vampire Debt

Death Game

Werewolf Dens (Paranormal urban romance)

Shifter Wars

Moon Claimed

Wolf Roulette

The Darkest Drae (Dragon shifter romance)

with Raye Wagner

Blood Oath

Shadow Wings

Black Crown

The Tainted Accords (Royal fantasy romance):

Fantasy of Frost

Fantasy of Flight

Fantasy of Fire

Fantasy of Freedom

Novellas:

Sin

Olandon

Rhone

Shard

Pirates of Felicity (Pirate fantasy romance):

Immortal Plunder

Stolen Princess

Pillars of Six

Dynami's Wrath

Veritas

Eternal Gambit

Mortal Trinity

Last Battle for Earth (Dystopian romance):

Earth's Warrior

Rebel's Crusade

Traitor's Mandate